GILDED DECEIT

Tracy Grant

This is a work of fiction. Names, characters, places, and incidents are either products of the writer's imagination or are used fictitiously and are not to be construed as real. Any resemblance to actual events, locales, organizations, or persons, living or dead, is entirely coincidental.

Gilded Deceit
Copyright © 2017 by Tracy Grant
ISBN-13: 978-1545053393
ISBN-10: 1545053391

NYLA Publishing
350 7th Avenue, Suite 2003, NY 10001, New York.
http://www.nyliterary.com

DEDICATION

In memory of Lescaut, the model for Berowne, and a wonderful inspiration for twenty years. Good night, sweet prince. We love you!

ACKNOWLEDGMENTS

Nancy Yost, my agent, has been an amazing friend to me and to Malcolm and Mélanie Suzanne and their family and friends from the first. Fervent thanks from the Rannochs and me, Nancy, for your support and wonderfully keen advice. Natanya Wheeler creates wonderful covers (this one being no exception) that evoke both the mood of the series and of each particular book to perfection, and also look remarkably like my image of Mélanie Suzanne Rannoch. Natanya also shepherds the book through the publication process with a skill that leaves me free to write. Sarah Younger looks after the books brilliantly on the print side and provides superb social media support. Adrienne Rosado is a wizard at subsidiary rites. Thank you, Natanya, Sarah, Adrienne, and everyone at NYLA—the Rannochs and I could not be in better hands.

Thank you to Kate Mullin, for the invaluable feedback on the manuscript and lively and inspiring discussions about the past and future of the Rannochs and their friends. Thank you to Eve Lynch, for the careful copy editing and answering countless questions about the finer points of grammar and style.

To all the wonderful booksellers who help readers find Malcolm and Suzanne, and in particular to Book Passage in Corte Madera, for their always warm welcome to me and to my daughter, Mélanie. Thank you to the readers who share Suzanne's and Malcolm's adventures with me on my Web site, Facebook, and Twitter. To Suzi Shoemake, Betty Strohecker, and Kate Mullin, for managing a wonderful Google+ Discussion Group for readers of the series, and to all the members of the group, for their enthusiasm and support, and making me see new things in the stories and characters. Thank you to Gregory Paris and jim saliba, for creating my Web site and updating it so quickly and with such style. To Raphael Coffey, for juggling cats and humans to take the best author photos a writer could have (and to my daughter, Mélanie, and our cats, Suzanne and Lescaut, for being so wonderfully cooperative over a two-hour photo shoot).

Thanks to my colleagues at the Merola Opera Program, for understanding that being a novelist is also an important part of my life. To the staffs at Pottery Barn Kids, Peek, and Blue Stove at Nordstrom, all at The Village in Corte Madera, for a friendly welcome to Mélanie and me on writing breaks. And to the staff at Peet's Coffee & Tea at The Village in Corte Madera and at Opera Plaza in San Francisco, for keeping me supplied with superb lattes and cups of Earl Grey, and keeping Mélanie happy with hot chocolate and whip cream and smiles as I wrote this book.

Thank you to Lauren Willig, for sharing the delights and dilemmas of writing about Napoleonic spies while also juggling small children. To Penelope Williamson, for support and understanding and hours analyzing Shakespeare plays, new works, and episodes of *Scandal.* To Veronica Wolff, for wonderful writing dates during which my word count seemed to magically increase. To Deborah Crombie, for supporting Malcolm and Suzanne from the beginning. To Tasha Alexander and Andrew Grant, for their wit and wisdom and support, whether in person or via email. To Deanna Raybourn, who never fails to offer encouragement and asks wonderful interview questions. And to my other writer friends near and far, for brainstorming, strategizing, and commiserating—Jami Alden, Bella Andre, Allison Brennan,

Josie Brown, Isobel Carr, Deborah Coonts, Catherine Coulter, Catherine Duthie, Alexandra Elliott, J.T. Ellison, Barbara Freethy, Carol Grace, C.S. Harris, Candice Hern, Anne Mallory, Monica McCarty, Brenda Novak, Poppy Reiffin, and Jacqueline Yau.

Finally, thank you to my daughter, Mélanie, for inspiring me, encouraging me, and being amazingly tolerant of Mummy's writing time. I am so excited you are beginning to make up stories yourself! I know you wanted to write something in the book yourself, so here it is ffdggfhzrjshtyryimmMhyyghdgtmmmmmmmmmmmmmmm mmm?yytyiuuiuuih

DRAMATIS PERSONAE

*indicates real historical figures

The Rannoch Family & Household

Malcolm Rannoch, Member of Parliament and former British agent
Mélanie Suzanne Rannoch, former French agent, his wife
Colin Rannoch, their son
Jessica Rannoch, their daughter
Berowne, their cat

Laura Fitzwalter, Marchioness of Tarrington, Colin and Jessica's former governess
Lady Emily Fitzwalter, her daughter
Raoul O'Roarke, Laura's lover, Suzanne's former spymaster, Malcolm's father

Miles Addison, Malcolm's valet
Blanca Addison, his wife, Suzanne's maid and companion

Lady Frances Dacre-Hammond, Malcolm's aunt
Chloe Dacre-Hammond, her daughter

Zarina, housemaid
Giacomo, manservant
Rodrigo, manservant

The Davenport Family

Lady Cordelia Davenport
Colonel Harry Davenport, her husband, scholar and former
British agent
Livia Davenport, their daughter
Drusilla Davenport, their daughter
Archibald Davenport, Harry's uncle

The Montagu/Vincenzo Family & Household

Bernard Montagu, Lord Thurston
Elena, Contessa Vincenzo, his mistress
Eliana Montagu, their daughter
Matteo Montagu, their son
Floria Montagu, their daughter

Kit Montagu, Thurston's son
Diana Smythe, Thurston's daughter
John Smythe, her husband
Selena Montagu, Thurston's daughter

Conte Vincenzo, Elena Vincenzo's husband
Sofia Vincenzo, their daughter
Enrico Vincenzo, their son

Tomaso, Conte Vincenzo's valet
Rosa, Contessa Vincenzo's maid
Hibbert, Diana's maid
Carlo, footman

Others

*George Gordon, Lord Byron, poet
*Percy Shelley, poet
*Mary Shelley, novelist, his wife

Margaret O'Roarke, Raoul's wife

Julien St. Juste, agent for hire

This royal throne of kings, this sceptred isle,
This earth of majesty, this seat of Mars,
This other-Eden, demi-paradise,
This fortress built by Nature for herself
Against infection and the hand of war,
This happy breed of men, this little world,
This precious stone set in the silver sea.

Shakespeare, Richard II, Act II, scene i

CHAPTER 1

Lombardy
August 1818

Jessica Rannoch clutched the worn velvet window ledge of the hired carriage and bounced on the seat. "Almost there?" she asked, face pressed to the glass.

Mélanie Suzanne Rannoch put a steadying hand on her daughter's back. "Not quite, darling. Soon."

"At least no one's chasing us." Jessica's brother, Colin, peered out the window on the opposite side of the carriage.

Mélanie's husband, Malcolm, turned his gaze to their son. "There's no reason for anyone to be chasing us."

"Yes, there is, we're running away," Colin pointed out, with the irrefutable logic of five.

"We're not exactly running away." Colin's friend, Emily, twisted the end of a red-blonde plait round her fingers. "It's

1

not like we're hiding in hampers or anything."

Mélanie cast a sharp look at Emily, incidents from her own past reverberating through her head. Just how much had Emily heard?

"We sneaked out of an inn in the middle of the night," Colin pointed out.

"Your parents had seen people they preferred not to converse with." Laura Tarrington, Emily's mother, spoke in the firm tone she had once used as a governess.

The seventh occupant of the carriage leaned back in the corner beside Laura, an amused smile on his face. Mélanie met his gaze for a moment. Raoul O'Roarke had made many escapes in the course of his career as a spymaster. In the years when he'd been her spymaster, she'd made a number at his side. Escapes far more hair-raising than their journey from London to France to Switzerland and into Italy. And yet, in many ways, this was the most harrowing of all those journeys. Because of the three children with them.

Jessica turned from the window to smile at the occupants of the carriage. "'Scape."

"Jess understands." Colin grinned at his sister. As if to punctuate the point, Berowne, the cat, lifted his head from Malcolm's lap and meowed.

Mélanie pulled Jessica into her lap, torn between laughter and tears. Considering that they—four adults, three children, and one cat—had spent weeks crammed together in carriages or on boats, they were managing remarkably well. Colin was right, they had slipped out of an inn in the middle of the night because Malcolm had spotted a fellow British agent. There had been a bit of intrigue in Switzerland when they stopped to visit her friend, Hortense Bonaparte, but they had resolved it. All things considered, their journey—their escape—was

2

going more smoothly than they had any right to expect. Soon they would be at the villa on Lake Como that Malcolm had inherited from his mother. Addison, Malcolm's valet, and Blanca, Mélanie's companion, had gone ahead to open the villa. Some of their familiar things would already be unpacked. The children would be able to run about. They could settle into some sort of routine. She should be relieved. But her throat was tight beneath the satin ribbons on her bonnet and her insides twisted beneath the twilled sarcenet of her traveling gown. For she knew full well the dangers they faced. And those dangers could be laid directly at her door.

The carriage skidded to an abrupt stop. Mélanie clutched Jessica and the carriage strap. Malcolm's hand tightened on her shoulder as Berowne yowled. Laura and Raoul steadied Colin and Emily. Malcolm and Raoul both moved, but they had scarcely pushed themselves to their feet when the door jerked open. A pistol barrel gleamed in the light of the interior lamps. A pistol held in the hand of a dark, masked man.

Mélanie's arms tightened round her daughter. Bandits were not uncommon in Italy, though they were more prevalent in the south. For that matter, they were not unheard of in Britain and certainly not in Spain, where she and Malcolm had lived during the recent war. This was not the first time they'd been held up. She met her son's gaze. Colin's eyes told her he remembered, though beside him Emily was the color of bleached linen.

"We have money," Malcolm said in an even voice. "This needn't be difficult. If you'll let me step outside and open our luggage—"

"You know damn well it isn't money we want," the man said in a low voice. "Hand it over."

Malcolm's gaze shot to Mélanie and then to Raoul. "It?"

3

"Don't play games. Hand it over and this can go easily."

Mélanie's gaze locked on her husband's. This was a scene they'd played before. They were agents, after all. Save that in this case they weren't carrying anything secret. Unless—But Raoul's gaze told her he wasn't either.

The lamplight leapt on the pistol as the man jerked it to the side. "Going to make this difficult, are you? Out. All of you."

Mélanie's gaze met Malcolm's briefly as he handed her from the carriage. They had weapons, but not on them and not loaded. And it wouldn't be safe with the children anyway. Colin was silent as he climbed from the carriage. Mélanie squeezed his hand and he gave her a quick smile. Emily was shaking and holding tight to Laura's hand, but her head was high.

The ground was soft from recent rain. The air smelled of loamy earth. They stood in a tight cluster, Colin and Emily between Mélanie and Laura, Malcolm and Raoul on the outer edges.

A second man had a pistol trained on their coachman.

"Down," the first man said to the coachman. He looked at his confederate. "We can go through the luggage if we have to, but it's my guess one of them has it on them. Search them. One at a time."

The second man moved towards Laura.

"Start with me." Raoul stepped in front of Laura. "You don't think much of us if you think we'd let the women hide whatever it is."

Actually, it might be very sensible for her or Laura to be hiding whatever it was. Assuming there really was something to hide. But the man took the bait, shook out the coat Raoul was handing to him, patted Raoul's shoulders, shook the

4

boots Raoul obligingly removed.

Jessica squirmed and let out a squawk. The first man sent a sharp look at Mélanie. Mélanie murmured to her daughter.

Hoofs pounded against the ground. A gunshot ripped the air. Not from their captors. The first man swung round on instinct. Malcolm sprang and knocked the man to the ground. His pistol scuttered across the leaves. Mélanie grabbed it, still holding Jessica. When she straightened up, Raoul had knocked the second man to the ground and was grappling with him. Laura grabbed one of Raoul's boots and hit the man on the head.

Footsteps thudded on the leaves. Malcolm's opponent scrambled to his feet and lurched into the trees. Raoul gave a hoarse cry and his opponent ran after his confederate.

A third man ran into clearing. Malcolm moved in front of the others.

"Are you all right?" The man spoke English, pure Oxbridge with no trace of an accent. He had an unruly shock of sandy hair, and even in the dim light, the Bond Street tailoring of his coat was apparent.

"You scared them off with a timely intervention." Malcolm dropped his arm round Mélanie's shoulders.

"I'd heard brigands were rampant in Italy, but somehow I didn't expect—" The young man shook his head.

Malcolm drew a soft breath. Mélanie could feel his calculations. They hadn't been ordinary brigands, but he wasn't ready to share that yet.

"My name is Montagu," the young man said. "We—my sisters and brother-in-law and I—" He broke off, peering at Malcolm through the shadows. "Rannoch?"

For a moment, Malcolm went taut as a bowstring. Mélanie felt the reactions shoot through him. Recognition, followed by doubt. They had been using aliases on their journey. But if they had been recognized, there was no help for it. "Kit? Last I saw you was in a field hospital outside Waterloo."

"I've sold out. Explanations later. We're on our way to our father's villa. It's just beyond those trees. We can give you shelter."

"Thank you," Malcolm said, "but our own villa—"

"That would be most welcome." Laura had her arms round Colin and Emily, but her gaze was on Raoul. "Mr. O'Roarke is wounded."

Raoul, Mélanie realized, was still on the ground. He drew a breath, but she could tell it pained him. "It's only—"

"It's not only a scratch," Laura said. "But even if it were, it could fester."

Malcolm's gaze moved from Raoul to Laura to Colin and Emily, silent but white-faced within Laura's arms. He nodded.

In the carriage, Jessica snuggled into Mélanie, arms like a vice round her neck. Colin and Emily watched intently as Laura used Raoul's cravat to bind a makeshift handkerchief bandage round his chest. Mélanie studied Raoul long enough to satisfy herself that he wasn't about to collapse from loss of blood, then turned her gaze to her husband. "Do you meet people from your past everywhere, darling, even in foreign climes? Did you go to school with Mr. Montagu too?"

Malcolm grinned, though his brows were drawn together. "Hardly. Kit's five years my junior. He was an ensign at the time of Waterloo. We met once or twice. He wasn't in Brussels much. I doubt you ever crossed paths with him."

"And his father is staying in Italy?" Laura knotted the cravat round Raoul's chest.

"I believe his father has been in Italy for over a decade."

6

Raoul's voice was hoarse but steady. "If I'm right about the names, his father is Lord Thurston."

Malcolm frowned. "I don't think I ever knew—There was some scandal, wasn't there?"

"When you were still at Harrow. Thurston left England and settled in Italy."

"Did he run away too?" Emily asked.

"In a sense." Raoul smiled at her. "There was a duel. And a lady he wanted to spend time with. Who lived in Italy."

"The children stayed in England with Lady Thurston?" Malcolm asked. "Unusual." It was not unheard of for aristocratic marriages to end, but usually the husband retained custody of the children. And if anyone fled the country it was usually the wife.

"I don't know the details," Raoul said.

And in front of their own children it was impossible to speculate.

"So we're being ourselves again?" Emily asked.

"For the moment." Malcolm smiled at her. "Easier that way, don't you think?"

"I suppose so." Emily frowned at the muddy toes of her shoes. "I liked Uncle Raoul being my daddy."

Raoul touched her hand. "What we call each other doesn't change how any of us feels, sweetheart."

Emily gave him a quick smile.

Colin's dark brows were drawn together. "I was afraid they'd try to take one of us away."

"What makes you think that, darling?" Mélanie shifted Jessica, who was pulling at her dress to indicate she wanted to nurse.

Colin met her gaze across the carriage. "Those men who stopped us in Paris tried to take Pierre."

7

Mélanie drew in her breath. "I wasn't sure how much you remembered." Colin had only been two.

"You stopped them," Colin said simply. "So I knew we were safe today."

Mélanie released her breath. She didn't dare risk a glance at Malcolm for fear she would cry. Colin's simple trust must mean they were doing something right. And it was a terrifying burden.

The carriage pulled up in a forecourt. White walls and columns flashed into view beyond the window. The coachman let down the steps and handed her from the carriage. A columned portico met her gaze, the white stone washed golden by the torchlight. Imitations of this type of façade were a standard feature of the English countryside, but the Palladian original never failed to take her breath way. The wind from the lake brought the scent of the water.

The coachman handed Laura down and then the others. Colin ran to Mélanie's side. Malcolm put a steadying hand at her waist.

Kit Montagu's carriage was already drawn up in the forecourt. Footmen in blue and gold livery hurried from the house to assist them. Mélanie had a brief impression of an entrance hall tiled in cool cream-colored marble and a gilt-railed staircase as they were conducted upstairs. There was still no sign of their host. Or a hostess. They had been running away from Malcolm's world, something she had felt no small measure of guilt about. Yet they seemed, for the moment at least, to have landed smack dab in the middle of it.

She could converse in Italian, though not as fluently as in French, Spanish, or German. Malcolm's Italian was quite good, and he was comfortable in the local Milanese. Raoul, predictably, could speak a number of Italian dialects without accent. Laura knew the least, though even she could make herself understood. Colin and Emily could already chatter away in the tongue with the ease of the very young.

The footman conducted them to a suite of well-appointed rooms. Laura took the children into one of the rooms where the footman promised to deliver refreshments directly. Malcolm went to speak with Kit, while Mélanie got out the medical supply box she'd retrieved from the coach and attended to Raoul's wound.

It was worse than he had let on, though not as bad as she'd feared. She shot a look at him. Raoul lifted a brow. "I was careless. And too slow. Not as young as I once was."

"You were reckless and as quick on your feet as ever." She secured a dressing over the jagged cut. "I thought—"

"We were in for monotony?"

"Yes. No. One type of it, I suppose."

"I don't think you or Malcolm need ever fear monotony."

It had been her greatest fear in their hurried departure from London. That once they were settled in Italy, in the idyllic but quiet villa, without Malcolm's work in Parliament, without her role as a political wife, boredom would set in. Malcolm would have all too much leisure to dwell on what he had lost. And that he had lost it because he had been forced to flee to protect his wife, a former Bonapartist agent who had originally married him to spy on him.

"I knew we'd meet other expatriates here." She kept her gaze on the bandage as she knotted off the ends. "But I didn't think, so quickly—"

"Thurston's been out of Britain for a long time," Raoul said. "And we've no reason to think the truth about your past has become generally known, in any case."

"No," Mélanie said, though she lived with that dread

9

whenever they got the English papers. After all, the rational part of her said, they had fled not because the truth of her past as a Bonapartist spy had come out in the open but because they had learned Malcolm's spymaster, Lord Carfax, knew it. Which gave Carfax an intolerable hold over both of them. All of them, for he almost certainly knew about Raoul's past, as well.

She cast a glance round the room. The plasterwork and marble tiles were unmistakably Italian. But the sofa Raoul sat on and the small table where she'd put her medical supply box were solid English oak. Odd the emotions evoked by that sturdy wood and the faint whiff of lemon oil. "I'll get used to it. I lived all those years without Malcolm knowing the truth. I lived all the months Malcolm knew the truth and our friends didn't. It's just a bit odd being Suzanne again." She snipped off the ends of the bandage. "Stepping back into old roles."

Especially when those roles had been smashed to bits.

CHAPTER 2

A footman directed Malcolm to a different wing, where he found Kit in a small sitting room hung with light blue silk. Kit had changed from his dusty travel clothes into cream-colored breeches, a dark coat, and a silver-striped waistcoat, and had a half-full glass of brandy beside him. He turned round at the opening of the door and took a quick step towards Malcolm. "I trust you have everything you need? Is there need to send for a doctor?"

"I don't think so. My wife's quite excellent at tending wounds."

"Yes, I remember hearing accounts of her talents. A ministering angel, one fellow called her."

"Don't tell Suzanne that. She'd cringe at the very words." Odd to be calling her Suzanne again. He was going to have to watch himself. Malcolm regarded Kit for a moment. "O'Roarke's wound isn't serious, as these things go, but it needed prompt tending. You have our deepest thanks."

"I could hardly have done otherwise. My father was most concerned when I told him." Kit moved to a table by the window with a set of decanters and poured Malcolm a glass of brandy. "They've held dinner back in anticipation of our arrival, and hope you can join us. Though I didn't consider—" Kit's gaze shifted from side to side. "If you're concerned about your wife and Lady Tarrington—"

"Why would I be concerned about Suzanne and Laura?" Malcolm took the glass Kit was holding out to him. "I suspect even O'Roarke will be in condition to sit at table."

"It's not that." Kit took a drink of brandy, then stared at a blue-and-white vase on the mantel, as though it could give him the words he was struggling for. "My father left Britain a decade and a half ago."

"I know. That is, I didn't, or I'd forgot, but O'Roarke did."

"Oh, God." Kit grimaced. The gaze he turned to Malcolm was that of a boy who has had his eyes opened too young to harsh truths. "So you know Father left my mother."

"Yes. It can't have been easy."

"He lives here with her. The Contessa Vincenzo. The woman—"

"He left your mother for."

Kit nodded. "Your wife—"

"I'm sorrier than I can say for what you and your sisters must have gone through, Kit. I'm sorry we've disrupted what must be a sensitive time for your family. But you must have seen enough of society by now to realize my wife and Laura would scarcely be shocked at sitting down to dinner with your father and the contessa. And certainly wouldn't judge them."

"Gentlemen's mistresses don't dine with their friends' wives."

"Not their acknowledged mistresses perhaps. But then I'd

12

hardly laud hypocrisy. Nor would my wife or Laura."

Kit released his breath. "You always said rum things, Rannoch."

"My parents remained married until my mother died. But it was hardly an easy relationship. For anyone. Including their children."

Kit scraped a hand over his hair. "I was at Eton when it happened. I don't know much. They tried to keep the details from us. I remember meeting her once at a house party at my parents' when I was home from school. But I never guessed—"

"One doesn't think those things about one's parents," Malcolm said, thinking of what he had and hadn't sensed about his mother and Raoul O'Roarke.

Kit nodded. "Then there were rumors. I ignored them at first. You know the sort of thing schoolboys say to torment each other."

"Quite." Echoes of taunts across the commons at Harrow resounded in Malcolm's ears.

Kit gave another curt nod, gaze on the blues and reds of the carpet. "I tended to be focused on my own concerns, as one is at that age. Then one night Father came to Eton." Kit nudged the andiron with the toe of his boot, as though it held untold secrets. "I'll never forget. They rousted me out of bed. Father had only visited a handful of times since I'd started school, and here he was arriving in the middle of the night. He told me he was leaving England. That he couldn't explain all of it, but it would be better this way for all of us. That I should be kind to my mother. And never doubt that he loved us." Kit stared out across the dark water of the lake as he said that last, repeating it as though from memory in a curiously flat voice. "I'm not sure he'd ever used those words before. Not that he was a bad parent. Just not—effusive. Any more than most of my friends' fathers were."

"Mine certainly wasn't." At least not his putative father, Alistair Rannoch. O'Roarke, in his own way, had been more affectionate, though Malcolm hadn't learned the truth of their relationship until recently.

"As the days went on, I pieced together bits of it. There was a duel, I think, though they hushed it up pretty well." Kit downed another swallow of brandy. "Mama wouldn't talk about him at all. But somehow I learned he was living with the contessa."

"When did you see him again?" Malcolm asked.

"Tonight."

Malcolm drew a breath.

"He left during the Peace of Amiens. Then war broke out again, and it was hard to travel. He did write." Kit hunched his shoulders, pulling the glossy black fabric of his coat and putting Malcolm in mind of his friends David and Simon's schoolboy nephews. "My mother seems all right. Has her friends, fusses about the girls' come-outs and the like. For weeks—months—at a time I'd forget—" He shook his head. "With the war, plenty of chaps don't have fathers."

"Different knowing one has a living father somewhere one can't see."

"I suppose so. To own the truth, I can't credit it. He was Lord Thurston. He is Lord Thurston. To walk away from his responsibilities for—"

"Love can be a powerful emotion."

Kit met Malcolm's gaze with the look of one who did not yet fully understand the meaning of the word. "But whatever she means to him—"

"I assume she means an incalculable amount. They've

both given up a great deal to be together."

Kit tossed down the last of his brandy and stared into the glass. "There've been times I thought I never wanted to see him again. But I'm not a boy anymore. There's no sense in holding grudges," said the young man who, to Malcolm, still seemed little more than a boy.

"A very adult attitude," Malcolm said.

Kit crossed to the decanters and splashed some more brandy into his glass, shoulders hunched. "I wasn't sure about bringing the girls. Especially Selena. She's only eighteen. But she can be very insistent. She said it was her right as much as mine or Diana's."

"She had a point."

"I suppose so."

Malcolm crossed to Kit's side and clapped him on the shoulder. "I doubt you'll any of you regret seeing him. Or the contessa."

Kit looked at Malcolm with the gaze of an untried soldier on the eve of his first battle. "I wouldn't for the world have had you go through what you went through tonight, but it's actually rather a relief to have you here. A bit of a buffer. I suppose that makes me a coward."

"Nothing cowardly about wanting to ease into things."

Kit met his gaze. "I've faced battle. But I learned what to expect. This is—"

"Uncharted territory."

Kit took a long drink of brandy. "Quite."

Mélanie looked up from closing her medical supply box as her husband came back into the room. "They've invited us to join them for dinner in half an hour," Malcolm said.

"They?" Mélanie asked, fastening the brass closure.

"Lord Thurston and the Contessa Vincenzo. The woman he left Britain and his whole life for." Malcolm looked at Raoul. "Are you all right, O'Roarke?" He put up a hand. "Why am I asking you? Is he all right, Mel?"

"He will be." Mélanie sent Raoul a mock-sharp look that wasn't entirely in fun. "With proper rest."

Laura came in from the adjoining room. "A sensible-seeming young maid is sitting with the children. They seem quite matter-of-fact about the whole thing." Her gaze fastened on Raoul.

"I'll live," he said, smiling into her eyes.

"If I doubted that, I wouldn't have left the room." She echoed the smile and dropped down on the sofa beside him.

Malcolm perched on the edge of the table near where Mélanie sat on the floor. "Kit and his sisters haven't seen their father since he left Britain fifteen years ago."

"Dear God." Laura said.

"Quite. Though Kit says it's a relief to have us here as a buffer. Dinner and a night's sleep and we'll be off to our own house. We'd have seen them at some point in any case."

"I'm not objecting." Mélanie leaned against her husband's legs and twisted her head round to look up at him. "You're always the one who's more cautious than I am. But we still don't know what the devil the thieves were so convinced we had."

"No." Malcolm shot a look at Raoul. "You didn't—"

Raoul lifted a brow. "Smuggle dangerous information with everything else we're facing?"

16

"Are you telling me you wouldn't if you thought it important enough?"

Raoul gave a faint smile. "Possibly. But in this case I didn't."

"Something convinced them we had it," Mélanie said.

"You think they knew who you were?" Laura asked. "And assumed you must have something of value? Because of your position or because you were agents? Or were they—"

Mélanie met her friend's gaze. "Were they looking for a party of English travelers?"

"And the Montagu party were the actual targets?" Raoul asked. "Interesting."

Malcolm frowned. "I didn't know Kit well, but he didn't strike me as the sort to be carrying secret documents. Though you'd think by now I'd know better than to take anyone at face value."

"And the sisters and brother-in-law?" Mélanie asked.

"The younger sister is eighteen. The elder is just younger than Kit and has been married for some years."

"Of course there's another possibility." Raoul draped his arm across Laura's shoulders without seeming to pull on the wound in his side. "Assuming the bandits were looking for an English party, they were actually trying to find Thurston, on his way home."

Laura looked at her lover. "He wasn't—"

"An agent? Certainly not, at least far as I ever knew. He wasn't even particularly politically active. But people can change."

Mélanie got to her feet and shook out the creased folds of her traveling gown. "If we're dining with them, we'd all best dress."

They scattered to their chambers and went through the

17

business of dressing for dinner. Except for their stay in d'Arenberg with Hortense Bonaparte, they hadn't been in the habit of fully dressing for dinner since they'd left Britain. Some nights she'd not change at all, other nights she'd put on a dinner dress or even an evening gown for morale's sake but leave her hair tumbling down her back. Tonight, without Blanca to assist her or time to heat her curling tongs, Mélanie twisted her hair into a chignon and wound her side curls round her fingers. She stared at her reflection in the dressing-table looking glass. The high standing lace collar of her rose sarcenet gown framed her face. Pearl and diamond earrings swung from her ears. Pearls glowed round her throat. Ivory gloves lay on the dressing table. Subtle changes, but taken all together she was Suzanne Rannoch, the political hostess and wife of a duke's grandson, again, not Mélanie Suzanne Lescaut Rannoch, the former spy in exile.

"Do you need help?" Malcolm was tying his cravat with quick competence, if without Addison's flair.

"No, I managed all the strings." Mélanie reached for her gloves. They were, after all, only stepping back into the world in which they had lived for five and a half years. When Malcolm had essentially given up that whole world for her, the least she could do was keep her qualms about stepping back into it to herself.

CHAPTER 3

Mélanie picked up the amethyst Norwich shawl Malcolm had given her last Christmas and a beaded reticule Hortense had given her when they left d'Arenberg, and they went next door to check on the children. The maid, a young woman with a direct, friendly gaze who also struck Mélanie as sensible, assured them she would stay with the children until they returned from dinner. She had produced a doll and blocks from somewhere and Emily and Colin were already building a block castle and attempting to keep Jessica from knocking it down.

"It's odd not to have dinner with you," Colin said, when Mélanie went over to scoop up Jessica before she could toddle into the tower.

Mélanie touched her son's hair. "It's just for tonight." Except for their stay in d'Arenberg, the children had been accustomed to dining with their parents on the journey. "We can make our own rules at the villa."

Colin grinned. So did Emily. Then she ran across the room as Laura and Raoul joined them.

A few minutes later, the footman who had shown them to their rooms returned and conducted the adults back downstairs, where he opened a pair of double doors onto an airy salon with French windows opening onto the terrace. White and gold walls set off crimson silk upholstery and soared to a ceiling where cherubs disported. A tall man with a keen blue gaze and sandy hair that was still thick, an older version of Kit, came towards them. "Welcome. Always glad to meet new neighbors, though I'm sorry for these circumstances."

A slender woman, with thick dark hair coiled round her fine-boned face, stepped to his side.

"May I present the Contessa Vincenzo?" Thurston said.

"Contessa." Malcolm bowed, as did Raoul. "Thank you for having us in your home."

The contessa gave a warm smile. "We are delighted to have you, and only sorry for what you have been through, as Bernard said. Have your children settled in?"

"They are hardy travelers," Mélanie said, shaking hands with the woman for whom Thurston had abandoned his life and family and all he was. Much as Malcolm was now doing, though they had their children with them. Thurston and the contessa stood a handsbreadth apart, not quite touching, but the intimacy between them was palpable. A stranger entering the room would have known them for a couple. On closer terms than many married couples within the beau monde.

"I had some of our children's toys sent in," the contessa said.

So they had children of their own. Half-siblings to Kit and his sisters. Young enough to still play with blocks and dolls.

20

Thurston waved them to chairs and a sofa by the French windows, open onto the warm evening air. "You're traveling on the Continent?" he asked, as they disposed themselves about the room.

"It seemed a good time to make a journey," Malcolm said in an easy voice, settling back on the sofa beside Mélanie. "We haven't had much chance to travel free of my work."

"Italy has much to recommend it." Thurston's voice was equally easy.

Mélanie settled her skirt and shawl and folded her gloved hands round her reticule. Thurston commented on the dangers of bandits in the countryside. The contessa asked after their journey and remarked on the temperate summer weather. In many ways it was similar to countless evenings Mélanie had spent since she'd become Malcolm's wife. Save for the fact that they were all exiles, for reasons acknowledged and unacknowledged.

Malcolm responded to questions from Thurston about Britain with no indication that he was wondering when he'd see his homeland again. Laura accepted condolences on the deaths of her husband and father-in-law with an equanimity that offered no clue to her true relationship with either of them. Raoul, who had always had a knack for blending into any setting, gave an excellent impression of being a British gentleman rather than a revolutionary.

The footman threw open the double doors again to admit a young woman with thick honey-blonde hair looped and curled round a heart-shaped face, and a taller, slighter, younger woman with glossy brown ringlets and a direct blue gaze. They were followed by Kit and another young man, perhaps a few years older, with close-cropped brown hair and stiff posture.

21

Thurston got to his feet. So did the contessa, though she hung back as Thurston went forwards to greet his children. The children he hadn't seen in a decade and a half. They had had their first reunion earlier, while Mélanie, Malcolm, and the others were upstairs, but judging by the way Thurston paused a few feet off and the formal nods that were exchanged, much remained unexpressed.

It was Kit, not his father, who presented his sisters, Diana and Selena, and Diana's husband, John Smythe.

Chairs scraped discreetly against the thick pile of the carpet as the company rearranged themselves.

"We're so very grateful to you for making the journey," the contessa said. "You stopped in Milan on the way here?"

Diana smoothed her skirt over her knees. She wore pale blue crêpe, cut fashionably but with a much more modest neckline than Mélanie's rose sarcenet. Or the contessa's dark red silk. "We had a very agreeable time. My husband's godmother's sister is living there, and we wanted to call on her," she added, as though an explanation for why they had spent time in Milan first was called for. Her gloved fingers tightened on the blue crêpe, perhaps at the realization that calling on a godmother's sister before a father might seem odd.

"We met Lord Byron." Selena leaned forwards, her face brightening, cherry-colored ribbons bouncing on her shoulders. "And his friends Mr. and Mrs. Shelley. Mr. Shelley is a poet, as well." She glanced at Thurston. "They're all exiles like you."

John Smythe frowned at his young sister-in-law. "It's not precisely the same, Selena."

"I don't see how," Selena said. "The Shelleys seem to have left partly because of their debts and to see Byron, but it also

22

must be because of all the scandal about his first wife killing herself and the two of them having a baby before they married. And everyone knows Byron left because of the scandal with his wife."

Smythe drew a sharp breath. Lord Byron had left Britain in the wake of the breakup of his marriage of scarcely a year, amid accusations by his wife of sexual depravity rumored to involve other men and possibly his half-sister.

"Lord Byron and the Shelleys were very kind to us," Diana said, in a tone intended to end the conversation. "Though of course we don't move in their circles. Literary circles, that is."

Her husband cast an apologetic look at Thurston. "Abroad. Fellow Englishmen. Couldn't escape the connection."

"Of course not," Thurston said. "We haven't met the Shelleys yet, but we have met Lord Bryon several times. Very entertaining fellow."

Selena put up her chin. "They said they may come to Lake Como later in the summer."

"Then we shall certainly invite them to call," the contessa said. "All the English on the lake are very friendly."

Kit turned to Malcolm, like one seeking a refuge from sniper fire. "You were at Harrow with Byron, weren't you, Rannoch?"

"We overlapped," Malcolm said. "I didn't know him well. But then, I tended to keep to myself at school. I believe our friend Simon Tanner knows the Shelleys."

"The playwright?" Selena asked. "Who writes the plays the censor shuts down?"

"Occasionally." Malcolm smiled, though talking about Simon could not but stir thoughts of why they had left

23

Britain.

Selena returned his smile. "There are so many interesting people in Italy. Even if a lot of the ones we've met so far are English. I'm so glad I insisted Kit and Diana bring me. Though to own the truth, I don't think Mama wanted me left home alone with her."

Her mother's name hung in the air, like smoke from a silent shot.

"How is she?" Thurston asked.

For an instant, Diana's gaze met Kit's. "She has her friends," Diana said. "She enjoyed Selena's come-out."

Selena snorted. "She nearly strangled me a dozen times. If—"

"She's just redone the London drawing room," Diana said.

"It's rather hideous," Selena said. "Too much Egyptian. But she seems to like it, and it did keep her busy." She glanced round at the crimson upholstery and the rich but subdued tones of the Aubusson carpet. "I must say you have much better taste, Contessa."

"You're very kind," the contessa said. "I understand the fashion is quite different in England."

Silence fell over the room. Pity it was the wrong time of day for tea, Mélanie thought. They all could have used something to do with their hands.

"Such a difference between what works for entertaining and what's good for a family," Laura said. "My sister-in-law has been struggling with what to do with Trenchard House." She met Mélanie's gaze for a moment. Mélanie could almost hear the laugh her friend must be biting back. Who would have thought the Trenchard family would ever be a source of small talk to smooth over another family's difficulties?

24

"Very true. I confess we tidied away a few toys in anticipation of our guests." The contessa smiled at Laura and then turned her gaze back to her lover's children. "Your brother and sisters wanted to wait up. But we weren't sure how late it would be. I hope you'll have time with them tomorrow."

"That will be lovely," Diana said with a bright smile. "We've heard so much about them."

"Not really," Selena said. "I mean, where would we have heard it? Except for letters from—" She stared at Thurston, carefully plucked brows drawn together. "I don't know what to call you."

Thurston hesitated a moment. "You were quite proud of yourself for having mastered 'Papa' the last time you saw me."

"I was three."

For a moment, in Thurston's gaze, Mélanie thought she caught a flash of what he had lost. Then he gave one of his easy smiles. "Just so. You're quite welcome to call me Thurston if you prefer. Or Bernard."

"I'll think about it," Selena said.

Thurston inclined his head. "You were quite sensible, even at three."

"We're pleased to be here, sir," Smythe said into the silence that followed. "We were sorry you couldn't be at the wedding."

"'John." Diana shot a look at her husband.

"No sense avoiding the fact that it would have been distinctly awkward," Thurston said. "But I was sorry not be there, as well."

"Kit's going to be married," Selena said.

Thurston turned his gaze to his son. "Wonderful news. My felicitations. May I ask your betrothed's name?"

Kit shifted on the sofa. "It's not official yet."

Thurston leaned back on the settee, one arm trailing along its back, just barely brushing the contessa's shoulder. "You needn't feel you need to share anything you don't wish to. But I'm delighted to hear you've found a lady you can love."

"If you ask me, he's not in the least in love with her," Selena muttered.

"Selena!" Diana said.

"I don't think Kit would say any differently. Would you, Kit?"

"I'm very fond of her," Kit said in repressive tones. "We have every chance of being happy together." He looked at his father. "It's Elinor Dormer. She was only a child when you left. But you know the family."

"Of course. George Dormer and I were at school together."

"Elinor and I've always got on well. I think it's been apparent to both of us for some time that we'd be a good match."

"Mama seems quite happy with the idea of Elinor as her daughter-in-law." Selena looked at her father. "Does that set you against the match?"

"Of course not." Thurston met his daughter's gaze without blinking. "Your mother has always had excellent instincts."

"We're delighted to welcome her to the family," Diana said.

"And we're none of us romantics," Selena said, "given our parents' example. I suppose it could have gone the other way and made us all convinced that anything that caused you to abandon your family must be worth it, but it doesn't seem to have worked that way. I shouldn't worry, though. Kit isn't the

26

sort to desert his family."

The door opened again on the silence that greeted this pronouncement. A stout man with gray-streaked dark hair and a young woman whose delicate features and wide cheekbones were like a copy of the contessa's own stepped into the room.

Again, both the contessa and Thurston got to their feet, but it was the contessa who stepped forwards. "Just in time for dinner." She turned to the others. "My daughter, Sofia, and her father, the Conte Vincenzo."

Malcolm, Raoul, Kit, and Smythe all bowed.

Selena was staring. "Your husband?" she blurted out, less this time to create a reaction than out of genuine disbelief, Mélanie thought.

Thurston looked with a smile from his daughter to his mistress's husband and daughter. "We're all quite friendly these days. Elena and I are very grateful to Vincenzo for bringing Sofia to stay with us."

Mélanie felt Malcolm's stillness beside her. Hard not to be rooted in fascination; at the same time one was aware of a distinct desire to disappear into the tapestry sofa cushions.

"It may be hard for you young people to understand," Vincenzo said, "but though there was a time Thurston and I were scarcely the best of friends, as one grows older one begins to see the folly of such quarrels."

"The folly of believing in fidelity?" Selena asked.

"Selena!" Diana said. "Please excuse my sister."

"On the contrary," Vincenzo said. "I've always admired plain speaking. The folly of trying to hold on to what is no longer one's to keep."

Selena frowned, then cast a glance at Sofia, who was sitting decorously, her face a study in careful serenity. "So you

27

grew up—"

"Going back and forth between my parents," Sofia said.

"We didn't realize you'd all be here at the same time when you first wrote of your visit," the contessa said to Kit and his sisters. "I hope you don't mind."

"Of course not." Kit drew a breath. "We're all family in a way."

"Quite so." The contessa smiled.

Vincenzo settled back in his chair and turned to Malcolm. "Prince Metternich speaks highly of you."

In the breakup of the Napoleonic empire, Italy had once again become a mishmash of states. Lombardy, where Lake Como stood, and Venetia were part of the Austrian Empire. Malcolm, who had crossed swords with the Austrian Chancellor, Prince Metternich, at the Congress of Vienna, gave a smile that would have appeared free of irony to all but those closest to him. "The prince is kind."

"On the contrary. I've never known Metternich to give idle praise." Vincenzo's smile was equally pleasant, but the gleam in his eyes made Mélanie quite sure he knew more than a bit about their adventures at the Congress.

"How lovely to have friends in common." The contessa turned her gaze to the door. The footman had just stepped back into the room. "It seems dinner is served."

CHAPTER 4

Music drifted through the blue-framed French windows from the salon. Mozart. The contessa was at the pianoforte. Mélanie and Laura had gone upstairs to look in on the children. The rest of the guests had wandered onto the terrace. The footmen had lit lanterns that cast warm light across the stone. Malcolm paused for a moment, hands on the balustrade. The lapping of the lake sounded below. He looked out over the long, winding ribbon of water. It was not, would never be, the same as Dunmykel Bay at his home in Scotland, but there was a certain magic in water, and the lake had its own memories for him.

Thurston stopped beside him. "I never get tired of the view."

Malcolm turned to smile at their host. "I can understand why."

Thurston met his gaze. "I'm sorry you had to arrive in the midst of our—family drama."

"I'm no stranger to family drama. I'm sorry we added to the complications for you."

"On the contrary. Having you here probably made things a good deal more restrained than they might otherwise have been." Thurston cast a glance down the terrace. Raoul was making conversation with Conte Vincenzo while Selena looked over the balustrade, and Kit, Diana, and Smythe spoke with Sofia. Then he glanced through the French windows at the contessa at the pianoforte. His gaze softened. For a moment, it held the glow of a young man in the throes of first love. "I never expected it," he said in a low voice. "Oh, I'd had—adventures—before. But I never thought an amorous impulse could make me forget what I owed to my family. To my name."

He looked at Malcolm as though he expected Malcolm to understand. Which Malcolm did, in a way, though he wasn't given to thinking in that manner himself. He gave a slight nod.

"Then I met Elena." Thurston shook his head, a trace of the wonder of unlooked-for love still in his gaze. "I'd never known anything like it." He shot a look at Malcolm. "I think you know something about that."

"Do you?"

"I've seen the way you look at your wife."

"It took me by surprise, as well."

"I couldn't imagine leaving her. I couldn't imagine what I felt for her going away. For a while I simply ignored thoughts of the future in that blind way young lovers do. That men my age—or even the age I was then—should know to avoid. Then Vincenzo tumbled to the truth." Thurston's brows drew together as he looked down the terrace at his mistress's husband, laughing at something Raoul had just said. "I can't

30

really blame him. If it had been my wife—not that I can imagine Maria—Though perhaps that's a failure on my part. You may not think it to have seen him tonight, but Vincenzo was far from a complacent husband at the time. Of course, I had no choice but to meet him."

Malcolm bit back the comment that there were a number of alternatives to fighting a duel. He abhorred dueling, but he had once accepted a challenge himself.

"Vincenzo winged me, but it wasn't serious. We could have hushed the whole thing up. Very nearly did. It wasn't the actual duel itself, so much as that it forced me to face our options for the future." Thurston turned to Malcolm with a gaze that seemed oddly to will him to understand. "I couldn't set Elena up in a house in Half Moon Street and visit her after an evening at White's. Divorce—I might have gone through with it, but Vincenzo would never free Elena, so there was no point in even considering it. Leaving seemed the only option." He drew a breath. "Taking the children would have uprooted them from everything they knew. And I'd already dealt enough hurt to Maria as it was."

"It can't have been easy," Malcolm said.

"You're a good father, Rannoch. I suspect you despise me."

"I think you and the contessa were in a hellishly difficult situation."

Thurston gave a quick, defensive smile. "I wasn't counting on war breaking out again. On travel becoming almost impossible. Not that it would have been easy to return in any case."

"Do you miss it?" Malcolm asked, before he could think better of it.

Thurston's eyes narrowed. "Not as much as I'd have

31

thought. The rain. The dashed dull evenings at the club. The same people one's known since the nursery, encountered again and again. And yet—sometimes. A good cup of tea. The scent of the grass after it rains. The taste of sherry before riding to hounds. Some things will never be the same." He smiled again, the same armored smile. "Don't tell Elena."

"I wouldn't dream of it."

Mélanie and Laura had come out onto the terrace. Laura's shawl slipped from her shoulders as she crossed the terrace. Kit hurried to retrieve it.

"You knew Kit when he was in the army?" Thurston asked.

"A bit. He's a fine young man."

"He'll do well by the family. Though I could wish—" Thurston jammed his hands in his pockets. "I didn't really think about it before I married Maria. What I was committing to. What I was giving up by committing to it. I fear Kit is making the same commitments without understanding either."

"Not everyone finds what you found with the contessa."

"No. But am I wrong to want my son to have the chance to try?"

"Have you thought of talking to him?"

Thurston cast another glance at his son. "Given his current view of me, I rather suspect my talking to him would only convince him all the more of the wisdom of adopting the opposite course of action."

Conte Vincenzo took a puff on his cigarillo and leaned against the stone balustrade of the terrace. "Beautiful place here. Used to visit friends in the lake district fairly regularly. But then for quite a few years after"—he let out a puff of smoke and watched it dissipate in the warm evening air—"after Elena left me, I avoided the whole region like the plague."

"Understandable." Raoul braced his hands on the balustrade. He'd refused Vincenzo's offer of a cigarillo. He'd never acquired a taste for them, for all his time in Spain.

Vincenzo glanced through the French windows to the salon where the woman who was still his wife sat playing the pianoforte, bathed in the warm glow of lamplight. "There was a time I'd have sworn Thurston and I would never sit down at table together." His gaze moved down the terrace to his wife's lover, talking with Malcolm. "I quite liked Thurston when I first met him. Before I tumbled to what was happening. I should have seen it sooner, of course. But one doesn't think of one's own wife—Are you married, O'Roarke?"

Raoul's fingers tightened on the moss-covered stone. A simple question that stirred a tangle of guilt and regret. "I haven't lived with my wife in twenty years. By mutual choice." Though it had been quite obvious to him when Margaret fell in love with another man and took him to her bed. Obvious and, in a way, a relief.

Vincenzo gave a grunt, half of sympathy, half of acknowledgment. "Children?"

For a moment, Raoul was keenly aware of Malcolm, a dozen paces down the terrace talking to Thurston. Of Colin and Emily asleep upstairs. "No." At least not with Margaret.

"Easier that way, perhaps. Hard for Sofia and Enrico to be without a mother."

"It's the greatest challenge, I would think, when a marriage disintegrates." Or when the children were born

33

outside the marriage.

Vincenzo grimaced. "Counterproductive really, trying to raise a girl without her mother. And no point in making Sofia suffer for her mother's mistakes. Besides, at a certain point, one starts to feel a bit of a fool. Trying to retrieve a woman who has no desire to be one's wife anymore. What's the point, really? It's not as though I've gone unconsoled." He cast a glance round the terrace and grinned. "To own the truth, at times I think it's easier, living alone, not having to keep up appearances with one's wife. Do you find that true?"

Raoul drew a careful breath. Laura had come onto the terrace. Kit Montagu was retrieving her fallen shawl. He wished he could cross the terrace and take her hand in the easy way he'd been able to on the journey. "In some ways. My wife and I were spectacularly unsuited. We each saw the other as something we weren't or we'd never have married in the first place."

Vincenzo's brows drew together. "Can't quite say what I saw Elena as. Save obviously a very pretty girl. Fancied myself in love with her when we married. Believed in fidelity and the rest of it. But as one grows older love begins to look more and more like an illusion, don't you find?"

"Love's never been a word I've used easily," Raoul said with truth. Though he wouldn't say that meant he didn't believe in it. Quite the reverse in fact.

"Wise man," Vincenzo said, deaf to the subtext. "Life's easier without the illusions, all in all. Though I suppose Thurston and Elena must still believe in love. Hard to have given up what they have if they didn't. I'm happy enough to leave that nonsense to them now. And I can't say I envy Thurston what he'll have to go through with his children."

"They can be pardoned for feeling abandoned."

34

Vincenzo regarded him, cigarillo held in one hand. "I thought you'd be in sympathy with Thurston."

"I am, to a large degree. But I can see how the situation could appear quite different from his children's perspective." Without shifting his gaze, Raoul was aware of Malcolm shoulder to shoulder with Thurston. For all his own sins, he'd never gone even a year without seeing Malcolm. Or Colin. They'd probably not have noticed, but he would have. Keenly.

"Thurston admitted to me once that he'd always feel guilty for walking away from it all. Not just his children, but his position and responsibilities at home. I was surprised he confided in me. But I suppose after a fashion we're friends now." Vincenzo's gaze went from Thurston to the younger generation, separated by the length of the terrace. "I think he hoped this visit would improve matters. But I can't help but worry it will bring old hurts to the surface."

Mélanie stepped through the French windows into the salon and paused, leaning against a chairback, until the last notes of "Soave sia il vento" died away.

"That was lovely," she said softly.

The contessa laughed and turned round on the pianoforte bench. "Are your children asleep?"

"Yes, which is rather remarkable. They none of them settle down easily."

"It's always so challenging when children's routines are disrupted."

"Mine have never been used to much of a routine, for better or worse. Colin was born in Lisbon and went through

Spain to Paris, London, Vienna, and Brussels before he turned two. And our house in Paris was attacked the night Jessica was born."

"You've had an adventurous life." The contessa got to her feet, gathering the folds of her flowered silk shawl about her. "Ours has been quite contained for many years." Her gaze went to the French windows. Laura had gone over to Selena and was attempting to coax her to join the others. "I'm sorry you had to see tonight."

"It's hardly the first family drama we've been in the midst of. To own the truth, I think we were all relieved to be on the outside for once."

The contessa smiled and gestured towards two chairs set on either side of a small marquetry table. "I knew it would be difficult. I thought I had no illusions. But I didn't quite envision—"

"It's difficult to envision." Mélanie dropped into one of the chairs. "I suspect the children will settle in. Selena reminds me of my husband's sister when he returned to Britain after years abroad. At first she seemed determined to push him away." Mélanie could still see the anger in Gisèle Rannoch's gaze and hear the sharpness of her voice. "I think because she couldn't forgive him for being gone for so long and was also terrified she'd let herself care about him only to have him leave again."

"That must have been terribly hard." The contessa sat opposite Mélanie. "For you as well as your husband."

"I think it made Malcolm question the years he'd spent away."

"Without those years he wouldn't have met you."

"No." Wouldn't have tied himself to an enemy agent, wouldn't now have to flee his country and give up his career,

36

his home, his family and friends. "Fortunately Malcolm and Gisèle have mended their relationship," Mélanie continued, keeping her voice steady. "They're excellent friends now. I think perhaps that was what Gisèle wanted all along but was afraid to reach out for."

"I hope that happens with Selena. I think it may be easier for her than for Kit and Diana. They're so very polite, but they seem so much more—I suppose one would say armored. Diana in particular."

The contessa was a shrewd judge of character. "Give them time," Mélanie said. "I don't think one ever really stops needing a parent."

The contessa nodded, her gaze going back to the terrace. "I so want Bernard to have time with his children." She spread her hands over her lap. "It can't make up for what he's lost, but at least it will give him a foundation for the future. He's given up so much. Because of me."

Mélanie kept her hands steady on the folds of her shawl. "He doesn't look like a man who regrets it. And you gave up a great deal for him, as well."

"But we're in my country. Bernard would say Italy is his country now. He'd say it doesn't really matter. But he'll always be an Englishman."

Mélanie's gloved fingers tightened on her shawl. How often had she said the same about Malcolm? "Have you had time with your children?" she asked. Outside, Sofia was laughing at something Kit was saying. Even her laughter was decorous, as if she kept herself contained somehow.

The contessa's gaze also went to her daughter. "More than Bernard's had with his children. It was—difficult at first. Vincenzo was angry and keeping Sofia and her brother Enrico from me was a way to express that anger. I even paid

37

their nurse to bring them to meet me in the piazza in secret for a time."

Mélanie suppressed a shiver. In a life not short on terrors, losing her children was one of the things that most haunted her. "It must have been very difficult."

"And you wonder how I could have done it?" The contessa's gaze lingered on her daughter, but she seemed to be seeing into the past. "I've wondered myself at times. A dozen times I changed my mind. I couldn't imagine how I could be happy away from my children. Or away from Bernard. And then I learned I was expecting another child. And my husband couldn't be the father."

"So you didn't have a choice."

"Not really, not in the end. But Bernard did. And he chose me." She touched a ring she wore on her left hand, a ruby set in a gold band. "I'll never forget that."

She drew a quick breath. "But with time, Vincenzo relented. Sofia and Enrico come to us for months at a time now. And Vincenzo visits." She shrugged. "He was always a proud man, but not a fool. At our age he probably sees the folly of holding a grudge. Two middle-aged men dueling over a middle-aged mistress seems the stuff of comedy, not romantic drama. I understand he has a quite lovely mistress set up in Milan who is ten years my junior. And I suspect he thought it would help for Sofia to have her mother's influence. Though she's a very easy child. Too easy, I sometimes think. It's as though she's afraid of repeating her mother's mistakes."

"Children often react against their parents," Mélanie said. And then wondered what that might mean for her own children. It might depend on how much of the truth they knew about their mother when they reached adulthood.

38

When she tried to imagine that far ahead, the possibilities shimmered before her eyes, like images at the onset of a headache.

"I shouldn't complain," the contessa said quickly. "We're far more fortunate than most."

"It's admirable that you've worked it out so well," Mélanie said. "And it should give you hope for Lord Thurston and his children."

"In my optimistic moments. But I think the English take these matters more seriously than we do on the Continent."

Mélanie gave the question honest consideration. She might be lying about her past, but she wasn't lying about being an outsider in the English ton. "They take appearances more seriously," she said. "Gentlemen may set up their mistresses fairly openly, but they don't go about in society with them. And ladies certainly don't go about with their lovers. Not if the relationship is known. But as long as everyone can pretend to turn a blind eye, it's amazing what goes on."

"You're kind," the contessa said in a matter-of-fact voice. "Or brave, or both. I know in London it would be scandal for you to sit at table with a gentleman and his mistress."

Oh, dear God, if this kind woman knew the truth of her past. "Nonsense," Mélanie said. "We'd never take such tiresome conventions seriously."

"Perhaps not. But I suspect my husband's children do. Kit was quite concerned, I think, about you and Lady Tarrington being exposed to me." The contessa smiled with composure and smoothed her hands over her lap. "Which I suppose should make me all the more grateful that he and his sisters are here at all."

CHAPTER 5

Mélanie sank down on a gold silk settee in the bedchamber that had been allotted to her and Malcolm, Jessica in her arms. Jessica still woke to nurse before her parents went to bed. Was it her imagination, Mélanie wondered, settling her daughter at her breast, or was Jessica more insistent about nursing since their lives had been disrupted by their abrupt departure from the only home she could remember?

Malcolm patted Berowne who was curled up on the bed. "Not the day I envisioned when we got up this morning."

Mélanie rocked Jessica in her arms. "Odd to find oneself in the midst of someone else's nightmare."

"A reminder of how fortunate we are." Malcolm gave a quick smile. "Not that we need reminding." He tossed his coat over a chair and began to unbutton his waistcoat.

Mélanie studied her husband. Impossible to ignore certain parallels. "You talked to Thurston quite a bit after dinner."

"I think perhaps he relished having someone outside the family to speak to." Malcolm tossed his waistcoat after the coat. "He said he left not so much because of the scandal as because he couldn't figure out a way for the contessa and him to be together in Britain. Appalling to have to choose between the person one loves and one's children." Malcolm unwound his cravat and stared at the strip of linen. "I don't know what I'd have done if I'd met you after I'd married someone else and had children."

"I do. You'd have been honorable and stayed for your children, whatever the state of your marriage."

Malcolm folded the crumpled cravat into neat quarters. "Not that I'd have taken the risk of marriage if I hadn't met you."

"Oh, but you would have, dearest." Mélanie studied the familiar, determined bones of her husband's face, at once strong and fragile. "You'd have come to the aid of some other girl who needed you."

Malcolm smoothed a crease from the cravat. "I've said it before, sweetheart. Coming to your aid was an excuse to propose to a woman I desperately wanted, despite my qualms about my fitness to be a husband."

"You're underestimating your chivalry, darling. I'm quite sure that with or without your feelings being engaged to the same degree, you'd still have come to some other girl's rescue." It haunted her, sometimes, what girl he might have married if he hadn't met her. A girl from his own world. A girl who wasn't an enemy agent. A girl who wouldn't have forced him to flee his country and career, his friends and family.

"And then I'd have met you. At some point. On a mission in the Cantabrian Mountains. In Lisbon, with you in disguise. In Brussels, before Waterloo. In Paris, afterwards. And you'd have turned my world upside down. And probably acquired all sorts of British secrets in the process."

He smiled as he said it. That was what Malcolm did when it came to her past. Smiled and laughed in a way that at once defied and acknowledged her past betrayals. That offered a way to go on while accepting that they'd never really escape the past.

Mélanie smoothed her fingers over their daughter's still wispy hair. "However we might have met, I'm no contessa. You could have set me up as a mistress with relatively few raised brows."

"Don't, Mel." Malcolm's voice cut with a force that hadn't been there when they discussed her spying. "However we might have met, whatever my circumstances or your own, that's not a way I'd ever have seen you. That's not what I'd have wanted from you. What I'd have wanted between us."

She swallowed. "I'm sorry, darling. You know how I feel about conventions."

"I don't give a damn about conventions. I'd have happily lived in so-called sin with you. I think I could be happy with you anywhere. But I'd never be happy hiding you and our relationship away like a sordid secret."

"Gentlemen's mistresses in Mayfair are a fairly open secret, dearest."

"Even so." He set the cravat on the chair and folded his arms across his chest. "You underrate yourself sometimes, sweetheart. And me. However I'd met you, I know what I'd have wanted between us. Whether or not we could have had it."

She swallowed again. This time, her throat was raw with unshed tears. "I love you, Malcolm."

He grinned. "That's a relief. Considering what you've

42

given up for me."

"What we've given up for each other."

Malcolm moved to the settee and dropped down beside her and Jessica. "Thurston doesn't seem to regret what he's given up. On the contrary. He expressed concern about his son entering a marriage that seems to be motivated by something other than love."

"I can understand." Mélanie shifted Jessica in her arms. "Though I can also understand the younger generation of Montagus being wary of grand passion."

Malcolm cupped his hand round Jessica's head. "Selena reminds me of Gisèle when I first returned from the Continent. Quick to lash out lest she be betrayed into showing any feeling."

"I said much the same to the contessa." Mélanie blinked at the image of Gisèle, her husband Andrew, and their baby son at Dunmykel. Not because they weren't ridiculously happy but because she couldn't be sure when they would see them again. "And I told her what good friends you and Gisèle are now."

Malcolm shot a look at her.

"She confided in me about some of the challenges of their life here. I think she was looking for a confidante."

"I think Thurston was, as well. And perhaps Conte Vincenzo, judging by how long he talked to Raoul."

"The contessa is worried about everything Thurston's given up for her."

"I don't think he regrets it." Malcolm looked down at Jessica. "Though I can't imagine how he's gone on for so long separated from his children."

Raoul dropped his coat over a chairback. The bedchamber he'd been allotted, with handsome walnut furniture and terra-cotta walls that conjured thoughts of Renaissance frescoes, felt cold and dark despite the warmth of the night, the glow of a brace of candles, the moonlight spilling in through the window. For years he'd been used to sleeping alone. On missions. At home, or whatever passed for home. But these past months he'd got used to slipping into Laura's room (or on occasion climbing in through her window), then slipping out before dawn. Not the most comfortable of existences, but the delights were undeniable.

And then, in recent weeks, he and Laura had been traveling as husband and wife. It had been Laura's suggestion at first. Safer to put the adults in two rooms with the children between them. They were unlikely to encounter anyone they knew. She'd had a good point, though he'd protested about what the children might think. Laura had returned that the children were sharp eyed and they weren't going to be able to conceal their relationship forever. Better not to make too much of it. Which he'd accepted. Triumph of impulse over sense. Not for the first time.

But at least staying at inns, concerned about pursuit, it had made a certain sense to stay close. At the villa, all logic and prudence dictated he should remain where he was and see Laura in the morning.

But when had he ever listened to logic and prudence?

Besides, said a voice he didn't quite want to acknowledge, once they got to Malcolm's villa and were settled, his excuse for remaining would be gone. He'd never meant to be gone from his work in Spain this long. The country was on the verge of an uprising against the restored Royalists, and he was in the midst of setting up a network. The prospect of departure made every night that much more precious.

He tested the latch on his window and eased the sash up. A breeze greeted him, still warm despite the hour. For a moment he could feel the cool damp of an English evening. How odd to be missing it.

He could hear the lapping of the lake, but no other sounds. The other windows were dark or at least the curtains were drawn. Only two windows down to Laura's. He swung a leg over the sill, pulled himself up, and pushed the window closed. He gave his eyes a few moments to grow accustomed to the dark, then reached out to grip the smooth stones while his toe found a hold in the grout below. His wound gave a twinge of protest. Proof he was growing soft. He'd engaged in much more strenuous activity with much worse injuries.

He inched across to the next window, took a moment to breathe, then started for the faint glow behind the curtains that was Laura's room. A handhold, a foothold, another inch—

"What the devil are you doing here?" someone demanded in Milanese.

Raoul went still, flattened against the wall. The voice sounded startlingly close, but after a moment he realized it came not from the house, not even from the terrace, but from the edge of the lake below. Someone must have walked along the lakeshore to the villa. Or pulled up in a boat. By one of those freaks of sound, the voice carried so clearly it seemed to be speaking in his ear, though the speaker no doubt thought he was private. Years as an agent had taught Raoul to be wary of such traps.

45

"I needed to see you," another voice responded, also in Milanese. "We're moving the timeline up."

"Why—"

"Thurston has a shipment coming in. So the trade will happen soon."

"When?"

"We can't be sure. You'll have to watch. Investigate. If you're having qualms of friendship—"

"Friendship? For Thurston?" The first voice gave a rough laugh. "You know what I think of him. But—"

The voice cut off abruptly, as though the speakers had moved away from the pocket where sound carried. Raoul stayed where he was, though it was doubtful he'd be able to hear them again, and the trees below the terrace should guarantee he was screened from view wherever they were.

Still, it gave him ample opportunity to run those voices through his head. Both men. The voice that had warned that Thurston had a shipment coming in was a voice Raoul would swear he had never heard before. But the other voice, the one that had given the rough laugh at the idea of feeling friendship for Thurston, was familiar. Raoul had heard it only a few hours before, making conversation on the terrace below.

It belonged to the contessa's husband, Conte Vincenzo.

Laura did up the blue satin ribbon at the neck of her nightdress. Her candle cast a small circle of light on the polished floorboards and the purples and reds of the Turkey rug. The rest of the room was in shadow. Odd, when she had slept alone for so much of the past five years, to find the bedchamber so particularly empty now. Even when her relationship with Raoul began, he'd been gone much of the time and she'd only had memories to warm her, along with confused thoughts about what was between them and what it meant.

But these past weeks they'd been able to live like an acknowledged couple. Cut loose from society, away from most people they knew, they'd existed in a sort of world out of time. A world in which they could ignore the issues that would always keep them from being the sort of couple Malcolm and Mélanie were. Society's opinion, his wife, his work, his scruples about the danger that work could put her and Emily in. She'd always known they'd have to face those issues eventually. He couldn't stay in Italy forever. But once they were at the Rannochs' villa, they'd have a bit more time together. This night shouldn't feel such a wrench. And yet—

A faint creak sounded behind her. She spun round to see Raoul climbing over the windowsill.

Relief, delight, and alarm washed over her in a deluge. She ran to his side. "For God's sake, darling—"

"Don't tell me you aren't glad to see me." Raoul dropped to the floor and pushed the window closed. "I need to rest my back before I climb the walls again."

"You're wounded." She put a hand on his arm and peered at his gray silk waistcoat to see if any blood had seeped through.

"I've directed skirmishes and scaled battlements with worse."

"Yes, but those were things you had to do."

He bent his head and kissed her. "Define 'had to.'"

Laura leaned in to his embrace for a moment, then drew back. "I think I should check the dressing—"

"By all means. Do take my shirt off. Not to mention the

47

rest of my clothes."

"You're in no condition—"

"You may have to do most of the work, but I assure you I can manage." He tugged loose the ribbon on her nightdress and pressed a kiss to the hollow of her throat.

This time Laura closed her eyes and wrapped her arms round his neck. Honestly, there was no arguing with the man...

Much later, curled carefully against his uninjured side, she propped herself up on one elbow and looked down at him. He was smiling, but there was a faint furrow between his brows, as though he was trying to puzzle something out. "Raoul? Is something wrong?" she asked. And then immediately thought better of it, because if he was puzzling over their future, it might have been better not to speak. Not pushing each other had always been one of the unspoken rules between them.

"Not wrong." The warmth in his gaze as it met her own brought a rush of reassurance. But the furrow between his brows remained. He tucked one arm beneath his head and laced the fingers of his other hand through her own. "I overheard something on my way here, and I still can't make sense of it."

Laura listened as he recounted the conversation he'd overheard between Conte Vincenzo and the unknown man. "Good God." The night had been odd enough, but her attention had been focused on the family drama unfolding before them. "So Vincenzo has an ulterior purpose for being here?"

"So it seems."

"And Thurston—Is he smuggling?"

"It's possible. There's a lot of smuggling across the Swiss

border. I suppose he could be storing goods. It certainly sounds as though he's bringing something in secretly. I'm damned if I know what to make of it. Or what, if anything, to do about it."

Laura tightened her grip on his hand. "Darling, at least—"

"Don't worry, I think we've all learned something about the folly of keeping secrets." Raoul drew her hand up to his own and kissed her knuckles. "We'll tell Malcolm and Mélanie in the morning. Meanwhile, we have a bit of time before I have to climb back out the window."

Mélanie choked on a swallow of strong Italian coffee. One of the discreet footmen had brought a tray to their room in the morning. The four of them—she, Malcolm, Raoul, and Laura—were gathered round the low table where she'd put her medical supply box last night, and Raoul had just finished recounting the conversation he had overheard. "You could have started bleeding all over the walls and fallen on the conspirators."

"I'd have fallen on the terrace. Not that there was any danger of that."

Malcolm clunked his own cup down on the blue-and-yellow-flowered tray. "Good God. You're sure it was Vincenzo?"

"I don't forget a voice," Raoul said.

"No, you wouldn't." Malcolm shook his head. "What the devil is he involved in? He certainly gave an excellent impression of getting on with Thurston last night."

"Yes, that seems to be something of a sham." Raoul reached for his coffee and frowned into the cup. "But except for that one comment about what he thought of Thurston, he sounded more like a man on a mission than a man seeking vengeance against his wife's lover. A mission connected to whatever this shipment is that Thurston is receiving."

Mélanie leaned against the sofa, elbow on the sofa arm, chin on her hand. "Could he be buying art from abroad?" Napoleon had appropriated art treasures from all over the Continent. The restored Royalist government in France was less than eager to return them, and other treasures had found their way into a variety of hands through the wars that had engulfed the Continent. More than one case they had investigated had involved art that had found its way into unexpected hands.

"There are some handsome pieces in the house," Malcolm said. "But most of it looks Italian or like English pieces Thurston brought with him. Nothing—at least nothing we've seen—would suggest that sort of smuggling." Nothing on the level of the collection assembled by his putative father, Alistair Rannoch, though Malcolm avoided speaking of Alistair in general. "On the other hand—"

"The bandits who stopped us last night," Mélanie said. "They were after some sort of treasure."

"And whether that's jewels or paintings or information, it hard not to imagine a connection to whatever shipment Thurston is expecting. Of course sometimes the most seemingly obvious connections prove to mean nothing at all." Malcolm took a sip of coffee. "Italy's said to be crawling with agents these days. We're back in Metternich's sphere, after all."

They had had their luggage surreptitiously searched more than once on the journey. It probably wasn't anything to do with them personally, Raoul had said the first time it happened. The Italian states jealously guarded their borders and foreign travelers tended to be viewed with suspicion as potentially bringing dangerous political ideas with them. On the other hand, it was entirely possible Prince Metternich knew they were in Austrian territory. Mélanie and Malcolm had cause to know how extensive his network of informants and agents was.

"Vincenzo made it clear he's friendly with Metternich," Mélanie said. "Do you think he's one of Metternich's agents?"

"I can imagine stranger things," Malcolm said. "But except for generally keeping an eye on a British expatriate, I can't see why Metternich would have much of an interest in Thurston. Unless there's a great deal we don't know about Thurston."

Laura picked up the coffee pot and refilled their cups. "If Thurston is smuggling, Vincenzo could be trying to find proof. But the part about 'the trade' sounds like more than simple payment for goods."

"So it does." Raoul reached for her hand. "And the conversation shows Vincenzo's friendship with Thurston is a sham, at least on the conte's side."

"Leaving the question of what, if anything, we say to warn Thurston." Malcolm frowned. "And it's difficult to say anything without mentioning the shipment."

Mélanie reached for her coffee. "It might be interesting to see how he reacts to that."

"It might." Her husband met her gaze. "If we were interested in investigating whatever's going on."

"We're going to be living a handsbreadth away from them, darling." Mélanie took a swallow of coffee. Hot. Bracing. It did have a way of making one feel alive. "I don't see how we can avoid being caught up in whatever is going on, at least to

51

some degree."

Malcolm gave a faint smile and tucked a strand of hair behind her ear. "You're itching for something to keep you busy."

"Don't say you aren't. And we need to learn what was behind the bandits holding us up, in any case. If they weren't looking for Thurston or Kit, they may have really been looking for us."

Malcolm picked up his coffee and took a meditative sip. "Thurston's been generous. Shown us hospitality at a difficult time. If he is a target of Metternich, I'm inclined to be sympathetic. And we don't know for a certainty that he's doing anything underhanded. I think we owe it to him to warn him that Vincenzo may have some sort of agenda." He looked from Raoul to Laura. "I can do it without mentioning just how you overheard Vincenzo and his confederate."

Laura stirred milk into her coffee. "Not that I'm particularly concerned if he did learn the truth. We're rather beyond that, and he of all people shouldn't cast aspersions."

"We're never going to be completely beyond it," Raoul said. "And *I'm* concerned."

"That," said Laura, "is because you're overprotective. To the point of becoming sadly conventional."

Raoul laughed, "I think it's the first time I've been called sadly conventional."

"There's a first time for everything. No one should know that better than you."

Malcolm swallowed the last of his coffee and got to his feet. "I'll talk to Thurston before breakfast. There may be a perfectly logical explanation."

"Oh, darling," Mélanie said. "Haven't you learned there's never a perfectly logical explanation?"

52

Malcolm found Thurston in his study, a handsome apartment with a view of the terrace. It had a more English look than the rest of the house. A solid oak desk, chairs covered in bottle-green leather, hunting prints on the wall. As though Thurston had packed up the contents of one room in his London house and had them shipped to Italy. Or perhaps, Malcolm thought, Lady Thurston had sent them after him.

"Ah, Rannoch." Thurston looked up from a stack of papers on his desk. "I trust you all slept well." He set down his pen and waved a hand towards the bottle-green chairs. "How's O'Roarke this morning? He gave an impression of being in admirable condition last night, but I have the sense he's good at giving that impression."

"He is." Malcolm smiled and closed the door. Thurston had unwittingly given him the opening he needed. "O'Roarke's wound shows no sign of infection and he insists he feels well. But the wound troubled him last night." Malcolm dropped into one of the chairs. "He didn't come out and admit it—you're right, he's not the sort who would—but he wasn't able to sleep. He went downstairs and took a turn on the terrace in the middle of the night. Sure sign his wound was troubling him."

Thurston gave a faint smile. "I'm only surprised he admitted it to you."

Malcolm settled back in the chair and crossed his legs. "I'm not sure he would have done, but he overheard something that concerned him."

"At that hour?" Thurston's brows drew together. "If you mean an assignation—"

"No. I imagine O'Roarke would have kept that to himself. Two men were talking down by the edge of the lake. O'Roarke didn't hear much, and he hesitated to pry, but he heard one of them say something about planning something. O'Roarke couldn't identify the first man, but he's quite sure the second was Conte Vincenzo."

Thurston scarcely moved a muscle but Malcolm heard his indrawn breath.

"It could mean nothing, of course," Malcolm said. "Words taken out of context can easily be misinterpreted. But O'Roarke and I thought you should know."

"Thank you, Rannoch." Thurston released his breath and gave a smile that was just a bit too practiced. "There was a time I'd have been only too ready to believe Vincenzo was plotting all manner of things against me. But I think he and I are at a point now where I can talk to him about it. A bit odd, but as you say, there's probably an explanation. It could be a surprise party, for all we know. Still, I'd prefer to be aware of what O'Roarke overheard. I appreciate your telling me, Rannoch."

Malcolm inclined his head. "It's what I'd want in your position."

Thurston got to his feet. So did Malcolm. He was quite sure Thurston wasn't as sanguine about Vincenzo's words as he let on. But what Thurston did now was up to him. Malcolm had passed along the information. The prudent course was to stay out of it. If his mind was already racing ahead with dozens of questions, it was a habit from investigations.

Thurston aligned the papers on his desk. One paper slipped to the side. Thurston picked it up and tucked it back in the stack, then walked round the side of the desk.

"Breakfast should be laid out on the terrace."

Malcolm nodded, smiled, and followed his host from the room. Thank God for training to fall back on. Somehow he knew what to do and say. Because his brain had gone numb. He hadn't seen enough of the paper Thurston had tucked into the stack to make out the words. But he recognized the handwriting. He had known it from boyhood. It was familiar from family letters, official dispatches, and coded communications.

It belonged to his former spymaster, Lord Carfax.

The man they had fled Britain to escape.

CHAPTER 6

Mélanie's first view of the Rannoch villa was through the window of the carriage. She had been there once before, but for all they were in the midst of—their flight from Britain, the bandit attack, the unexpected tangle at the Thurstons'—the sight of the villa stopped her breath for a moment. White stone glittering against a blue sky. Green hedges surrounding it, the blue of the lake below. She'd never thought herself the sort to be sentimental about houses. But then, the daughter of traveling players, she'd never known a stable home, even in her happy childhood.

She glanced across the carriage at Malcolm. He'd been quiet since they'd left Thurston's villa. Even at breakfast, when he'd come back from his talk with Thurston about Vincenzo. They'd had no opportunity for private conversation. She wondered at the memories this house held. Not as many, surely, as Dunmykel or the house in Berkeley Square, but it had been his mother's, and her past was a tangled weight Mélanie was still coming to appreciate.

Two figures stood beneath the columned portico and descended the steps to greet them as their carriage drew up in the circular drive. Blanca, her companion and maid, wore a loose muslin gown and had her dark hair tumbling down her back, fastened back with a ribbon. Her husband, Miles Addison, Malcolm's valet, was formally attired in coat, waistcoat, cravat, and breeches. Addison was punctilious about the forms, but with the summer weather they were going to have to do something about it. Even Malcolm and Raoul wore lighter clothes.

"I'd forgot what a really warm summer feels like." Blanca ran forwards as they climbed from the carriage. The wind pulled back the folds of her gown, revealing her pregnancy. She was visibly more advanced than she had been when they parted in d'Arenberg.

Colin and Emily tumbled from the carriage and flung themselves on Blanca. "We missed you!" "The baby looks bigger." "Bandits attacked us!" "Daddy tackled one." "Mummy grabbed his pistol." "Laura hit one with a boot." "Uncle Raoul fought them with a sword."

"It was a knife," Raoul said, climbing from the carriage. "And they used it on me, not the other way round. But I'm fine, though my pride's a bit bruised for being so slow."

Addison's gaze flickered over their party. "It seems you had an eventful journey."

"We're all in one piece." Malcolm swung down from the carriage last, Berowne draped over his shoulder.

"The house is in good order," Addison said. "I don't think we'll need a large staff. We've hired an excellent woman from the village to cook and two of her daughters to clean. And Giacomo and Rodrigo here to help out." He nodded at two

57

young men who had emerged from the house and hurried to take charge of the luggage.

"There's a cold collation laid out on the terrace," Blanca said. "Wait until you taste the tomatoes."

The entry hall, tiled in ivory and burgundy marble, was blessedly cool in the afternoon heat. The walls were hung with fifteenth-century tapestries and paintings from medieval to modern. The statues that lined the hall looked centuries older. An open gallery edged with a gilt railing ran round the first floor and the ceiling rose two stories to exquisite Renaissance frescoes. The house was older than Thurston's villa and simpler in some ways, yet the art treasures were finer. An exquisite jewel. A retreat from the world. And now their home for the foreseeable future.

Mélanie saw Raoul hesitate as he stepped over the threshold. With a shock of surprise, she realized the house held memories for him, as well. A Madonna that looked to be late fourteenth century hung on the wall that faced the terrace. And opposite it, an oil of a fair-haired woman in a filmy white gown, leaning against a stone balustrade. Painted at the villa. Why had it never occurred to her that Arabella Rannoch might have brought Raoul here?

Malcolm's gaze went to the picture, as well, though he didn't break his stride.

They stepped through French windows onto the terrace, which, unlike the one at the Thurston villa, was covered, offering delightful shade from the afternoon heat. Red roses spilled from pristine white planters. Arabella Rannoch had cultivated exquisite gardens at all her houses. Stone steps wound down the hillside to the lake. Laura, the only one of them who hadn't seen the house, paused and drew a breath. "Dear heaven. Your family have a knack for picking beautiful

58

spots, Malcolm."

"I take no credit for it." Malcolm gave a crooked smile, though his gaze still seemed clouded to Mélanie.

The generous breakfast at the Thurston villa had only been a few hours before, but the children fell on the bread and cheese and sliced tomatoes with gusto. Mélanie sipped a glass of chilled Trebbiano and nibbled a piece of bread. She looked out over the lake. Wooded mountains soared above the water, unexpectedly wild, setting off the manicured beauty below. Offering protection. Or closing one in.

She'd thought she'd grown accustomed to the style in which Malcolm lived. But there was something about the villa that brought it all tumbling back. This wasn't a house for entertaining, the center of a political career, like the Berkeley Square house, nor a vast estate with numerous tenants, like Dunmykel. It was a place for lingering over a cup of coffee in the morning or a glass of wine in the evening, not for hosting political dinner parties or late night strategy sessions or entertaining the countryside at a harvest festival. It was a playground for adults, designed for pleasure. The very things that made it an ideal retreat made the thought of long-term life here close her throat with terror.

Raoul and Laura walked to the balustrade to look at the view of the lake. Malcolm listened to Addison's report on the condition of the property with every appearance of interest. But when the children asked to go down to the lake, Malcolm looked from Addison to Blanca. "Could you take them down? They're longing to see it, and there's something the four of us need to discuss."

"Of course." Addison scooped Jessica up. "There's a perfect spot for sand castles."

Laura had packed hats and sand toys within easy reach.

Within a few minutes, the children were outfitted and the little party was off, Jessica on Addison's shoulders, Colin and Emily clinging to Blanca's hands and pulling her along in their eagerness.

"Good practice for Blanca and Addison," Mélanie murmured. Hard, now Blanca and Addison were about to become parents and were very much a married couple, to remember there'd been a time they'd attempted to conceal their very relationship from their employers. She turned to Malcolm. The afternoon light caught the seriousness in his eyes. Whatever was going on, it was worse than she had supposed. Something far more than the memories the villa contained. If she hadn't been so caught up in her own qualms, she'd have noticed much earlier. "Darling? What is it?"

He moved to her side and raised her hand to his lips. "I'm not sure how long we can stay here."

She scanned his face. "Why—"

"I saw something when I went to talk to Thurston." He drew her over to a metal sofa piled with tapestry cushions. Laura and Raoul sat in chairs opposite them. The sun glittered off the lake, but shadows filled the terrace where they sat. Malcolm leaned forwards and recounted his interview with Thurston and the letter he had glimpsed on Thurston's desk.

"Lord Thurston is working with Carfax?" Laura asked in pardonable disbelief.

"We don't know that." Mélanie looked from Laura to Malcolm to Raoul. "We just know that Carfax wrote to him."

"It doesn't matter," Malcolm said. "It means we aren't safe here."

"For God's sake, darling, where do you suggest we go? France and Spain aren't safe. We can't keep running."

"We can avoid living next to a spy of Carfax's."

60

"We aren't running from Carfax. That is, we're running because he knows about me, but he told you that though he couldn't protect us, he wouldn't expose me himself."

"For God's sake, Mel, don't tell me you believe the man."

"Of course not. But I think it would be folly to run just because—"

"Just because the head of British intelligence is spying on us?"

"Darling." She seized his hands. "I didn't quarrel with leaving Britain. I admitted it was the best choice. But we can't keep running every time we face a whiff of danger. It isn't always the best option."

"Damn it, Mel, I know you're always ready to run risks—"

"This isn't about that—"

"No? Do I have to remind you what we're risking?"

"Of course not. But we're not in England. Carfax can't have me arrested. Nor can anyone else."

"If you think that would stop Carfax—"

"It wouldn't," Raoul said, "but it would make it harder. Assuming he wanted to move against you."

"Christ, O'Roarke," Malcolm turned to his father. "I thought you'd be on my side."

"My dear Malcolm. If you imagine I'm fool enough to choose sides—But think about Carfax for a moment. Thurston and Carfax are roughly of an age. They probably knew each other before Thurston left the country. Carfax may very likely have guessed you'd come here. If so, he might have written to Thurston for information. It doesn't necessarily mean there's any particular connection between the men."

"Except that we have whatever shipment Vincenzo claimed Thurston is expecting, and the bandit attack," Malcolm said, his voice even but with a grim edge.

61

Laura was fingering a fold of her green-sprigged skirt. "It's not my decision. I'm not the one in danger. But if Carfax is tracking you, it's likely he'll be able to find you wherever we go." She looked from Malcolm to Mélanie. "You're very good at what you do, but—"

"Point taken," Malcolm said. "Go on."

"Wouldn't it be better to stay and try to learn what he's planning? We know someone connected to him. Which is more than we might have if we went somewhere else."

Malcolm drew in and released his breath. "You're a very astute woman, Laura. And you said all that without telling me I've reacted like a fool."

"You reacted like a man very concerned about his family."

"I should have been prudent enough to think a few steps ahead. We haven't a prayer of surviving against Carfax if we don't." Malcolm dug a hand into his hair. "But I think we have to at least consider that Thurston may be working with Carfax."

"It would be like Carfax to make use of an expatriate," Raoul said. "And assuming you were right in your theory that Vincenzo may be working for Metternich, this would explain why Metternich would be interested in Thurston."

"But Thurston's been living quietly here for fifteen years," Laura said. "What information could he give Carfax?"

"Reports on the expatriate community perhaps," Raoul said. "It's amazing who comes to Italy. Princess Caroline lived near here until recently."

Malcolm dug a hand into his hair. "You think Carfax had Thurston sending him reports on the prince regent's estranged wife? Carfax almost certainly is getting reports on her. From more than one agent. But she left for Pesaro a year ago."

62

"She was perhaps the most notable British expatriate on the lake, but there are others Carfax might find of interest," Raoul said.

"Could that be the shipment?" Laura asked. "Money Thurston is being paid? Is Vincenzo planning to intercept the payment?"

"Or whatever information the payment is for," Mélanie said.

Malcolm was frowning. "You're right. Carfax's network is so vast—vaster even than I realized, as we learned before we left—we were almost bound to run into one of his agents at some point. I just deceived myself into thinking one of the benefits of our leaving Britain was that I was free of Carfax."

Raoul leaned forwards and put a hand on Malcolm's shoulder. "You don't work for Carfax now. Not in any conceivable way. You may not be free of him, but the dynamic has shifted."

"I can't believe he'd care that much about what we're doing now."

"I think you're underestimating his interest in you." Raoul squeezed Malcolm's shoulder and sat back in his chair. "But I don't think he's using Thurston to lure you back."

Mélanie smoothed a crease from the sheer lavender muslin of her gown. "At least now we're likely to be invited back to Thurston's villa."

Malcolm turned to her. "Mel—"

"You'd rather break in in the middle of the night? Obviously we need to get a look at his papers. Unless you've decided not to worry about Carfax?"

Malcolm stared at her for a moment, then began to laugh. "My God, sweetheart."

"What?"

"You've got us in the midst of an investigation."

"It's the logical course of action."

Malcolm put his head in his hands.

"What?" Mélanie asked.

"Ever since we left London you've been saying the quiet in Italy could be our undoing. Bandits held us up last night and seemed to think we possess something of value. Our neighbor is connected to Carfax and receiving secret shipments. One of his guests is plotting against him. His house is full of people from two different families who can barely be civil to each other." He looked up at Mélanie, torn between laughter and desperation. "I don't think you need fear being bored, sweetheart."

Laura stepped back onto the terrace after going upstairs to take off her spencer and exchange her bonnet for a wide-brimmed hat to wear to the lake. Raoul was alone on the terrace, arms resting on the balustrade, gaze on the lake below. He looked round with a quick smile as she closed the French window. "Malcolm and Mélanie have gone down to the lake. I could hear shouts of delight from the children."

"Emily is going to love living so close to the water." Laura joined him at the balustrade. "We have a lovely room with a view of the lake. There's a room that can serve as the night nursery between ours and Mélanie and Malcolm's."

Raoul's gaze darted over her face. "You're sure about this?"

"Sharing a bedchamber with you? I've rarely been so sure of anything."

"It's not the same as when we were stopping at inns—"

"The children know. Addison and Blanca know. I don't give a damn about who else knows. Besides, I don't want you climbing any more walls. At least not until your wound is healed."

"In the villa I could simply rap at your door."

"I'm a greedy woman, darling. I want the whole night with you. I flattered myself you wanted the same."

He smiled and dropped an arm round her shoulders. "And so much more."

Laura tilted her head back so she could look up at his face past the brim of her hat. He was still smiling, but something about the angle of his back when she stepped onto the terrace had betrayed a more serious mood. "You're more worried about Carfax than you let on to Mélanie and Malcolm."

Raoul's brows drew together. "I think you're right that Carfax could have someone watching them anywhere. Better to be here where we can watch the watchers. And I do think it's possible Carfax simply wrote to Thurston because he guessed Malcolm would take the family to the villa and wanted to keep an eye on them. But taken together with the bandits and what I overheard from Vincenzo, I suspect it's more complicated and Thurston is more than simply an innocent instrument to Carfax. Though I'm damned if I can put the pieces together yet." He tightened his arm round her. "At least it means I won't be leaving for Spain for a bit."

"Darling." Laura turned in his arm and put her hands on his chest. "You must know how happy that makes me for all the complications. But I don't ever want to be a reason—even part of a reason—that you avoid doing what you think you must."

His gaze shifted in that way it sometimes did when he looked at her, as though he was sorting through both past and future. "You aren't," he said, in an oddly flat voice. "I warned you of as much at the start."

"You didn't need to warn me," she said. "It's not anything I'd ever want. And I know it would destroy both of us."

"You're a remarkable woman, Laura. But then, I've always known that." Raoul smiled again, a smile that at once warmed his face and drew a shade over his thoughts. "But you can't blame me for being glad we have more time." He glanced out over the water. "I'd have liked to bring you to Italy under different circumstances. But we can still take advantage of the circumstances in which we find ourselves." He shrugged out of his coat and slung it over one shoulder, then took her hand and drew her over to the stone steps cut into the hillside. As the steps wound down to the lake, she could catch an occasional glimpse of the children, the Rannochs, and Blanca and Addison on the beach at the lake's edge below. The topiary bordering the path gave way to more rustic greenery as they descended. Laura looked down at the blue lake, the green grass, the birds soaring over the water. "I can't quite take in how beautiful it is here."

"Yes. A place out of time." Raoul paused for a moment, gaze moving over the blue water and white sand. "I've always loved this view in particular."

Something in his tone more than the words made Laura pause. "You used to come here with Arabella Rannoch."

He looked up at her over his shoulder, still holding her hand. "Once or twice. Or perhaps a bit more often."

"Does Malcolm know?"

"We actually brought him here more than once when he was small, but I doubt he remembers it. I haven't talked to him about it. I doubt Fanny has. She's probably the only other person who knows. But I can't speak to what he may have guessed."

The portrait of Arabella Rannoch in the villa's entry hall danced in Laura's memory. Fair hair. Fine-boned face. Restless, glittering, discontented eyes. Eagerness in her smile belied by the discontent, as though she had a great thirst for life and already knew she'd be disappointed. She'd been Raoul's lover for over twenty years. "Did she buy the house—"

"For us?" Raoul shook his head. "Oh, no. Her father bought it years before. And I doubt I was the only man she brought here."

He could say it so casually. And yet he didn't take relationships casually. At least he didn't seem to, for all he was always careful to give her an out and warn her about the limits of what he could offer.

Laura gathered up her muslin skirt with her free hand and followed Raoul down the steps to a small stone terrace cut into the hill partway down, concealed from the house by the hillside above. Roses spilled over the wall and a wrought iron table and chairs invited one to enjoy the view.

"One of my favorite spots on the property," he said simply.

"I can see why." She took in the setting for a moment, the rippling water of the lake, the scent of the flowers, the warmth of the sun on her face and arms. And yet— "It must be difficult," she said. "The memories."

As often happened, she was afraid she'd pushed too far, but he gave a quick smile. "Arabella wasn't very happy. It made for a lot of challenges. But she was happier here than most places. In fact, some of my best memories of her are here." He gave another smile. "I'm sorry. Not perhaps the best thing to say to you."

67

"I asked."

They were on the flat terrace but he was still holding her hand. His fingers tightened round her own. "It's a long time in the past, sweetheart." He drew her hand up to his lips and kissed it. "Nothing to do with us."

"It's a part of who you are." Arabella was a part of who he was, but she didn't quite want to say that.

"You're the last person I should be talking to about this."

"No. I'd like to understand." Rather to her surprise, she realized it was the truth.

He drew a breath, gaze on the water. "I still remember my first glimpse of her. At that point in my life, I'd never met anyone who seemed so alive."

"Across a ballroom?" Laura could hear Harry Davenport, in an unguarded moment, talking about his first glimpse of Cordelia.

"Picking the lock of Lord Glenister's desk. At a house party." Raoul dropped his coat on one of chairs and leaned against the balustrade, back to the lake. "I couldn't sleep and had taken refuge in the library next door."

"You caught her?"

"Yes, to her eternal shame, I think. She was looking for information about the Elsinore League."

"Did she tell you so?" Laura asked. She knew Arabella's life's work had been unearthing the secrets of the League, a mysterious club begun by a group of powerful young men with the aim of manipulating the world to their own advantage. Malcolm said his mother had very likely married Alistair Rannoch, one of the founding members, as part of her effort to expose and checkmate the League. Arabella had drawn Raoul into her quest. Years later, Laura's lover, the Duke of Trenchard, had blackmailed her into spying for the

Elsinore League. Which meant that, for a time, Laura had worked for the group Arabella and Raoul were dedicated to stopping.

"She didn't tell me about the League that night," Raoul said, "but she told me enough to catch my interest."

"In more ways than one." Laura perched on the balustrade beside him.

He smiled. "I'm not blind. She was a beautiful woman. But I'd met beautiful women. I'd never met anyone like Arabella. I offered my services to her before I really understood her quest."

Laura studied her lover in the midday sun, the creases and shadows in his face unmistakable, trying to see him as a young man. "You must have been just out of university." His eyes would have been as quick and brilliant as ever, but surely his gaze hadn't contained as many ghosts.

"I was actually about to go back to Paris for my last year. Arabella came to Paris that winter. That was where she told me about the Elsinore League. And where our relationship progressed in other ways, as well. It was then that she first brought me here."

Laura stared, doing sums in her head. "Was Malcolm—"

"Conceived here? I think so." Raoul hesitated a moment. "Arabella wasn't my first lover, but I suppose you could say she was my first love."

"Love" wasn't a word they used between them. Or that Raoul used often at all. And yet it was another aspect of his words that lingered in her memory. "When Arabella recruited you in her fight against the Elsinore League—was that when you first became an agent?"

"Yes. I knew I wasn't happy with the way the world was ordered, but I hadn't yet thought about how I might work to

69

change it. Once I was working with Arabella, being an agent in other ways seemed possible, as well."

"You were twenty."

"Nineteen. Arabella wasn't much older, though she'd already been married to Alistair Rannoch for over a year."

Putting him in much the same situation she was in now, inextricably intertwined with a married lover. "You didn't ever consider—"

"Asking her to run off with me? I did. Once. When I found out she was pregnant."

Laura stared at her lover, a possible alternate life he might have lived dancing before her eyes. "Does Malcolm know?"

"That I explicitly asked her? I don't know that it would serve any purpose. I didn't care for convention, and I thought society was easily defied. Arabella was a creature of society. If I'd been older, I'd have realized she'd never consider turning her back on it. Or on her quest to expose the Elsinore League. She was perhaps the center of my life at that point. I don't think I was ever the center of hers."

She caught echoes of loneliness beneath the matter-of-fact tone. She wasn't sure she'd ever plumb those depths. She touched his arm lightly, afraid to intrude. "Was that when you met Margaret?" Strange to say his wife's name.

"A bit later. After Malcolm was born I felt I needed to draw back a bit. Not from him—I visited whenever I could—but to avoid scandal. And to avoid rousing Alistair's suspicions. But it didn't end things. I was in France for much of the time. Arabella and I met here more than once in those years. We brought Malcolm here." His gaze moved round the terrace again. For a moment, Laura was sure Arabella Rannoch seemed so close he must have felt he could reach out and touch her. "It holds a lot of happy memories. But not

70

all. Arabella had moods. It was years before I understood she was ill. I kept thinking I should be able to shake her out of them. Sometimes for days she couldn't leave her bed. And then other times she'd be convinced she could do anything. And I was hardly enough for her then, either."

"She had lovers." It was fairly common knowledge about Arabella Rannoch.

"Some in pursuit of the Elsinore League. Some simply because it amused her. Or because she was seeking escape. Or a way to quiet demons I couldn't begin to understand. It wasn't as though we'd made any promises to each other. But I wasn't as understanding as I should have been. Then Arabella and I quarreled. I didn't admit I was jealous, though that was probably part of it. I told her she was destroying herself. She said that wasn't any business of mine. Which I thought showed my place in her life. Which perhaps it did. Malcolm was seven. I'd nearly lost my life in the Terror, which has a way of throwing things into perspective. "

"And you wanted children of your own. That is, children that you could openly be a father to." Somehow that had never occurred to her.

He turned his head to look at her. "Is that so surprising?"

"No. Yes. That is, I'm not really used to seeing you as a father. I mean, I see you as Malcolm's, but—" Actually, she increasingly saw him as Emily's, but it didn't seem the time to say so.

He gave a twisted smile. "It hasn't seemed much of a possibility for years. But in those days—for a time I had delusions I could put down roots. One of my more spectacular failures." He drew a breath. "Margaret read. She was curious about the world. She seemed interested in the causes that drove my life, though I later realized that was

71

mostly to shock her parents. But perhaps most important, I couldn't imagine her screaming or throwing a scent bottle at me or staring blankly at the wall for hours on end. I felt as though I could see my life with her, for years on end. It was a long time before I realized she seemed so stable because underneath the rebellion she was terrified of change." He hesitated a moment. "I meant to be faithful. I actually was until it was clear the marriage was over to all intents and purposes."

"I don't doubt it."

He gave another, quick smile. "I don't know how a realist like you can have such touching faith."

"I know you. I know how seriously you take promises. Even unstated ones."

"If I hadn't been chasing a dream of a life I was never suited for, I wouldn't have dragged Margaret into an untenable situation."

The shifting breeze brought laughter and indistinguishable voices from the lakeshore. Laura looked down. Malcolm and Addison appeared to be building a sandcastle with Colin and Emily. Blanca was sitting in the shade of a myrtle tree while Mélanie held Jessica's hands and let her walk in the water. "You and Margaret never—"

"She lost a baby, the first year we were married." His voice, flat and precise, carried echoes of loss. "None after, despite trying. Not that having a child would have resolved our problems. It would only have made it more difficult for me to leave. Instead, I started spending more time in Dublin and London and Paris. Margaret and I had a blistering quarrel in the months before the '98 uprising. When I returned from my next trip it was clear she'd begun a love affair with her childhood sweetheart. He owns the neighboring estate, and the woman he'd married was an invalid by then. It seemed best for all of us that I make myself scarce. Then I was caught up in the uprising. Arabella helped me escape in the aftermath. When we resumed our relationship I was no longer a young man inclined to romanticize things." He met Laura's gaze. "Yes, I know it's hard to imagine me—"

"On the contrary. In many ways you're still inclined to romanticize things."

"Gammon."

She tucked her hand through his arm. "I know you."

He touched his fingers to her hand. "We went on for another decade. I started to understand her illness, though I still couldn't figure out how to help her." He looked over his shoulder at the water below. "I fished her out of the lake once. I bandaged her wrists another time. I told her what it would mean to her children to lose her. What it would mean to me. She said she understood. But I don't think any of it really had an impact."

Laura tightened her fingers round his arm. "I doubt anything you said would have made a difference."

"Perhaps." He looked into her eyes for a moment, his own unusually without armor. "But the devil of it is, one tends to be arrogant enough to think one should be enough. In the end, I don't think she could bear being out of control. Her suicide attempts weren't when she was in the depths of depression but when she felt herself slipping away."

"It must have been unbearable to lose her after so many years."

"Yes." She was relieved he didn't try to deny it. "Especially not being able to tell anyone what losing her meant. Not being there." He hesitated. "Not knowing what it was doing to Malcolm. The world seemed a less vital place."

"And being here—"

"I've learned to remember the good times. A lot of them were here. And if bad times were as well, I've learned to live with those. One has to or one would go mad."

"It's the risk," she said. "Of caring so much." Which she never had, not until recently.

Raoul looked down at her, his gaze gone unreadable. "For so long she was there. A part of my life I kept going back to. A promise. A sort of worry. But we never—" He slid his arms round her and rested his chin on her hair. "I'd never have simply drunk in the moment with her like this."

Malcolm shrugged into his dressing gown and watched his wife smooth the covers over Jessica. Addison and Blanca had found a cradle in the villa, walnut with puppies and kittens painted on it, and had it set up in the room Malcolm and Mélanie used when they arrived. Jessica was tucked in under her favorite white blanket that had been a gift from his aunt Frances. Mélanie wore her seafoam silk dressing gown, the ivory lace on the sleeves falling back along her arm as she bent to press a kiss to Jessica's forehead. If he focused on them and somehow shut his senses to the ornate plaster moldings, the cherry silk hangings, the warm breeze wafting through the open window with the scent of roses, he could imagine they were in Berkeley Square.

Mélanie straightened up and turned to him with a smile as dazzling as her diamond earrings. "Addison and Blanca arranged the rooms splendidly. Colin and Emily seem quite comfortable in the night nursery. But then they're both used to changes of location."

He glanced round their bedchamber. His shaving kit was on the chest of drawers, a carved walnut piece more ornate than the one at home. Her dressing case stood open on the dressing table, with several cream pots, her silver brush and comb, and a velvet jewel case already in residence on the ebony-inlaid surface. Mel had been making a home in different lodgings for most of their marriage, after all. They had really only had a settled home for a little over a year. One could say this move had more continuity about it than change.

"We can make some changes as we settle in." Malcolm moved to the chest of drawers, where Addison had also left a bottle of whisky along with a pair of Venetian glasses that gleamed crimson in the lamplight. "There's no reason you shouldn't redo anything you like."

Mélanie moved to his side, her dressing gown and unbound dark hair stirring about her. "I quite like the house as it is." She hesitated, her gaze flickering over his face. "Unless you want to change anything?"

She had redone the Berkeley Square house largely to get rid of the ghosts of his parents, though making it theirs had had other advantages. "It's different here," he said. "I wasn't here that often, but most of my memories of it are happy. And I was never here with Alistair. In fact, I don't know that he ever came here." Malcolm thought back to the moment they had all stepped into the villa that afternoon. The shock of how vivid his mother's presence still was amid the tile and plaster and marble, the relief of finding no echoes of the man he had grown up calling father. And other things he had noticed, as well. "Though after today, I suspect O'Roarke did."

"So do I." Mélanie drew a breath. "That is—"

"He was as aware of Arabella as I was, walking into the

house. He was probably here with her more than I was. I never thought of it much—one doesn't think of those things about one's parents—but it's an obvious place for them to have come. Poor devil. I don't imagine the memories are all easy ones."

Mélanie curled her hand behind his neck. "They can't be for you, either. I never thought—Darling, would you rather have gone somewhere else?"

His slid his arms round her waist. "The villa was my idea. I rather insisted upon it, as I recall."

"Because you were being practical and it was part of your escape plan. An escape plan you made when we all hoped we'd never have to put it into effect." She tilted her head back and looked up at him. "We needed to leave Britain. You have a beautiful house in another country—"

"*We* have." He tucked her fall of hair behind her left ear.

"We have, then. It seemed practical to come here. That doesn't mean there might not be other reasons for going somewhere else."

"Just a few hours ago you told me we couldn't keep running."

"That was because of Carfax. I don't think we can find a place free of Carfax. But we could find a place without memories."

He smoothed her hair back on the right side and pressed a kiss to her temple. "And I love you for it, beloved. But I told you, my memories here are quite happy. Less complicated than O'Roarke's, I suspect."

Mélanie put her hands on his chest, gaze fastened on the braid on his dressing gown. "I know it's complicated."

She didn't define what "it" was, but then there really wasn't any need to. He put a hand under her chin and tilted

76

her face up. "I'm glad he's here. Truly."

He felt the sigh of relief that ran through her, though her gaze continued thoughtful. "I suppose the news about Carfax means he won't be off to Spain as quickly as he intended."

"Yes, well, that's a side benefit. Whatever we may be facing from Carfax, it rather pales against the risk O'Roarke's up against in Spain."

Mélanie's eyes widened. "He's only doing what he's always done."

"My point precisely." Malcolm turned to put one of the glasses of whisky he'd poured in her hand. "How many times have you seen him almost die?"

Mélanie took a sip of whisky. "He never—"

Malcolm saw the memories flash through her eyes.

"Quite." He reached for his own glass. "We may have to run again, but I don't think we're in imminent physical danger from Carfax. Not that I'm discounting the bandit attack."

Mélanie lifted her glass and touched it to his. "It could be worse. We have a beautiful home and enough to keep life interesting."

Malcolm looked at his wife's face. The quiet and what it would do to them had been her greatest fear about their exile, he knew. The bruised look to her gaze had nothing to do with the traces of blacking left round her eyes. "Surely we don't need Carfax to keep life interesting." His voice came out more forced than he intended.

Mélanie took a sip of whisky, her brows drawing together. "I've been fighting Carfax most of my adult life, one way or another. But I hate to cede that much power to him."

"So do I." He brushed his fingers against her cheek. "We'll be all right, sweetheart." His gaze went to Jessica in her cradle and then the door to the new night nursery. "We have

77

everything that's essential to us and we'll take it with us wherever we go."

"Of course, darling. We're in a ridiculously lovely spot with just enough intrigue to keep us occupied. And if I grow bored, I can always redo the house."

"Don't even joke about it. I can't bear to think I've brought you to decorating houses."

"You haven't brought me anything but happiness, darling. Besides, I quite like decorating houses."

She gave another smile, more dazzling than the first. The bruised look was gone. On the journey across the Channel, Malcolm was the one who hadn't wanted to talk about their departure from Britain and the reasons for it. But now, the brilliance of Mélanie's gaze showed polished armor buckled tight over any qualms she might be feeling. He put a hand against the side of her face. "Sweetheart—"

Mélanie set down her glass and wound her arms round him. "I can think of one way we can make this room truly ours, darling." She kissed him, lightly but with the promise of more. "There's more than one type of distraction, dearest."

CHAPTER 7

Three weeks later

Mélanie lifted her hair from her neck. She'd left it down, reveling in the lack of confining pins, but it was already warm, even at ten in the morning, even in the shade of the terrace. She reached for her coffee and took a sip. For all the luxury she and Malcolm had lived in for much of their married life, they'd rarely lived lives of leisure. Vienna, Brussels, and Paris had all been hothouses of political and military intrigue with schedules crammed with balls, receptions, picnics, concerts, military reviews, nights at the theatre and opera. At the most seemingly frivolous gathering, treaties were negotiated over glasses of champagne, papers smuggled in picnic hampers or passed behind potted palms, borders drawn on napkins beside plates of lobster patties and chilled asparagus. Even London was a constant round of political dinners, balls with parliamentary colleagues, diplomatic receptions, evenings at Almack's, where several of the patronesses also happened to be at the heart of the political world. Scotland was quieter, but there were the tenants to visit, harvest balls and holidays fêtes to plan, village festivals to attend. It was rare for her to wake without a long list of things to do, entertainments to plan, calls to make, engagements to keep.

This was different. They lingered over breakfast on the shaded terrace until close to noon, a medley of English, French, and Italian papers (out of date to varying degrees) beside pots of strong coffee, plates of fragrant pastries and fresh fruit, vases of brilliant flowers from the garden. In the afternoon they would wander down to the lake or take a walk on the hillside or read in the cool of the library or nap on the sofas with the children or the cat cuddled beside them. They often dined outside on the terrace while the children ran about. Malcolm played the piano. She sang. They organized puppet shows with the children. It was an idyll in every sense of the word. At times she wanted to drink it in and will it never to stop. And at other times she wondered how long it would be before she went mad.

She glanced at the smiling faces round the table and wondered, not for the first time in the past three weeks, if the others felt the same.

Laura looked up from the *Morning Chronicle*. "Reading between the lines, Lady Derby appears to have run off with the music master."

"Perhaps we'll meet them in Italy." Malcolm looked up from *Le Moniteur* and bent to pet Berowne, who was napping in a patch of sun. "D'Artois's people are grumbling about Bonapartists still lurking in the government."

"They never stop." Raoul had Jessica on his shoulders so she could pick a leaf from the cypress tree that overhung the terrace.

"There was a disturbance during the electioneering at Durham," Laura said. Mélanie saw her friend go still as the words left her mouth.

"To be expected." Malcolm reached for the coffeepot to refill their cups. "Rupert writes that there was a near riot at Westminster."

Rupert Caruthers had managed to preserve Malcolm's seat for him in the general election. For how long remained open to question. Mélanie reached for her coffee and took a quick sip. A little too quick. It burned her tongue. She looked up to see Zarina, one of the two girls who helped in the house, coming out with a fresh pot of coffee and a sealed paper. "This just came, signora."

"Perhaps it's from Cordy." Mélanie felt her spirits lift at the thought. The Davenports were already on the Continent. They'd reach Lake Como within a fortnight. But when she took the paper from Zarina, the hand was far more careful than Cordy's slanted, exuberant script. The letter did not appear to have gone through the post and the writing was in Italian. She slit open the letter. "Thurston and the contessa have invited us to a picnic. Wednesday next."

"All of us?" Colin looked from the terrace floor where he and Emily were feeding breakfast to a variety of dolls and toy animals arranged on a checked tablecloth Zarina's mother had given them from the kitchen.

"Yes." Mélanie smiled at her son. "The contessa specifically includes all of us in the invitation. Apparently some others with villas on the lake will be there, but she says it will be a very informal party." She looked from Malcolm to Laura to Raoul. "Just the opportunity we needed."

A week after their arrival at the villa, they had invited the

Thurston party to dine as thanks for their hospitality. The evening had been convivial enough and quieter than the one they spent at Thurston's villa. The Montagu/Vincenzo party seemed to have recovered their surface equilibrium. No further sweeping confidences were made, despite Mélanie making a point to take the contessa on a tour of the house and Malcolm taking Kit into the library to show him some of the Duke of Strathdon's first editions. They had parted with talk of seeing each other again soon, but the contessa's prettily worded note of thanks mentioned that they would be living quietly for a time so the family could have time to get know each other and she hoped the Rannochs would understand.

Raoul moved to the table, Jessica still on his shoulders. "There will definitely be more opportunities there than here."

"The contessa says we will picnic on the lakeshore," Mélanie said. "That should mean the house will be fairly empty."

"You want to go through Thurston's study?" Raoul swung Jessica down from his shoulders into his arms and gave her a roll from the table.

Malcolm was frowning. "It's the obvious place to find information about his dealings with Carfax."

Mélanie leaned across the table. "I know you don't like invading someone's privacy, darling—"

"It's not that." He looked up at her with a quick smile. "I'm trying to work out which of us can most easily do it."

Mélanie met her husband's gaze across the breakfast dishes and felt an absurd rush of relief. "Oh, thank God," she said.

"What?" Malcolm asked.

"You've been bored too."

Malcolm grinned. "How could I be bored with you? But

82

there's no denying it's good to have a focus."

"Which is as close as Malcolm Rannoch comes to admitting the need for action."

Raoul wiped crumbs from Jessica's face, which made her giggle. "There's no denying it's the sort of exercise that sharpens the brain."

"Meaning you've been going mad." Laura looked up at him with a smile of mock frustration.

"Of course not." Raoul gave Jessica a strawberry. "Only worried about growing rusty."

"You have as much chance of growing rusty as a steel blade, Raoul O'Roarke," Laura said. "But I'll admit that finally being able to take action is a distinct relief. What can I do?"

Malcolm regarded the breakfast things as though he were seeing enemy terrain. "Thurston's the main one we need to keep occupied. It's probably easiest for me to engage him in conversation, given our past interactions. With Raoul as backup. Two ladies going into the house should seem unremarkable." He looked at Laura for a moment. "I assume you had practice at this sort of thing when you lived in our house working for the Elsinore League."

"For my sins, yes." Laura returned his gaze steadily.

Mélanie looked at her daughter, reaching to take another strawberry from Raoul's fingers. "We'll bring Jessica with us."

"Mel," Malcolm said, "you can't take her—"

"On a mission? We've taken both the children on missions, darling. But it's not as though this is a dangerous mission, for all we're all absurdly excited about strategizing it. If Thurston bursts in and finds us, it will be embarrassing and potentially give him information to take to Carfax, but we won't be in any actual danger. And with Jessica, we may be able to pass the whole thing off as looking for a place to

83

soothe a tantrum or change a nappy. Besides, this way you and Raoul won't have to keep an eye on her while you're distracting Thurston."

"She's right." Raoul plucked a strawberry stem from Jessica's fingers.

"I know." Malcolm sat back in his chair and reached for his coffee. "She usually is."

Champagne glasses clinked on the lower terrace at Thurston's villa. Unlike the classical formality of the upper terrace, this one was done in terra-cotta with tables tucked into niches beneath vine arbors. An imitation rustic playground, like Marie Antoinette's at Petit Trianon. Laura tightened her grip on Raoul's arm as she negotiated the steps cut into the hillside. Emily and Colin had run ahead with the sure-footed agility of the very young. Malcolm and Mélanie, carrying Jessica, were behind. Laura was grateful for the support of Raoul's arm for more than just the tricky steps. She still had to brace herself going into company. Although, she realized, as they reached the bottom of the steps, surely the tangled story of her past hadn't reached the expatriate community in Italy yet. She shouldn't have to deal with the exclamations of horror, the sympathy barely veiling patent disbelief at the supposed memory loss that accounted for her four-year disappearance. She drew a breath as they reached the bottom step. As though he understood, Raoul turned and gave her a quick smile.

The contessa and Thurston emerged from the throng of gauzy muslin dresses, wide-brimmed straw hats, and pale blue coats on the terrace. "We're so glad you could join us." The contessa smiled at Colin and Emily. "My children are particularly excited you're here." She drew forwards her children, fourteen-year-old Eliana, nine-year-old Matteo, and six-year-old Floria.

Eliana smiled shyly, but with her mother's poise, and offered to show Colin and Emily the lake. The contessa and Thurston drew the adults into the crowd. Whatever they had said about living a retiring life, they were easy hosts now, producing glasses of champagne, introducing the Rannoch party to their neighbors, a mix of British expatriates and Italian aristocrats. Kit and Sofia hurried over to greet them. Vincenzo nodded to them from one side of the terrace, Diana and Smythe from the other. Even Selena turned from a party of young people to wave. Whatever their private situation, the family had managed to put on an assured public face.

The crowd shifted in front of them. Laura's eye was caught by a slender woman with glossy brown hair dressed in loose ringlets across the terrace. Something about the lines of her jaconet gown and blue shawl and the style of her chip straw hat immediately told Laura she was British, though not anyone Laura recognized from London society. She glanced towards Mélanie to see if she recognized the woman and then realized Raoul had gone statue-still beside her.

Laura looked up at her lover. His gaze was fastened on the dark-haired woman. "Dar—" For some reason Laura swallowed the endearment. "Do you know her?"

The gaze Raoul turned to her held shock, apology, and something else that was perhaps fear. "It's Margaret."

CHAPTER 8

Mélanie heard Raoul's voice, and for a moment felt herself rooted to the ground. Margaret O'Roarke, the woman to whom Raoul was legally bound, the shadowy presence who had impacted decisions Raoul had made and limited choices he had, but who had never quite seemed real. Mélanie had wondered about her, especially in the early days of her own relationship with Raoul, but mostly with a sort of disbelief at the idea that Raoul had ever done anything as conventional as marry, anything that had committed him so fully and irrevocably, at least in the legal sense, to a person rather than his cause and work. When she'd tried to picture Margaret, she'd imagined either a brilliant seductress or a stodgy matron, neither of which image seemed quite right. She'd hadn't pictured this attractive and stylish woman, not much older than Laura, who could be anyone she might meet in a Mayfair drawing room.

The contessa, who had turned to speak with a footman,

rejoined them and noticed the direction of their gazes. "Do you know that lady? I just met her this afternoon. She's a guest of the Chipperfields. Margaret O'Roarke from Ireland." She cast a quick glance at Raoul. "O'Roarke. I didn't think—Is she a connection of yours?"

"You could say so." Raoul turned to the contessa with an easy, armored smile. "We happen to be married, though we haven't lived together for two decades."

"Oh, dear," the contessa said. "If I'd had any notion I'd have warned you. I didn't know her name until she arrived with the Chipperfields."

"It's quite all right," Raoul said. "If she's staying nearby, we were bound to meet. We're adult about the situation, as you should appreciate, Contessa."

"None better, Mr. O'Roarke. And no matter how adult and civilized one is, it's never quite as easy as it seems. I'm so sorry for putting you both in this situation."

"Better not to make too much of it, I think," Raoul said. "But we should speak, to show we can."

Margaret had caught sight of Raoul. She went completely still for a moment, much as Raoul had done. Raoul inclined his head to her. Then he turned and gave Laura a quick smile, released her arm, and moved across the terrace.

Jessica, who had been observing the scene with bright eyes, stirred in Mélanie's arms. "Strawb'rry," she said.

"Quite right." Mélanie forced her gaze to her daughter. "We need to feed you."

Malcolm's hand closed on Laura's elbow. "Let's find a place to sit."

Keeping her gaze firmly on Jessica, Mélanie moved to a table set with refreshments and filled a plate with strawberries. Out of her peripheral vision, she did notice that

Raoul and Margaret were speaking with apparent civility. Nothing she could do, save try not to draw unnecessary attention to them. She drew a breath and carried Jessica over to the cushioned wrought metal sofa where Malcolm and Laura were sitting.

Laura was sitting with her back very straight, hands folded in her lap, gaze fixed on a planter box spilling trailing vines over the balustrade. She looked like a princess turned to ice from one of the children's storybooks.

Malcolm tightened the hand he still had on Laura's elbow. "Deep breaths can help."

"It's—"

"I know." He got to his feet, snagged three fresh glasses of champagne from a footman passing with a tray, returned to the sofa and put a glass in her hand. "I'm sure Raoul is as shocked as you."

Laura took an automatic sip. "It shouldn't matter so much. That is, I always knew about her, so I don't know why meeting her matters so much. It's just—"

Mélanie took one of the champagne glasses from Malcolm. "It's funny, this isn't how I thought she'd look. Not that I can precisely say what I expected. She never quite seemed—"

"Real," Laura supplied.

"Yes," Mélanie said.

"I recognized her at once," Malcolm said.

"You met her when you were a child?" Mélanie asked.

Malcolm nodded. "She's little changed from the woman I remember meeting as O'Roarke's bride, though she couldn't have been much more than twenty then, maybe not even that. She couldn't be more different from my mother. In that sense, she's precisely what I'd have expected in a woman

88

Raoul married."

Mélanie took a sip of champagne. Jessica was happily engaged eating strawberries in her lap. Mélanie put a hand on Laura's arm. "I'm so sorry. But it doesn't change anything, you know."

"No. Except that now she's a real person." Laura took another sip of champagne, willing her fingers to be steady.

"A real person from the distant past," Malcolm said.

"Who will always be a part of his life."

"She hasn't been a part of his life for years," Mélanie said.

"Not obviously. But you know him. He doesn't make commitments lightly."

Mélanie's gaze jerked to her former lover, now in seemingly easy conversation with his estranged wife. They were standing only a few feet apart. Raoul was leaning against one of the terrace pilasters, booted feet crossed at the ankle. Probably only she, Malcolm, and Laura could read the tension in the set of his shoulders and the angle of his head. She wasn't used to thinking of commitments when it came to Raoul, at least not personal commitments. To his cause, yes. To his agents. Not to individuals for personal reasons. Or so she had thought. There was his commitment to Malcolm. To Laura. To the children. To herself, in ways she was only just beginning to understand.

Laura swallowed the last of her champagne. "I think—"

She broke off at a stir and a murmur in the crowd round them. Someone new seemed to have come onto the terrace, but seated they couldn't see who it was. Of one accord they got to their feet. A man with wavy dark hair, finely molded features, and a full-lipped mouth stood by the base of the stairs, accompanied by a tall, thin man with shock of curly brown hair and a slight woman with reddish blonde hair drawn back from a pale face set in a strained expression.

"Good heavens." Selena pushed through the crowd and stopped beside them, transfixed. "He actually came."

"I forgot," Malcolm said, a somewhat bemused expression on his face. "How he can command a room."

"Who is he?" Laura asked.

"Byron," Selena said, with a sigh that sounded almost happy.

"That must be Mary and Percy Shelley with him," Mélanie said.

"Yes," Selena said, still staring at Byron. "I didn't think they'd actually accept the invitation."

"So that's the mind that invented Frankenstein," Laura murmured. "That intrigues me more than Byron."

The crowd shifted. The contessa brought Byron and the Shelleys over to Selena and the Rannoch party. There was probably nothing she could have done more likely to win affection from her lover's daughter. Selena actually spared the contessa a brief smile before staring transfixed at Byron. Byron bowed over her hand and said he was pleased to see her again. His gaze held a mixture of amusement, enjoyment of the admiration, and a touch of kindness for a starstruck young girl that slightly improved Mélanie's opinion of him.

"Rannoch." Byron held out his hand to Malcolm. "I suppose I should say something about it being good to meet a fellow Harrovian so far from home."

"Spare us," Malcolm said, shaking Byron's proffered hand. "I don't think either of us has ever had much use for old school solidarity."

"Very true." Byron's gaze moved to Mélanie. "I heard you were lovely and brilliant, Mrs. Rannoch, but it seems reports have underrated the first and, I suspect, the second, as well."

"You're very kind, Lord Byron. But you must have learned not to judge by appearances."

"Perhaps I have a particularly keen eye for seeing beneath appearances, Mrs. Rannoch." He smiled at Jessica in her arms. He stretched out a hand. Jessica grasped hold of his fingers, fascinated. "Charming. I have two daughters myself. Of course I'm not able to see Ada." He tossed this out as something of a challenge, referring to his legitimate daughter who lived in England with her mother, Byron's estranged wife. "But little Allegra is a delight. She's with the Shelleys' little boy and Mary's sister just now."

Thanks to their friend Simon Tanner, who was friends with the Shelleys, Mélanie, Malcolm and Laura knew that Claire Clairmont, Mary Shelley's stepsister, was Allegra's mother. But even the Shelleys, who moved in a bohemian set, had been at pains to conceal her parentage, beset by rumors that Shelley himself was the father. Mélanie wondered if those rumors, as well as the scandal over Shelley's first wife's death, had played a role in the Shelleys' decision to leave Britain. One way and another, so many of them seemed to be fleeing something in Britain.

Percy Shelley had fallen into conversation with Malcolm. Laura turned to Mary Shelley, carefully averting her gaze from Raoul and his wife on the other side of the terrace.

"I suppose this was bound to happen." Margaret regarded Raoul with that gaze he remembered so well, especially from the last days of their marriage. Coolly formal and yet with a knife's edge of anger underneath. "It's rather remarkable we've avoided it for so many years. There's no sense pretending it's anything but excruciatingly awkward."

"It needn't be. I think we've said all the awkward things we have to say to each other." Raoul folded his arms and studied the woman he had married twenty-three years before. There were fine lines about her mouth and eyes he didn't remember, but more, her face had a set look, as though the years had taught her to armor herself. The years and her experiences, of which he was very much a part. Yet the elegant bones of her face were the same, her skin still glowing, her eyes bright, her figure trim beneath the demure lines of her gown. "You look well. I had no notion you were on the Continent."

"There's no reason you should. We're hardly in communication. I don't pay particular attention to where you are, but I had a vague sense you were dividing your time between Spain and London."

"I was until recently." Raoul rested his shoulders against a pilaster in a deliberate pose of nonchalance. "I was visiting Malcolm and Suzanne Rannoch when they decided to go to the Continent. I thought I would come with them on my way back to Spain."

She raised a well-groomed brow. "Spain by way of Italy? You used to be more direct."

"I'm not in any particular hurry."

"No? In the old days you always seemed to be in a hurry." Her gaze moved across the room. "She's very lovely."

"There are a number of lovely women present."

"Don't be tiresome, Raoul, my instincts at reading people haven't faded. It was quite apparent from the way you were holding the arm of that striking woman with the titian hair."

"I believe you mean Lady Tarrington. She's a widow who is a good friend of the Rannochs and is also traveling with

92

them."

"You needn't explain. I'm scarcely in a position to criticize. Though I am rather surprised that a romantic attachment took you so far away from your work."

"My dear." He kept his voice even and light. "You don't know that I don't have work in Italy."

"True enough. I know little at all about you. Though, if you're traveling with the Rannochs, am I to assume Malcolm Rannoch knows the truth?"

For all his suspicions, he went still. "Malcolm has always known I'm a friend of his family's."

"Oh, Raoul. Did you really think I didn't know?"

Raoul met her hard blue gaze. The quickness of her mind was one of the things that had always fascinated him. "I wasn't sure. And you never said."

"You never confided in me. I always wondered if you would have done if you'd loved me more."

"Margaret—" He put out an involuntary hand, then let it fall to his side. "You can't think it was that."

"No? Don't love and trust go hand in hand?"

"It wasn't my secret to share."

"And Arabella Rannoch meant an incalculable amount to you. That much was clear the first time I saw you together. That house party at the Duke of Strathdon's three months after we were married. Odd as a bride to realize one's hostess is one's husband's mistress."

"Arabella wasn't my mistress," he said, not flinching from Margaret's gaze. "Not then. Not while you and I were married in any real sense of the word."

Margaret returned his gaze though her own remained armored. He knew that look from the quarrels at the end of their marriage, though it seemed to have cooled, like iron hardening to steel. Less burning, but tougher. "There was a time I wouldn't have believed that. But with a bit of distance—it has the ring of truth. You always took some loyalties seriously. Perhaps to excess."

He remembered that house party. He'd wondered at the time if it was a mistake to accept the invitation. But he'd told himself it would lead to more talk if he suddenly stopped socializing with the duke and his family, and they were going to encounter Arabella at some point in the confined society in Ireland where she spent much of her time. And he'd wanted to see Malcolm. That, more than anything, had driven him. "Are you saying you spent our whole marriage thinking—"

Something softened a fraction in Margaret's gaze. "No. Not entirely. I wasn't sure. But you can't deny you were still in love with her."

It wasn't a word he used now save in extreme moments, when all other words failed him. It wasn't a word he had used easily then, though he had vivid memories of telling Margaret he loved her. What the words had meant to him. What he had thought they meant. "I would have denied I was at the time," he said in a low voice. "I'd convinced myself what was between Arabella and me was over." He drew a breath. "For someone whose stock in trade is deception, I can have a remarkable capacity to deceive myself. I'm sorry, Meg."

For a moment, the hardness in her gaze wavered. "For what it's worth, I wasn't really over Desmond either. We were a fine pair."

For a moment he saw her in the days of their courtship. Not so different, in many ways, from now, but her gaze had been wide and eager, open to the world, not closed and careful as it had become. "I was almost a decade older than you. I should have—"

"Little sense in refining upon the past. Isn't that what you always say? In any case, by the time I'd watched you play catch with Malcolm Rannoch and read him stories, I was quite sure he was your son. Partly from his appearance. But mostly from your attitude towards him."

Raoul drew in and released his breath. "I couldn't—"

"No, you couldn't turn your back on him. Or at least you wouldn't." Margaret tilted her head to one side in a way that brought a shock of memory. "I respect that. I respected it even twenty years ago, though my feelings were somewhat more confused." She regarded him for a moment, and he had the sense that Margaret, who had always been so certain of how she saw the world, was trying to puzzle him out. "I think you always wanted children more than I did."

It seemed so long ago, those dreams of a family life he'd briefly nourished, born out of what he couldn't have with Arabella, out of what he almost had with Malcolm, out of the devastation of the Terror. And yet her words stirred more recent images. Laughter round the breakfast table. Emily's hair beneath his fingers. Laura's head resting on his shoulder. "Perhaps I did, once." It seemed wholly inadequate, but what else could he say?

Margaret continued to watch him. The brim of her hat shadowed her face, but he felt the pressure of her gaze. "If we'd had a child, would you still have left?"

"If we'd had a child would you have wanted me to stay?"

Margaret drew a sharp breath.

"I wouldn't have walked away from a child, Meg," he said after a moment. "But I wouldn't have given up fighting for what I believed in. Having a child wouldn't have changed the issues between us."

The fingers of Margaret's left hand curled inwards. "If you

95

could have just—"

"Shut my eyes and put up with a world I find intolerable?"

"You're never going to stop, are you? No matter what destruction you leave in your wake."

He controlled an inwards flinch. In the wake of recent events, her words cut to the bone. "One hopes one grows better at minimizing the damage. But my convictions haven't changed. You should understand that. I don't think yours have, either."

"One of these days you're going to get yourself killed."

"Everyone dies sometime."

She shook her head. "How in God's name could we ever have thought—"

"I live with a number of regrets. Very much including the life I pulled you into."

Her shoulders jerked straight. "I'm not a victim, Raoul. I manage."

"I'm glad for whatever happiness you can find."

She gave a dry smile.

"How's Desmond?" he asked.

She lifted a brow. "Are you trying to prove how broadminded you are?"

"I never had anything against Desmond. We don't have a great deal in common, but he's a very decent man."

"He's had a difficult few months. Lucy died in March. A chill, though her health had steadily declined."

"I'm very sorry." Desmond Quennell's wife Lucy had been bedridden over twenty years ago after a riding accident.

Margaret nodded. "I thought I'd come to terms with my guilt about Lucy, but I confess this made it worse. I came abroad partly to give Desmond some time." She hesitated a moment. "He's going to meet me in Rome in a month."

96

It was more than Margaret would once have openly admitted about her relationship with Desmond Quennell. "I'm glad. Italy's a place to see with someone one loves." Raoul watched her for a moment, a hitherto unlooked-for possibility occurring to him. He'd only asked her once, years ago, and she'd made it very clear she had no interest. But given the change in her own circumstances—"Meg, now that Desmond is free, do you think you'd ever—"

Margaret stared at him for a moment, then gave a brittle laugh. "Are you asking if I want a divorce? To start my life over at my age? A bit late for that, surely."

"Don't talk nonsense, Meg. I don't know that it's ever too late for a fresh start."

"You always had a mad belief in lost causes."

"You and Desmond have years you could enjoy openly together."

"Mired in scandal? Little as you care for convention, you must know what it would mean to me to live my life as a divorced woman." She watched him for a moment. "Don't tell me you want to be free?"

"And if I did?"

She gave a short laugh. "We both made our choice two decades ago. A bad choice, but we have to go on living with it. You've admitted you're scarcely in a position to offer any woman a settled life, in any case."

"Very true."

Margaret continued to watch him in silence. "Of course, if you were that determined, you could always try to divorce me."

"Openly accuse you of adultery?" He straightened up and stepped away from the pilaster. "My dear Margaret, if you think there's a chance in hell I'd do that after everything else

I've put you through, you know me even less well than I thought."

CHAPTER 9

Byron accepted a glass of champagne from a passing waiter and smiled at Mélanie. Malcolm and Laura had fallen into conversation with the Shelleys, leaving the two of them more or less on their own. Byron had followed Mélanie when she moved to settle Jessica in a nearby chair with more strawberries. "It's a great tragedy that we haven't met before, Mrs. Rannoch."

"I only lived in Britain for a bit over a year. Though I've heard rather a lot about you."

"Oh?" He raised a brow.

"Cordelia Davenport is one of my best friends."

"Cordy?" Byron gave a rueful laugh. For a moment, he looked like a schoolboy who has been caught out. The effect was disarming, even though she was quite sure he was aware of it. "Then perhaps I should be relieved you risked shaking hands with me."

"On the contrary. Cordy is aware enough of her own foibles not to cast aspersions on others."

Byron scraped a hand over his hair. "I stand corrected. The truth is I'd have been better served turning an eye on Cordy than on her friend Caro. She's living with Davenport again, isn't she? Cordy, that is."

"Yes, since Waterloo. They have two daughters. I think they're very happy."

Byron shook his head in disbelief. "Domesticity. Apparently it equals happiness for some."

"It's not the only sort of happiness. But it can be surprisingly agreeable."

"It's hard to imagine Cordelia Brooke—Cordelia Davenport—being happy with such a tame life."

"I think Cordy is very much aware of what she has and how hard-earned it is. And I don't think she considers life with Harry Davenport at all tame."

He raised a brow. "People can surprise one. But my own experience suggests that while one may appreciate the lure of a settled, quiet existence, actually living in such a state for a sustained length of time is a different matter entirely. You look as though you might understand that, Mrs. Rannoch."

Sitting by the blue of the lake. Feeling a rush of excitement simply at the prospect of breaking into Thurston's study. "I'm not nearly so complicated as you imagine, Lord Byron."

"On the contrary. I'm a good judge of people, Mrs. Rannoch, and I don't think I'm underestimating you in the least. Some people aren't made for a quiet life."

Mélanie plucked a strawberry stem from Jessica's fingers before she could drop it on the ground. "I have two children, Lord Byron. My life isn't in the least quiet."

"You're a friend of Simon Tanner's, aren't you?" Percy Shelley said to Malcolm.

"Since Oxford."

Shelley nodded. "I can't claim as long an acquaintance, but I consider him a friend, as well. I've always admired his plays. And his other writing."

"Simon has a brilliant way with words. Though I've heard him wax lyrical about your poetry. With good cause."

"Good of you, Rannoch. I've read some of your speeches, as well. I don't think much of Parliament, but it's good to know there are men like you there."

"I'm not there now." Malcolm took a sip of champagne. His throat had gone unaccountably tight.

"But you'll be back, surely."

"Difficult to say. Right now we're enjoying life in Italy."

Shelley ran a gaze over him. Malcolm could see the other man calculating the things that might have made them run. Debts. Scandal. Disillusionment. He couldn't possibly hit on the truth, though the second option wasn't far off. Nor, in a way, was the third.

"Italy has much to recommend it, I suppose," Shelley said. "But I can't imagine a man like you being happy here indefinitely."

"It's surprising what one realizes makes one happy, given enough time. You must understand the lure of a scholarly life."

"In theory." Shelley cast a glance about. "When I first met Mary, I thought we could be happy on nothing. Time goes on and one realizes it's a bit more complicated."

"I don't think one can ever find happiness in another person. Not entirely."

Shelley's gaze lingered on his wife, like a man looking for a lost illusion. "I thought it would help Mary to be here. Distraction. New surroundings." He drew a breath. "We recently lost our baby girl."

Malcolm swallowed as though he'd been dealt a blow to the gut. "My dear fellow. I'm so very sorry."

"You'd think it would bring two people together. That no one else could understand our grief. Instead, it seems harder to talk than ever."

"I imagine you're grieving in different ways."

"Perhaps. If she'd just talk to me—"

Malcolm saw Mélanie's bright gaze, heard her brittle voice, talking with charming laughter of anything but her own feelings. "There are times when talking is the hardest thing to do of all. Even between married couples. Perhaps especially between married couples."

Shelley met his gaze for a moment and gave a slow nod.

Laura smiled at Mary Shelley. After a polite greeting, Mary had seemed to sink into herself. Her husband was engaged with Malcolm, and Byron had moved a bit off with Mélanie and Jessica. "*Frankenstein* kept me up into the early hours of the morning," Laura said. It had, in fact, kept her company on a long night when she was particularly missing Raoul. "I'm not a fanciful woman, but I confess it gave me chills and had me reluctant to put out my candle."

"You're very kind," Mary Shelley murmured. "I'm glad it seems to have been well received."

Writers, in Laura's experience, were usually eager to discuss their work, but Mary seemed to be an exception. At least at present. Laura glanced about, searching for a topic of conversation. "It's lovely here," she said.

"Yes." Mary Shelley cast a listless glance over the lake, eyes vacant. "We thought about taking a house here. It seems centuries ago, but it was only last spring. A different world." She rubbed her arms. For a moment it seemed she wasn't going to say more, but then she added in a quick monotone, "They brought me here because they think it will be a distraction. As if pretty views could distract one from—" She put a fist to her mouth. The vacant look was gone from her eyes, replaced by naked despair. "We lost our baby girl. I still can't comprehend it."

"I'm so very sorry." Laura put out her hand in unconscious sympathy and touched Mary's arm. "I can't imagine anything more dreadful." Emily, Colin, and Jessica were all very sturdy, but losing children was a reality parents lived with every day. Laura felt it whenever one of them caught a simple cold, and she could tell both the Rannochs were feeling it, as well, though none of them put it into words. It had haunted Laura in the years Emily was away from her, the fear that her child, taken from her mother at birth, subjected to the long voyage from India to England, might have died in the first months of life. Or later, in whatever cold refuge the Duke of Trenchard had placed her in.

Mary pleated a fold of her shawl between her fingers. "One replays everything. What if we hadn't left England, what if we'd stayed in Switzerland, or taken different lodgings, or I hadn't had to bring her to join Percy and my stepsister in the wretched heat—We lost our first baby three years ago, when she was only a few weeks old. I don't think one can be a

103

parent and not worry about losing a child, but it's so much worse than one can imagine when it actually happens. I keep feeling as though people are staring at me as though I'd done something wrong. Or don't want to get close to me because I represent their deepest fears."

"If so, they're being nonsensical," Laura said, in a firm, governess voice. "Life can be a great muddle, and I can't come close to truly appreciating what you've been through, but I do know it's folly to blame oneself."

Mary met her gaze. "No one's ever put it that way. Have you—"

"I've never been through anything this dreadful. But I do know what it is to replay decisions and torture oneself with what might have been."

Mary glanced at their host and hostess. "It's odd. When Percy and I first went abroad four years ago, we weren't married. He had left a wife behind in England." Her eyes darkened. Percy Shelley's first wife had killed herself a year and a half ago. "Like Lord Thurston," she added quickly. "Now I suppose we're considered a respectable married couple, though it doesn't seem that way. I used to think I didn't care a bit for marriage. But I don't deny it does make a difference."

Laura forced her gaze not to stray to her own lover, who was still talking to his wife. "Even if one doesn't care a scrap for the morality of it—which I confess I don't—I suppose it means something to be able to acknowledge the relationship in front of the world."

Mary's eyes widened, as though she was surprised to find this seeming English aristocrat spouting opinions as bohemian as her own.

"Hiding one's feelings can seem exciting, but in the end I

104

think it grows a bit tiring," Laura said. "And if one loves someone, one tends to want to share it with one's friends and family." Simple things. Holding hands in public. Entertaining guests together. Claiming the person instead of prevaricating about the relationship. As she was doing now with Mary. "Still, as long as one can acknowledge it to those one's closest to, and knows it oneself, I think that's what really matters." God knows it was easier now, in Italy, living with Raoul openly in the household at the villa.

"I hadn't thought of it quite that way." Mary smoothed her skirt. "We lived together openly. It seemed romantic. But then there we were living in pokey lodgings, with Percy invited to see people but not able to bring me with him. My own father didn't speak to us for two years."

"Society is much harder on women in these things than on men. It's most unfair."

Mary's gaze settled on Laura's face, as though, through the fog of grief, she was again reevaluating her opinion of the other woman. "My mother didn't believe in marriage. Because of all the restrictions it puts on a woman. But then when she was expecting me she agreed to marry my father. It does make a difference for children."

Laura firmly checked the impulse to slide her hand to her abdomen. "And yet the contessa and Lord Thurston's children appear quite happy." She glanced at the three children playing on the shingle with Colin and Emily.

"Their father is a wealthy man," Mary said. "That helps. And they're living in retirement here. But it will close off options for them in society." She gave a harsh laugh. "I sound a dreadful hypocrite, don't I, talking about society's opinions? But I've learned that it's one thing to defy the world for oneself, and quite another when it comes to one's children."

105

Laura's gaze went to Emily, wriggling her bare feet in the sand. "I'm a mother myself. I understand. Though, when I look at society's options for my daughter, sometimes I think I'd prefer her to be on the outside."

Mary's brows rose. "I never quite thought—"

"It's a difficult world," Laura said. "Marriage puts a woman legally under her husband's thumb, but society isn't kind to women who don't marry. I know Juliette Dubretton. She was in much the same situation as your mother. In the end she married Paul St. Gilles when they had children."

"I've met her," Mary said. "Their marriage seems happy." A note of half wonder, half bitterness tinged her voice.

"I think marriage is always a challenge. I can't claim to have been very good at it myself. My husband died, almost five years ago now," Laura added.

"I wasn't thinking. That is, when I heard your name—"

"There's no reason you should know. And unlike your tragedy, it's in the past." Not that she could precisely call Jack's death a tragedy for her.

"It seems so romantic," Mary said. "Giving up all for love, finding the person who can complete one. But in the end, married or not, there are bills to pay, and meals to plan, and the laundry to see to." She cast a quick glance at her husband, talking to Malcolm. "Percy believes in freedom. In politics. And in one's personal life. He doesn't think love should fetter one."

"My husband had a similar attitude," Laura said. "Though he wasn't as consistent. His politics were quite conventional, but he certainly didn't believe the marriage tie should fetter him." She regretted the wrongs she had done Jack. She was sorry for his death, in the way she'd be sorry for any loss of life. But she shuddered at the prospect of her life today were she still married to him. Would she have taken Emily and run off to Italy with Raoul? In a heartbeat.

Laura glanced across the terrace and met Mélanie's gaze. It was time to extricate themselves. They had a study to break into.

Mélanie shifted Jessica on her hip and willed herself not to hurry. Half the trick of carrying off a break-in was acting as though one had a perfect right to be where one was going. If anyone noticed two ladies leaving the party with a toddler, they would probably assume they were seeking somewhere to change her nappy. Laura, in fact, carried a large black canvas bag they used for just such supplies, though it was also useful for concealing other objects. The contessa had made the whole thing easier by hurrying to their side and explaining where the ladies' retiring room was. Fortunately, she hadn't offered to accompany them.

Easy enough to climb the terrace steps. A bit trickier, once inside the tile-floored cool of the villa, not to turn towards the ladies' retiring room but down the passage Malcolm had explained led to Thurston's study.

"Kitty." Jessica pointed to a white cat curled by the feet of a jeweled lady in a farthingale and ruff in a sixteenth-century oil.

A maid, passing through the entrance hall with a tray of olives and tomatoes, paused and smiled. Mélanie smiled back with assurance. As soon as the maid was out of sight, she started in the direction Malcolm had indicated. After all, if anyone stopped them they could plead confusion about the floor plan of the villa.

Three doors down the passage. It seemed to take longer than it should have done. They heard footsteps in the entrance hall again, went still, then moved forwards when no one approached. Laura eased open the door of the study, and then nodded to Mélanie over her shoulder.

It was like stepping back into England. The oak and leather, the hunting prints. If she were designing a stage set meant to instantly conjure an English gentleman's study, it would look much like this. The room revealed a huge amount about what England and his old life still meant to Thurston. For an instant, Mélanie wondered what Malcolm would have brought with him from Berkeley Square if he'd had time.

Laura set down the canvas bag and took Jessica from Mélanie's arms. "See the pictures, sweetheart? Yes, there are horses. And a doggy." Laura glossed over the dead stag in one of the prints. "And look at the trees."

Mélanie moved to Thurston's desk. His papers were arranged in neat stacks. The pen, inkpot, and penknife were chased silver and looked to be Italian—gifts from the contessa, perhaps? She flipped through the first stack of papers, taking care to keep them in the same order and alignment. Though if the letter from Carfax really was sensitive, it seemed unlikely it would still be there.

A variety of bills from tailors and dressmakers in Milan. Correspondence with his steward in Britain, which indicated that Thurston still took an interest in his estates. A letter from Kit about the forthcoming visit, much creased as though it had been read many times. A drawing of flowers and a puppy, which appeared to have been made by Thurston's youngest daughter.

The drawers contained older paperwork about the estate, some carefully worded, carefully filed letters with Lady

Thurston about the children's education. More bills, also neatly filed, apparently all paid. Thurston didn't appear the sort of aristocrat who was constantly holding creditors at bay. Nothing from Carfax. She closed the bottom drawer, looked at the inlaid writing case atop the desk. The inside held only a spare inkpot and pen nibs. But the gilded bottom of the case was unusually thick. She felt along the edges and it sprang back to reveal a secret compartment.

Mélanie flipped through until she found Carfax's distinctive hand. Not as familiar to her as to Malcolm, but they had received enough letters from Carfax (not to mention papers she had gone through in Malcolm's dispatch box in the old days) for her to recognize it. She took paper and a pencil from the black canvas bag and quickly copied out the contents, scarcely taking time to absorb the words.

My dear Thurston,

Make sure you have receipt of the package. Trust is all very well, but I prefer to have the goods in hand. I hope we have no difficulties as we did last time.

On another note, you may encounter Malcolm Rannoch and his family. I believe they will be coming to stay at Malcolm's villa on the lake. Malcolm, as you know, was one of my abler agents for years, though he isn't currently in my employ. I'd appreciate your keeping an eye on him. Raoul O'Roarke is probably traveling with the party, definitely someone to pay attention to, as well. As is Suzanne Rannoch. As far as I know, the purpose of their trip is personal, but with that group one never knows. Malcolm is not precisely the ally he once was. And I've never trusted O'Roarke. Don't do anything rash, but send reports.

Yours, etc...

Carfax

Mélanie copied down the last word, her mind tumbling with speculation even as she told herself there'd be time for that later.

"Mel," Laura said in an intense whisper. But Mélanie had already heard it as well. Footsteps in the passage outside. She pushed the secret compartment closed, snatched up her paper and pencil, scanned the desk to make sure the papers were back in their original place. Laura already had the black bag in hand. Without even exchanging a glance, they slipped through an adjoining door, which opened onto the villa's library.

Laura moved to the windows, holding Jessica, who seemed to understand the need for silence. Mélanie lingered by the door, ear to the ornate panels.

"I fail to see why we needed to leave the party." Though muffled by the door panels, the voice from the study sounded like Conte Vincenzo.

"Because I don't want there to be any chance Elena overhears this." That was definitely Thurston. A thud indicated the study door being pushed shut. "I know why you're really here, Vincenzo. We can stop prevaricating."

"I don't know what you're talking about." Vincenzo's voice was flat and even.

"You can tell your friends it's no sense sending you to spy on me. I'm on to you. And you're not going to get what you want."

"My dear Thurston." Mélanie could almost imagine Vincenzo folding his arms across his chest as he spoke. "You've always had a tendency towards the dramatic. I've often wondered if that's what attracted Elena. Women do like a touch of romance, even if it's based on nonsensical imaginings."

"I know you were talking with a confederate the night you arrived."

110

"Who—"

"Overheard you? Quite."

"Difficult to think back that far, but I sometimes go for a walk before bed. Sometimes I encounter one of the locals and exchange a few words. If something was misunderstood—"

"Vincenzo. Whatever else you think of me, surely you don't take me for a fool."

"No, I believe you were the one who took me for a fool. When you seduced my wife."

"Is that what this is about?" Thurston's voice held an edge of realization. "You've never forgiven me for Elena, so now you're seeking a way to bring me down?"

"Just because you're besotted with Elena doesn't mean you should overrate her value to me."

"I'm not. To own the truth, I always thought the fact that you didn't appreciate her was a large part of the problem—"

"*The problem?* If you're blaming me—"

"Aren't both parties usually to blame when a marriage falls apart?"

"Is that what you told your wife?"

"I don't deny wronging my wife. But I wouldn't say either of us loved the other by the time I met Elena. I thought the same was true of you and Elena. But I begin to wonder if I got it all wrong. If you're this angry fifteen years later—"

"My dear Thurston. I'm not angry in the least. My pride may still be a bit piqued that you took advantage of me—"

"Elena and I fell in love. I thought you understood that now."

"Still calling it that at your age?" Vincenzo gave a coarse laugh. "Suit yourself. You know, I'm actually sorry she came between our friendship. She was only a woman, after all, and in the end proved to be a loose one. In the end, wives and whores aren't all that different. But I suppose you know all about that, now Elena's your—"

The sound of a fist connecting with flesh put an end to Vincenzo's remark. The thud that followed indicated the conte had fallen to the floor.

"That sensitive, are you?" Vincenzo said in an equable voice. "It seems I've hit a nerve. Are you afraid she'll play you false too?"

"I won't throw you out," Thurston said. "For Elena's sake. I don't want her ever to know the man you are, in any sense of the word. But tell your friends they won't get anywhere here. You'd best be off on another mission. Now, if you'll excuse me, I should return to my guests."

The sound of the study door slamming shut echoed into the library. A few moments later, the door opened and closed again. Footsteps sounded in the passage. Mélanie turned from the door to Laura, who had been playing silent peek-a-boo with Jessica at the far end of the room. Without speech, they slipped from the room and out into the passage.

CHAPTER 10

As his wife and daughter and Laura climbed the stairs to search Thurston's study, Malcolm turned and glanced round for his host. Thurston made it easy for him, catching his eye and crossing the terrace towards him. "Rannoch. Elena told me about O'Roarke's wife. Devilish awkward for both of them. Sorry we didn't know in advance."

Malcolm gave a smile designed to be easy. "O'Roarke's more capable than most of dealing with awkwardness. I imagine any woman who married him is, as well."

"For all the years and all my supposed sangfroid, I can't say what I'd do if my wife walked onto the terrace. Run like a schoolboy, I fear. All very well to pen civil letters. Quite another thing to face someone with whom one has such a tangled history in person. Have O'Roarke and his wife been much in contact?"

"Scarcely at all, I think."

"Easier that way, perhaps." Thurston cast a glance at the contessa, his gaze softening. "To own the truth, I don't know how Elena and Vincenzo manage. People say I made a sacrifice leaving my country for Elena, but in some ways I think I took the easy way out. I got a clean start. She has to face her past every day." He shook his head, as though shaking off the thought. "I trust you're all settling in well."

There was no reason, Malcolm told himself, to take Thurston's comment as anything more than a polite inquiry, whatever the segue. Unless, of course, Thurston was gathering information for Carfax and knew precisely why the Rannoch family had left Britain. "Capitally," he said. "It's a long time since we've had a holiday. The children don't know what to make of so much sunshine. And I'm sometimes not sure how to fill my days."

"You'll be back in Parliament soon enough."

"Quite." Malcolm mustered an easy smile.

"If—"

"Kit, you beast, you can't make me!" Selena ran across the terrace, knocking over a stand with a champagne bucket.

Guests sprang back. Thurston made to run after his daughter and skidded on the spilled champagne and broken glass. Malcolm steadied him as Selena ran down the steps to the beach. Kit ran up behind them. A splash sounded from the lake. Emily screamed. Malcolm ran to the terrace steps, but O'Roarke had already vaulted over the balustrade. Malcolm got to the beach to see O'Roarke pulling a dripping Selena out of the lake.

"Thank you, Mr. O'Roarke." Selena looked up at him with the sort of hero worship O'Roarke tended to inspire.

"Selena—" Thurston took a step towards his daughter.

"I'm all right, Papa. I just lost my footing and stumbled into the water. Mr. O'Roarke got me out. I'll go up and change." Selena marched past her father and brother and the

114

interested gazes of their guests.

"I can't thank you enough," Thurston said to Raoul. "Let us get you a change of clothes."

"No need. I have no desire to drip on your floors. I'll just remove my boots for a bit. Good excuse to play in the sand with the children." Raoul dropped down on the bottom step and began to remove his boots with Malcolm's help. Colin and Emily helped tug too.

Thurston turned to his son. "What the devil—"

"I didn't mean to set her off, sir, I just told her not to keep asking where Byron had got to—"

Father and son climbed the terrace steps. It was only a few minutes before Raoul had his boots off and was building a sand castle with the children. "I've got this," Malcolm murmured to Raoul.

"Sure?"

"Not difficult." Malcolm climbed the terrace steps again. When he reached the terrace, Thurston was still talking to Kit. Malcolm started across the terrace, keeping Thurston in view, when he caught sight of a dark-haired young man descending the stairs.

"Enrico!" The decorous Sofia ran across the terrace and flung her arms round the young man.

A smile broke across the contessa's safe. "*Caro!* I wasn't sure you'd arrive before the party was over."

Enrico released Sofia and bent to kiss the contessa's cheek. *"Buongiorno, Mama."* He inclined his head to Thurston, who was coming forwards to shake his hand. "Sir." He turned to Vincenzo on the other side of the terrace. "Sir."

The young man had the makings of a diplomat, Malcolm thought, as the contessa introduced them to her son, just arrived from Milan. The crowd moved and eddied. Greetings were exchanged, hands shaken. Kit made a point of coming forwards to greet Enrico.

By the time the crowd shifted again, there was no sign of Thurston.

Mélanie met her husband's gaze as she and Laura returned to the terrace. Relief flashed in Malcolm's eyes. "Thank God," he said, coming up beside them. "I lost Thurston."

"We know," Mélanie said, with a bright smile meant to indicate to observers that she was talking of inconsequential nothings. "Though it proved very interesting."

"My blood runs cold." Malcolm took Jessica from Mélanie's arms.

Laura's brows drew together. "Wasn't there a champagne bucket there?"

"It's been an eventful time down here. Selena Montagu quarreled with her brother and stumbled into the lake. O'Roarke fished her out. Which gave him an excellent excuse to build sand castles with the children while his boots dry."

While Laura took Jessica to walk in the sand, Malcolm and Mélanie moved to the balustrade. Mélanie waved to Colin and Emily. The sand castle was proving truly elaborate, with four turrets and a moat. Eliana, Matteo, and Floria were engaged in the project, as well.

Mélanie undid the clasp on her reticule, drew out the paper on which she'd copied out Carfax's letter, and slid it along the balustrade towards Malcolm. Better for him to see it while they were still at the villa and could seek more information. Who knew when they'd see Thurston again?

Malcolm scanned the words quickly. "More or less what

we expected. Though Thurston and Carfax seem to be more than acquaintances. What the devil is the package? Is Thurston collecting intelligence for Carfax?"

"I don't know. But there's more." Mélanie told her husband about the argument they'd overheard between Thurston and Vincenzo.

Malcolm frowned. "I knew Thurston was holding something back when I told him what O'Roarke overheard Vincenzo saying. Vincenzo's 'friends' Thurston talked about could be the Austrians. But who the devil is Thurston working with?"

She shook her head. "Is Thurston dabbling in Italian politics? Perhaps on Carfax's behalf?"

Malcolm stared out over the lake, his frown deepening. "I've heard talk of a network of Italian revolutionaries who operate in extreme secrecy. We know Carfax sent guns to rebels in Naples to get information about the Elsinore League. Perhaps Thurston was embroiled in it and Vincenzo is working with the authorities in Naples. Or for Metternich, who could well want to stop revolutionaries in another Italian state. Or Carfax has turned on the rebels and Vincenzo is working with them, though Vincenzo scarcely strikes me as the ally of revolutionaries."

"Unless Metternich's playing some deep game trying to undermine Naples," Mélanie said.

"Yes, that's a possibility. Though anything remotely connected to revolution is anathema to Metternich."

"Whatever's going on, it's clear the past isn't settled between Thurston and Vincenzo."

"No," Malcolm agreed. "But then, the past rarely is settled, is it?"

Mélanie held Jessica's hand as her daughter dug her toes into the sand. Hard to remember six months ago Jessica had just been getting her feet under her. On the fog-drenched, rain-lashed paving stones of Berkeley Square. In air filled with damp and soot and the rhythms of the English language. In a country she might grow up not even remembering.

"You and your daughter make a charming picture, Signora Rannoch."

Mélanie looked up to see Conte Vincenzo approaching along the beach. She was walking Jessica to give her daughter exercise and herself time to think, but Vincenzo had fallen neatly into her investigative sights. A bit too neatly? "Warm water," she said. "Quite a novelty after Britain. We have a beach at our house in Scotland"—how odd to so naturally refer to Dunmykel as her house—"but the water is frigid."

Vincenzo drew up beside them, inclined his head, and tipped his hat. "I trust you are enjoying your stay in Italy."

Holding Jessica by one hand, Mélanie held out her other hand with the sort of demure-flirtatious smile she had long since mastered in diplomatic ballrooms and political salons. The smile of a loyal wife who could still charm her husband's colleagues. "How could I not enjoy a stay in such an idyllic setting, with such warm and welcoming people?"

"Charmingly spoken." He fell in step beside her and Jessica as they walked along the edge of the lake. "But I remember how it was when I went abroad. To England"—he coughed, perhaps at the associations—"and other places. You must miss Britain."

"Of course, at times." Mélanie stopped as Jessica bent

down to pick up a shell and gravely study it. "But we're very happy here." Which was more or less true on both counts.

"You must have left many friends behind. I trust you've been able to write?"

"It's one of my most frequent occupations on our lovely lazy days here." Mélanie accepted the shell that Jessica was holding out to her. "We expect our friends the Davenports to pay us a visit any day now."

"How delightful. But, as it happens, it's another friend of yours I'm concerned with."

"A friend of mine?" Mélanie repeated, tightening her grip on Jessica, who was tugging to toddle towards the water. She wasn't sure she'd heard Vincenzo aright.

"I think he could be called that. Though there are cruder terms I could use. Julien St. Juste."

For an instant, the sand and water and her daughter's bonneted head swam before Mélanie's eyes. Her blood had turned to ice, but she said, without dignifying Vincenzo's comment by turning to look at him, "Julien who? I'm afraid I don't know whom you are talking about."

"Come, Signora Rannoch. There is no need to play the innocent with me. I know far too many details of your past."

She had played this scene so many times it was almost comical. Save that for all they were on the run, the danger was still there. Made all the sharper by the feel of Jessica's small hand in her own. She picked up a striped rock Jessica was reaching for and gave it to her daughter, then straightened up and smiled at Vincenzo. "I think you must have me confused with someone else. As you can see"—she smiled down at her daughter—"I've been quite busy with domestic pursuits in recent years."

"Yes. Very impressive how you manage to juggle it all,

Signora Rannoch. Or should I say Signorina Lescaut? Or, simply, the Raven."

Mélanie lifted a brow. "That sounds like something out of a novel."

"It wasn't I who invented the alias. I assure you I have no desire to share the details of your past. Provided you do as I ask."

Mélanie picked up Jessica and settled her on her hip. She could go on fencing with him, but at this point it was probably more important to find out what he wanted. "Which is?"

"Get a message to Julien St. Juste."

She wouldn't have thought she could grow colder, but ice stabbed through her pintucked bodice. At the same time, she had a lowering suspicion she should have seen this coming. "My dear Conte Vincenzo. Even if I knew who that was and where to find him, why on earth would I do as you ask?"

"My dear Signora Rannoch. Surely I do not have to remind you of the consequences if you do not?"

Mélanie detached Jessica's grip on the satin ribbons that fastened her hat and gave Jessica her reticule to hold. "But if you really know my supposed history, you must be able to guess at the reasons for my being in your charming country. The corollary being that such threats no longer carry the weight with me that they once did."

Vincenzo's gaze moved over her face. "You may be on the run from Britain, but the truth of your past isn't out. And if you wish to maintain a prayer of hope of returning to Britain, you don't want it to be."

For a moment, Mélanie had a vivid sense of the salt breeze off the Channel. "Who says I want to return? It isn't my country."

"You may not wish to do so. But you'll never convince me

120

your husband doesn't."

Jessica had the steel clasp on the reticule open and was pulling out Mélanie's comb. Mélanie put the comb in her daughter's hand and snapped the reticule closed. "What do you want with Julien St. Juste?"

"That's our business."

"Our?"

"The people I'm working with."

Mélanie watched Jessica push back her bonnet and tug the comb through her sparse hair, then lifted her gaze to Conte Vincenzo. "Are you so afraid to say the name of the Elsinore League?"

This time she had the satisfaction of seeing shock in his gaze, and a flash of fear. "I beg your pardon?" he said. "The name sounds very English."

"Yes, you're the first foreign member I've met. Assuming you are a member and not a hired helper."

Anger flashed in his gaze. "I assure you—"

"So you are a member. Interesting."

"'Snore," Jessica said.

"Just so. Nothing to fear from putting it into words." Mélanie pulled Jessica's bonnet up, pressed a kiss to her daughter's forehead, and put Jessica on the sand. "Hasn't it occurred to you I may be more afraid of Julien than of you and the Elsinore League?"

"We have a mutually beneficial proposition to present to him."

Mélanie gave a peal of laughter. "My dear Conte Vincenzo. If you intend to make any sort of alliance with Julien, I pity you. Take some advice from one all too well acquainted with him—run in the opposite direction."

"I think Signor St. Juste will be very interested in what we have to offer. But that will be between him and us. You need merely make the introduction."

"There's no 'merely' with Julien St. Juste."

"Don't prevaricate, Signora Rannoch."

Jessica was digging the comb into the sand. "You must give me time. I'm not even sure where to find Julien."

"I can give you until tomorrow afternoon, Signora Rannoch."

"What a splendid sand castle." Mélanie dropped down on the sand beside Raoul, Colin, Emily, and the younger Montagu children, Jessica in her lap. The castle now boasted eight towers, shell doors, stick flags, and a handsome moat filled with water with a slab of stone for a drawbridge.

Jessica stretched out a hand.

"Build us a carriage, Jess." Colin was learning to distract his sister.

"Here, I'll help." Emily began to help Jessica shape the sand.

"We can find round stones for wheels," Eliana said.

Raoul's gaze flickered over Mélanie's face, but he waited until Malcolm, whose eye Mélanie had caught crossing the terrace, dropped down beside them. With the children chattering about the castle, they had a bit of cover.

Mélanie fixed a bright smile on her face for any onlookers and kept her gaze on the castle. "Conte Vincenzo is working for the Elsinore League."

"What?" Malcolm at least managed to moderate his voice, though he couldn't keep the shock from his eyes.

"And he wants me to contact Julien."

"Oh, my God," Malcolm said.

"Yes, that was more or less my reaction. Or he threatened to expose me. The same tiresome threats I heard from Fouché and Lord Craven. Hardly the threats they once were, but not exactly nothing."

Malcolm's hand closed on her arm.

"What does he want with St. Juste?" Raoul asked in a level voice that concealed an effort few would notice. "Or, rather, what do the Elsinore League want?"

"I don't know. He said he had a mutually beneficial proposition."

Raoul gave a short laugh.

"Again, that was my reaction. If they want to talk to Julien so much, I don't know why they can't just find him."

"He's not the easiest man to find," Raoul pointed out.

"Precisely. So how am I supposed to do it?"

Raoul regarded her for a moment. "St. Juste would respond to a message from you."

For a moment, Mélanie could hear Hortense Bonaparte's voice. *He was half in love with you on that journey into Switzerland.* And Julien's. *In the right circumstances. With the right woman. You could come close.* She shivered. And then forced a smile to her face. "I don't know why everyone is so determined to exaggerate my importance to Julien."

Malcolm's hand slid down her arm to twine round her own. "I only met the man once," he said. "And I agree with O'Roarke. Which doesn't help us with what to do." He cast a seemingly casual glance about. "Vincenzo's bound to know you're talking to us."

"He'd guess I would, and he didn't say not to." Mélanie cast a glance at the children. "At least now we know who the friends are that Thurston warned Vincenzo about. Perhaps

123

Thurston was gathering information on Conte Vincenzo's activities for the Elsinore League for Carfax—No, that doesn't really fit with what Carfax said about the package."

"No, it doesn't." Malcolm dug his free hand into his hair. "The immediate problem is how to respond to Conte Vincenzo."

"I could contact Julien."

Malcolm's brows snapped together.

"Julien can take care of himself," Mélanie said. "And he might actually want to hear whatever the Elsinore League have to say to him. Though the thought of Julien and the Elsinore League combining forces—"

"Quite," Raoul said.

"I could defy Vincenzo," Mélanie said. "The bit about exposing me might be bluster. But it might not. And if they made the truth of my past public, we'd never be able to go back to Britain."

"Carfax makes it impossible for us to go back in any case," Malcolm said. "But it would affect our lives here." He looked at Raoul. "And your options in Spain. If it was known you were working for the French, not the guerrilleros—"

"You don't need to take me into account." Raoul righted a shell door in the castle that was tilting. "But I agree it's not advisable to lightly cut off options."

"How long did he give you?" Malcolm asked.

"Until tomorrow afternoon," Mélanie said. "And whatever I tell him, we need to learn more about what the devil the Elsinore League want with Julien. Do you think the Elsinore League recruited Vincenzo when he was in Britain?"

"It's entirely possible," Raoul said. "Although I do know from Archie that they have some international members. But Archie's never been able to determine names or details about

124

them."

Malcolm picked up a stick from a pile the children had made and dragged it through the sand. "We arrive here, in supposed seclusion, to be attacked by bandits. And then rescued by Kit, who takes us to his father's villa. Where we learn Kit's father is in communication with Carfax. About us. And Kit's father's lover's husband is working for the Elsinore League. Who happen to be an enemy of both us and Carfax."

"You can't be suggesting this all centers round us," Mélanie said. "I'm always ready to see patterns, but that doesn't even make sense. Carfax may have written to Thurston because we were coming. The bandit attack may have been set up to catch us. Kit could conceivably be working with his father. But Vincenzo and Thurston aren't allies. Raoul heard Vincenzo plotting against Thurston, Laura and I heard Thurston confront Vincenzo. Besides, Thurston is connected to Carfax, and Vincenzo to the Elsinore League, and Carfax is the League's sworn enemy. Even more than he's ours. So, how on earth—"

"I know." Malcolm stared at the stick clutched between his fingers. "But it's suspicious. How could Vincenzo have known we'd be here? Was it just a lucky accident that he happened to be so well positioned to try to blackmail you?"

"Someone in the Elsinore League who knew we'd left Britain could have guessed we'd come to Italy, just as Carfax did," Mélanie said. "With our stop in Switzerland, a letter could have reached Conte Vincenzo in time for him to arrange to be here."

"And it's coincidence his wife's lover is working for, or with, Carfax?"

"Thurston's working for Carfax could have driven Vincenzo to seek out the League," Raoul said. "Or the other way round, I suppose."

Malcolm dropped the stick in the sand. "South America looks rather appealing just now."

"Don't," Mélanie said, only partly in mock horror. "We can't keep running."

"Besides, someone connected to Carfax would be bound to be there," Raoul said.

"That," Malcolm said, "is all too true."

Mélanie drew her legs up in the sand and locked her arms round her knees, pulling the ivory lace of her skirt taut. "I think I should meet Vincenzo tomorrow. Say I agree, but need more time. Try to draw him out."

Malcolm grimaced and glanced at Raoul.

"Probably our best option," Raoul said.

"Why is it always you who has to meet with villains?" Malcolm muttered.

Mélanie reached out and squeezed her husband's hand. "Because I have much more experience with betrayal than you do, dearest," she said with the brightest smile she could muster.

Malcolm's grip on her hand tightened. "You're not going alone."

"Honestly, darling. It's not as though he's a threat—"

"Nevertheless. If—"

A scream from the other end of the beach drowned out his words.

CHAPTER 11

Jessica screamed in response to the scream and leapt into Mélanie's arms. Malcolm met his wife's gaze for a moment. "Go," she murmured, stretching out her arms to gather in Colin and Emily, while she gave a reassuring smile to the Montagu children. Malcolm exchanged a quick look with Raoul and the two of them sprang to their feet and ran down the beach.

The scream had come from round a small bend where the house jutted almost to the water and the beach curved round it. Malcolm and Raoul rounded the point to see a woman in a blue dress and straw hat standing at the water's edge, hands to her mouth. Diana Smythe, Malcolm realized. Her gaze was trained on a man, knee-deep in the water, bent down to lift something floating in the shallows, shoulders straining against the well-cut seams of his coat. The sunlight flashed on crimson in the water round him.

Lord Byron. And what he was trying to lift was another man, with a knife protruding from his chest.

Malcolm and Raoul plunged into the water. Byron was holding the man under the arms. Malcolm and Raoul each seized one of his legs. It was only then that Malcolm realized the man was Conte Vincenzo.

They got Vincenzo to the beach and laid him in the sand, all three of them breathing hard. Malcolm dropped down in the sand and put his fingers to Vincenzo's neck, though the vacant look in the man's eyes told its own story. He looked at the other two men and Diana and shook his head.

"Oh, God," Diana said. "We were walking along the beach, we came round the point and then we saw him. Who—? How—?"

"How is almost certainly that someone plunged a knife in his chest. As to who—Did you see anyone else?"

Diana shook her head.

"No one," Byron said. He was staring down at Vincenzo, eyes glazed with shock, but also with the look of one noting details. A writer's reaction, Malcolm had learned from watching Simon. "How long has he been dead?"

"Difficult to tell with his being in the water." Malcolm said. "But my wife was talking to him little more than half an hour ago."

Footsteps pounded on the sand. Thurston, Mélanie, the contessa, and Sofia ran round the side of the villa. They all came to a halt as they took in the scene before them. Sofia rushed forwards, tripping over her muslin skirts, and flung herself down beside her father.

"I'm sorry, Donna Sofia." Malcolm touched her shoulder. "He was dead when we found him."

Thurston walked up to the group clustered round the conte and stood staring down at him with uncomprehending eyes. "There's been a terrible accident."

"It isn't accident in the least." Sofia put a hand to the side of her father's face, then stared up at her mother's lover and her mother, who stood stone-still beside Thurston. "Someone murdered him."

Thurston drew a breath that sounded like smashed glass.

Malcolm pushed himself to his feet. "Mrs. Smythe and Lord Byron found the conte. My wife spoke with Conte Vincenzo half an hour ago." He met Mélanie's gaze for a moment. "Have any of you seen him since?"

Thurston passed a hand over his hair. "No. I don't think so. It's difficult—"

"Quite," Malcolm said. "Time to talk later. We should get Conte Vincenzo in the house without disturbing the guests. I assume there's a side entrance we can use?"

Thurston nodded, then drew another breath of smashed air. "Dear Christ, what are we supposed to do? Do I have to tell my guests not to leave?"

"I don't think that would be very successful," Malcolm said. "And we know where to find them. For now I'd say there's been a tragic accident." He looked at Sofia. "I know it's not an accident. But for the moment, we want to forestall panic."

Sofia was still kneeling beside her father, but she met his gaze, comprehension in her own. Then she pushed herself to her feet and went to her mother. The contessa's arms closed round her daughter. It wasn't clear who was comforting whom. Mélanie moved to Diana Smythe, who was also standing as though transfixed, and touched her arm. Diana's fingers closed round Mélanie's own.

Malcolm, Raoul, Thurston, and Byron lifted Conte Vincenzo and carried him to the door Thurston indicated. Mélanie hurried ahead to open the door. And they carried

129

Conte Vincenzo into the shadows on a golden day that had suddenly turned crimson.

CHAPTER 12

At the contessa's instructions, they laid Conte Vincenzo on a sofa in a small ground-floor sitting room. The contessa produced a sheet from somewhere to wrap him in. In the contessa at least, shock had given way to composure. Sofia also seemed to have herself well in hand. Diana Smythe looked number than either the victim's wife or daughter, but by the time they had settled Vincenzo, some color had returned to her cheeks.

Thurston and the contessa went to speak with the guests. Sofia, Byron, and Diana Smythe followed them. Malcolm exchanged a look with his wife and father. Instead of following the others, the three of them of one accord made their way back to the strip of beach where they had found the murdered conte.

Mélanie closed her arms over her chest. The wind blew the fragile ivory lace and muslin of her gown against her legs. Her straw hat slipped back against her shoulders, held only by its rose satin ribbons. "Scarcely more than an hour ago I was talking to him," she said in a low voice. "Walking on the beach, holding Jessica's hand. I wasn't happy with what he asked of me. Truth to tell I wished him at the devil. Metaphorically. But I never wanted—"

Malcolm closed his arms round her. "Whoever attacked him, for whatever reason, thank God it was after you and Jessica were well away." He pressed his lips to her forehead, and then looked at Raoul. "You didn't—"

Raoul raised a brow, though his face was uncharacteristically white. "I'm a spymaster, not a murderer."

"Given the provocation—"

"Far too many complications. Besides, morality aside, if I resorted to murder every time the past threatens to come out, we'd leave a trail of dead bodies in our wake that would rival John Webster."

Mélanie lifted her head from Malcolm's shoulder and gave a choked laugh. "And without Conte Vincenzo it will be harder to learn what the Elsinore League want with Julien."

"Quite. And I was on the beach with the children when he was killed," Raoul said.

Mélanie turned in Malcolm's arms and cast a glance round the beach. "So many of us milling about, I suppose it's folly to hope there are clues left."

"Probably," Malcolm said. "But I thought we should at least check."

The sun-warmed sand was not good for footprints and, as Mélanie had said, so many of them had walked over the beach it was impossible to search out new prints. But in the damp sand near the water's edge, a bit further down from the spot where they'd pulled Vincenzo from the water, Malcolm spotted some drops of crimson. "It looks as though Vincenzo was stabbed here," he said. "Then pushed into the lake. Or dragged, but that would leave the murderer soaking wet, which seems unlikely considering the killer almost certainly came from the house."

Mélanie glanced over the lake. "Vincenzo could have had a rendezvous with a contact. The Elsinore League connection makes that more likely. Someone could have come by boat, sticking close to shore, and not been seen by the guests on the terrace. But you'd think Byron and Diana Smythe would have seen the boat escaping."

"I was on the beach with the children for a good hour before the body was discovered," Raoul said. "Byron and Mrs. Smythe didn't pass me. So they must have gone the long way round the villa."

"Which is suggestive." Malcolm met his father's gaze. "Particularly with a man like Byron, and a pretty woman. Selena was asking where Byron had got to when she quarreled with her brother, so Byron and Mrs. Smythe were likely gone for some time."

"Definitely suggestive," Mélanie said. "Especially given Diana Smythe seems such a decorous wife. But not necessarily connected to the murder."

"But still interesting." Malcolm scanned the beach.

"I didn't get a good look at the murder weapon," Mélanie said. "But it looked like an ordinary knife."

"It was." Malcolm had removed the knife from Vincenzo's chest as discreetly as possible. "It could even have come from the kitchen here."

"Vincenzo didn't walk past us on the beach, either," Raoul said. "So he must have gone round the long way or through the house. Which suggests he didn't wish to be seen, whether he was meeting someone from the house or from the outside."

Malcolm cast a glance at the house. "And whoever killed him must have gone through or round the house, as well. Or come from outside. Of course, it's also possible he slipped away to meet someone and someone else killed him. But if so, that person took care not to be seen as well."

"And then rejoined the party?" Mélanie stared at the blood in the sand. "If they sprang back after stabbing him, and Vincenzo staggered backwards—Perhaps the killer didn't push him into the lake, perhaps he staggered and fell. It's possible the killer wouldn't have been sprayed with blood or lake water. At least not too obviously."

Malcolm nodded. "Probably impossible to inspect everyone. We can see what we can note before the guests leave."

Mélanie met her husband's gaze. "We're investigating."

"I don't see how we can do otherwise, do you? Though we don't have any official authority."

"Thurston is already relying on you," Raoul said.

Malcolm gave a quick smile. "Yes, I was trying to lay the groundwork." He looked between Raoul and Mélanie. "We all have motive. We'll have to investigate without that coming out."

"Quite like old times," Mélanie said.

Thurston passed a hand over his hair. The self-assured man appeared quite out of his depth. Not surprisingly. Most people went a lifetime without confronting murder. "God in heaven. I never thought that—"

"One doesn't," Malcolm said.

They were in Thurston's study, the same room in which

Malcolm had glimpsed Carfax's letter in what now seemed another lifetime. After the guests had departed, Thurston had asked Malcolm and Mélanie if he could speak with them.

Mélanie poured a glass of brandy and put it in Thurston's hand. "It's not a solution, but it will help."

Thurston took a swallow of brandy and looked between them. "You've handled this before."

"Yes." Malcolm didn't even try to deny their role as investigators these days. In this case, he was counting on their reputations preceding them.

"So you can look into it. Find out what happened to Vincenzo."

"There'll be authorities," Malcolm said.

"Italians. Austrians. I need someone I know. Who speaks my language."

Malcolm gave a crisp nod.

The door opened on the end of their exchange and the contessa came into the room. "I can get you a list of the guests." Her voice was crisp and level. "And I assume you'll want to talk to the servants, as well."

Thurston crossed to her side. "Elena. This isn't fit for you—"

"It happened in our house, Bernard. We have to deal with it. Thank God we have friends to help us." She looked from Malcolm to Mélanie. "We are quite out of our depth, you see."

"Of course we can help, Contessa," Mélanie said. "I am so very sorry. I know you hadn't lived together for years, but he was the father of your children."

"Thank you. I— " She swallowed, her eyes bright. "It is difficult to take in."

Thurston kissed her forehead. "My darling, there's no need—"

135

"There's every need." The contessa pulled back from his embrace. "I need to keep busy, Bernard."

"It can be one's salvation at such a time," Mélanie said.

The contessa nodded. "I've asked the servants to assemble belowstairs. One of the kitchen maids had hysterics, but otherwise everyone is being quite sensible. More sensible than I am, I fear."

"The children—" Thurston said.

"Lady Tarrington was with them, bless her. And now Sofia is. They're calmer than I thought."

"Children can be very practical at times like these," Malcolm said.

The contessa nodded and swallowed. "If we hadn't had the party—"

Malcolm crossed to her side and touched her shoulder. "It wasn't an accident. If Vincenzo had an enemy, that enemy would most likely have found him, whatever you had done."

The contessa gave a shaky nod.

Malcolm looked between the couple. "If you're able to answer a question—do you know of any enemies Vincenzo had?"

Thurston's brows drew together. "I fought a duel against the man once. But even then I wouldn't have called myself his enemy, though he might have called me his." Thurston stared into his glass as though he didn't quite realize he held it. "The truth is, though he visited with the children, I can't claim to have known him well."

"Nor I," the contessa said. "Despite the fact that I'm married to him. Was married to him." She shivered and shook her head in disbelief. "It doesn't change anything for Bernard and me. Bernard isn't free to marry. Not that that would have mattered—But I don't see how anyone could even claim we wanted him dead."

Leaving aside the fact that Thurston had quarreled with Vincenzo an hour before the murder. But this wasn't the time to ask about that. Thurston might order them off the investigation before it started.

Not to mention that one rather lost one's investigative edge if one admitted to spying. "Could we have a look at Vincenzo's room before we leave?" Malcolm asked.

Malcolm cast a glance round the chamber that had been Conte Vincenzo's. A handsome room with mahogany furniture and hangings of dark blue Venetian silk. Vincenzo had not brought a great deal with him, as one might expect of a man not planning a long stay. A single trunk, a dressing case, and shaving kit. All elegant and obviously expensive. Malcolm discovered a false bottom in shaving kit, but the compartment was empty.

"Nothing but clothes in the trunk," Mélanie said. "But I think Vincezno has had a woman in his bed since the linen was last changed." She straightened up from the bedclothes holding a long dark hair.

Malcolm examined the hair in the light from the windows. No obvious hints of red or blonde or gray. "Presumably not the contessa's," he said. "Perhaps one of the servants."

"Vincenzo seemed the sort of man who would take advantage of the maids." Raoul, who had been tapping on the paneling, went to kneel beside the fireplace.

"That could yield interesting information if we can discover whom." Malcolm gave the hair back to Mélanie who folded a piece of paper about it and tucked it in her reticule.

"Unless of course Vincenzo smuggled a woman into the house in secret. Which could also have all sorts of implications."

"Ashes in the grate," Raoul reported from the fireplace. "In the middle of summer. Ground up carefully with the poker, so there's nothing left to read. The sort of care one would expect of an Elsinore League member. It probably means we won't find anything hidden elsewhere, but we should finish looking."

A search of the walls, furniture, and bedding did indeed reveal no hidden information, though Mélanie retrieved something shiny and silver from beneath the night table.

"It looks like a waistcoat button," Malcolm said, as she held it up to the light of the window.

"Yes, I think it is," she said. "But I went through all the clothes Vincenzo brought with him, and there are no buttons missing on his waistcoats or any other garments. I suppose it could be a spare his valet dropped, but I wonder if it didn't come from a visitor." She wrapped the button in another piece of paper and tucked it into her reticule, as well. "Perhaps Addison can ask Vincenzo's valet."

They finished their search, but the room yielded no further clues. Malcolm cast a last glance about. For all they had learned about Conte Vincenzo today, in many ways the man remained a cipher.

Laura was sitting on a settee on the lower terrace, Jessica snuggled in her lap, Colin and Emily curled up on either side of her. Raoul dropped down on an arm of the settee. "We'll be able to go soon. Malcolm and Mélanie are just having another word with Lord Thurston and the contessa and some gentleman from the local authorities who've just arrived. You're all being quite amazing. Not that I'd have expected anything less." He tweaked one of Emily's curls, touched a hand to Colin's shoulder, then put a hand on Jessica's head.

Jessica lifted her head from Laura's shoulder long enough to smile at him. "Home." She buried her face again.

"Just so," Raoul agreed.

Colin was frowning. "Mummy and Daddy are going to Investigate, aren't they?"

"I imagine so," Raoul said. "Does that bother you?"

"No." Colin shook his head vigorously. "It will feel like home."

"Quite right." Raoul touched his fingers to his son's cheek and nodded.

The carriage ride back to the villa was mostly silent. Jessica curled up in Mélanie's arms. Colin climbed into Malcolm's lap and Emily into Laura's. None of the children said much, though Colin looked up at Malcolm and said, "I'm glad you're Investigating."

Mélanie smiled across the seat at her son as she stroked Jessica's hair. There would undoubtedly be questions later, but with luck when they got home (was the villa home now?) they'd be able to get the children settled and then properly discuss the events of the day. She couldn't yet make sense of the thoughts tumbling in her brain.

The local podestà, more or less the equivalent of a magistrate, and the commander of the nearby Austrian garrison had arrived at the Thurston villa just before they left in response to Thurston's summons. Both had said, with surprising alacrity, that they welcomed the Rannochs' involvement. Without quite saying so, they had made it clear that they vastly preferred to leave the task of questioning British expatriates, and as much of the investigation as possible, to Malcolm and her. The garrison commander had added that he knew of the murder they had investigated during the Congress of Vienna and that Prince Metternich held them in high esteem. Odd how things could change. For much of that investigation, Malcolm had been a suspect himself, and at one point Austria's chief of police had arrested him. But it was true that by the conclusion of the investigation, Metternich had considered himself in their debt.

It seemed an age since they had left the villa, as though they should be returning in darkness. But when they pulled up in the forecourt, the evening sun gleamed rose gold on the white columns. And on another carriage that stood in front of the villa.

Mélanie stared in bewilderment. As she watched, the door of the villa burst open and a small, blonde person came running out.

Colin understood first. "Livia!" he cried, jumping up on Malcolm's lap.

CHAPTER 13

Colin tumbled out the carriage door as soon as he could and ran to hug Livia Davenport. Emily was close behind. By the time Malcolm handed Mélanie from the carriage, Cordelia and Harry (with two-year-old Drusilla on his shoulders) had followed Livia from the house.

Still holding Jessica, Mélanie ran to hug Cordelia. It hadn't been so very long since they had seen the Davenports, but somehow having them here now bridged her two worlds, the separation from home, the sense of exile. Tears pricked her eyes.

"I'm sorry," Cordelia said, "we got here sooner than we anticipated. The girls were so excited they didn't mind traveling long hours."

"We couldn't be happier," Mélanie said truthfully. Jessica pressed a damp kiss to Cordelia's cheek, then started wriggling to get down. Mélanie set her on the ground and she ran to throw her arms round Drusilla, whom Harry had swung down from his shoulders.

"You've come at an excellent time," Malcolm said, as Raoul handed Laura from the carriage. "We have an investigation we could use help with."

A gleam lit Harry's eye. "Well, then. Best go inside and tell us about it."

In the end, it was some time before they could update Harry and Cordelia. But once the children were settled on the terrace with Blanca and Addison and plentiful food, the adults were able to settle in the grand salon and share the events of the day. Or rather, of the past four weeks, leading up to this shattering day.

"Good God," Cordelia said. "I thought you were escaping."

"Agents don't escape." Harry frowned into his glass of Brunello. "Conte Vincenzo was working for the Elsinore League?"

"That much is without question." Mélanie rubbed her arms. For the first time in the midst of an investigation, she didn't have to hide her past from Cordy and Harry. Liberating, and yet it left her feeling strangely exposed. As though all her secrets were piled on Arabella Rannoch's Savonnerie carpet for her friends to pick through. "He told me. Or at least admitted it when I put the pieces together."

"And Thurston is working for Carfax?" Cordelia looked from Malcolm to Mélanie to Raoul.

"For him or with him." Mélanie reached for her wine. "In the letter Laura and I looked at, Thurston was making some sort of trade or purchase for Carfax. Carfax was concerned about having 'the goods in hand.'"

"With Carfax that could mean anything," Harry said.

"Quite," Malcolm said. He was on one of the burgundy-and-gold-striped sofas beside Mélanie, his arm stretched out to trail against her shoulders. "Carfax also wanted Thurston to keep an eye on us. How we managed to choose to escape here of all places—" He put up a hand. "I know, I know. Carfax has agents everywhere."

Cordelia kicked off her kid slippers and drew her feet up onto the edge of the settee. "But Lord Thurston already knew about what Conte Vincenzo was doing for the Elsinore League. Or trying to do. When Suz—Mélanie and Laura overheard them in the library it sounded as if he'd known for some time. So it doesn't make sense he'd have killed him today."

"Not unless he uncovered new information after we overheard him," Mélanie said.

"It was also clear from the quarrel that the two men have never been on the sort of easy terms they displayed to the world." Laura took a sip of wine. "Old resentments can fester. Though again, it seems odd that it came to a head today. I mean, if Thurston were going to lose his temper and attack Vincenzo, you'd think he'd have done so in that confrontation in the library. He did knock Vincenzo to the carpet."

"Perhaps the murder was only meant to look like a crime of passion," Malcolm said. "Suppose Carfax wanted Thurston to get rid of Vincenzo. Thurston wouldn't have wanted to do it in the house."

"So he killed him by the lake?" Mélanie turned her head to look at her husband. "With a house full of guests? It seems risky."

"But whoever did it wasn't seen," Malcolm pointed out. "And a house full of guests provides the cover of lots of

143

suspects. I could certainly see Carfax ordering Thurston to get rid of Vincenzo."

"Darling, you can't blame Carfax for everything."

"No, but given what he's done lately, it's hard to imagine the man has any limits." Malcolm's voice was easy but his gaze had a hard gleam.

"You know about letting personal feelings cloud the issue," Mélanie reminded him. "Besides, whatever Carfax's cryptic words in that letter mean, it's difficult to interpret them as an order to murder."

"There is that," Malcolm acknowledged. "Though we don't know what other letters he may have sent to Thurston recently." He looked at Laura. "Did you ever hear mention of anyone Italian in the Elsinore League?"

Laura shook her head. "But though I listened as well as I could, mostly I followed orders." Her gaze went through the French windows to her daughter, playing hide and seek on the terrace with the other children. Blackmail over Emily had kept her working for the League for four years.

Raoul leaned back in a corner of the sofa across from the one where Mélanie and Malcolm sat, his arm round Laura. "Thurston's an obvious suspect because of the history between the two men and their present tensions. But he's hardly the only one. "

"You'd think I'd be inured to it by now, but I don't like to think it of any of them," Laura said. "Lord Thurston can be quite charming."

"So he can," Malcolm said. "I felt that charm myself. Right at the moment I looked down at his desk and saw Carfax's letter."

"Vincenzo's son arrived just before the murder," Raoul pointed out.

"Sweetheart." Laura swung round to look at him. "You're not suggesting—"

"I don't think it's the likeliest explanation," Raoul said. "But he does reap an obvious benefit from his father's death. Assuming, of course, that he wants to be Conte Vincenzo and all that goes with it."

"It sounds as though the podestà and the Austrian commander gave you carte blanche to question the guests," Harry said.

"Yes, they more or less turned the investigation over to us," Malcolm said.

"Isn't that surprising?" Cordelia asked. "I know many of the guests are British, but Conte Vincenzo was an Italian aristocrat and a friend of Metternich's. One of their own, to both the Italians and the Austrians."

"And if anything goes wrong with the investigation, if the questions or results ruffle any feathers, if word gets back to Metternich, we'll be the ones blamed." Malcolm gave a faint smile. "The podestà and the Austrian commander both struck me as shrewd men."

"What do you know about the other guests at the picnic?" Harry asked.

"Some Italians, but mostly a collection of expatriates and their guests." Raoul reached for his wineglass. "Including the woman I'm married to."

"Oh, dear," Cordelia set her glass down. "I'm so sorry."

"The awkwardness is no more than I deserve," Raoul said. "But I'm sorry for the position it put Margaret in. And Laura."

Laura reached up and twined her fingers round the hand that was resting on her shoulder. "I can take care of myself."

"That I know full well." Raoul squeezed her hand. "Margaret is a complicated woman and God knows she's

145

surprised me, but I doubt she's ever even heard of the Elsinore League."

"Lord Byron was there," Mélanie said. "Along with Percy and Mary Shelley. In fact, he discovered the body."

"Byron discovered the body?" Cordelia demanded.

"In the company of Kit's very pretty and very married sister," Malcolm said. "With whom he had evidently wandered some distance away from the guests for a considerable time."

"Oh, God." Cordelia put her head in her hands. "I'm supposed to try to see him. Caro gave me a letter to deliver to him. Not a letter that I want to deliver or I suspect that he has any desire to receive, but I suppose I should at least make the attempt."

"He was rather more rational than I anticipated," Mélanie said. "Though I imagine he's quite mercurial."

Cordelia made a face. "I don't know who is worse for drama, he or Caro."

"We're going to have to talk with him, in any case," Malcolm said. "He may remember more about the murder as the shock wears off. But it's difficult to imagine him associated with the League either."

Cordelia frowned. "I can actually see the secrecy of the Elsinore League appealing to Byron. But he couldn't be further from their politics. And I credit him with enough actual belief that he'd cavil at being a member. Though it wouldn't be the first time I've given Byron more credit than he deserved."

"If it didn't stop him, I would think it would stop the Elsinore League," Raoul said. "They have members with a more liberal bent—Caroline Lamb's father Bessborough for one, and your uncle Archie. But none perceived as being as radical as Byron. At least, not as far as they know. They don't know the full truth about Archie's politics. And even if they thought they could make use of Byron, I think they'd have seen a risk in his penchant for public display."

"I can only imagine," Cordelia said. "In fact, I should quite like to wish Byron on the Elsinore League. Unlikely as it seems."

"But we don't know about others at the party," Harry said. "The Elsinore League's reach is deep. Vincenzo could have been using the party as cover to meet with a confederate. We know he has at least one here whom O'Roarke overheard him talking to."

Malcolm grinned across the salon at his friend. "God, I've missed you, Davenport."

An answering grin warmed Harry's face. "Not half as much as I've missed you, Rannoch." He frowned. "I knew I'd miss Archie when we said goodbye to him, but I didn't realize I'd be wanting his insights into the Elsinore League." Harry's uncle, Archibald Davenport, was an Elsinore League member who for years had worked undercover with Raoul and Arabella Rannoch to expose the League's secrets.

"We could certainly use your uncle's insights," Raoul agreed. "But it's true the League are ruthless enough to turn on their own. I didn't recognize the voice I overheard the night we arrived among any of the guests today, but I didn't speak with all the guests."

Cordelia linked her arms round her knees. With the frothy muslin flounces of her skirt spilling over the delicate ivory and burgundy pattern of the settee, she looked as though she were lounging after a day of frivolity, but her face had the concentration of an investigator. "Do you think Julien St. Juste knows the Elsinore League are looking for him?"

"Conte Vincenzo didn't seem to think so," Mélanie said. "But knowing Julien, I'd say it's entirely possible."

Cordelia smoothed one of the links of her diamond bracelet. "I've never met him. But from what you've described it sounds as though he wouldn't cavil at killing if he thought it the best solution to the League's searching for him."

Mélanie met her friend's gaze. "You've grasped Julien perfectly, Cordy. I should have thought—The truth is, he could have been at the party in disguise and I can't even be certain I would have recognized him."

"Nor can I," Raoul said. "He's also entirely capable of blending in with the servants. I can't see him killing Vincenzo just because the League are searching for him, but depending on why they're searching—"

"Quite, to quote my husband," Mélanie said. "I can even see sympathizing with Julien's killing Vincenzo depending on what the League were after. And I'm not inclined to sympathize with anyone killing anyone. Or to sympathize with Julien at all."

"They can't expect you to get the message to St. Juste by tomorrow now, can they?" Cordelia said. "That is, there's no one to report to."

"No," Mélanie agreed. "But knowing the Elsinore League, they'll get another message to me shortly."

"A bit tricky," Harry said. "Whoever sends the message will be revealing a connection to the League. And they have to know that you're investigating."

"It's unusual for them to come out of the shadows as much as Vincenzo did," Laura said. "Which says something about how determined they are to find Julien St. Juste."

"Determined or desperate," Raoul said.

Harry picked up his wineglass and twisted the stem

148

between his fingers. "They're almost sure to realize that all of you benefited from Vincenzo's death."

"Darling," Cordelia said.

"We have motives," Malcolm said. "It's quite true."

Harry met his friend's gaze. "We know none of you killed Vincenzo. But the Elsinore League might jump to the opposite conclusion."

"And though they can turn on their own, they've also been known to avenge their own," Raoul said. His gaze went to the children on the terrace for a moment, and Mélanie saw the flinch in it, though his tone was calm. "I've thought of it. We're going to have to be on our guard."

"It's mad, isn't it?" Cordelia said. "What all of you have to live with."

"You already knew that," Mélanie said.

"Yes, but it's worse than I realized."

"Much worse," Mélanie agreed.

"Oh, you know what I mean by worse, dearest," Cordelia said quickly. "More challenging. I can't believe you've been going through all this and I didn't have the least notion of it."

"I'm glad you know," Mélanie said. "I can't tell you how much more comfortable it makes life."

Cordelia smiled. "It must have given you a headache working out what you could and couldn't tell us." She took a sip of wine. "I remember the Thurston scandal. I was still in the schoolroom, though old enough to be dreaming of my debut and starting to take a keen interest in grown-up scandals. The Thurston scandal was the talk of the schoolroom for weeks. Julia and I would steal the papers and look through articles we weren't supposed to read. We thought the only drawback was that all the key players were so middle aged." She laughed. "They must have all been about

149

the age we are now. Odd how one's perspective changes. I'm afraid we were rather heartless. We quite wanted there to be a divorce because we loved reading about crim con trials. The duel kept us going for weeks." She shook her head. "One doesn't realize what capital one is making out of human misery at that age. I didn't dream that in a few years—"

"We'd be giving schoolgirls scandal-sheet fodder to pore over ourselves?" Harry asked with a raised brow.

Cordelia met her husband's gaze and reached for his hand. "In a nutshell."

"What about the younger Montagus?" Mélanie asked.

Cordelia laced her fingers through Harry's. "I didn't know any of them well. Talking of my own scandals, when Diana made her debut I wasn't much invited to the sort of entertainments to which mamas took their unmarried daughters. But I remember she married John Smythe. It was one of the matches of the season. Lady Thurston made quite a fuss of the wedding, perhaps in case any of the old scandal was revived."

"I met Kit once or twice in the run-up to Waterloo," Harry said. "Likable lad. And so, of course, not the sort a bitter fool like me was likely to spend much time with. I remember thinking he was just the sort of idealist who was likely to turn into cannon fodder at the first volley. I was relieved to learn he hadn't."

"There are plenty of tensions in the Thurston family," Malcolm said. "But it's difficult to see the young Montagus blaming Vincenzo for the family drama."

"Could Kit have learned Vincenzo was working against his father?" Cordelia asked.

"It's hard to see either Thurston or Vincenzo mentioning the Elsinore League to Kit," Malcolm said. "Though I

150

suppose Kit could have seen Vincenzo doing something he thought betrayed his father." He looked from Harry to Cordelia. "I'm sorry you've landed in the midst of this."

"On the contrary," Harry said. "We're glad to be here to help."

Cordelia tightened her grip on her husband's hand. "The truth is we've both been going a bit mad without the distraction of your investigations."

CHAPTER 14

The sky had faded from pink to green, but childish voices still echoed across the terrace. The table had become a fort, and Harry was helping Colin, Emily, and Livia strategize an attack. Bedtimes had never been very exact in Berkeley Square, and, if anything, were even later in the freedom of Italy.

Raoul moved to stand beside Malcolm.

"How much of a risk do you think the Elsinore League are?" Malcolm asked his father.

"Difficult to say. Especially as we don't know who's involved and what they're after. Save that they do seem singularly determined."

"And if Julien St. Juste gets wind of it, he could show up here."

Raoul nodded, with the look of one who'd been turning the possibility over. "I wouldn't be surprised."

"Or do you think Mel was right and he's already here?"

"I'd like to think we'd know it. But Mélanie's right. I can't swear I'd recognize him in every disguise." Raoul hesitated a moment. "I don't think he'll like Mélanie being made into a pawn."

"Nor do I. I saw him with her in Hyde Park last June. Only a few minutes, but it was enough."

"For what?"

"To determine that the man is half in love with my wife. Maybe more so."

Raoul met Malcolm's gaze in the shadows of the terrace and the shifting light of the lanterns.

"You have to have known," Malcolm said.

Raoul's gaze scarcely shifted, but it showed acknowledgment. "If anything, it's got stronger. Not that it would necessarily stop St. Juste from all sorts of actions that could harm Mélanie and her family. But I think he'll protect her, all other things being equal. Especially after that last meeting in Hyde Park." Raoul paused a moment, his gaze going down the terrace to the children and Harry and then beyond them to Mélanie, Laura, and Cordelia with the younger girls. "St. Juste wouldn't be the only one to find his priorities changing with the end of the war. Though I don't think he has any intention of anything approaching settling down. But my guess is he'll be more of an ally against the Elsinore League than otherwise."

"Unless he wants to take on whatever they want him for."

"There is that." Raoul touched Malcolm's arm. "With everything that's happened, I haven't had a chance to thank you. For supporting Laura when I had to go speak with Margaret. I hated walking away from her. I hated the way the whole thing unfolded."

"Awkward for everyone, very much including you. Laura understands." Malcolm hesitated. "I recognized Margaret at once."

Raoul swung his head round to meet Malcolm's gaze. "I wasn't sure you remembered."

"You were—important to me." He hadn't quite been ready to admit just how important until recently. He fixed his gaze straight ahead, picking out the words the way Jessica had picked out her steps when she was learning to walk. "I knew it was significant that you'd married, though I couldn't quite have said why." He risked a sideways glance at Raoul. "I think I knew Mama was upset, though I didn't understand the reasons."

Raoul's mouth tightened, as though to hold back some emotion perhaps not even he could have defined. "At the time I thought she was relieved."

"You're good at reading people, O'Roarke, but you may not have been the best observer in this situation."

"Perhaps not. I'm not sure I was ever the best observer of Arabella, in any case." Raoul continued to watch Malcolm. "Whatever was between your mother and me, I never meant to walk away from you. I know I didn't—"

"Tell me? No, you couldn't very well, considering you couldn't articulate what you were trying to be to me in the first place. But you kept on visiting. Thinking back, that means rather a lot. I'm sure it didn't make the rest of your life easier."

"My dear Malcolm. There were times when my visits to you were the one thing that kept me sane."

Malcolm stared at his father. For all the ways they'd come to know each other recently, Raoul could still shock him.

Raoul lifted a brow. "Surely there've been times you've felt the same about Colin and Jessica."

"Yes, but—" Malcolm paused, frowning, turning over bits of the past.

"I didn't do as much for you as you do for your children. It's a fair point. It doesn't necessarily change the feelings."

"It's not that. You had—other priorities." Whatever he had meant to O'Roarke—and he was coming to realize it was a great deal more than he had realized at the time—the center of Raoul's world had always been his work.

Raoul turned, leaning against the terrace balustrade. "One set of priorities doesn't necessarily drive out another. My work kept me going many times. It also put me in despair more than once. You never put me in despair. Quite the reverse, in fact. I wasn't willing to give up my time with you. I thought things were sufficiently over and done with between your mother and me that Margaret wouldn't guess. I underestimated both the echoes between Arabella and me, and Margaret's astuteness. She guessed about Arabella and me, though I didn't know it until today." He hesitated a moment, fingers taut against the stone. "She also guessed that you're my son."

Malcolm pictured Margaret O'Roarke's hard-eyed gaze today, and then a mistier image of the young woman he remembered as Raoul's bride. "That must have—"

"It was only one small additional complication between two people who couldn't have been more ill suited." Raoul picked up a leaf from the balustrade and twirled it between his fingers. "There's no reason she should share the information with anyone. Margaret's still angry at me, but she's not vindictive."

Malcolm nodded, hesitated, then asked a question he'd been mulling since their departure from London. "Do you think Carfax knows?"

Raoul's eyes narrowed, though evening shadows now slanted across the terrace. "I've wondered that myself. I know

155

of no particular reason to think he does. Save that he's Carfax and has a way of knowing things."

"Quite."

"You know him much better than I do."

Malcolm considered the question he had pondered many times in the past. "I'm not sure. He definitely has an interest in you. He's tried to get information about you from me, and he seems to know there's a connection between us. His interest in you could be accounted for by your activities in Ireland and Spain, and he could connect you to me simply because of the family connection. But I doubt it."

Raoul nodded. "Carfax's own interest in the Elsinore League borders on obsession, as we saw three months ago. It would be a wonder if he hadn't known Arabella and I were investigating them, and that could lead to his learning other things."

"Quite." Malcolm rested his hands on the balustrade behind him. "I'm almost certain Carfax knows Colin isn't my biological son. He's all but said so a few times—in the nicest possible way, implying he'd do his best to divert any gossip. But if he knows you were Mel's spymaster, it wouldn't be a huge leap for him to guess you're Colin's father. Especially if he knows you're my father, which accounts for the resemblance among the three of us."

Raoul's mouth tightened. "The same occurred to me on the boat across the Channel. I think we have to assume he knows, or has guessed."

Which, given how much else Carfax knew, shouldn't be bothering Malcolm as much as it was. Perhaps he'd simply reached a tipping point. Or perhaps—"Carfax is fond of the children. I don't think he'd lightly make use of the truth of Colin's parentage. But he didn't lightly make use of the truth about Mélanie either." His gaze went to the fort where Colin and Livia seemed to have barricaded themselves against Emily and Harry, then back to his father. "If Carfax thought the truth about Colin could gain him some advantage—"

The lamplight caught the fear in Raoul's gaze, carefully banked. "My thoughts exactly."

Malcolm drew a breath. "We're going to have to tell Colin the truth."

Raoul's face went marble-still in the gathering twilight. "For God's sake, Malcolm. We can't even think about it for years."

"We shouldn't tell him for a few more years—unless we're forced to. But there's no question that we'll have to tell him eventually."

Raoul's gaze shot to Colin, holding up a wooden sword, then back to Malcolm. "You have an admirable love of truth, Malcolm. But in this case I think we need to consider carefully—"

"Think, O'Roarke. If Colin learns the truth from anyone else—"

"It would be harder. Granted. But he may never learn the truth at all."

Malcolm gave a short laugh. "After what we've been through these past weeks, is that really a risk you're willing to take? Besides—" Malcolm drew a breath of the warm night air. "I think he deserves to know."

Raoul's gaze darted over Malcolm's face. "As I said, you have a love of truth."

"This is more personal. In Colin's shoes, I think I'd want to know the truth."

Raoul's gaze went steady as still water. "Are you saying you wish you'd known the truth?"

"Yes, actually. But I can see why you and my mother didn't tell me. This is different. Colin is surrounded by people who love him. And I think—"

"What?" Raoul asked.

"I think you deserve for Colin to know the truth."

The stillness extended to every muscle in Raoul's body. "I don't deserve anything, Malcolm. Unless you mean I deserve the anger Colin might well feel towards me if he knew the truth."

"If I thought Colin would be angry, I wouldn't suggest we tell him. I don't think it could destroy the bond between you. And I think he deserves to know the nature of that bond. He'll be able to handle it."

"You sound very sure."

"I am. He's my son. And yours."

"I'm sorry." Raoul leaned against the closed bedchamber door. "Sorry you had to go through that. Especially without warning."

So much had happened that day that it was a moment before Laura realized he was talking about Margaret. "It was hardly your fault. And it's not as though I haven't known about Margaret from the first." Although, as Mélanie had said, in a way she hadn't seemed real until now. Laura had been keenly aware of the fact that her lover was married, but the person to whom he was married had been as shadowy as an offstage character, more literary device than person.

She studied Raoul in the light of the bronze lamp on the table by the bed. His gaze was dark with concern, but that concern was all for her. Whatever his response on his own account, it was held carefully inside, buried beneath layers of control, like so much of what he felt. As always, she hesitated to push against the boundaries he set. And yet the terms of their relationship were shifting. He might still hesitate to impose on her, but that didn't necessarily mean he didn't need more. "It must have been fiendishly awkward. For both of you."

He gave a wry smile. "For years I've been armored against meeting her. In Dublin. In London. Even in Paris after Waterloo. But I confess, in Italy it was the furthest thing from my mind. Just as meeting me seems to have been the last thing she expected. Poor Margaret."

"It can't be easy for you, either."

He hesitated, stepped into the room, pulled off his coat and stared down at the pale tan fabric. "We'll be thrown together inevitably, especially after today. But we're both adults. And she's not as angry with me as she once was. Or at least the anger doesn't burn as hot." He draped the coat over a chairback. "We've been married for twenty-three years, but we've been strangers for most of that time. Difficult now to believe I ever—"

And yet, he had tried to build a life with her. They had shared a home, had hoped for children, had gone about in society as a couple, had entertained guests together. She might not be the most important person in his life, but she was the only woman he had tried to build a life with in that sense.

"Most of the time it's all too easy for me to tuck Margaret away as one of the—many—mistakes of my past. Seeing her today"—his hands closed on the chairback—"I couldn't avoid the reality that for twenty years she's lived a life that's been constrained from what it should have been. Because of me."

159

"She agreed to marry you."

"She was eighteen. I was twenty-seven. How I could ever have been so deluded—"

"People in love have delusions."

He met her gaze for a moment. "It's hard now to believe that I ever fancied myself—" He drew a breath, twitched a crease in the coat smooth. "I found out today that Meg guessed about Arabella and Malcolm."

"You never told her?"

He passed a hand over his hair. "I was terrified of Malcolm learning the truth. And given Arabella's state of mind—"

"You must have trusted Margaret then," she said, and then nearly bit the words back.

"I did, then. But you know me, I've never shared secrets lightly." He shook his head. "Margaret seems to think I'd have told her, if I'd loved her more. I told her that was nonsense. But I wonder—God knows. I'm sorry I didn't realize she guessed, though it wouldn't have made a difference in the end." He paused, then added, "She guessed about you, as well. I don't seem to be very good at hiding my feelings."

"Margaret is obviously a very astute woman." Laura closed her arms over her chest. She'd have said it didn't make a difference. Yet, it was a reminder that her lover legally belonged to another woman. She glanced round the room. Raoul's shaving things were on the chest of drawers beside the straw hat she had worn to the picnic. Their dressing gowns were draped over the foot of the bed—his, paisley; hers, sapphire blue. His boots and her Roman sandals leaned against each other beside the chair. It was their room, a shared space they hadn't had until Italy. That she had never had before with anyone, certainly not her husband.

160

"I'm no stranger to guilt," Raoul said. "But I never felt it where Alistair Rannoch was concerned. Because whatever had been between him and Arabella—never much, I think, at least on Arabella's side—was over long before anything began between Arabella and me. I'm sure I needn't tell you to feel the same way about Margaret. She admitted she had no right to be jealous."

"I hope she's happy."

"So do I. God help me." He dug his fingers into his hair. "Desmond Quennell's wife died last spring. Margaret's lover. She'd been injured in a riding accident two decades ago. Her health had deteriorated even more. A sad story."

"How dreadful. Though perhaps it will make it easier for Margaret and Mr. Quennell to be together. Which must be a source of guilt in and of itself."

"Yes, I suspect it is." Raoul drew in and released his breath. "Margaret isn't interested in a divorce so she can remarry. I asked."

Laura stared at him. "I had no notion—"

"Of course not." His voice was neutral and matter of fact, relaying information, careful not to add more. "Margaret made it clear to me years ago that she wasn't interested in ending our marriage. But with Quennell free, I thought it might make them happier." He hesitated a moment, then added, carefully not changing his inflection, "I thought it might make us happier."

She drew a quick breath. "I've never asked you—"

"I know, sweetheart. And, as Margaret pointed out, I'm scarcely in a position to offer a woman a settled life. But you can't blame me for wanting the right to pledge myself to you before the world."

It was the first time he'd talked about marriage as more

161

than a hypothetical he couldn't offer her. For a moment she couldn't breathe. "I don't give a damn what the world thinks."

"I know full well you don't, beloved. It's a large part of why I love you."

For the second time that day, though for very different reasons, she felt herself rooted to the ground, frozen in shock, the world rushing away about her, the unexpected ringing in her ears.

"Past time I said it, don't you think?" he said in a mild voice.

She went to him and slid her arms round him.

"You can't have doubted it," he said into her hair.

No, not really. But it was amazing how different it was hearing it put into words. She kissed him. "I love you," she murmured against his cheek, framing the words with care. "I've loved you for far longer than I'd have admitted. I should have said it. I—" Was afraid of making an emotional demand? Or of defining their relationship by words that could seem hackneyed? Or of making herself vulnerable?

He took her face between his hands. His fingers trembled against her skin. "Sometimes the most overused sentiment is the only way to say what one feels."

Mélanie closed the door of the night nursery and leaned against the panels. "Stepping into someone else's nightmare. I said that the night we arrived. And I felt guilty then that I was relieved to have a problem to solve. It's only got worse now. The look on the contessa's face—"

Malcolm poured a glass of whisky and put it in her hand. "Damnable."

Mélanie took a sip of whisky. "And yet I know what Cordy meant." Despite Vincenzo's blackmail attempt—or even because of it—she'd felt her mind come alive all day, from the break-in through the aftermath of discovering Vincenzo. Investigations had always been an escape, something she and Malcolm could share and lose themselves in, despite the secrets between them. Now, it could be an escape from the damage wrought by those secrets.

Malcolm poured a glass of whisky for himself. "We're more caught up in the investigation than we thought we were that first night."

She dropped down on her dressing table bench and took another sip of whisky. Smoky. Bracing. A reminder of home. "Which is all the more reason we can't run from it."

"I wasn't suggesting we do so. Not that we could if we wanted to." He took a drink of whisky and stared at the red glass for a moment, as though appreciating the irony of drinking Scots whisky out of Venetian glass. "In truth, I probably wouldn't want to even if we weren't so entangled, but Vincenzo's threats to you make it imperative that we learn the truth." He watched her for a moment.

"I'm all right, Malcolm. And we're a match for whatever the Elsinore League may try."

"Oh, yes, I think so." He lifted his glass to hers. "Though I can't deny my pulse is beating faster."

"That can make one think more clearly."

"As long as one doesn't give way to panic." He took another drink of whisky. "Hard to remember, now that Margaret O'Roarke's presence at first seemed the greatest shock the day held."

Mélanie's fingers tightened round her glass. She could see the three of them on the beach, looking for clues. They were

163

friends now. Allies. Family. But at times she still felt she was walking on ground more fragile than the translucent glass in her hand. "I never thought much about the fact that Raoul was married. I never thought much about marriage in general." She swallowed. "I'm sorry—"

"It's all right. It was a shock for all of us. Including O'Roarke."

She looked at him for a moment. "You talked to him? Did he tell you—"

"How he felt?" Malcolm gave a crooked smile. "When does O'Roarke ever do that? But he admitted to being shocked. And concerned about the situation he put Margaret in. And Laura. I'm not sure he'd have talked to me so much if he hadn't wanted to—warn me, I suppose."

"Warn you?" She was still coming to terms with the fact that Raoul talked to Malcolm as much as to her these days.

Malcolm dropped down beside her on the dressing table bench. "It seems Margaret guessed that I'm Raoul's son. Raoul didn't know she suspected until today."

Shadowy images of a past she was just beginning to understand swirled in her head. "I imagine he's cursing himself for a fool for not realizing. Though I can see why he kept it to himself. He doesn't share things easily. Like his son." She looked up at Malcolm. "I can't see Margaret—"

"Telling anyone? No, it doesn't seem likely. And even if she did, I'm not really worried about the truth about my relationship to Raoul coming out. But it did make me realize—" He took her hand and stared down at their interlaced fingers. "Raoul agrees Carfax probably knows the truth about my parentage. He knows I'm not Colin's biological father. We now know he almost certainly knows Raoul was your spymaster."

164

"You think Carfax knows Raoul is Colin's biological father?" She kept her voice steady, but she had to fight off a shiver as a chill shot through the pomona green silk of her dinner dress.

Malcolm's fingers tightened over her own. "Given the man he is and the pieces of information he has, it would be shocking if he hadn't put it together."

"And you think he's waiting to use it against us?"

"I think he *will* use it against us, if he thinks it could further his ends. It doesn't mean he definitely will find use for it, but we have to be prepared. Just as we have to be prepared for someone else to put the truth together."

Now that she knew Malcolm was Raoul's son, the resemblance between them seemed so pronounced she wondered she hadn't seen in sooner. The deep-set eyes that burned with thought. The flexible mouths. The sharp-boned faces and the way they had of carrying themselves, loose limbed yet contained. Colin looked more and more like both of them the older he got.

"Sweetheart—" Malcolm stroked his thumb over her fingers. "In a few years, we're going to have to tell Colin the truth."

This time her blood seemed to turn to ice. She had spent so long determined to keep layers of truths buried that it was difficult to comprehend telling the truth. She stared into her husband's tender, steady gaze. "Darling—"

"Better for him to hear it from us than from someone else. And better for him to know the truth. If we tell him in the right way, he'll understand."

"My God, Malcolm. You can be such an optimist."

"Sometimes."

She took a drink of whisky. It burned her throat. "He's

happy. He loves us. He loves—" She couldn't quite say it.

"He loves Raoul? Yes, he does. That's partly why I think he'll be able to handle learning the truth."

She stared down at their linked fingers. "Everything we've been through. Everything we've—everything I've—done. And yet, somehow the children are happy. It's such a fragile balance."

"It will shift how they see us," Malcolm agreed. "But not necessarily for the worse. Since when have you of all people been afraid of change?"

Her fingers tightened round her glass. She was keenly aware that she could snap it in two. "I know what we have, darling. I know how hard-won it is."

He watched her for a moment. "Don't you want the children to know the truth of who you are?"

She drew a breath sharp enough to break her corset laces. She could hear Colin only yesterday asking her, as he often did these days, about her parents. And her own reply, a fairy tale about her fictional family, with whatever details of her own real parents she could manage worked in. Used as she was to maintaining a cover story, it was still a challenge to remember the details, to file away the bits of embroidery she added with each story she told. "Of course I do. But it's a terrible secret for them to have to keep."

"Which is why we'll wait until they're older."

"Darling." Mélanie turned to look at her husband. The candles on her dressing table cast flickering light over his face. His eyes were dark with concern and yet steady with confidence. "Has it occurred to you that if they learn the truth, they may well see me as the woman who betrayed their country and their father?"

"I doubt it." Malcolm's tone was even and matter-of-fact.

166

"Not given the way they both already question things. Besides, by the time they're old enough for us to tell them, they may well not see Britain as their country anymore."

She turned her head away. "Damn it, Malcolm—"

"There's no particular reason they should," he said. "Neither of them was born there. It's not their mother's country. Jessica may not even remember it."

Mélanie could keenly recall a moment on their first visit to Britain four years ago, after Napoleon's first abdication. Colin had wanted one of the Royalist Bourbon flags that vendors were selling in Hyde Park, and Lady Frances had bought one for him. The sight of it clutched in his small hand had cut her in two. So why did the thought of the children growing up alienated from Britain now tear at her with a physical wrench? "It's still their father's country."

"Well, yes. And I suppose I want them to know that. Though at the moment I'm more aware that it's the country I had to flee."

"Because of your wife."

"Because of my spymaster. Who claims to be working in the country's interests. I walked away once before."

"Because of your family."

"Mostly. I'd probably never have gone back if it weren't for you. So, in a sense I'm where I might have been a year and a half ago anyway."

"Malcolm—"

"I almost didn't go back when I left the diplomatic corps, you know. We talked about where else we might go, and I came closer to considering it than I admitted even to you. A fresh start had an appeal. I wasn't sure it was fair to inflict what I'd have to face in Britain on you. I was afraid of what it might do to us. Of the person I might become. The person I

167

did become, to a degree. At the same time, I had this absurd sense I had to face the past. And as much as I didn't want to put you through that, I could never have done it without you."

"Darling—"

He tightened his grip on her hand and carried it to his lips. "That's the thing, sweetheart. For all we've been through, I'm not sorry we went back. If I never see Britain again, I won't have to live with the questions I lived with before we returned. I'll always be grateful to you for getting me through that."

Tears stung her eyes. "I didn't get you through anything you couldn't have managed much better without me."

"That's where you're wrong, beloved. And why I can be happy now. I wonder how Thurston and the contessa's children feel," he added after a moment. "There've never seen Britain and likely never will."

"And yet their father's still an Englishman," Mélanie said.

"More than I will be in fifteen years, I suspect. Being an agent comes in handy when one has to blend into a new country."

"Being an agent has to do with the surface."

"And changing the surface can change what's underneath. You should know that better than anyone."

"In a way. But it hasn't changed whom I was born, as you just pointed out."

"No. But you always believed in your cause more than I did in mine. If it can even be called that."

"Oh, Malcolm. You've always believed in it."

"What? If you mean the Crown—"

"The sceptred isle, the other Eden, the demi-paradise—"

"I'm Scots."

168

"It's the same island, darling."

"We'd have to ask Shakespeare what he meant."

She shook her head. She knew on some level that being away from his country would always tear at him. And she knew with the same certainty that he'd never admit it.

"The children won't have the same view," he said. "They may not be particularly attached to any country, which isn't a bad thing."

"We can't—"

"I don't know who's more afraid, O'Roarke or you. Though in Raoul's case I think it's partly that he doesn't think he deserves—"

"What?"

"To have Colin think of him as a father in any way."

She tightened her grip on his hand. "You're Colin's father."

"Of course. And I'm not afraid Colin will think differently about me. But O'Roarke is his father too. Not in the same way, perhaps, but in a very real way. I think they both deserve to know that."

For a moment, she couldn't speak. She put a hand out and touched his face. "Dearest—"

"I'm not being self-sacrificing, Mel. What Colin has with Raoul doesn't change what he has with me. And they already have a relationship, in any case."

She closed her eyes for a moment, blinking back tears. For all the dangers their future held, in some ways it was the secrets within their family she feared the most.

Malcolm slid his arm round her shoulders and pulled her to him. "We'll muddle through it, sweetheart. We've managed to do that rather well for nearly six years. And we won't tell them anything without all of us deciding together."

169

That was the good thing now. That they could share information, and make decisions in the open.

Most of the time.

CHAPTER 15

Harry set down his coffee cup. "Where do we start?"

Malcolm glanced round the table on the terrace. The breakfast things had been cleared and the children had retreated to the terrace floor and Colin and Emily's castle, leaving the adults to a fresh pot of coffee and a council of war. "I should see Thurston," Malcolm said. "I'm still working out how much to reveal to him." He looked at Harry. "Come with me?"

"Thought you'd never ask."

"And I should see Byron." Cordelia added more milk to her coffee, then looked at Mélanie. "Can you put it to good use by coming with me and talking to him?"

"And the Shelleys," Mélanie said. "They should all be keen observers. They may have seen something and not realized it."

"You'll all be fine without me." Raoul stared into his coffee cup. "I should—"

"You need to see Margaret," Laura said.

Raoul met her gaze. "I don't have to. But—"

Laura took a sip of coffee. "She'll be shocked by what she witnessed yesterday. You should make sure she's all right. And you can also find out if she saw anything. If you married her, I imagine she's a keen observer, as well."

Raoul lifted his coffee cup to her in a silent toast. "You're a remarkable woman, Laura."

"I'm a woman who's very sure of what she has. I wouldn't dream of staying out of the investigation, but I think for today I'd better stay with the children. They're a bit unsettled from yesterday. If—"

She bit back what she'd been going to say next because Zarina came out of the house with a letter, which she presented to Mélanie.

Mélanie slit open the letter and smiled. "It's from Lady Frances."

"Let me guess," Malcolm said. "She's passing on theories about our disappearance in a thinly veiled attempt to get information."

Mélanie's smile deepened as she scanned the letter. "Actually, she's in Italy."

"*What*—" Malcolm said.

"With Chloe and Archie. Apparently, they left a few days after Harry and Cordy and the girls and are traveling faster. They should be here in a day or so."

Malcolm shook his head. His aunt had always been good at surprising him, but this pushed things even for his experience of her. "Aunt Frances and Archie are traveling together? I suppose neither of them has ever worried much about the forms."

"But Archie would have a care how things appeared for

Lady Frances's sake," Harry said. Mélanie was still smiling, with surprised delight. She folded the letter closed, hesitated a moment, then looked from Malcolm to Harry. "Frances writes that she and Archie are going to be married."

Malcolm felt a smile break over his own face. "My word. Good for them. She's always sworn she'd never marry again."

"Archie's often sworn he'd never marry at all," Harry said. "But I think neither was quite anticipating the other."

Mélanie set the letter beside her coffee cup, fingers resting on the folded paper for a moment. "And they're expecting a child."

Malcolm and Harry stared at her.

Raoul's lips twitched. "If you're going to say you thought they were too old to indulge in such activities, you will seriously insult at least one person at table."

"Of course not," Malcolm said. "But—" She was his mother's sister, one of the parental generation, a grandmother before his own children had been born. And he, who prided himself on his open mind, had been viewing her in a particular way.

Laura picked up Berowne, who had jumped on the table, and put him in her lap. "I don't think Lady Frances is more than ten years older than I am."

"I think she'd prefer that we not make a great fuss about either development," Mélanie said. "That's why she wrote in advance. She says they were considering marriage before she realized she was with child. Or at least Archie was. Apparently, he insisted she tell me that."

"That sounds like Archie." Harry was grinning. "It will be good for him to be a father."

Malcolm looked at his wife. "Do you know when—?"

"The baby's due? No. But she says they plan to be married

173

in Italy. To be with the family. And, I suspect, to make the timing a bit ambiguous."

"A wedding, how splendid." Cordelia glanced at the children, still absorbed in their game. "Chloe's wonderful with the girls and Colin and Jessica. She'll make a splendid big sister."

"It's a good change to have something to celebrate," Malcolm said. He met his wife's gaze across the table. Mélanie was still smiling. But the look in her eyes told him she was thinking what he was thinking. Good as it would be to see Frances, Archie, and Chloe and celebrate with them, their arrival would also bring questions. And they were going to have to figure out how to answer them.

"Manon sends her love," Cordelia said. She and Mélanie were walking on a lakeside path to the villa that Byron and the Shelleys had taken. It was the first real chance they had had to talk on their own since the Davenports' arrival. "We saw her as Lady Teazle just before we left. They built her pregnancy into the story quite beautifully. And, not surprisingly, she's one of those women who continue to look exquisite while expecting."

"Not surprising in the least." Mélanie smiled at the thought of her friend and then swallowed a pang because she wasn't there to share the joy and excitement of Manon's pregnancy. "When did you last see Bel?"

"Not long before we left." Cordelia put up a hand to adjust the brim of her hat, though the shadow that crossed her face seemed to have nothing to do with the light. "She and Oliver gave a musicale. A detached observer would never have guessed anything was wrong between them. And even though she knows I know, she doesn't talk much to me. I don't think she talks much to anyone. But one can read the signs. Especially having been through the breakup of a marriage."

For a moment, Mélanie could hear Oliver and Isobel Lydgate and their children laughing in her drawing room. Three months ago. Along with Isobel's brother David and his lover Simon Tanner. Before the secrets of the past and the machinations of Isobel and David's father, Lord Carfax, had smashed so much. "You don't think—"

"That Bel will leave Oliver and run off with another man? No. She's not me. And even I wouldn't have done it after I had children. But one can see the cracks in the marriage. And also—" Cordelia drew a breath. "I hesitate to read too much into it. Or to assume they are like Harry and me. But I don't think the relationship is entirely without feeling. On either side."

Mélanie drew a breath. "I used to think so. I didn't read them well in the past." She thought back to days shopping with Isobel, taking the children to the park, writing out cards of invitation. The things she hadn't said and hadn't noticed. "I hate that I'm not there. Not that I could do anything to help them if I were."

"You could be someone for Bel to talk to. Oliver too. But I think they'd both be the first to say they have to resolve their own problems."

Mélanie nodded. "One always wants to think one could help." She drew a breath. She was wearing only the lightest of corsets beneath her muslin gown, but she could feel the laces biting into her skin. "David wrote to Malcolm. He didn't say a lot—he wouldn't, he knows letters can be intercepted—but

175

he sent his love to all of us. I think it meant a lot to Malcolm, though he isn't ready to talk about it. I don't know that he ever will be."

Cordelia's gaze darkened with a concern she didn't try to deny. "We've seen them mostly with the children. So there are things we don't say. That perhaps they wouldn't want to say, in any case. But David and Simon seem more comfortable with each other."

"Simon's written to us twice. Mostly about the children and his plays. But reading between the lines, things seem easier." Mélanie drew another breath, again aware of her corset laces. "I so desperately hope so. I can't bear to think of the damage extending to them."

"They're together," Cordelia said. "With the children. I haven't seen David so much as dance twice with an eligible girl. And, according to Bel, he hasn't been to see Carfax except at large gatherings. You know David. He has a lot to work out, and he isn't likely to share it with anyone."

"He might share it with Malcolm. If Malcolm were there. If I hadn't come between them."

Cordelia stopped walking and gripped Mélanie's arm. "You didn't come between them. Carfax did. And from David's writing to Malcolm and what I've observed, I'd say things are already mending."

"Starting to. I hope." Mélanie squeezed Cordelia's hand. These were her problems. There was a limit to what she could burden Cordy with. "We seem so far away from all of it. It's another world here, in so many ways."

"It must be a relief not to have to pretend all the time," Cordelia said, as they started to walk along the path again.

Mélanie hesitated, gaze on a pair of ducks gliding along the lake. "Yes, in a way. I don't think I realized until we were

176

gone. What it's like not to be in society every day. Pretending I was born in a different world, with different beliefs. At the same time—" She frowned, not quite able to put it into words.

"There's nothing to hide behind?" Cordelia asked.

Mélanie turned to her friend. "That's it precisely. At home"—she shook her head—"Funny. There was a time not too long ago I'd have sworn I could never call Britain home. At home I had so many roles to hide behind. Even after Malcolm knew the truth. Political hostess. Pamphlet writer. "

"Fashion plate."

"Not really."

"There's a hat at Madame Leroux's called The Suzanne."

"Dear God."

"It's very pretty. Satin straw with sea-green ribbons. But I didn't mean to change the subject. You don't have a role to play here?"

"Not so much. So I can't ignore what I've done. Especially not when we're all living with the consequences of it."

"You're living with the consequences of Lord Carfax's trying to interfere between David and Simon."

"In a way he couldn't have done if it weren't for me."

"He'd have found something."

"You sound like Malcolm."

"Malcolm is sensible."

"Malcolm is trying to keep me from going mad. And himself."

"Is he succeeding?"

"You know me. I'm not the sort to give way to the dismals."

"Suzie. Melly. You just said you couldn't ignore what

you'd done. I know a bit about that. I think it's at least half the reason I went so madly hurtling from lover to lover after Harry and I separated. Because I was afraid if I slowed down enough to think, I wouldn't be able to live with myself. What I didn't work out until years later is that feeling guilty doesn't help anyone."

"And so you stopped feeling guilty?"

Cordelia wrinkled her nose. "I try to make Harry think I have."

"Thank God for your honesty, Cordy."

"What are friends for?" Cordelia gave a twisted smile. "Always easier to give advice than to follow it oneself. But it's not just about what you owe to Malcolm and the children, you know. It's about what you owe to yourself."

"I hardly think—"

"I realized when Harry and I reconciled that I couldn't expect him to live with me if I couldn't live with myself."

Mélanie gave a laugh that came out just a shade sharper than she had intended. "Cordy, darling, if there's one thing I know how to do, it's live with myself. I've been managing for nearly a quarter century. I daresay I shall contrive to go on."

Cordelia looked at her for a long moment, but didn't press the matter.

Mélanie looked out over the wind-ruffled blue of the lake. One of the ducks had dived underwater, tail feathers in the air. "London society is exhausting. It's a relief to be away from it, as I said. But I also miss it. More than I'd have thought possible. I actually found myself thinking that the little season will be starting soon. We'll miss what Emily Cowper does with her ball, and the speculation at Holland House, and the opening of Almack's, of all things."

"You're very good at it," Cordelia said. "And for all the

idiocy, there's something about the bustle that makes one feel tremendously alive."

"A good word for it." The ducks had come up onto an outcropping of rock, shaking the water from their feathers. "God help me, there are even times I miss planning menus and working out seating arrangements."

Cordelia laughed. "It is a challenge that would test the tactical abilities of most generals, I think. Never let it be said London society is entirely without intellectual exercise."

"Perish the thought. Sometimes even as I gnashed my teeth, I realized the challenge kept my skills fresh."

"You're missed. If you knew the speculation—"

"Oh, dear." Mélanie stared at her friend. "I hadn't thought—"

"Well, yes, there is the story you ran off with another man and Malcolm followed. Or in some cases that you followed because Malcolm ran off with a mistress. Or possibly another man."

"How broadminded of the gossips."

"And then there's the version that Malcolm had to flee the country because he fought a duel."

"With whom?"

"A political opponent. Or an unnamed lover of yours, I'm afraid."

"And I fled with him? Out of guilt? No, don't. We've talked enough about guilt."

"It's not very logical," Cordelia said. "There's also the more prosaic version that he had unknown debts that sent you both out of the country. Andrew wrote Harry a rather amused letter when the rumors reached Dunmykel. He said a part of him was itching to deny them, but he suspected you and Malcolm would find them useful."

179

Andrew's friendly face shot into Mélanie's memory. "We should be at Dunmykel now," she said. She saw the children as she had left them on the terrace. If they were still in Britain, they'd be in the gardens at Dunmykel playing with Andrew and Gisèle's baby son.

Cordelia touched her arm. "You'll see them again."

Mélanie nodded. Andrew and Gisèle and little Ian could come to Italy. Aunt Frances and her daughter Chloe and Archie would be here soon. Allie and Geoff and their daughter Claudia and all the friends and family they had left behind could visit eventually. "It should be safe enough. Provided no one learns the truth."

"Even if they did learn it," Cordelia said firmly. "They'd stand by you."

"It wouldn't be safe for them to do so," Mélanie said. It wouldn't be safe for Cordelia and Harry either, though she wasn't prepared to have that argument with her friend. Or to contemplate a loss she wasn't sure she could support.

Cordelia, as usual, saw more than Mélanie intended. "Harry and I aren't going anywhere. If we have to take up residence in Italy ourselves."

"That's not funny, Cordy."

"Actually, it sounds quite delightful." Cordelia gestured towards the lake, the steep wooded hills, the blue sky. "How could one quarrel with this? It's too perfect. And at the same time it holds the most intriguing mysteries."

Harry looked sideways at Malcolm as they walked towards the Thurston villa. "Thurston's doing some sort of errands for Carfax."

"So it appears."

"And we know Carfax sent guns through Whateley and Company to rebels in Naples recently. In exchange for information about the Elsinore League. Vincenzo was working for the Elsinore League. Difficult not to wonder if Thurston had a role in transferring the guns. Or the information. Or both."

Malcolm nodded. "I need to figure out how much to confront him with."

"We've always been good at playing a scene by ear."

"I'm counting on that."

They walked in silence for a few moments longer.

"We saw David and Simon just before we left," Harry said. "They sent their love. David's words. The sort of thing David wouldn't say if he didn't mean it."

"He wrote to me." Malcolm drew a breath, because he wasn't prepared to say more yet, even to Harry. David's letter had been more than he expected or hoped for, but it couldn't erase the past. David's anger when he learned the truth about Mélanie, his inability to accept her loyalties, or that Malcolm not only forgave but in many ways admired her.

"I think—" Harry hesitated, and Malcolm realized with a shock of surprise that his friend was wondering how much to reveal. "David and Simon are considering leaving the country and taking the children."

Malcolm stopped walking for a moment and stared at his friend. Of all the people he was close to, David was perhaps the one most rooted to Britain. "Leave England? For how long—"

"Until it's safe to come back. Which, David said, may not be until his father dies." Harry watched Malcolm for a moment as Malcolm took this in. "David said you and

Mélanie had the courage to protect your family, and he could learn from your example. If using the truth about Mélanie to drive a wedge between him and Simon doesn't work, Carfax is likely to try to control David though the children."

David and Simon had been raising David's late sister's children since the spring. Harry was right, Carfax was all too likely to try to use the children to bend David to his will. Still——Malcolm shook his head, still trying to see his childhood friend, defined for so long by his role as heir to an earldom, contemplating leaving Britain and all it meant to him. "David said nothing about it in his letter."

"He wouldn't. He knows the letter might be read."

Malcolm grimaced. "It's damnable. We've always been somewhat careful in writing, but when I was out of Britain before, we didn't know how much we had to fear from Carfax."

"David told me in confidence," Harry said. "After taking precautions not to be overheard that were worthy of an agent. He wanted advice about leaving the country quickly if they had to. I haven't even told Cordy. Though I did put David in touch with Bertrand."

Stable, duty-driven David contemplating turning his life upside down. Which Malcolm had feared he would do, but not in this way. "I was afraid——"

"That Carfax's strategy would work and David would contemplate taking a wife? So was I. But it seems to have had quite the opposite effect. And to have convinced David that the only way to keep safe from what his father may try next is to leave."

"He'll miss England," Malcolm said. "Far more than I do."

"He'd miss Simon and the children more."

182

"Yes." To his own surprise, Malcolm found himself smiling. "I'm only surprised he realized that before it was too late. I seem to have not given him enough credit."

"I think—" Harry hesitated. "Perhaps we're all realizing what's truly important to us." He coughed. They had both said more than they usually would. But then, nothing was usual these days.

"What can I do?" Malcolm asked. Funny, had he ever said that to Harry before?

"Welcome them if they come to see you. Which I think they will. But you've already done an immeasurable amount by giving David an example of how to set priorities."

"I'm not sure David would agree."

"I think David might surprise you."

Malcolm nodded, not trusting himself to speak.

"Mélanie looks well," Harry said.

"She's trying very hard to convince everyone of that," Malcolm said. "Including herself."

Harry shot a sideways glance at him. "Has it been very bad?"

"She calls me 'darling' about fifty times a day."

"My dear fellow."

"She spends hours arranging flowers. Thank God for the business with Thurston or we'd both have gone mad, I think." He shook his head. "That was Mel's fear. I have to confess she was more right than I wanted to admit when we first left Britain. Tragedy strikes our neighbors, and I'm aware of a shameful relief."

"You have to miss—"

"Oh, yes." Images shot through his head in quick succession. Striding through the halls of Westminster. Rising to speak in the House. Rotten Row on a summer morning.

The plane trees in Berkeley Square etched against a twilight sky. The glow of lamplight in the library windows as he climbed the steps to the house. Sharing a glass of whisky with David and Simon in the Albany. "I even find myself nostalgic for Brooks's on occasion, God help me."

"And I don't suppose it helps that you don't feel you can say so. About any of it."

"Have I told you you're damnably acute, Davenport?" Malcolm stared across the lake for a moment. "It's not easy being an exile. You know that as well as I do."

"But we lived largely among our own people in the Peninsula and Brussels and Paris," Harry said. "Much as I claimed to disdain any memory of home, I think a part of me found it comforting."

Malcolm met his friend's gaze. "Quite. I chose not to go back, but I knew I could. I didn't fully appreciate how hard it must have been for Mélanie in Britain until we came here. Even now, we're surrounded by expatriates. I don't have to lie about who I am, or my past, or what I believe in."

"But you have more leisure to reflect on what you lost than Suzanne—Mélanie—did in Britain."

"Perhaps."

"Malcolm." Harry hesitated a moment, drew a breath, touched Malcolm's arm. "I love Mélanie like a sister. You know that." He gave a faint smile. "And I can count on you not to take it the wrong way. But she'd be the first to say you have a right to be angry."

Malcolm studied the beautiful landscape in front him. Green grass, blue water, white columned houses. Their refuge and their prison. "I'm angry with Carfax. I'm angry with myself for not having anticipated his move. I'm angry with David, at times, though he reacted precisely as I thought he would. And even if he'd reacted differently, we'd still have had to leave. But as for Mel—My being angry with her wouldn't be very productive."

"Productivity has nothing to do with it." Harry stopped walking and swung round to face Malcolm. "Look—I know full well how corrosive it can be. You heard me rant about Cordy often enough in the years we were apart. I didn't handle it very well. Any of it. I cringe when I think of the things I said. But I don't think denying I was angry would have resolved much, either. I'd have probably let my feelings spill over at just the wrong moment."

Malcolm gripped his hands together behind his back. The blue of the water wavered before his eyes. "I'm not—You had a right to be angry. No, listen," he added as Harry started to protest. "You know how I love Cordy, but you could be pardoned for wishing she'd never done the things she did to you. I can't say that about Mel. For one thing, if she hadn't, we'd never have met at all. For another, if she hadn't, she wouldn't be the woman I love. Even if she'd stopped spying sooner—which wouldn't change the mess we're in now—I can't say I'd have wanted that. Part of what I love about her is her convictions."

Harry nodded. "I love that Cordy's willing to defy the world. The truth is, if she'd left Chase and stayed with a husband she didn't think she loved, she wouldn't be the woman I love either." He shook his head. "Funny. I don't use the word 'love' much. Even now. It doesn't seem adequate somehow. Though there's no other word to really take its place."

Malcolm drew a breath of the warm, rose-tinged air. When one has kept one's feelings bottled up for so long, it's difficult to put them into words, even in one's own head.

"Without Mel, I don't know that I'd ever have come back to Britain. Oh, I'd have had to when Alistair died, but I might well have left again once I'd sorted his affairs and put someone in charge of the properties. I might well be an exile still. I'd almost certainly never have stood for Parliament, settled in Berkeley Square. I'd never have had the life we built there."

"And because of her you had to leave it," Harry said softly.

Malcolm released his breath, as though letting go of something held tight within him. "In a nutshell." He stared at the well-worn ground of the path ahead. The sun was warm on his back. It should be comforting, but now it was a reminder of the cold damp he had left behind. "I'm far happier in this exile than in that other one. Far happier than I ever thought to be. Far happier perhaps than I have any right to be. If we'd gone right from Paris to this—But I can't forget that other life we had for a time." He drew another breath, his throat tight with words he still wasn't sure he wanted to speak. "And, irrational as I know it is, I suppose at times I am angry."

Harry touched his shoulder. "You wouldn't be human if you weren't. I'm rather relieved to know you are. Being very human myself."

Malcolm met his friend's gaze for a moment. "If she ever knew—I don't think Mélanie would do anything differently if she had to do it again. I think she'd say she's not sure, but if it came down to it, I suspect she'd make the same choices. But I also don't know that she's ever going to be able to forgive herself."

"Which is what really scares you." Harry made it not quite a question.

"Even Mélanie Suzanne has to have a breaking point,

186

though I've never seen it. Not quite. Not even when I remember Waterloo in light of what I now know. Or last December, when I learned the truth." He watched a sailboat on the lake, white sail against blue water. "To see something eating away at one's wife and be powerless to stop it. To know one's the cause of it—"

"Malcolm, for God's sake."

"I am the cause, even if an unwitting cause."

"In the sense I was the cause of trapping Cordy in a marriage she wasn't fit for. Not then. All right."

Malcolm dug his fingers into his hair. "She won't talk to me about it. If I try to push her to talk, it will only make it worse. For now we have the investigation. When that's resolved—Mel doesn't do well without activity."

"Neither do you."

Malcolm felt himself give a reluctant smile. "That's what she would say. But I think I'm better suited to living with my thoughts. I've done it for much of my life. Mel has a tendency to rush into danger."

"You don't think she'd—"

"Go off to Spain with O'Roarke and plot a revolution? No. She wouldn't leave the children. She wouldn't leave me, I don't think, even for a few weeks or months. But she may drive herself mad. To the point where she takes some crazy risk just to feel alive. And what she fears is that I'll blame her."

"It sounds as though occupation would be good for both you," Harry said. "More investigations?"

Malcolm looked down the hillside at the gleaming sand of the beach where the children loved to play. "The idea was to keep our family safe."

"You're the best of fathers, old fellow. But the children will be better off if both their parents avoid going mad."

Malcolm had a keen image of Mélanie grabbing Jessica's hands as their daughter darted into the water. "It stops my breath sometimes. Not what we've lost, but what we have. And how much we have to lose."

Harry nodded. "I know what you mean. I can't imagine my life without Cordy. Though I'm not sure this is the life she'd have chosen."

"My dear fellow." Malcolm turned sideways to look at his friend. "You can't possibly doubt that Cordelia loves you."

Harry's mouth twisted in the way that had been so characteristic in the Peninsula, though with less bitterness. "I think she does, though when I married her the idea of her ever feeling that way seemed as out of reach as the moon. But—there are different types of love."

"As many as there are people to feel it, I imagine," Malcolm said. "That doesn't make one stronger than the other." He saw Cordelia an hour before, holding Livia and Emily by the hand. "Cordy's happy."

"I think she is. I know I am. She feels guilty, of course, and tries to make things up to me, much as I try to stop her—"

"Harry, for God's sake, that's not—"

"That's part of it," Harry said, with the clinical detachment of a scholar appraising a complicated bit of translation. "Much as I hate it, I can't deny it helped bring us back together. We discovered we had more in common than we thought at first. We both love Livia, though I made a hash of being a father for the first three and a half years—"

"Talk about guilt."

"Yes. It can work both ways. Now we have Drusilla to love as well." He shifted his gaze to stare out over the water. "I wanted Cordy the moment I saw her, as I'd never wanted

188

anyone or anything. Wanted her at any price, even knowing she was desperately in love with another man and would probably never do more than tolerate me. It was damnable of me to have trapped her in a marriage, knowing how she felt. I can see that now. But it doesn't change how I felt. That I'd have loved her no matter what, no matter the circumstances. I'd love her no matter what she did to me," he added, with the faint surprise of a scholar unearthing an unexpected fact. "It's hard to imagine Cordy ever being mad enough to feel that way about me. After George Chase, it's a miracle she lets herself love at all."

"Harry, you can't think that George—"

"I don't think she still loves George," Harry said, with the precision of one writing Q.E.D. "I do think she loved him as she'll never love again."

"She loved him foolishly."

"Wholeheartedly."

Malcolm drew a breath of the fragrant, almost too-perfect air, considering and abandoning a dozen possible responses. He'd never loved that way, with the wild, crazy abandon of youth. He'd once felt he'd done Suzanne—Mélanie—a great wrong, denying her that sort of love. He'd never be a Romeo climbing Juliet's balcony. Unless it was to steal documents from her jewel case. Even now, knowing the truth of Mélanie's past, knowing what they had together, he still sometimes wondered if she deserved more. "I'm perhaps the last person to speak to this," he said at last. "By the time I let myself admit I was in love with Suzette—Mel—we'd been married over two years and were parents. We were in the midst of a Congress and then a war. I was being pulled by Castlereagh and Wellington and Carfax, and increasingly angry at the direction I was being pulled in. While at the same time, I suspect I let my duty come before my wife and son far too much. I was on the field at Waterloo when it wasn't even my fight."

"Speaking for myself," Harry said, "I'm rather glad you were."

Malcolm shot a look at his friend. "So am I. But I don't think I ever had it in me to be a Romeo, and certainly not by the time I met Mel. And yet—I don't think I could possibly love her more wholeheartedly than I do."

Harry clapped him on the shoulder. "I don't think so either."

Malcolm cleared his throat. Some things were damnably hard to articulate, though he could articulate them more to Harry than to most. "What I'm trying to say is that there are different types of love. Some may be more—ostentatious than others. But not necessarily stronger."

Harry grinned, though a touch of yearning lurked in his eyes. "You're a good friend, Rannoch."

"And you need to learn to appreciate what's in front of you, Davenport."

"Oh, but I do. I'm struck dumb by wonder every day." Harry's gaze went back to the lake. "It's a funny thing. Having the moon in one's fingers and at the same time feeling it's still out of reach."

CHAPTER 16

Margaret was standing by the terrace balustrade in the villa where she was staying with her friends, the Chipperfields. Even now, almost twenty-four hours after the murder, her face was like bleached linen. One hand gripped the railing as though she feared she could not support herself. Raoul crossed to her side and took her hands in an unthinking clasp. "It can't but be a shock. And a tragedy. But whatever happened, it was directed at Conte Vincenzo. There's no reason to anticipate further violence."

Margaret's gaze fastened on his face. For all she'd feared violence in the United Irish Uprising, she'd never actually confronted it. At least, not in their time together, and he doubted since. "I was talking to him. Less than an hour before—"

"I know." He squeezed her hands. Images shot before his eyes. Blood sprayed on a plaster wall in Paris. Friends dying in his arms in Ireland. Lying in a pool of his own blood in a Spanish plaza, consciousness fading as he stared into the blazing sun. Waterloo, where he'd been so soaked with blood he couldn't tell where his own left off and others' began. "I find it a shock myself. And I've been through more of it."

Margaret jerked her hands from his clasp. "Did you have anything to do with this?"

"With what? With Vincenzo's death? Good God, Meg, I'm a lot of things, but I'm not a killer."

"Aren't you?" She closed her arms across her chest. "You can't deny you've killed."

More images came thick and fast. Blood spurting from a sword cut. Shock in an opponent's eyes. A chasseur falling from a desperate pistol shot. The numbing roar of battle. "Not like this. And whatever you think of me, I had no reason to kill Vincenzo." Actually, that wasn't true, strictly speaking, but he wouldn't have killed Vincenzo to put an end to his threats to Mélanie. Murder was not his idea of an acceptable solution. Though, if he could have killed Fouché in Paris three years ago…

Margaret turned her head away, staring at the lake, the same lake in which they had found Vincenzo's body. "I don't understand the world you live in."

"I know it. But in this case, the events aren't about my world." Which also wasn't entirely true, given that Vincenzo had been allied with the Elsinore League.

"Am I supposed to trust you?"

"I've given you precious little reason to, I admit, but I don't see why I would lie about this." Which in and of itself was a lie.

"Is that why you came here? To reassure me?"

"To make sure you're all right. And if you're up to it, to see what, if anything, you remember from yesterday."

Her brows rose. "Why—"

192

"I'm helping the Rannochs investigate."

"The Rannochs?"

"They've done it before, more than once. Malcolm was an intelligence agent and he investigated more than one murder during the war. Suzanne worked with him."

She shook her head. "I suppose I shouldn't be surprised, given that he's your son. But Mrs. Rannoch must be a remarkable woman."

"She is."

There, at least, Raoul told the unvarnished truth.

"And you think I—"

"You were always a good observer, Meg. And you said you were talking to Conte Vincenzo."

"Yes, briefly." She smoothed a hand over her hair. "We found ourselves standing together as the crowd milled about. You know how it is at a large party. He asked how I found Italy. He mentioned he'd never been to Ireland, but he'd heard it was beautiful. He was very polite. But a bit distracted. Then he—" She broke off.

"Yes?" Raoul asked in a neutral voice.

"He apologized for being distracted. He said—" Margaret hesitated again. "He said he'd just had the misfortune to come across his daughter kissing his host's son."

Raoul stared at his wife. "Sofia Vincenzo was kissing Kit Montagu?"

"Yes, the conte was most distressed about it. Any father would be, and I suspect it was worse because Mr. Montagu's father ran off with Sofia's mother." Margaret's gaze flew to his face. "You don't think—"

Raoul touched her hand. "It's too early to think anything, Meg. But I'm glad you told me."

"Rannoch." Thurston crossed his study to greet Malcolm, hand extended. His self-assurance had settled back over him like armor. He shook hands with Harry when Malcolm introduced him, saying, "I remember your uncle. He was the devil at cards."

"He still is," Harry said. "You'll be able to see for yourself in a day or so. He's on his way here."

Thurston gestured to a sofa and chairs by the windows. "Needless to say, we're all still in shock. Sofia and Enrico haven't said much. Neither has Elena. But then, for all the stereotypes about emotional Italians, she tends to talk least when things mean most to her. This reminds me of how things were when we first came here."

Malcolm saw his wife, arranging a vase of flowers with every appearance of cheerful interest. "Sometimes I think talking is the hardest thing for a couple."

"Quite." Thurston dropped down on the sofa beside Malcolm. "You must have questions for me."

"Yes, actually."

Harry had moved to one of the chairs, but he said, "Your grounds look splendid, Thurston. I can easily go and explore them."

Thurston waved a hand. "I may be an exile, but I still get reports from home, Davenport. You were in military intelligence and you investigate with Rannoch. I'm sure he'll update you. You might as well hear the answers straight from me."

Harry gave a faint smile and settled into the chair.

"Did you ever get a chance to ask Vincenzo about the

conversation O'Roarke overheard the night we arrived?" Malcolm asked.

"Oh, that." Thurston passed a hand over his face. "Seems a century ago. Yes. All a misunderstanding, as I suspected."

Malcolm regarded Thurston. His look of mild confusion was perfectly done. "I could almost believe that. Save that when I came into your study the next morning, a letter you'd received fell to the floor. And I caught sight of the hand. It came from Lord Carfax."

Thurston met his gaze, no chink in the armor. "Like Archibald Davenport, I've known Carfax for years. He writes to me from time to time. He let me know you might be coming to Italy."

"I could believe that as well," Malcolm said. "Save that I got a look at the letter." Leaving aside the fact that he'd only done so a month later, when his wife broke into Thurston's study and copied it out. "Carfax was much more direct in what he wanted you to do. And he also made it plain you were negotiating something for him. Before I left Britain I learned Carfax had traded guns to rebels in Naples in exchange for information. I think you assisted him."

Thurston regarded him for a long moment. The armor was still in place, but his gaze had the look of one reevaluating terrain as the weather shifted. "I should have known. You're obviously a genius at ferreting out information. To own the truth, I half thought I should make a clean breast of it the moment you walked into the house today. I should have listened to myself."

"I think I understand," Malcolm said. "Carfax can be very persuasive. He recruited me once. I was mired in working for him before I quite realized what I'd committed to. He recruited you to do errands for him?"

"It's a bit more complicated." Thurston leaned back on the sofa, one arm along the carved back, in every appearance of control, though he'd been caught out. His gaze moved out the window over the terrace, the hillside, the lake. "It's expensive, running two households. Improving the estate at home. Paying for Kit's school fees and the girls' governess while educating the younger children here. Keeping up the villa and our house in Milan. Elena was used to living in a certain style. I couldn't deny her that, when she'd given up so much for me. And I suppose I was used to living in that style, as well."

Malcolm studied the man he'd come to like and, in some ways, identify with. "You were smuggling guns to support your two families."

Thurston lifted his shoulders in an elegant shrug. "I saw a need. Someone with ties to England, living on the Continent in the midst of the war and the blockade. Sometimes it was a matter of getting past the blockade. Sometimes a question of finding a buyer for weapons left over after an army retreated, or for a surplus that fell into someone's hands. I had connections to people fighting on both sides."

"Meaning you could arm both sides," Harry said.

"Shocked?" Thurston looked from Harry to Malcolm. "You were both spies. I didn't take either of you for as much of a Crown-and-country sort as my son. Surely you saw the war's complexities in the course of your work. Carfax complains you're both a bit too friendly with the opposite side."

Malcolm willed himself not to alter so much as a breath. There was no reason to think Carfax had risked giving Thurston such a valuable bargaining chip as the truth about Mélanie. He might have done, of course, if he wanted

196

Thurston to watch them. But, if not, Malcolm wasn't about to tell Thurston. "I'm well aware of the complexities of any war, and perhaps particularly the one we were all fighting for the past decade and more. But one could make the argument that selling weapons to both sides merely furthers the conflict."

Thurston gave a short laugh. "The conflict was going to go on with or without me."

Which was very true. But Malcolm wasn't sure it changed the nature of his objection. "So Carfax found you?"

"There were times he wanted to funnel weapons, and sometimes other things, to various people on the Continent. Usually to allies. Occasionally to enemies with whom he'd made deals. I don't know that I'm the only person who handled such transactions for him, but I handled quite a few. He set up—"

"A shipping company called Whateley & Company. I learned about it just before I left Britain. A few months ago, Carfax had a shipment of guns destined for rebels in Naples. I assume that's the shipment you're in the process of handling?"

"One of them. It's been a complicated process. Information for a trial shipment and then more weapons for more valuable intelligence."

"Intelligence about the Elsinore League."

Thurston's gaze settled hard and steady on Malcolm's face. "If you know about the League, you must understand why Carfax would go such lengths for such information."

"I'm increasingly unsure I understand anything when it comes to Carfax. The exchange was supposed to take place at the picnic?"

Thurston nodded.

"Who was your contact?"

197

"I don't know." Suppressed frustration broke through in Thurston's voice. "The Carbonari play everything close to the chest. Possibly the only organization more secretive than the Elsinore League. The papers were supposed to be left under the third urn on the left corner of the terrace. I know it sounds like something out of a lending-library novel, but it actually wasn't a bad plan. It's similar to how we traded information before. And the papers were there. I saw them during the party. Not long after that whole business with Selena tumbling into the lake. I was waiting for a better time to retrieve them. When I finally thought to do so, after we discovered Vincenzo, they were gone."

"So it was someone at the party. Can you narrow it down from the earlier exchange?"

Thurston shook his head. "I can't be sure they used the same person for both."

"Do you know what the information was?"

"A list of members of the Elsinore League."

Malcolm drew a breath. Harry whistled.

"Quite," Thurston said.

"Do you think Vincenzo took them?" Malcolm asked.

"I was watching him all day."

"You knew he was a member of the Elsinore League?"

"I discovered it. I was arrogant enough to think I could outwit him. But if he did manage to take the papers, you didn't find them on his body." Thurston's voice held just the faintest of questions.

"No," Malcolm said. "You may not believe me—"

"For the moment I choose to. We need some sort of framework to work in. And I like to think I could tell if you'd found them, though you're probably a skilled enough agent I couldn't."

"It's possible Vincenzo stole the papers and the killer retrieved them," Harry said. "It's difficult to imagine his death is unconnected to all this, though of course it could be."

"Did the contessa know Vincenzo was working for the Elsinore League?" Malcolm asked.

"Elena? Of course not."

"So sure?" Malcolm asked in a soft voice.

"You think I don't know the woman I live with?"

"I think many of us don't know the person we live with, at least not entirely. But I take it you at least didn't tell the contessa."

"Of course not. She's had enough to deal with when it comes to Vincenzo."

"And her daughter?"

"Sofia?" Rather to Malcolm's surprise, Thurston didn't laugh the idea off. "You saw the sort of man Vincenzo was and his attitude towards women. Can you imagine him confiding in his gently bred daughter?"

"It doesn't seem likely. It doesn't mean Donna Sofia couldn't have learned the truth on her own."

"Sofia's clever, takes after her mother. But I've seen no hint that she knew anything of the sort."

"And the contessa's son?"

Thurston's brows drew together. "Enrico's a decent young man. I hope to God his father hasn't pulled him into the Elsinore League. But I can't be sure."

"And Kit?"

Thurston drew back on the sofa. "What about Kit?"

"Does he know about the Elsinore League? Or your gun smuggling? Or both?"

"You can't imagine I'd have told my son about either."

"No? You just gave a very cogent defense of your work

selling guns."

Thurston smoothed his cuff. "It's not work I'd care to have my son follow me into."

"And did you want his help outwitting the Elsinore League?"

"You've seen more of Kit in recent years than I have."

"You've had four weeks with him since his arrival. You're obviously on much easier terms than the night we met."

"I hope so. But I don't want him anywhere near the Elsinore League."

Malcolm sat back on the sofa. "I'd like to find the list of Elsinore League members. As I suspect you would."

"Quite." Thurston met his gaze with a look of acknowledgment, almost amusement. "But I don't expect we'd do the same thing with that list."

Malcolm returned his host's gaze. "It's true," he said. "I might hesitate now to turn it over to Carfax. But I don't think either of us wants it floating about."

Thurston inclined his head. He reached out and adjusted the cuff of his coat sleeve. "I realize, of course, that this gives me an excellent motive to have killed Vincenzo, either on my own or at Carfax's behest. And I don't expect you to choose to believe me, as I chose to believe you."

"It's certainly a possibility we have to consider," Malcolm said, matching his host's tone. "Among others."

Thurston inclined his head. "And I realize this will probably sound as though I'm trying to turn suspicion away from myself. Which I suppose I am, in a way. But, at the picnic, just after I spoke with Vincenzo, I saw him down the beach talking with another man. I was too far away to hear them, but from their gestures it was plain they were arguing."

"Did you recognize the other man?" Harry asked.

200

"Yes." Thurston paused, fully aware of the import of what he was saying. "It was Diana's husband, John Smythe."

CHAPTER 17

"It's good to see you, Cordy." Byron pulled out a chair for her at the wrought metal table on the terrace of the villa where he was staying. They were alone. Mélanie had stayed inside with the Shelleys. "Whatever else it's done to you, it's plain that domesticity hasn't dimmed your beauty."

"And life abroad hasn't dulled your propensity for poetic license."

"You have a glass, Cordelia. You must know that in this, at least, I speak the unvarnished truth."

Cordelia sank into the chair, aware of the glance Byron shot at her ankles as she settled her flounced skirts.

Byron poured two glasses of pale white wine and retreated to a chair across the table from her. Cordelia took a fortifying sip of wine. "I have a letter for you." She undid the steel clasp on her reticule.

Byron took the sealed paper between two fingers and regarded it as though it might bite him. "Let me guess. She made you promise to put it into my hands personally."

"Can you doubt it?"

He peered at the seal. "She didn't seal it with her own blood, did she?"

"It doesn't look that way."

"Or tuck a lock of her hair inside?"

"I can't speak to that."

Byron set the letter on the edge of the table where he couldn't accidentally brush against it. "Why didn't I have the sense to look at you, rather than Caro, Cordy?"

"You know perfectly well why. You and Caro could each give each other something no one else could."

"What?" He sounded genuinely interested.

"Notoriety."

He gave a short laugh. "If you think I wanted—"

"Didn't you?" Cordelia held his gaze with her own. "You may not have enjoyed all of it, but you can't tell me you didn't relish being the talk of London just as much as Caro did."

Byron flung himself back in his chair and gave a shout of laughter. *"Touché, ma belle."* He stretched his legs out, feet crossed at the ankle, and slouched his shoulders. "I'll grant you there may be a touch of truth in what you say. But anything becomes wearing with time. Even notoriety. Caro and I are at the point where it's become tiresome."

Cordelia looked steadily into those dazzling eyes. "Caro still loves you."

He laughed again. "Caro doesn't know the meaning of the word."

"Does anyone, really? I think it means different things to all of us. Which is why it can cause such hellish complications when two lovers define it differently."

Byron reached for his wineglass, took a slow sip, and regarded her over the rim. "Do you and Davenport define it

203

the same way?"

"I think so. Now. To be honest, I don't think I'll ever deserve to be loved the way he loves me. But I'm doing my best to live up to it."

Byron's gaze settled on her face for a moment while his fingers tightened round the stem of his wineglass. "I'm not sure what's odder. To see you professing such devotion or to see Harry Davenport, of all people, the object of it."

"Harry is a remarkable man. But I believe we were talking about you and Caro. If you have a scrap of decency—which I'll own is open to question—you'll send her a reply that's not too encouraging, but not the crushing set-down I know full well you can deliver."

"I thought you wanted her to be done with me."

"I do. I think William is ten times better a man than you and actually loves her, whereas I'll grant your meaning of the word is highly open to interpretation, and changes with the wind. But Caro isn't letting go. A dismissal will only send her into a depression, or make her more determined than ever, or encourage a grand tragic gesture. I can only hope a temperate response from you will temper her own feelings."

"Have you ever known Caro to be temperate about anything?"

"Rarely, I admit." Cordelia gripped her glass but didn't lift it to her lips. "I care about her, Byron. I think you used to, too. Unless it was all a sham."

Byron took a sip of wine and twisted his glass between his fingers. "I doubt the parody Caroline painted of me in *Glenarvon* would show much sympathy. Any sympathy. But I'm not quite the monster she portrayed me as. I'll try to pen something that won't worsen the situation. God knows we're long past the point where an amusing scandal turns sordid. I'll

204

even let you read the letter before I seal it. I don't allow editorial advice to many, you know."

"I'm honored." Cordelia met his gaze across the table. "Thank you."

Their gazes locked for a moment, the gazes of two people who cared for Caroline Lamb and had tried in different ways to pull her back from the edge.

Byron gave a quick nod and took another drink of wine. He shifted his shoulders in the chair, facing her square on. "Your friends the Rannochs are looking into Conte Vincenzo's murder."

"Lord Thurston has asked them to assist the authorities. They've done it before, both in London and on the Continent."

"And you and Davenport have worked with them."

"On occasion. I own I enjoy the adventure."

"That sounds more like Cordelia Brooke." Byron flung his head back against the chintz cushions in the chair. "Out with it, Cordy. You didn't just come here to deliver Caro's letter. What do you want to ask me about the murder? Am I a suspect?"

"I suppose, to a degree, everyone who was at the party is a suspect."

"My word." Byron's brows lifted. "A murder suspect. I've certainly been accused of being capable of that and worse in the past."

"Don't give way to delusions of depravity. There are many with actual motives to have killed Vincenzo."

"But?"

"You discovered the body. And you're a good observer."

"So I flatter myself. I suspect there's nothing like a bloody corpse to send all thoughts of metaphor and allusion rushing from one's mind."

"It must have been a shock for Diana Smythe, as well."

"Yes, I imagine it was. She's probably seen even less death in her life than I have."

"She's very lovely."

He looked up and gave a lazy smile, which somehow gave Cordelia the sense he was donning armor. "My dear Cordelia. Are you implying something?"

"My dear Byron. Does it really need implying?"

"Do sit down, Mrs. Rannoch," Mary Shelley said.

"Thank you. I don't mean to impose myself on you, but I wanted to give Cordelia and Lord Byron a bit of time alone to discuss their friends at home."

"You mean to exchange grimaces over Lady Caroline?" Percy Shelley asked. He had risen when Mélanie came into the salon and was still standing with punctilious good manners. "Sorry," he added, a bit abashed. "But I know how she drives Byron mad, and I can't imagine she's an easy friend for Lady Cordelia."

"I don't think she makes life easy for anyone," Mélanie said, moving one of the walnut chairs. "Very much including herself."

Shelley nodded. "I think one of Byron's great fears has been that she'll follow him to Italy."

Mélanie considered the determined Lady Caroline Lamb. "I wouldn't put it past her. She isn't the sort to let a lot stand in her way, whether it's convention or the logistics of travel. But she is living with her husband now."

"Marriage can fetter one." Mary moved to the table,

where a tea service was set out. "That is, hold one in check. That is, I mean—"

"I think your meaning is clear," Shelley said in a voice that was level but not unkind.

Mary met her husband's gaze for a moment. "There's no denying a married person doesn't have the same options a single person does."

"No." And then, quite suddenly, Shelley reached out and touched his wife's cheek, as though he was reaching for the past.

Mary touched his fingers for a moment, then turned her attention back to the tea. "Not that a single woman has a great deal of freedom. At least, not if she wants to maintain any sort of veneer of respectability. Lady Tarrington had some very interesting thoughts on that."

"Yes, Laura would." Mélanie accepted a cup of tea from Mary.

"Milk?" Mary asked. "It's odd, how fond I've become of tea since we've been out of England."

"I find I crave it, myself," Mélanie said, "even though I'm not an Englishwoman. And the sound of English, and the English papers, and all sort of things I'd have sworn I wouldn't miss."

"Yes, it can be quite a relief to hear one's own tongue." Mary handed a cup of tea to her husband.

Mélanie stirred milk into her tea. "You saw the Montagu party in Milan?"

Shelley settled back into a chair and took a sip of tea. "You're curious, naturally, since you're investigating the murder."

Mélanie met his gaze. "Lord Thurston has asked us to look into the murder, that's true. And, of course, it does mean

207

anything to do with the family is of interest."

Mary lifted her cup to her lips and took a careful sip. "In England, I doubt we'd have associated with them. We hardly moved in the same circles."

"Thurston's a baron. My father was a baronet," Shelley said, for all the world as though he weren't an avowed Radical.

Mélanie hid a smile behind her teacup. She'd heard much the same from French revolutionaries with aristocratic pasts. It could be hard to entirely repudiate the world one was born to.

"You know what I mean," Mary said. "They go to Almack's. Selena talked about being presented at Court. It's not our world." She looked at Mélanie. "Your world isn't, either. But—"

"I'm an émigrée," Mélanie said. "I'm an outsider wherever I go."

Mary gave a faint smile of acknowledgment. "But here we found we had a surprising amount in common just by virtue of the fact that we all came from England. We dined with them a few times."

"Young Montagu has a decent sense of poetry," Shelley said. "So does Selena, actually, though mostly she couldn't take her eyes off Byron. Fortunately, Byron had the sense to behave himself. At least, as far as—"

Shelley bit back the words.

"At least, as far as Selena was concerned?" Mélanie finished for him.

Shelley met his wife's gaze for a moment. Mary picked up her spoon and stirred her tea, as though to give herself something to do with her hands.

"Diana Smythe?" Mélanie asked. "Or Kit Montagu, or John Smythe?"

"You don't shock easily, do you, Mrs. Rannoch?" Shelley said.

"I see no particular reason to be shocked by two people indulging in a love affair. Though, if it was Mr. or Mrs. Smythe, the presence of their spouse would complicate the situation. Logistically, if not morally."

Shelley gave an unexpected grin. "Simon Tanner said you had a remarkably flexible mind."

"That's a lovely compliment." Mélanie took a sip of tea and let the memory of Britain wash over her. "Diana Smythe and Byron discovered Conte Vincenzo's body together."

"It was Diana," Mary said. "Not as bad as Selena. But I'm afraid she took it too seriously. As women are inclined to do with Byron."

"Did Mr. Smythe know?" Mélanie asked.

Mary and Shelley again exchanged glances. "I'm not sure," Shelley said. "For her sake, I hope not. I don't think he's the easiest husband."

"What makes you say that?" Mélanie asked, though she wouldn't necessarily disagree, based on what she'd observed.

"She had a bruise on her cheek one morning at breakfast," Mary said. "The day after we met them, so if her husband gave it to her in a quarrel, it wasn't over Byron. Not then."

Mélanie's fingers tightened round the delicate handle of the teacup. Memories from her days in the brothel shot through her mind. The shock of pain, the numbing sting of powerlessness, worse in many ways than the pain itself. And a wife was arguably even more powerless than a whore. Legally, there were few limits on what her husband could do to her.

Mary Shelley met Mélanie's gaze. She couldn't possibly see the whole truth, but she understood more than Mélanie intended. "It's appalling," Mary said. "What a husband can do

209

to a wife and leave her no recourse. It's why my mother likened marriage to slavery."

"Your mother had an excellent point," Mélanie said. "A wife is quite dependent on her husband's good character."

"And shouldn't have to be," Shelley said. "I quite agree."

"I think it caught Byron's interest," Mary said.

Shelley shot a look at her. "You think—"

"Byron genuinely was concerned," Mary said. "And, also, he likes to cast himself as a rescuer. You can't deny he likes to cast himself as a lot of things."

Shelley frowned in consideration of his friend.

Mary Shelley was a keen judge of people. Not surprising in a skilled novelist. "You think he wanted to protect Diana Smythe?" Mélanie asked.

"I think Byron likes to be the hero of whatever drama is playing out. Or sometimes the villain. But in this case the hero role suited him. I only hope it didn't cause Diana more difficulties with her husband."

"They were reasonably discreet," Percy said. "Especially for Byron."

Mary shot a look at her husband. "We knew."

"We're used to Byron. They'd wander off on walks together when we were all on an outing, but mostly they stayed in sight. Once or twice we're quite sure she and Byron were alone for an afternoon, but there's no reason to think Smythe knew."

"Do you think Diana Smythe being here had anything to do with Byron wanting to come to Lake Como?" Mélanie asked.

Percy reached for his tea. "Doubtful. When Byron's—"

"Done with a woman, he's done?" Mary finished for her husband with a twist of her lip. "Usually. But in this case the affair didn't end because Byron was tired of Diana. It ended because the Montagu party left. I'm not sure Byron's interest had run its course. He likes to be in control of a love affair."

Mélanie added more milk to her tea. Difficult to see how any of this might relate to Conte Vincenzo's murder, but if Byron and Diana Smythe had resumed their relationship, if Vincenzo had learned of it for some reason—"Do you think Byron and Mrs. Smythe had met by the lake before the party?"

"I doubt it," Percy said. "Byron—"

"Oh, but they did. I'm quite sure of it," Mary said. "Two days before the party. I took a walk by the lake. I saw Byron in the distance walking with a woman. I couldn't see her face, but from the way she carried herself, I'm almost positive it was Diana Smythe."

Percy shook his head, but didn't appear overly surprised.

"Did you see anyone else that same day?" Mélanie asked.

Mary frowned. "There were a couple of men fishing. And just before I saw Byron and the woman, I passed Conte Vincenzo—" She broke off, realization washing over her face.

"Are you suggesting Vincenzo saw Byron and Diana Smythe and that one of them killed him to keep him from talking about it?" Percy demanded.

"It's one possibility," Mélanie said. "It seems rather farfetched, but we need to at least consider it."

Percy frowned. "Knowing Byron, he'll probably be pleased to find himself a murder suspect."

"Surely Diana wouldn't—" Mary shook her head. "Here I am suggesting a woman wouldn't be capable of what a man might do. My mother would be horrified."

"Could a woman have done it?" Percy asked. "Purely physically?"

"I think so," Mélanie said. "Whoever it was almost certainly took Conte Vincenzo by surprise."

Mary shivered. "I know it will sound odd, given the stories I write. But I can't quite bear to imagine—"

"It's different," Mélanie said. "Confronting the reality." Though she herself had been confronting that reality for close to a decade. In the war. In the investigations she undertook with Malcolm. Most of the time she could remain detached and pragmatic. But she'd never quite got used to it. Which was probably a good thing. Though it was odd that something she encountered in the course of the two things that gave her solace and escape and defined her life remained a source of horror in unguarded moments.

Mary nodded.

"Someone killed him," Percy said. "Someone we were drinking champagne and eating strawberries with."

"Most likely," Mélanie said. "It could have been one of the servants."

Percy's brows rose in surprise.

"Or just possibly an outsider. But given what we know about the day, it's most likely the murderer was one of the guests." She looked from husband to wife. "Can you think of anything else you saw that day that might be relevant? Or anything you learned about the Montagus in Milan?"

Mary shook her head. "The main person I remember talking to at the party was your friend Lady Tarrington. She was very kind and understanding. About our children." Mary drew a sharp breath and tossed down a sip of tea, fingers white round the brilliant Italian porcelain.

Percy frowned and traced a line in the tile floor with a booted toe. "It's hard to see how it could be remotely relevant to Conte Vincenzo's murder."

212

"Anything to do with anyone connected to that day could be part of the puzzle," Mélanie said.

Percy looked up from contemplation of the tiles and met her gaze. "It was something Kit Montagu said. And then a bit Selena let slip in her chatter. I don't think the young Montagus were here just to see their father. I think something compelled them to leave Britain."

Byron looked up as Mélanie stepped onto the terrace. "I was wondering when you'd join us, Mrs. Rannoch."

"I've been having a delightful talk with Mr. and Mrs. Shelley," Mélanie said.

Byron got to his feet and drew out a chair for her. "But now you have questions for me."

Mélanie sank into the chair. "I didn't realize how well you got to know the Montagu party in Milan."

"You and Cordelia think alike. I've just been answering similar questions from her." Byron poured Mélanie a glass of wine. "We spent time with them. One tends to gravitate towards other expatriates." He set down the decanter with a flourish. "Odd, now I think of it, since I was quite pleased to see the last of Britain."

"The Shelleys say it was a bit more than simple conversation between fellow expatriates." Mélanie accepted the glass of wine and took a sip. "At least when it came to Mrs. Smythe."

"The fair Diana? Having left Britain behind, why would I have a taste for British matrons?"

"To add to your list," Cordelia murmured into her wine.

"Mr. and Mrs. Shelley both were convinced of what was

213

happening between you and Mrs. Smythe," Mélanie said. "It would be purely between you and Mrs. Smythe, save that Mrs. Shelley thinks she saw the two of you walking by the lake three days ago, and that Conte Vincenzo may have seen you, as well."

Byron stared at her for a long moment, realization dawning in his eyes. "Good God. I really am a murder suspect."

"Don't enjoy it, for God's sake," Cordelia said. "She's quite in earnest. She'll investigate you and turn over your secrets. And if you didn't do it, she'll waste valuable time. Besides, though you might quite like to be at the heart of a murder investigation, I'm going to do you the credit of thinking you don't want to drag poor Mrs. Smythe into the midst of one."

Byron took a sip of wine. "I'm very fond of Diana. But as it happens, she isn't my mistress."

"Simply denying it won't get you anywhere, you know," Cordelia said.

"You may not credit me with sense, Cordelia, but do credit me with a bit of understanding." Byron set down his glass. "Diana Smythe is a lovely woman. Under other circumstances I might have been tempted. If she'd given me the smallest sign that that's what she wanted from me."

"According to the Shelleys, you spent a good deal of time with her and slipped off to meet her in secret more than once," Mélanie said.

"I don't deny it. I said I was fond of her. I don't think I'd be going too far to say I count her a friend."

"Are you saying you slipped off to meet a beautiful woman in secret merely to talk?" Cordelia demanded.

"My dear Cordelia. Are you falling into the trap of

214

assuming the conventional explanation is the correct one?"

"With you, it usually is. Just as it once was with me."

"Touché, my sweet. We're birds of a feather. Or were, before you settled for domesticity." Byron twirled the stem of his glass between his fingers. "Under other circumstances I might have been tempted to see if I could make Diana fall in love with me. But I didn't want to taint what else was between us."

Mélanie took a sip of wine. Byron was enjoying this. Which wasn't a bad thing, so long as he went on talking. "What was between you?" she asked.

"Diana wanted my professional advice."

Mélanie stared at Britain's foremost poet. "Diana Smythe is writing poetry?"

Byron gave a faint smile. "She asked me one afternoon, with the shyest smile, if she could show me a poem. I can't tell you how I cringed. The romantic scribblings of schoolgirls and young matrons that I've been asked to look at—But in such confined society and with so little to do, I agreed. I thought I must be mad. But the poem was—rather extraordinary."

Mélanie pictured Diana Smythe's pretty, decorous face. "Does her family know she writes?"

"No. And she doesn't want them to."

"Writing poetry is hardly considered unladylike," Cordelia said.

"The nature of these poems would be," Byron said. "Some are quite frank about subjects ladies aren't supposed to discuss at all. I wondered, in fact, at the man who had inspired such passion. Somehow, I don't think it was John Smythe."

"I take it he didn't know about his wife's writing either?" Mélanie made it a genuine inquiry. She wanted to see if Byron

215

shared the Shelleys' appraisal of the Smythes' marriage.

"No." Byron gave a short laugh, but his mouth went taut. "Smythe's the sort who has little appreciation of poetry. Or women. He either ignores Diana or orders her about. I'm quite sure he gave her the bruise on her cheek the morning after we met the Montagu party."

Cordelia drew a breath of outrage.

"Did she tell you so?" Mélanie asked.

"Not in so many words. But reading between the lines, I doubt it was the first time he'd struck her. A woman with her mind and talent, tied to a man like that—"

"Does her brother know?" Cordelia asked.

Byron reached for his wineglass. "I don't think so. Damn it, it's an intolerable situation. If it was my sister, I'd want to know."

"Did you tell him?" Mélanie asked.

Byron shook his head. "Though I've been sorely tempted. I tried to convince her to talk to her brother about her poetry when I gave her advice on her poems. She has a wonderful sense of metre and a great economy of words, but sometimes she needs help with structure."

"You met her by the lake two days before the picnic?" Mélanie asked.

Byron nodded. "She'd written some new poems. Inspired by the family drama, I rather think."

"Do you think Conte Vincenzo could have observed you?"

"Oh, yes." Byron flicked a bit of lint from his coat. "He stopped and talked with us."

"What did he say?"

"How fine the day was, as I recall. All the while, I have no doubt, making the sort of assumptions about us that Percy

216

and Mary made." Byron flung his head back. "So, even though I'm not Diana's lover, I suppose I do have a motive. I certainly didn't want him to mention seeing us to Diana's husband."

"Nor did Diana, I imagine," Mélanie said.

Byron's head jerked up. "Diana wouldn't—"

"My dear Lord Byron. In an investigation, as in art, lack of imagination can be fatal. Was Conte Vincenzo alone?"

"At that point."

"You saw him speak with someone else later?" Cordelia asked.

"After he moved off down the lake, I kept an eye on him. I wanted to see if he was watching us. He walked some way off, then stopped to talk to a lady. It looked as though it was not a casual meeting. They each stopped as though they expected to see the other."

Byron had a good eye for detail. "What did she look like?" Mélanie asked.

"She wore a muslin gown sashed in blue and a wide-brimmed straw hat." Byron's gaze moved from Mélanie to Cordelia. Both were dressed similarly, save that Mélanie's ribbons were rose colored and Cordelia's seafoam green. Such a toilette was close to a uniform for ladies about the lake during the day. "Her hat shielded her face," he continued, "and they were too far away for me to make out her features, in any case. Most of her hair was hidden by the hat, as well. It might have been anything from blonde to dark brown. It could have been the contessa. Or their daughter. Or Selena Montagu. Or either of you, for all I could tell."

"Did they speak for a long time?" Mélanie asked.

"I don't know, because they moved into the shelter of some large rocks, as though they didn't wish to be seen. But I don't think it was a tryst." He paused for a moment. "They appeared to be arguing."

Lord Byron was no fool. He had a flair for the dramatic, but whatever thrill he might find in being a suspect himself, he had just neatly delivered another suspect into her hands.

CHAPTER 18

Raoul walked from Margaret's villa to the Thurston villa, to be informed that Signor Kit was on the lower terrace. He descended the stairs to the scene of yesterday's party to find young Montagu at the balustrade, looking out over the lake. Kit turned round at the footsteps, a little late, as though he had scarcely heard in his abstraction. "O'Roarke. Rannoch and Davenport are in the study with my father. I can take you up."

"Thank you." Raoul crossed the terrace to the balustrade. "But it's actually you I came to see."

Kit's brows rose. "Happy to talk. But I didn't know Vincenzo well. Which doesn't make it any less of a shock."

"You must be concerned for Donna Sofia."

Wariness shot through Kit's posture, though his gaze remained easy. "Of course. And her brother."

Raoul regarded the younger man. So far he was showing more skills at dissembling than Raoul would have expected in one who wasn't a trained agent. "Vincenzo confided in one of the guests, Montagu. That he caught you and his daughter embracing."

Kit's eyes widened. For a moment he looked like the schoolboy he'd have been not so very long ago. "Oh, God, I should have realized—He was furious. But I didn't think he'd talk about it. Not to a guest he didn't know well, at least."

"No, that surprised me too. A sign perhaps of how shaken the conte was."

Kit nodded. "It was unpardonable of me. To take advantage of Sofia so."

"Did you take advantage of her?"

"I—" Conflict shot across Kit's face. The instincts of a gentleman who feels he has crossed a line warring, perhaps, with the memory of mutual passion. "I never meant for it to happen. We neither of us did."

"One often doesn't," Raoul said, remembering a night in an inn in Maidstone when he and Laura had crossed a line he'd thought was uncrossable.

"I fully intended to marry Elinor," Kit said.

"Intended?" Raoul asked.

Kit drew a sharp breath. "I thought I could see my life stretching out before me. I thought I'd have precisely what I wanted. Precisely what I needed. I never thought—Love seems such a simple word. But it's not at all, is it?"

"Anything but. And I'd say the more one feels it, the less simple it seems."

Kit nodded. "I noticed she was pretty that first night, of course. How could I not?" The words spilled out, as though having begun to speak he found it a relief to share his tangled feelings. "But it wasn't then. It was later, when we began to talk, when I saw how kind she was to her sisters and brother, to my sisters—even to Selena, for all her behavior." He hesitated. "Of course we talked about what it was like growing up, with our parents separated."

"You share a unique perspective. I imagine it meant a great deal to find someone who'd gone through the same thing."

Kit nodded. "All these years of only really being able to talk to my sisters, and a lot I couldn't say to them. I can't tell you what a relief it was. But that wasn't why—That may have got us to talk, but I'm quite sure I'd love Sofia if we had no other connection between us." He glanced away, stared down at the paving stones for a long moment, looked back at Raoul. "I struggled against it. I know you don't know me well, O'Roarke, but I hope you'll believe I had enough honor to do that. I knew it was wrong, that it flies in the face of what I owe my family, my name—"

He broke off, face twisted with the torment of the very young struggling to find their way.

"She's not your sister," Raoul said. "Not even your stepsister. Not legally, and you didn't grow up together in any sense. And you aren't married to Miss Dormer. It sounds as though you aren't even officially betrothed."

Kit dragged the toe of his boot over the tiles. "It hasn't been announced. But it's understood between our families. Elinor would be hurt."

"Not a happy circumstance. But better perhaps to be hurt than to be tied permanently to a man who doesn't love her."

Kit frowned, as though this way of looking at it hadn't occurred to him. "I don't think Elinor expects love. I don't think she's in love with me."

"But would she want a life with you, knowing you were in love with someone else?"

Kit stared into the distance, his frown deepening. "I never

thought of marriage being —"

"Being based on love? No, I don't suppose you did, given your parents' marriage. But then, you saw what came of that. Is that what you want for yourself and your children?"

"I wouldn't leave a wife and children." Kit's voice was low and fierce.

"Perhaps not. But growing up with parents who live together—or at least occupy the same house when they can't avoid it—but don't love each other is far from ideal. Take it from one who grew up in such a household."

Kit cast a quick look at him. "I'm sorry."

"I survived. But it made me determined not to marry without love. If I married at all, which didn't seem likely for some time. And then when I decided to risk it, I wasn't very good at making it work."

Kit's gaze skimmed over his face. "Are you sorry you tried?"

Raoul drew a breath of the warm, perfect air. Sorry he'd married Margaret and put them both through hell? How could he not be? Sorry he'd tried to form bonds that by all rights a spy should be better off without? How could he be sorry, for all the risks? Without those bonds, life would be scarcely worth living. "I don't live a life very suited to domesticity. That doesn't stop me from wanting things. And having known love, I don't think I'd ever settle for the counterfeit." He hesitated a moment, but Kit deserved more, for reasons that went beyond the investigation. "The woman I married was at the party yesterday. She's the one Conte Vincenzo confided in, as it happens."

Kit's eyes widened.

"She has a sort of calm about her," Raoul continued. "That may have made it easier for Vincenzo to talk to her. As

222

to me, we've been separated for two decades. Longer than your parents. I thought I loved her when I married her, but the truth is I was running. From things I was afraid of. From feelings that were too complicated."

"That's not—"

"No? Perhaps it's not the case for you. Only you know what you have with Donna Sofia. But if a life together is what you both want, there's no reason you can't have it."

Kit drew in and released a breath. The breath of one hovering on the edge of hope, able to see it, afraid to grasp it. "We'd both be going against our families."

"Sometimes that's necessary. But for what it's worth, your father appears to have grave concerns about your marriage to Miss Dormer. You might find him an ally. The contessa as well."

"Perhaps. But Vincenzo will never—that is, he would have never—" Kit spun round to face Raoul, realization dawning in his eyes. "This gives me a motive to have killed him, doesn't it?"

"In theory." Raoul kept his gaze steady on Kit's own. "You're hardly the only one."

Kit gave a quick nod. "I can't imagine—I love Sofia. I want a life with her." He drew a breath, as though it steadied him to have said it. "But not built on her father's death. I'm sure you don't believe me—"

"Whatever I believe," Raoul said, "I have to investigate."

Kit nodded again, more slowly.

The truth was, Raoul had a hard time seeing this young man as a killer. And yet, Kit had shown himself a man of action, and he was a trained soldier. If he'd quarreled with Vincenzo, it wasn't beyond possibility to think he might have turned to violence. Love could be a powerful motivator.

And it was quite clear Kit loved Sofia Vincenzo.

"Lord Thurston has been smuggling guns for fifteen years?" Mélanie asked. They were gathered on the terrace of the Rannoch villa after their various morning excursions, sharing bread, tomatoes, wine, and information while Blanca and Addison took the children to the lake.

"At least for a decade," Malcolm said. "And quite unapologetic about arming both sides."

Cordelia took a sip of wine, frowning over another piece of information. "And this list of members of the Elsinore League—actual names—disappeared during the picnic?"

"According to Thurston," Harry said. "I'm not sure how far I'd trust him, but at present I don't see why he'd be lying about that."

"To think it may have been there under an urn, where any of us could have picked it up if we'd known," Laura said. "The Elsinore League would be furious. Even the members don't know the names of all the other members."

"Their passion for secrecy is rivaled by that of the Carbonari," Malcolm said. "We know someone at the party was an agent of the Carbonari, but we have no way to determine who." He looked at Raoul. "Have you had dealings with them?"

Raoul shook his head. "My network has never extended to Italy. I've heard rumors about them, but little more than you. I've rarely seen such secrecy. And I speak as a spy."

"Tell them what you told us on the walk back from Thurston's," Malcolm said. "About Kit."

Raoul relayed his interview with Margaret and her

revelations, and his subsequent talk with Kit. "I confess I quite lost my investigative detachment," Raoul said. "In favor of not wanting to see two young people throw their lives away."

Malcolm shot a look at his father. "It's all right. We saw through you a long time ago. But it does give Kit motive. And Donna Sofia, I suppose."

"She looked horrified when we found her father," Mélanie said. "Not that that's necessarily a guarantee of anything. Diana Smythe looked horrified too. And her story proves to be a bit more complicated." She exchanged a look with Cordelia and they proceeded to update the others on their talks with the Shelleys and Lord Byron.

"Byron's no fool," Mélanie said. "He was enjoying the drama and intrigued at the thought of being a murder suspect. But he also knew what he was doing in offering me up Conte Vincenzo's mysterious lady."

"Do you think he was telling the truth?" Malcolm asked.

Mélanie exchanged another glance with Cordelia. "I think so," Cordelia said. "It's not that Byron isn't capable of lying, but I don't think he felt backed into a corner enough."

"The specificity felt real," Mélanie said. "He's a good observer. And I suspect he's telling the truth about not being Diana Smythe's lover."

"Yes, that's outlandish enough that it has the ring of truth," Cordelia said. "But it doesn't change the fact that Conte Vincenzo very likely jumped to the wrong conclusion when he saw them together, just as the Shelleys did."

"They were only walking," Malcolm said. "And they were known to be acquainted. They could have said they were both out for a stroll and encountered each other and walked together."

225

"They could," Mélanie said. "But we now know John Smythe is given to violence. And men who are are often given to jealousy, as well."

"I should have thought of that," Laura said. "For all Jack's deficiencies as a husband, at least he wasn't given to jealousy or violence."

Raoul was studying Laura with carefully veiled concern. In the course of their investigation into the murder of her lover, the Duke of Trenchard, they'd learned he'd hit his wife Mary. And he'd also been violent with a young actress Raoul had helped escape him in Paris decades before.

Laura met her lover's gaze. "Trenchard hit me once. Not when we were lovers. Much later. When I didn't want to follow his orders on behalf of the Elsinore League." She rubbed her arms. "It's dreadful, that feeling of powerlessness."

Raoul's fingers curled round the arm of his chair. "If the Duke of Trenchard hadn't got himself murdered, I'd—"

"You don't believe in capital punishment," Malcolm reminded his father.

"No. And killing him seems too easy. He deserves something much worse."

Laura reached for his hand. "It was only once. But the fear of it lingered. If John Smythe regularly took his anger out on his wife—I can see her fearing something that would set him off."

"One wonders if that could be what Vincenzo and Smythe quarreled about at the picnic when Thurston saw them. Smythe refusing to believe Vincenzo's accusations, perhaps? At least at first." Raoul's mouth was still grim.

"The quarrel gives me an excuse to talk to Smythe." Malcolm's expression was equally grim. "I must say I rather

226

relish the prospect of interrogating him."

"Cordy and I can talk to Diana," Mélanie said. "Cordy's Byron's friend, that should help." She looked at Laura. "Can you come with us? You have experience—"

"Of being hit?"

"Of being in an unhappy marriage."

Laura nodded.

"And we should talk to Donna Sofia, as well," Cordelia said.

Malcolm twisted his wineglass between his fingers. "The person who discovers a body is always of interest. As Laura knows, to her cost. It can be a misleading avenue to follow. But Vincenzo could have come upon Byron and Mrs. Smythe again at the picnic. Could have made accusations. If Byron had a knife and then stumbled into the water when Diana screamed—that would have neatly got rid of any blood spattered on him, and he's the one person at the picnic, other than Raoul and me, who could look disheveled after the murder without rousing suspicion." Malcolm looked at Cordelia. "Would Byron kill to protect Diana Smythe?"

Cordelia frowned. "Byron would like to position himself as the sort who'd kill in passion, but I think he's too self-absorbed to do so under most conditions. And he has an odd detachment that would stop him if morality didn't. But—it was odd the way he spoke about Diana Smythe. I've heard him talk about a number of women, and I've never heard him talk in quite that way before."

"He obviously feels she has a rare talent," Mélanie said. "I doubt he feels that about many people. Whereas, I imagine there are any number he wants to take to bed."

"Does take to bed," Cordelia said. "That's Byron in a nutshell. And he was genuinely appalled at John Smythe's

227

behavior. If he confronted Vincenzo, asked him to keep quiet, and Vincenzo said he wouldn't—" She broke off, as though the reality of what she was saying about the man she had known half her life had washed over her. "I think it's possible."

CHAPTER 19

"It's kind of you and your husband to try to learn what happened to poor Conte Vincenzo," Diana Smythe said. She had received Mélanie, Laura, and Cordelia in a salon on the main floor of the house, with blue silk wall hangings that echoed the color of the lake and windows open onto the balmy air.

"'Kind' is not a word people often use about investigations," Mélanie said, settling herself in one of the silk-covered straight-backed chairs.

"We're going to have to answer questions from someone," Diana said. "Easier with someone we know, who speaks our language. That is, the language of some of us." She frowned, as though puzzling out that "us" had become not just the Montagus but the Vincenzo family, as well.

"Our sympathies," Mélanie said. "I know you hadn't known Conte Vincenzo long, but it must still be a shock."

Diana nodded. "I think the hardest is seeing Sofia and Enrico lose their father. We've become quite fond of them, especially Sofia, whom we've known longer." She pleated a fold of her muslin gown between her fingers. "We grew up without our father. But this makes me realize how very different knowing he was in another country was from not having him at all. We had his letters. We always believed one day we'd see him again."

"I didn't see my own father for years," Laura said. "But yes, it meant something to know he was still there." She met Diana's gaze for a moment. "I don't know how much you've heard of my history, but I also once discovered a murder victim."

"The Duke of Trenchard," Diana said. She would know, of course. The murder had been the talk of London.

"Yes. He was dying when I found him, and beyond help. It shakes one, being so close to violent death."

Diana nodded. "There was nothing we could do for Conte Vincenzo when we found him. Not that we knew that at first. We thought someone had fallen into the lake. Then I saw the knife. That was when I screamed."

"You and Lord Byron had been walking on the grounds?" Mélanie asked in a conversational tone.

Diana's fingers tightened for a moment on the blue-sprigged fabric of her skirt. "Yes. Lord Byron was kind enough to offer to walk with me. He learned when we met him in Milan that I've never cared much for crowds."

"You must have a great deal in common," Mélanie said. "I understand you write poetry."

Diana Smythe's gaze widened and then went shuttered. Much the way some women might respond if they were accused of having a lover.

"We spoke with Byron," Cordelia said.

Diana's fingers curled inwards. Her nails must be digging

230

into her legs through the sheer fabric of her gown. "And he told you—"

"Not willingly. But Mrs. Rannoch can be very persuasive. And it's as well he finally admitted it. Before, we were inclined to put a rather different construction on your friendship with him."

Diana colored but did not look away. "I know. Others put the same construction on it, as well. Byron was concerned about how my husband might react. But I found it almost a relief. There are some things I prefer to keep private. That I can't bear to have violated."

Whereas she'd endured other forms of violation? "Lord Byron also said your husband—isn't the easiest man to be married to," Mélanie said. "So did the Shelleys."

Diana drew a breath, glanced away, looked back at them.

"I knew a man like that," Laura said. "It's amazing the control that can come with such crude behavior. I think that was what I hated most of all. That sheer force could have an impact on me."

A shudder ran through Diana, stirring the knots of ribbon on her sleeves. "I think Byron and the Shelleys got it within a few days of meeting John and me. Whereas, my own family—" She shook her head, her mouth twisting.

"I think sometimes it can be harder to see it with people one's close to," Cordelia said. "Because one doesn't want to."

"There is that." Diana rubbed her arms. "And Byron and the Shelleys are writers. They have the imagination to fill in the gaps." She stared out the window across the lake for a moment. "It's odd. I was so sure I didn't want the marriage my parents had. I didn't want to marry a man who'd leave me for a grand passion. And if, by any chance, I chose wrong, and my husband did leave me, I didn't want him to be a man I'd

231

pine for." She fingered the end of her gauze scarf. "I don't know that my mother ever had a grand passion for my father—one never likes to think those things about one's parents—but I know he hurt her. I didn't want to be hurt." She gave a rough laugh at the irony contained in the word. "John seemed a good choice. I'd known him half my life. I thought his greatest flaw was his lack of imagination. But I thought that very flaw would make it unlikely he'd fancy himself madly in love with anyone. And that it would equally keep me from ever caring too deeply for him." She cast a quick glance at the other three women. "I expect I've shocked you."

"No, I assure you," Mélanie said.

"I've seen the way you look at your husband, Mrs. Rannoch. It was apparent moments after I walked into the salon that first night. And I've seen you with Colonel Davenport in London, Lady Cordelia. The idea of marrying a man precisely because one thinks one won't love him must seem mad."

"I married Jack Tarrington because we were caught in a compromising situation," Laura said in a calm voice.

"When I married Malcolm I scarcely knew him," Mélanie said. "I was alone and stranded by the war. He offered me his protection."

"And I married Harry when I'd lost the man I thought I loved and was certain I'd never love again," Cordelia said.

Diana's eyes widened.

"Cordy and I were lucky," Mélanie said. "Lucky beyond words. Laura, not so much. But we can all understand choosing a marriage partner because one wants to be safe. Only I don't think you found a lot of safety."

Diana put a hand up to pull a ringlet free of her pearl

earring. "I've never been tempted to love John. I was right about that. But I don't think I understood him very well. He may lack imagination in some things, but he's certainly able to imagine transgressions on my part. I sometimes think I misjudged John. That he cared more than I realized and is angry I can't respond. "

"Some people are very angry on their own," Mélanie said. "And don't know how to express that anger."

Diana met her gaze. "The first time he struck me I was more shocked than anything. He promised it would never happen again. I told myself it was an aberration. He was even more agreeable for a time. But then it happened again. And again. It's more often now. I simply do my best to ignore it."

"You didn't think of telling your family?" Cordelia asked.

Diana's fingers tightened. "I did tell my mother the first time. She was concerned. But she told me to keep John happy and it wouldn't happen again. To avoid scandal, which our family had had far too much of. To—" Diana drew a sharp breath. "To be happy I had a husband."

Mélanie's nails dug into her palms. "Your brother—"

"Kit was away with the army at that point. But even after he came back—He'd be angry, I think. In fact, I'm quite sure of it. But would it really serve anything for my brother to plant John a facer? Except to create a scandal that would engulf Kit." Her mouth tightened. "John is damnably clever. He'd find a way to make it seem Kit's fault."

"A separation—" Laura suggested.

"My mother wouldn't stand for it. She'd say I was tarnishing Selena's chances. And she might well be right. We already have one scandal hanging over us. More than one young man who showed an interest in me pulled back after his parents had a few words with him. Father being gone

233

raises all sorts of questions about us, from our personal stability to the safety of our fortune. And Kit doesn't have his own household to take me into. Even when he does, I wouldn't impose myself on him and a new bride in the early days of matrimony. And for all the unpleasantness—perhaps I prefer having my own household, even with John, to being a guest in someone else's."

"I can understand that," Mélanie said. She'd been on the streets, but she'd never been a guest in someone else's household. But she could imagine the need for independence, or what passed for it, at any price.

Cordelia gripped the arms of her chair. "It's appalling. There must—"

"I assure you, I'm not a complete victim," Diana said. The gaze she turned to them was steady but hard as frozen water. "I don't let John touch me in the ways that really matter to me. I have my poetry to escape into."

"Were you writing before you married him?" Mélanie asked.

"Yes." Her eyes lit. "But I've done more since."

"You never thought of showing your family?" Cordelia asked. "It's not considered scandalous for a woman to write."

"I was afraid John would find a way to ruin it for me." Diana drew the folds of her scarf about her shoulders. "I wanted to keep one part of my life that was mine alone, where John couldn't touch me. That I could shape to my liking. You don't know how often that's been the salvation of my sanity."

"I think I have a glimmering of understanding," Mélanie said. She was beyond fortunate in her life, but there were times when it mattered desperately to her to have something of her own to hold on to.

Diana met her gaze in a moment of understanding. "And

yet I can't imagine defying society. Being like Mary Shelley. Or her mother."

"Even they married eventually," Cordelia said. "And it's harder to defy society when one is in the midst of it. Amazing how much belonging can matter. Or seem to matter."

"Meeting Byron—" Diana stared out over the water, fingers pressing against the fragile gauze of her scarf. "Perhaps if I hadn't been writing, if he hadn't been a poet, I'd have been more susceptible to him in—in the way a number of other women have been. But all I could think was here was a man whose poetry I'd long admired, reading my poetry, talking to me about it. At first I was dumbstruck. Then I simply wanted to drink in everything he had to offer."

"He's obviously very impressed with your work," Mélanie said. "I think he thought it far more important than anything else that might develop between you."

"I dream about different things now," Diana said. "I imagine people reading my work. It means more to me, but it's not enough somehow to hold it to myself anymore." She folded her arms across her chest. "Yesterday at the picnic we'd walked the long way round the house to talk about a poem I'd given him. It seemed harmless enough. We weren't hiding. Then we came round the side of the building and saw Conte Vincenzo." She shuddered.

"You also saw him when you were out walking two days before," Mélanie said. "Alive, that time."

Diana nodded with no attempt at prevarication. "Yes, that was the day I gave Byron the poem we were discussing yesterday. Conte Vincenzo stopped and spoke with us. Byron was concerned about the construction he might put upon seeing us. I pointed out we were only walking in the open air."

"Byron said Vincenzo spoke with a lady after he spoke

with you that day," Mélanie said.

"Yes. We couldn't see her face. Byron was also concerned because it might be someone we knew. But we couldn't make out her features or even her hair color, and in the end it seemed folly to linger. We weren't doing anything wrong."

"And if your husband had learned of it?" Laura asked softly.

Diana's shoulders tightened. "John could well have jumped to the wrong conclusion. But I wasn't going to hide because of that."

"Lord Thurston saw Conte Vincenzo arguing with your husband at the picnic," Mélanie said. "Do you know what it was about?"

Diana's eyes widened in seemingly genuine surprise. "No. But if Vincenzo had told John about seeing me with Byron, I'm quite sure I'd have—felt—John's reaction. He hasn't indicated anything to me. He hasn't—lost his temper." The pause spoke volumes about what John Smythe losing his temper meant.

Which emphasized how desperate both Diana and Byron might have been to prevent that happening.

"There's one other thing," Mélanie said. "The Shelleys were under the impression that you and your brother and sister might have had reasons for leaving Britain other than seeing your father."

Diana's eyes widened. "Surely seeing our father should be reason enough."

"It could be. It doesn't mean it's the only reason."

Diana glanced away, hesitation in the way her fingers twisted in the ends of her scarf.

"I can't compel you to tell us, of course," Mélanie said. "But you might prefer to do so rather than to have us ask

236

further questions."

Diana drew a breath and met Mélanie's gaze. Resolution closed over the uncertainty in her eyes. "I can't tell you anything, Mrs. Rannoch. Because there's nothing to tell."

Malcolm and Harry found John Smythe bent over a billiard table, cue in hand. He finished his shot, bouncing it neatly off one corner. "Rannoch." He straightened up, still gripping the cue. "And you must be Davenport. Think I've seen you in London—crush of the season, don't you know—though we've never been introduced."

Malcolm felt his friend's instinctive hesitation as Smythe extended his hand, but they'd neither of them have survived in the worlds of diplomacy and the military if they hadn't learned to shake hands with people they held in distaste. "Just arrived. My sympathies."

Smythe gave a curt nod. "Hard to take it in. Didn't know Vincenzo well. Feel a bit of out of place in a household of mourning, truth to tell. Sought refuge here." He cast a glance round the billiard room. "It's a capital table. Thurston had it shipped from England in pieces." He looked back at them. "Sorry, you wanted to talk to me? I heard you're investigating."

"Lord Thurston asked my wife and me to offer what assistance we could," Malcolm said. "And the Italian authorities have indicated we can be of help. Davenport and his wife have worked with us before."

Smythe's brows rose, perhaps at the mention of wives working with them, but he merely said, "Happy to do my bit, of course. Don't know what I can tell you. We're all more or less strangers here."

"You'd met Conte Vincenzo in Milan. And you and Conte Vincenzo were seen arguing at the picnic."

Smythe drew a breath. "Oh, that."

"Yes, that."

Smythe glanced away, drummed his fingers on the edge of the billiard table, looked back at Malcolm. "I wouldn't have called it arguing. But I did feel I would not be doing my duty did I not give him a warning."

"About what?"

Smythe cast a glance about, then looked between Malcolm and Harry. "I can count on you both not to tell tales?"

"We're neither of us given to idle tales," Malcolm said. Which didn't answer for what they might do with information that was relevant to the investigation.

Smythe gave the sort of curt nod that implied man-to-man confidences. "I didn't care for Vincenzo's attentions to my wife."

Malcolm frowned, going over details of what he'd seen between Conte Vincenzo and Diana Smythe. Very little beyond pleasantries came to mind. "I don't recall—"

"It was mostly in Milan. Look, Rannoch. Davenport." Smythe turned, leaning against the table. "I have to look out for Diana. She's an innocent. We all know she didn't have a father to guide her growing up. And what influence she did have from her father—" He shook his head. "She's scarcely seen anything of the world."

"Nor have you, I would think, with the war," Harry said.

"What? Oh, well—not quite the same thing. Not at all." Smythe coughed. "Told Kit it was a mistake to bring the women to the Continent. One could guess at the sorts of

238

things they'd be exposed to. But they were both insistent. Kit's usually sensible, but he said they had a right to see their father. That it might cause more talk if they didn't go. Never been very good at holding out against my wife's wheedling. I imagine you both know something about that."

"I wouldn't call it wheedling," Malcolm said. "I've learned the value of listening to my wife."

Smythe gave a short laugh. "I can't exactly say the same. But of course once we decided to come I thought it was my duty to look out for Diana, and Selena too. Diana was too guileless to understand Vincenzo's innuendos. She doesn't know how things are done abroad."

Out of the corner of his eye, Malcolm saw Harry suppress a snort.

"One can misinterpret," Malcolm said. "I've seen that in the diplomatic world. Is it possible Conte Vincenzo was simply flirting in the way men do with married women?"

"It was more than that." Smythe's mouth hardened. "He'd take advantage of any excuse to offer her his arm or touch her shoulder. I could tell Diana was uncomfortable, for all she didn't truly understand."

"Unpleasant behavior. I can quite understand objecting to my wife—or anyone else—being treated in such a manner."

"Then you see why I had to say something to Vincenzo. Tell him to stay away from Diana." Smythe strode to the screen of ionic columns at the end of the table and returned his cue to the rack. "To own the truth, I thought he was an unpleasant fellow. Didn't much care to be in company with him. But I certainly didn't dislike him enough to kill him."

It made sense on the surface. Malcolm had no use for Smythe after the revelations about his treatment of his wife, and he wasn't much in charity with Smythe's attitude towards

239

women in general, but he could certainly understand taking offense to the type of behavior Smythe described in Vincenzo. And Smythe did not seem like the sort who would dissemble. Yet Malcolm could not shake the sense that Smythe was not being forthcoming about something.

A rap at the door punctuated Diana Smythe's sudden refusal to disclose more about the young Montagus' reasons for coming to Italy.

"Sofia and I are having refreshments on the terrace with the children, if you want to join us," Selena said, poking her head through the door. She glanced at the four women. "That is—I'm sorry to interrupt."

"It's quite all right." Diana got to her feet. "We're finished. If you'll excuse me, I think I'll see if the contessa needs anything."

Diana wasn't likely to reveal anything more in the immediate future. But Selena was a promising source of information. And Mélanie knew she needed to find a way to speak with Sofia Vincenzo. She, Laura, and Cordelia followed Selena to the lower terrace.

"Diana's been having a hard time," Selena confided. "Finding the body must have been beastly." She cast a glance up the stairs at the other three women, eyes wide and candid. "To own the truth, it still doesn't seem quite real to me. And I can't figure out what to say to Sofia, except to try to keep her company and distract her if she wants it."

Mélanie touched the younger girl's arm. "Those are both excellent things to do, Selena. You're being a good friend to her."

240

Selena wrinkled her nose. "It's funny, she does seem like a friend now. When we arrived here I'd never have dreamed that would be possible."

She led the way down the rest of the steps to the lower terrace, where Sofia sat with her younger sisters and brother, serving fresh fruit and lemonade. Floria, who was looking solemn, smiled at the sight of Mélanie, Laura, and Cordy. "Did you bring Colin and Emily?"

"Not this time," Mélanie said. "But I know they'd love to see you again soon."

"I know you're helping my mother and Lord Thurston," Sofia said. "Thank you."

"Mrs. Smythe said something similar," Mélanie said. "It's not the way investigations are usually greeted."

"Someone has to investigate," Sofia said. "And I want to know what happened to my father." She poured out lemonade and said nothing more about the murder, instead asking questions about Britain and enjoying the children's excitement at hearing about the Tower of London and Hampton Court. But when the refreshments had been consumed and Eliana proposed a walk on the beach, Sofia said, "Perhaps Selena and Lady Cordelia and Lady Tarrington could take you. I need to talk to Signora Rannoch."

Sofia watched her sisters and brother move off along the beach with Selena, Laura, and Cordy. "We're going to bury Papa here tomorrow morning. A quiet ceremony, which is just as well. There's no question of taking him home or summoning his friends with everything else going on. They said perhaps we could have him moved later, but I don't suppose it matters much."

Mélanie studied Sofia. Her expression was even more contained than usual. Her words were surprising from a girl

241

of her background, who presumably would care about both the trappings and meaning of family and church. "You can always decide later," Mélanie said. "It can be hard to think clearly when a tragedy like this has just occurred."

Sofia nodded. She looked at Mélanie for a moment, her gaze at once armored and direct. "I don't quite know how this works, but I'm sure you have things to ask me."

"I think there are things you could clear up for us." Mélanie waved to the children, then turned to Sofia, leaning against the terrace balustrade.

Sofia waved to the children as well, then faced Mélanie, back very straight. "I suppose you're going to ask if my father had any enemies. He was active in politics, so, as you can imagine, he had a number of enemies. Though his side had won in the war, so his friends were in power more than his enemies. And I don't know of anyone I would think hated him enough to kill him."

"Donna Sofia." Mélanie considered and abandoned a number of approaches in favor of plain honesty. There was nothing for Sofia to be ashamed of in her love for Kit Montagu. No need to make it into more than it was. "Before he was killed, your father confided in one of the guests that he'd seen you and Kit Montagu embracing. Mr. Montagu admitted his feelings for you to Mr. O'Roarke. Feelings I think are reciprocated?"

Wariness shot through Sofia. But then, to Mélanie's surprise, the younger woman gave a sharp laugh. "Is that what Kit said? That we're a pair of star-crossed lovers? He would put it that way, I suppose. And you thought I was an innocent young girl lost in love? It's an easy role to play. So many writers have written it. That may make it a cliché, but it also makes it a natural role to slip into."

Mélanie studied the younger woman. Sofia Vincenzo had hit on one of the truths of being an agent. Part of a successful cover story was tapping into natural assumptions about who one was. "You're not in love with Kit?"

Sofia hesitated a fraction of a second that spoke volumes. "That's not the reason we were meeting. I did kiss him. I found it quite agreeable. But I also found it useful to have others think we were in love."

"It makes for good cover," Mélanie said. Though cover for what remained a mystery.

Sofia cast a quick glance at her. "You've been an agent, haven't you? With your husband."

Mélanie nodded. What mattered for this conversation was that she'd been a spy, not which side she'd been spying for. "People tend to underestimate women. It's tiresome. But it also can be useful."

"Yes. So I've found." Sofia gripped the edge of the balustrade. "I can't remember a time before the war. But what's happened since—I can't bear to see my country going backwards. Breaking into pieces. Men like my father and the people he works with in power." Her fingers tightened on the stone. "My father counted Metternich a friend and supported Austrian rule. He said it was the best way to guarantee stability. Which meant protecting his estates and position." She stared across the lake at the mountains in the distance. "I didn't much care to be ruled by the French. But they were right to unify Italy. And right in many of their reforms." She cast a glance over her shoulder at Mélanie. "I suspect I've shocked you."

"No, I assure you." Mélanie kept her gaze steady. For years she'd been used to bottling up her political sentiments, but for some reason wariness shot through her. As though

243

this girl scarcely out of the schoolroom might see through her where some of the most sophisticated politicians in Britain and on the Continent had not.

Sofia lifted her chin. "Italy should be one country. One country that's a republic."

"I'd be the first to agree with you," Mélanie said. "But republics aren't in fashion these days."

"All the more reason to fight. And all the more reason we sometimes have to do so in secret." Sofia drew a breath. "I know I've been sheltered. But I read."

In some ways it was like looking at her own young self. Save that she'd been forged in fires Sofia could thankfully not imagine. "Donna Sofia. Are you working with the Carbonari?"

Sofia's eyes widened. "I heard you were quick. But I didn't quite realize—"

"It's a leap," Mélanie said. "But we know someone at the picnic yesterday was delivering information from the Carbonari. In exchange for certain goods."

"It wasn't I who—" Sofia bit back what she'd been going to say.

"Who was delivering the information? You didn't have it with you, perhaps?" An image from the picnic flashed into Mélanie's mind. Sofia clinging to her brother Enrico's arm, joy and, more than that, relief on her face. "Your brother brought the information from the Carbonari, didn't he?" she said. "Did you recruit him?"

This time shock leapt in Sofia's gaze. "How did you know?"

"I can see your determination. I've seen the two of you together. I can see who is stronger willed."

Sofia pushed a strand of hair behind her ear. "I wouldn't

244

say recruited, precisely. Enrico and I shared many of the same ideals growing up. But I perhaps took them more seriously before he went off to university. He made some friends who were more active than he was. I met them when he brought them home on holidays. I perhaps encouraged Enrico to get more involved."

"With the Carbonari."

Sofia cast a quick glance about the terrace. "Yes." She gave a faint smile. "I know the secrecy can get a bit silly. Like the sort of secret club schoolboys might form. But it's also true they face death if they're discovered."

"Believe me, I understand the danger," Mélanie said.

Sofia fingered a fold of her skirt. "My father's in an organization. I don't understand it precisely. It's not Italian, but what they want for Italy is the opposite of what we do. I've tried to learn more."

Dear God. This young girl, tough as she was, going up against the Elsinore League. "Did you learn more?" Mélanie asked.

"Not a great deal. But I was able to intercept some communications and copy them."

"The information the Carbonari were trading to Carfax came from you."

Sofia nodded. "I gave the copies I made to Enrico."

"Surely they were in code."

"Oh, yes. I broke the codes and gave them what I copied."

Mélanie had seen some of the Elsinore League's codes. Sofia Vincenzo was a formidable young woman. "You have a talent for this."

Sofia shrugged. "I've always been good with numbers. And it's nice to have something to do."

"I wish you could meet Malcolm's cousin Aline. She has a

245

talent for numbers as well, though she isn't as adventurous as you. So your brother gave your decoded papers to friends?"

"Yes. The Carbonari aren't really one group, you know. More a loose network. But Kit and his friends—our friends—have connections to a group in Naples. Who needed the weapons."

"And they negotiated with Carfax through Lord Thurston. Does Thurston know where the information came from?"

"Of course not. That's why we had to make the exchange secretly but in a large group, so he'd have no idea who left the papers."

"And your father? Do you think he suspected what you'd done?"

"No. That is—" Sofia went pale. "I can't imagine he wouldn't have taken action."

"Did you know he knew Thurston was passing information to Carfax? And that Vincenzo was trying to stop it?"

Sofia's fingers clenched on the muslin of her skirt. "No. That is, I didn't at first. Then, just before we came here, I intercepted another letter and decoded it. Papa's friends were warning him there'd been an information leak and Thurston was receiving papers from the Carbonari. But it didn't say anything about the leak coming from Papa. So I don't think he could have traced it to me." She bit her finger.

"And he said nothing to make you think he suspected?"

"No. But if you're asking if I killed him because I thought he was on to me, or because he was on to me and confronted me, then I'd say no in any case, wouldn't I?" Sofia put her hands to her face. "Damn. I didn't agree with him. I was angry at him for so many reasons. But I never wanted—"

246

"I know." Mélanie covered the younger girl's hand with her own. "Relationships are complicated. Especially for spies."

"I'm not a spy."

"My dear Donna Sofia. I beg to differ. You have shown yourself to be a formidable agent. And I mean that as a compliment."

Sofia turned her gaze to Mélanie. For a moment she looked like the very young woman she in fact was. "I just started out trying to gather information. Because it seemed important. Perhaps because it made me feel important. And then people used that information, which made it seem more important, and then before long—"

"It can happen that way. It was like that for my husband. He was clever, and before he knew it, he was an agent."

"But do you think anything I did—I don't believe in what my father stands for, but I couldn't bear it if anything I did led to his death. That's why I'm telling you this."

Her voice rang with sincerity. Which, as she herself had said, was precisely what she would strive for if she'd been behind Vincenzo's murder. Mélanie put an arm round Sofia and squeezed her shoulders. "Your father was a complicated man in a complicated situation. He had a number of enemies and had to have known the risks he ran."

"None of which means it wasn't my fault."

"At this point we can't be sure of anything."

Sofia drew a shuddering breath and nodded, as though Mélanie's words reassured her where she wouldn't have been able to believe a more general reassurance.

Mélanie met Sofia's gaze, at once trusting and worldly, feeling equal parts as though she was talking to her own younger self and to Jessica. "Tell me about Kit Montagu."

247

Sofia dragged a hand across her eyes. "It's funny, I've known about him for years. Enrico and I used to speculate about Lord Thurston's children. As I got older, I thought it was odd that we spent more time with their father than they did. I can scarcely remember Before, you know."

No need to ask what Before meant. "You'd only have been four or five."

Sofia nodded. "I think I remember my mother not being here. Odd that her absence is my first memory of her. And then being able to see her again. And the babies came and it started to seem as though Thurston was our father, as well." She hunched her shoulders, gripping her elbows. "He used to ask my opinion sometimes on the gifts he picked out for his children for the holidays. It seemed so odd. As strange as things were for Enrico and me, we still saw both our parents. And unless we compared ourselves with our friends, it really wasn't strange at all, because it was the only life we'd known."

"I sometimes think that about my children's lives. Their parents are together, but their lives are anything but conventional."

"And then suddenly we got word that Thurston's children were coming to visit. That was surprising enough. But then Enrico told me that Kit was part of a group in England who were reaching out to the Carbonari."

Mélanie pictured Kit Montagu's earnest face talking about the family estates and his practical marriage to his neighbor. "Kit is involved with a group of English Radicals?"

"They aren't as active as the Carbonari, but they share many of the same ideals. They wanted me to talk to him when he arrived at the villa, sound him out, give him some information and see what he had to offer."

"And you both thought a supposed love affair was good

248

cover."

Sofia's mouth curved with irony. "We scarcely even had to try. As I said, it's what people assume when two young people spend time together."

"It was more than assumption when your father saw you embracing."

Sofia's fingers closed on the embroidered folds of her gown. "It wasn't supposed to be—I was giving him information. Getting information from him. It wasn't supposed to be anything more. I didn't mean it to be anything more."

"It's not unheard of for spies to fall in love in the course of a mission. After all, in a world in which one lives on lies, whom else does one have things in common with?"

Sofia's gaze shot to Mélanie's face. "I didn't say—"

"No, I was reading between the lines."

Sofia glanced out over the water. "I thought love was childish. A preoccupation of other girls."

"I fell into that trap myself." Of course, that was after she had had her childhood ripped from her.

Sofia turned her gaze back to Mélanie's own. "Kit and I shared keeping secrets. We shared a childhood shaped by scandal on both sides of the Channel. But it was more than just having things in common. I like him. But more even—I feel alive when I'm with him. I feel like he understands me. So many things I thought were important go away and what matters is just that we're together."

"And Kit?"

Sofia's shoulders drew inwards again. "We haven't really talked. Not about the future. I think he's fond of me. I think he"—she lifted her chin and gave a faint, defiant smile—"desires me, though he wouldn't dream of putting it into words. But he has commitments at home. He's betrothed to Miss Dormer."

"Betrothals can be broken."

"Your husband strikes me as an honorable man. Would he have broken one?"

Mélanie opened her mouth, then closed it. She'd like to think Malcolm wouldn't have locked himself in a loveless marriage when his feelings lay elsewhere. But he took his word seriously. A lady could cry off an engagement. A gentleman wasn't supposed to. "I'm not sure. But though I have the utmost admiration for my husband, I don't agree with him in everything."

Sofia shook her head. "I never could understand my mother giving up everything for love. I think I understand it now. But I'm not sure—"

"That you'd do it yourself?"

"That I'd want someone I loved to do it."

CHAPTER 20

Selena watched as Floria and Matteo ran down the beach. Fourteen-year-old Eliana hung back for a moment, then picked up her skirts and ran after, dark hair streaming behind her. Selena grinned as though she half wished she could run after herself. She must only be about four years older than Eliana, Laura realized.

"I'm glad they can still be children," Laura said.

Selena nodded. "It's hard, I think. They knew Conte Vincenzo better than we did, but he wasn't their father or even an uncle, really. But he was their sister and brother's father, and they think of Sofia and Enrico as their sister and brother more than they think of us as their siblings. At least more than they used to." Selena stopped walking for a moment and wrinkled her nose, as though struck by the changing family dynamics in the Montagu-Vincenzo household.

"That's very perceptive," Laura said.

Selena gave her a quick smile. "I can't quite imagine how it

251

is for Sofia and Enrico, knowing they'll never see their father again. It makes me—" She drew a breath, glanced back over her shoulder at the villa. "It makes me glad I still have my father. Not that it makes me forget other things."

"I don't think one ever forgets," Cordelia said. "But one can learn to appreciate what one has. I lost my own father when I was about your older sister's age. We didn't always get on. But looking back, I'm grateful for the time I had with him."

Selena nodded. Her gaze moved past the house to the far end of the beach where Vincenzo's body had been found, the opposite direction from that in which they were walking. "It's hard to believe anyone hated him enough to—"

"I know." Cordelia touched Selena's shoulder.

Selena met her gaze for a moment. "Your sister was murdered, wasn't she? I'm sorry, I suppose I shouldn't talk about that—"

"It's all right," Cordelia said. "It's actually worse when people ignore it. Act as though Julia never existed. Or talk about her but just avoid mentioning how she died."

"It must have been—I can't imagine losing Diana. Or Kit."

"Worse when it's someone one is close to," Cordelia said. "But a shock to have violence touch the fabric of one's life, whoever it is."

Selena hunched her shoulders, pulling on the ruched bodice of her gown. "I keep thinking it must be someone from the outside. Or one of the guests we didn't know. But it probably isn't, is it?"

"It could be someone from the outside," Laura said. "But people the victim knows well are always the first suspects."

Selena nodded again, as though relieved at the honesty.

252

Her gaze went down the beach where the children, even Eliana, had taken off their shoes and were wading in the shallows. "It still looks just as beautiful as before yesterday. I didn't expect to like it here so much. I didn't expect to like the contessa or Sofia and Enrico. Or even Papa. Perhaps especially Papa. I didn't expect to like Italy. Odd how I could have been so wrong. Every morning the lake takes my breath away again. I always do this walk before breakfast. Funny, two days ago I thought how lucky it was I'd chanced upon Mr. Shelley or they might not have come to the party. That doesn't seem very important now. In any case, I daresay if I hadn't brought up the party to him, Conte Vincenzo would have—"

Laura exchanged a quick glance with Cordelia. "You saw Mr. Shelley talking to Conte Vincenzo two days ago?"

"Yes, they were just down the beach past where the children are now."

"Do you know what they were talking about?" Cordelia asked.

"No, they went rather quiet when I reached them. Truth to tell, I don't think it had been a very comfortable conversation—" Selena broke off and looked between Laura and Cordelia. "Oh, no, you don't think—Mr. Shelley's a *poet*."

"It may not have anything to do with it," Laura said. "But if Mr. Shelley knew Conte Vincenzo as well as it sounds, it would be worth talking to him."

Selena met her gaze and gave a slow nod.

Malcolm stared at his wife as she related her conversation with Sofia Vincenzo. Beside him, Harry was equally silent. They were on the upper terrace where Mélanie had found them after their interview with John Smythe.

"I don't know which of them I'm more surprised about," Malcolm said. "I suspected Sofia had hidden depths, but not to this degree. And Kit could seem quite conventional."

"Perhaps he is about some things," Harry said.

"Perhaps. Or my skills are rusty, or his are very good indeed."

"Sofia's certainly are," Mélanie said. "She reminds me of—"

Malcolm cocked a brow at his wife.

"—me," Mélanie finished.

He smiled, despite everything. "Formidable indeed."

"Raoul's going to be kicking himself for not seeing through Kit," Mélanie said.

"None of us tumbled to Julia being an agent in Brussels," Harry pointed out. "Not until it was right in front of us."

Malcolm shot a look at his friend. Davenport was never one to shy away from hard truths or memories. "True," he said. "Julia's skills impressed me, as well. But I suppose in this case—Kit and I seem to be more or less on the same side. He might have told me."

"That rather depends on what other secrets he's keeping," Harry said.

Malcolm pushed himself away from the balustrade. "I should talk to Kit."

"Alone, this time, I think," Harry said. "He's confided in you recently. You can build on that."

Malcolm nodded and turned to his wife. "Harry can tell you about our talk with Smythe. We didn't learn much. He has a plausible explanation for his quarrel with Vincenzo, but I'm not at all sure that's all there is to it."

"Diana confirmed Byron's story," Mélanie said.

"She's—I'm glad I didn't have to face John Smythe after talking to her. I'm going to be hard pressed to face him again."

Malcolm looked at his wife, saw John Smythe's self-satisfied face. He reached out and touched his fingers to Mélanie's cheek. She turned her head and pressed a kiss against his palm.

"What's that for?" he asked.

"Thank you for being you, darling."

"Smythe said he confronted Vincenzo over the conte's attentions to his wife," Harry told Mélanie when Malcolm had left the terrace. "Which is plausible, especially if Smythe is given to jealousy. But, like Malcolm, I thought there was more to it."

Mélanie nodded. This was the first time she and Harry had had a chance to talk alone since the Davenports' arrival. Though that morning, before breakfast, they had taken the children down to the beach. Mélanie could still hear Jessica and Drusilla giving shrieks of delight, each clinging to one of her hands, could feel the sand slithering beneath her feet and the wind catching at her skirt. Harry had swooped in, scooped up Drusilla in one arm, and caught Mélanie's wrist in a reassuring clasp.

"For lake water, it has a surprising tug," he'd said.

They'd run back up the shingle. Harry dropped down with Drusilla on one knee and took Jessica from Mélanie to put on the other. "I've missed this," he'd said, as Mélanie pulled sand toys from a basket to give to the girls.

"It's a long time since we've all played at the beach," Mélanie had said, though she had known that wasn't what he was talking about. "Not since Dunmykel last summer."

Now Mélanie cast a glance at Harry along the terrace. The walk here would have given him time with Malcolm, just as she had had time with Cordy. "I hope you and Malcolm had a chance to talk. I think he's desperately needed to."

Harry leaned forwards, elbows on the balustrade. "I imagine you do, as well."

Mélanie pushed a curl beneath the brim of her hat. "God knows I've had years to reflect on what I've done."

"I can't really imagine," Harry said in a low voice. "Because I don't think I could have pulled off what you did. But I came close enough that I have perhaps a glimmering of what you're going through. Malcolm does too, of course."

Mélanie met Harry's gaze. The gaze of one of her best friends. Who could almost be a brother. Who had once been an enemy agent. "But Malcolm would never have done what I did. Whatever he says."

"No," Harry agreed. "I don't believe he would have done. What you did is remarkable. As I said, I don't think I could have pulled it off. But I might have tried. Not out of conviction, as you did. For the escape. For the challenge." He looked down at his hands. For some reason Mélanie remembered Jessica putting a handful of sand in Harry's hand that morning and Harry letting it run through his fingers. "Hard to resist a challenge like that."

Mélanie looked into those steady blue eyes. "That was part of it. Just wanting to see if I could pull it off." It was a shameful admission, but one she felt Harry would understand.

Harry nodded, no judgment in his gaze. "If I'd had any such opportunity, I think I'd have seized on it as an escape. You know how desperate I was for escape in those days. And hard to find a more thorough escape than going deep undercover."

"I wasn't——" She bit back an instinctive retort, aware of the wind tugging at her hat. "I suppose perhaps in a way I was looking for escape. Not from the present so much as from the past. I'd have called myself a hardheaded realist. But I don't know that I liked the person I was very much."

Harry gave a twisted smile. "I know something about that. Quite a bit, actually. "

Mélanie looked out over the blue ribbon of the lake. She could see Laura and Cordy with Selena and the younger Montagu children. "Odd. In looking for escape, I found a happiness I wouldn't have thought possible."

"Funny how that can work." Harry's gaze was on his wife.

"I don't just mean Malcolm and the children," Mélanie said, watching the young Montagus run into the water. "Though that would be enough. But I also mean my friends."

Harry caught her gaze and held it, as though it was something fragile that could break. "Friends are a rare thing. I never really had them growing up. Odd how something one is quite sure one can do without can suddenly become essential."

Mélanie drew a breath that hit harder than she expected. "He's never going to admit to me how much he misses it."

"You were an exile for a long time," Harry said. "Perhaps it's not entirely a bad thing for you to be exiles together."

"You wouldn't wish it on Cordy," Mélanie said.

"No, but I'd happily share it with her." Harry cast a glance at his wife on the beach again, then touched Mélanie's wrist. "I don't think Malcolm could resent you if his life depended on it. But if for some reason he did, I flatter myself there's a good chance I'd see it."

257

Mélanie found herself smiling at the same time a lump lodged in her throat. "You're an amazingly generous man, Harry."

"You'll spoil my reputation." He grinned, and she had a memory of him with two toddlers in his lap. "Not that there's much of it left, in any case."

Malcolm surveyed Kit across the library where he'd found the younger man. "My compliments. Raoul O'Roarke is not an easy man to deceive, and he quite believed your impression of a young man in the throes of first love."

Kit set down the book he'd been reading and got to his feet. "I don't—"

"Spare us the protestations, Montagu. Donna Sofia confided the whole to my wife."

"Sofia—"

"She said she didn't want secrets to stand in the way of finding her father's killer."

Kit flushed. "I didn't mean—I couldn't tell O'Roarke the truth without betraying Sofia and her brother."

"I understand. Loyalties can be complicated. Though surely you realized O'Roarke would be sympathetic to your cause. As would I."

"I thought so. I've read some of your speeches and articles. But—"

"What?" Malcolm asked in the silence after Kit broke off.

"You work for Carfax."

Malcolm bit back a bitter laugh. "Not anymore."

Kit looked him squarely in the face. "Not officially, perhaps. But you can't pretend you don't still do errands for

258

him."

Malcolm returned Kit's gaze. Bitterness welled up on his tongue. "I did for some time, though with increasing reluctance. But Carfax and I quarreled just before I left Britain. I can't imagine ever doing his bidding again."

Kit's gaze sharpened. "Are you saying you left because of him?"

"In a manner of speaking."

Kit's brows drew together. "He's a dangerous enemy."

"Without question." Malcolm regarded Kit for a moment. There were five years between them, but for Malcolm those five years contained a vast journey, both in actions and in thought. "Are you part of the Levellers?"

Kit's shoulders straightened. "What—?"

"Do I know about the group? Not a great deal. But a bit from my friend, Simon Tanner. Some actors in his company are involved. I think Simon may be himself, more than he's admitted to me. They take their name from the seventeenth-century Levellers but they're a more educated group, more devoted, at least so far, to writing and talking than to taking direct action. Still, they've aroused government ire. Some pamphlets were confiscated a couple of months ago and the authorities were searching for the ringleader." Malcolm regarded Kit for a moment. "Is that part of why you left Britain?"

Kit met Malcolm's gaze without flinching. "We were planning to visit Father in any case. I actually wanted to stay and face things out, but my friends pointed out it would be safer for others if I weren't there to be arrested." He glanced to the side at one of his father's hunting prints—dogs, horses, a stone wall, a certain type of England. "I believed in what I was doing in the war. But I didn't much care for what I came

259

back to. Former soldiers without limbs, begging in the streets. Sleeping in Hyde Park. Corn laws that protect the incomes of those with property and deny bread to families. Including some of our own tenants. I think it was when I realized last Christmas that the holiday boxes we take them aren't just an indulgence but something they actually depend on for survival that I really got angry. I met up with some friends from university. We agreed we couldn't just sit back and watch."

"I had a group of friends like that in university," Malcolm said. "We talked and wrote. Carfax did us the honor of thinking us quite dangerous."

"I've read some of your articles," Kit said. "I can't tell you how much I admire them. But then you—"

"Went to work for Carfax. True enough. You could say I sold out everything I believed in. The truth is I was at a point in my life where I wasn't sure I believed in much. And I told myself I was working for my country. I hadn't thought through enough how I disagreed with my country's policies. And that even if my superiors did me the kindness of listening to me, I couldn't really influence them. So I left. I went into Parliament. Where at least I could speak my own mind."

"I've thought about it," Kit said. "But with the Tories refusing to advance any sort of reform, with even most of the Whigs opposed to universal suffrage—I wonder if any sort of hope of change that way is a delusion."

"I've heard the same arguments from others," Malcolm said. Notably, his wife and his father. "And I can't deny they can be powerful. I choose to believe even arguing on the fringe one can still nudge the argument along and make a difference."

"So you'll be going back to Parliament?"

260

For a moment, the loss was raw in his throat. "Probably not. But that's for my own reasons."

Kit's gaze skimmed over Malcolm's face. "Because of Carfax?"

"In part."

Kit shifted his weight from one foot to another. "My father's working with him."

Malcolm kept his expression neutral. "Did you know, when you left England?"

"No. That's the damned irony of it. I had no idea Father was anything but a dilettante enjoying life with his mistress. It was Sofia who told me." A crossfire of emotions shot through his gaze that had, Malcolm suspected, as much to do with his tangled feelings towards Sofia as towards his father.

"And your father and Carfax in this case were allies of your allies."

Kit nodded. "Hard to credit." He drew a breath. "I came to Italy to see my father. That's the truth. But the other Levellers convinced me it was a good time to make myself scarce, and I wanted to make contact with the Carbonari. I didn't know who my contact was until after I arrived. After that first night we all dined together. It was the next day that Sofia approached me. I'd never expected—"

"She's very disarming. It's part of what makes her so formidable. Part, but not all. She's obviously brilliant."

"One doesn't expect women—that is, gently bred women—I know your wife works with you, but—she's very different from my sisters and—everyone at home."

Such as the girl he intended to marry, though he couldn't quite bring himself to say it. "You wouldn't be the first spy to fall in love with a fellow spy," Malcolm said.

Kit's gaze shot to his face. "I never said—"

"No, I'm reading between the lines. You and Donna Sofia are obviously both expert at deception. But often the most successful deceptions work because they're grounded in truth."

Kit drew a long breath. "She's like no one I've ever known. We talk and strategize and I think of her as a comrade. Then suddenly I look at her and realize everything else she is."

Malcolm nodded, thinking of the moments still, almost six years into their marriage, when he'd look at Mélanie in the midst of plotting or strategizing or analyzing motives and find his pulse racing and his breath tight in his chest. He watched Kit for a moment. "You and Donna Sofia obviously have more complicated lives than I credited. But what O'Roarke said to you is still relevant. If the two of you want a life together, there's no reason you can't have it."

For a moment, Kit looked as young as he in fact was. "My commitment to Miss Dormer isn't a pretense."

"Knowing the man you are, I find it even more difficult to imagine you could be happy in such a relationship."

Kit glanced out the window, fingers curled round a carved oak chairback. "You never crave stability?"

Malcolm drew in and released his breath. "I think we all crave stability at times. Even my friend O'Roarke, who's led a far more adventurous life than I have. He married the woman he was speaking with at your father and the contessa's party. They've been estranged for two decades."

"The sort of life I'd have with Sofia—"

"You'd never be bored."

Kit grinned. "There is that."

"Did Vincenzo know what you and his daughter were really up to?"

"No!" Kit paled. "At least, I hope to God not. When he

discovered us, he seemed straightforwardly angry. But then, I suppose there was nothing straightforward about him. Still, I would think Sofia would have suspected—"

Which might be true. But if there were nothing straightforward about Vincenzo, that was doubly true of his daughter. And if Sofia had had anything to do with her father's death, she almost certainly would have kept it from Kit.

Though, of course, it was always possible Kit was more devious than Malcolm suspected and had had something to do with it himself.

CHAPTER 21

"K it said he might have trusted me earlier, except that I worked for Carfax." Malcolm smiled, but Mélanie could see the shock in her husband's eyes. They—she, Malcolm, Cordelia, Laura, and Harry—had gathered in a small salon at the Thurston villa with butter-yellow walls and flowered chintz upholstery that felt surprisingly English.

"Kit's put himself outside the system," Mélanie said. "Which is a surprise. But to him, I suppose you'd be—"

"Part of that system," Malcolm finished for her. "Quite. Rather how it once seemed to you, I suppose."

Mélanie drew a breath. Strange they were having this conversation in front of their friends. But good perhaps that they were. "I always trusted you, Malcolm," she said. "But it's true there are things I'd have hesitated to tell you." And there still were, though far fewer of them.

Malcolm nodded. "But, Kit's—"

"British." It was Harry who finished the sentence for him.

Malcolm met his friend's gaze. "Yes. Odd how that makes

264

a difference. Or perhaps not. Mel and I were on opposite sides during the war. I'm not used to thinking of groups like the Levellers as on the opposite side."

"You're in Parliament," Harry said. "They've run up against laws passed by Parliament even if you didn't vote for those laws."

Malcolm held Harry's gaze. "True."

"I've read articles by the Levellers," Laura said. "Some in the *The Phoenix*." The Radical newssheet had also published articles by Laura, Mélanie, and Malcolm himself. "Do you think Kit's reaching out to the Carbonari means they plan to become more active, instead of just writing about their views?"

"I don't know," Malcolm said. "I think there's a great deal we don't know about both groups. And, much as I admire both Kit and Donna Sofia, it gives both of them even stronger motives to have wanted Vincenzo out of the way. Both for political reasons and because their feelings for each other are clearly more complicated than either would admit."

"There's someone else who appears to have been at odds with Conte Vincenzo," Cordelia said. She and Laura described Selena's account of her meeting with Vincenzo and Percy Shelley, and the apparent quarrel between them.

Malcolm's brows drew together. "Obviously another talk with Shelley is warranted. But not tonight, I think. We should be getting home."

The contessa and Thurston came into the hall to see them off, with the good manners of hosts, though with a frankness that did not deny the reality of the situation. "Sofia said she felt better after talking to you, Signora Rannoch," the contessa said, pressing Mélanie's hand. "I don't know what you said to her, but I'm very grateful."

265

"Thank you, Contessa." Mélanie returned the pressure of the contessa's hand, unsure what else she could say.

Thurston thanked them all with an easy self-assurance that gave no hint of the revelations he'd made to Malcolm and Harry. Mélanie found herself wondering how much the contessa knew about his activities and how much he would now tell her.

The evening was balmy, the sky clear and still bright. They might have been out for a stroll. Save that as they walked back towards the Rannoch villa, Malcolm began to question Laura about her impression of the Shelleys at the picnic and what Mary Shelley had revealed about their acquaintance with Conte Vincenzo. Mélanie fell a bit back with Cordelia.

Cordelia was unusually quiet, gaze on the path before them. "I keep thinking about our interview with Diana Smythe," she said. She stopped for a moment and stared out across the water. " I always thought I understood why Juliette resisted marrying Paul even though she loves him, but I don't think I truly felt it until today. My God. As a girl, I thought marriage was my path to freedom. But it can be the most appalling trap. It *is* a trap, unless one has a husband who's decent enough not to snap it closed."

"I knew Malcolm was a decent person when I married him," Mélanie said. "But I also didn't expect the marriage to last. So I didn't think I was trapping myself." A few months ago she couldn't have said that to Cordelia. A relief to be able to frame the words.

Cordelia met her gaze and nodded. "I knew I was tying myself to Harry. Dangerous, in a way. A man who loved me so much. But I knew without even thinking about it that he'd never—" She shook her head.

Mélanie looked ahead at their husbands, walking on either

266

side of Laura. "There's so much trust involved. Far more than I ever appreciated."

Cordelia tugged the ribbons on her hat tighter. "The thought of any of our girls ever being so at the mercy—"

"I know." Mélanie's fingers clenched on the strap of her reticule. "We have to hope we're raising them to choose well."

"And know we'll be here for them if they don't," Cordelia said.

After a tedious and unproductive afternoon talking to guests from the party, Raoul returned along the lake to Arabella's villa. Malcolm's villa, he reminded himself. He rounded a curve to see the children gathered by the edge of the lake with Addison and Blanca. They were such a blur of movement that it was a moment before he realized there was a small brown-and-white dog and a fifth girl among them, taller even than Livia Davenport.

"Uncle Raoul!" Chloe Dacre-Hammond caught sight of him and ran down the beach, her blonde hair bouncing on her shoulders, her puppy frisking at her heels.

Raoul caught Fanny's youngest daughter and spun her round in a hug. "I swear you've grown in two months."

"Mama got me all new dresses before we left London. Two inches longer. We've been traveling ever so fast. We're having a baby, have you heard? That is, Mama and Uncle Archie are, and I'm going to be a big sister. I call him Papa now, but only when we're private because he says it would confuse people before they're married. Mama and Papa—Uncle Archie—that is. Emily says she calls you Daddy."

Raoul, bent down to pet the puppy, managed not to let his hand waver. "So she does. Sometimes. I take it as quite an honor. As I'm sure Archie does."

Chloe nodded with a gaze that saw rather more than he had had any intention of letting her see, but by then, Colin, Emily, and Livia had reached them while Blanca and Addison restrained Jessica and Drusilla. The children tugged Raoul down the beach. Fanny and Archie got up from the table and chairs in the shade of the myrtle trees where they had been sitting.

"You made good time," Raoul said, kissing Fanny's cheek.

"Fanny and Chloe are intrepid travelers." Archie clasped Raoul's hand.

Raoul looked between his two friends. "I couldn't be happier," he said. "For both of you."

"Hmph." Fanny tucked a guinea gold curl beneath the brim of her hat. "I'm glad my letter got here before we did. I was hoping to stave off the worst of the congratulations. We're long past the age for orange blossoms and cakes from Gunter's."

"Perish the thought," Raoul said. "But I don't see anything wrong with wishing two people I care about happy. You must know there are a great many people here who'll be happy with you."

"And some of us haven't done this before," Archie said. "You have to let me appreciate the novelty."

"If it comes to that," Fanny said, "I don't think I ever was in love with Dacre-Hammond. So it has novelty for me, as well. Not to mention being much more agreeable."

From Fanny, that was positively romantic. Raoul hid his smile.

"Uncle Archie!" Livia called, overlapping a cry of "Papa!"

from Chloe, and then, almost in unison, "You said you'd help with the castle."

Archie grinned. He looked quite ten years younger. "Duty calls. I suggest the two of you seize the chance to talk."

Raoul offered Frances his arm. "My felicitations, Fanny. It's splendid news."

Frances colored like a schoolgirl beneath her artfully applied rouge. "Goodness knows this isn't what I planned for my fifth decade." She curled her fingers round Raoul's arm. "But I can't deny I find the idea of a baby with Archie rather agreeable."

"Of course. A child with the person you love."

Frances paused on the first of the steps up the hill and put up a hand to the brim of her hat. "You're talking about love awfully easily."

"I don't think I've ever claimed not to believe in love."

"You've also never admitted to feeling it, so far as I can remember."

"But I've always believed in change, haven't I?"

Frances laughed. "It's good to see you smiling. And not talking twaddle about not being good for Laura Tarrington."

Qualms bit him in the throat, but he kept his voice light. "I'm not at all sure I'm good for Laura. But I'm quite sure I don't want to live without her."

"Thank God," Frances said. "You've always been the world's last romantic. Now at last you're talking like it."

Raoul put his fingers over Fanny's hand as they navigated uneven steps. "I suppose you'll hit me if I say the emotions of being with child have addled your brain?"

"Try me."

They had reached the terrace midway up the hill. Frances glanced about. "Arabella's favorite spot."

269

"Yes," Raoul said.

Frances went still for a moment, taking in not so much the lush greenery and the blue of the lake as the memories they evoked, he suspected. "It's good to see it again."

For a moment it was almost as though he could hear Arabella's silvery laugh above the stir of the breeze and the lapping of the water. "You'd think I'd be avoiding it, but I find myself coming here a lot. The memories haven't gone away, but it's easier to live with them somehow."

Frances touched her fingers to a late pink rose. "Perhaps because we've both found what she never could."

"What?" Raoul asked.

She gave him a quick smile, though her eyes were uncharacteristically serious. "Contentment."

She moved across the terrace. Raoul kept his grip on her arm and pulled out one of the chairs for her.

Frances shot a look at him. "You needn't look so concerned. I'm not going to break. And I'm not going to risk a fall. I may not have planned this baby, but I find I've already grown quite attached to it. Archie's being fairly sensible so far, but I count on you to intervene if he starts to look as though he wants to wrap me in cotton wool."

Raoul handed her into the chair. "He's never been through this before." For that matter, neither had Raoul, not really. Not being in a position to openly show an interest in how the mother of his child got on. "Archie will make a good father."

"Yes, I think so." Frances smoothed the folds of her muslin gown. "And after five children, I do finally seem to be learning how to be a good mother."

Raoul moved to the second chair. "You've always been a splendid mother, Fanny."

270

"Rubbish." She smiled at him across the table where he had so often sat with Arabella. "You have a much more instinctive knack for parenting than I do. But I've learned."

"You were very young when you had your first child."

"So were you." She watched him for a moment, gaze bright and steady beneath the shadows cast by the brim of her hat. "You aren't going to tell me, are you?"

"Tell you?" Again, Raoul kept his voice light.

"Why you and Malcolm and Suzanne have exiled yourselves."

Raoul drew a breath of the fragrant air. He had known this question was coming. You'd think he'd have a better answer prepared. "Fanny—"

"Archie knows. Or, at least, guesses. He says it's not his secret to share."

"It's not mine, either. Fanny, you're not an agent, but you've lived with agents enough to understand secrets."

"I understand that none of you thinks I'm to be trusted with them—not my nephew, not his wife, not one of my oldest and dearest friends, not my lover and the father of the child I'm carrying."

"My dear girl. I trust you better than most people I know. I also love you enough to feel a keen concern for your safety. Not to mention the safety of the child you're carrying."

"Just because I'm a woman—"

"It has nothing to do with the fact that you're a woman. It has everything to do with the fact that you aren't an agent." He watched her a moment longer, this woman with whom he shared so many secrets of his past, but who, as of yet, didn't know the greatest (worst) of those secrets. "I agree we're probably at the point where you should know, but they aren't my secrets to share. You should talk to Malcolm. I don't know

271

that it will make a difference, but I'll tell him I think you should know."

Frances released her breath. "That's more than I expected. In any case, looking at you at least, it seems your departure hasn't entirely been a bad thing."

"Not entirely," Raoul said, mornings and evening on the terrace echoing in his memory.

"And now you have this murder investigation. Addison said something," she added. "He was explaining where you all were."

"I know it may seem dangerous, but whatever happened to Conte Vincenzo, it's in the past, and there's no immediate danger now." He wasn't entirely sure of that, but there was no need for Fanny to know. "It's certainly a tragedy, but it's good for Malcolm and Suzanne to have occupation."

"And you."

"And me," he agreed. "Though it's taken some odd turns. Margaret's staying on the lake. She was at the party where Conte Vincenzo was killed."

Frances's finely arced brows snapped together. "Margaret is here?"

Fanny had known Margaret as a girl in Ireland. She'd warned Raoul when he became betrothed to her. He could still hear her voice. *I don't think you'll find what you're seeking. I'm not sure it exists for people like you.* And yet, Fanny had tried to be kind to Margaret as a young bride navigating the complex terrain of the society round the estates of Fanny and Arabella's father, the Duke of Strathdon.

"I was as surprised as you," Raoul said. "Margaret always seemed so settled in Ireland. But Desmond's wife died in the spring. It's apparently changed things for them. Though not to the extent that Margaret wants a divorce."

Fanny's frown deepened.

"It's all right," Raoul said. Though it wasn't, really. It wasn't, at all. "I never had any real expectation of her agreeing."

"It's not that. That is, I'm sorrier for your situation than I can say, but knowing Margaret, I never had much expectation of it, either. And I know perfectly well you can all take care of yourselves in the midst of your investigations. I agree it's good for all of you to have occupation. I should probably feel more grief for Vincenzo, considering I met the man and a human life is a human life, but the truth is I never liked him very well."

Raoul raised his brows. "I didn't think—You met him when he was in Britain with the contessa?"

Fanny nodded. "They drew quite a bit of attention in society that spring. A striking couple. And insular as the ton can be, they also can be quite fascinated by anyone who seems exotic." She drew a breath. "Margaret was actually at the party where the murder took place?"

"Yes. Damnably awkward, even before the murder. And of course Meg was in complete shock afterwards. Still was, when I saw her earlier today. She actually asked me if I'd had anything to do with it. Which tells you her opinion of me and my connection to anything to do with violence and destruction."

Fanny didn't smile or meet his gaze in acknowledgement as he expected. Instead, she smoothed her hands over her lap, pressing the sheer fabric of her gown taut, uncharacteristic tension in her ringed fingers. "Talking of secrets, this is one I'd have preferred stay buried. I know I enjoy gossip, but I never see much point in sharing information that can only cause hurt. But now—" She looked up and met Raoul's gaze.

273

He was reminded of Fanny as a teenager, struggling with how much to confide in him about Arabella, with how the confidences might hurt both him and her sister. Sometimes Fanny's delicacy of mind was surprising. "As I said, I saw a fair amount of Conte Vincenzo and the contessa when they were in England fifteen years ago. I was at a house party at the Grandisons', where Vincenzo was a guest. Without the contessa."

"Fanny," Raoul said, "are you saying that you and Vincenzo—"

"Good heavens, no. He wasn't really my type." Fanny kept her gaze on her lap. "But the thing is, Margaret was at that house party, as well."

"Are you sure? She never said anything about having met Vincenzo. I know Lady Grandison is her cousin, but Meg rarely leaves Ireland."

"I'm sure." Frances drew a breath. "And I'm sure she met Vincenzo." She looked into Raoul's eyes and spoke quickly. He was oddly reminded of Mélanie when she removed a bandage, quick and efficient to get the hurt over with. "Alistair was there, as well. I went to visit his bedchamber. I slipped out before dawn and saw Vincenzo leaving Margaret's room."

For a moment he couldn't make sense of her words. He stared at Fanny in what must, he realized, have looked like dumb stupefaction.

"You can't have thought she was celibate all these years," Frances said, in tones like a dash of cold water.

"Of course not. She was Desmond Quennell's mistress. Before we separated. For five years or more before you'd have seen her with Vincenzo."

"And you thought she was faithful to him when she
274

wasn't faithful to you?"

"No, of course not." He ran a hand through his hair. "That is, yes. That is, it's not the same thing. She'd been in love with Desmond since they were children, and our marriage was over when she went back to him."

"You're a strange man, Raoul O'Roarke. You pretend not to have ties to anything, but you've always taken your love affairs more seriously than the rest of us. Desmond Quennell may very well be the love of Margaret's life. It didn't stop her from marrying you. It didn't stop her from seeking distraction with Vincenzo nearly sixteen years ago. Because she was bored, or she'd quarreled with Quennell, or she just wanted distraction. I always thought she was much less of a romantic than you were. What matters for this investigation of yours are the facts. Margaret and Conte Vincenzo were lovers. For at least one night."

And Meg had revealed none of this at Thurston's party or when he'd spoken with her about the murder. Not that he'd have expected her to reveal a love affair. But she'd given no hint that she'd ever met Vincenzo. Vincenzo had given no hint that he'd ever met her. He'd even asked Raoul if Raoul was married, that first night when they spoke on the terrace at Thurston's villa. Reticence, because both Margaret and Vincenzo did not wish to call attention to their affair? Or something more complicated? If Vincenzo had been trying to avoid drawing notice to it, why had he asked if Raoul had a wife?

"My dear?" Frances was watching him closely. "I hate to tell tales about another woman. And I hate to cause you pain. I never thought it was relevant, so many years after you and Margaret had separated. But now—"

"You were right to tell me." Raoul slid his hand across the

275

table to grip Frances's own. "Thank you, Fanny."

"It's never easy to be deceived by those one thinks one knows, is it?" Frances said.

Raoul swallowed a bitter laugh, deep inside, where it cut like glass.

"No," he said, "it isn't."

CHAPTER 22

In the flurry of the Rannochs and Davenports returning, and greeting Fanny, Archie, and Chloe, it was some time before Raoul could follow up on Fanny's revelations. Which was probably good, as it gave him time to think. Not that time did much to make sense of this new side to Margaret. Or, more significantly, the lies she and Vincenzo had told.

Mélanie touched his arm as the company moved from the terrace into the salon. "What is it?"

"Am I that obvious?" he asked.

"Only to one who knows you, as you've often said to me."

He gave a faint smile. "Caught, *querida*. It seems I don't know the woman I married as well as I thought I did. Which is probably medicine I deserve. It's just lowering to realize one's been deceived in someone one thought one knew. Probably very good for me. But unsettling. Right now, I should talk to you and Laura and Malcolm before I talk to Meg."

Mélanie's gaze skimmed over his face, but she merely nodded and gathered up Malcolm and Laura while the others settled round the piano. The four of them moved into a side salon, a favorite room of Arabella's, with warm rose-colored walls and windows on three sides that let in the rose-gold evening light. Raoul recounted his talk with Frances as concisely as he could.

"I need to talk to Margaret," he concluded. "But I thought you should know first."

"I'm glad," Malcolm said. "If a bit surprised to find you so forthcoming."

"We've had too many secrets. And you should know in case Meg turns out to be a crazed murderer who attacks me when I confront her."

"That's not really funny," Laura said.

Raoul reached across the sofa to touch her hand. "Don't worry, sweetheart. Margaret's a lot of things, and I can't swear she isn't a killer. But I'm quite sure she has too much finesse to attack me. And I hope I have too much wit for her to succeed, if she did."

"Could Margaret have known about the Elsinore League?" Mélanie asked.

Raoul drew a breath. "I'd have sworn not. But I'd also have sworn she was loyal to Desmond Quennell and that she wasn't deceiving me at Thurston and the contessa's party."

Mélanie continued to frown. "There's more than one reason to slip in and out of someone's room in the middle of the night, as we all know. At this house party—suppose she was conferring with Vincenzo about something to do with the Elsinore League instead of sharing his bed?"

Raoul met her gaze. "And here I was locked into one way of seeing the situation. How often have I said that can be fatal? You're right. We have to consider that it's possible." He leaned forwards. "I may well need you to talk to Margaret and

278

make sure I'm not letting my feelings blind me one way or another. But I should talk to her first." He looked across the salon at Malcolm and then at Mélanie. "Meanwhile, there's something else for you to deal with. I think we're going to have to tell Frances the truth."

Malcolm drew a breath.

"He's right," Mélanie said. "She's the only one in the house who doesn't know. And if that wasn't difficult enough, we're in the midst of an investigation that touches on all sorts of aspects of the truth. We need to tell her before someone lets something slip or she works it out for herself."

Malcolm released his breath, frowning at the gold medallions on the Turkey rug. "Unfortunately, I'm afraid you're right. I know, to my sorrow, how difficult it is to keep things from her. I'm impressed Archie's held out against her as long as he has." He drew another breath. "I'll talk to her."

Raoul met his son's gaze for a moment and inclined his head. He squeezed Laura's hand, got to his feet, and touched Mélanie's shoulder. "Fanny will place the blame where it belongs. On me."

Mélanie looked up at him, her own gaze steady in the rose-gold light. "Marrying Malcolm was my decision."

"But she knows how much I knew. I'll talk to her when I get back." He gave a faint smile, though he knew full well how difficult that talk would be. "Assuming I can get a word in edgewise."

Laura caught up with him in the hall before he could leave the house. "Darling—"

"It's all right, sweetheart." He took her hand. "Fanny was going to have to know at some point. Better here than in London. And better when we can all talk in person, however difficult that may be."

Laura's gaze darted over his face, sharp with concern. "She's your friend."

For a moment he could feel the warmth of the sun when he and Fanny had sat on Arabella's terrace. "She is. And if I lose her friendship over this, that's my lookout. And no more than I deserve."

Laura put her hands on his shoulders. "I know I can't get in the middle. But I hate to see you hurt."

"I've been able to escape the consequences of my actions all too much. Time I accepted them, don't you think?" He bent his head and kissed her, sliding his fingers into her hair and holding her against him for a moment. "I'll be back, sweetheart."

"Well." Margaret got to her feet and set down her book. "We've met more in the past two days than in the past two decades."

"I'm sorry to inflict myself on you." Raoul set his hat on the table. They were on the terrace at the Chipperfields' villa once again. He had found Margaret reading. She was dressed for the evening in a pale gray gown edged with peach-colored ribbon and her hair was in an elaborate knot confined with silver combs. But surely it was his own changing perceptions that made her gaze seem harder, her mouth more firmly set. He was used to reevaluating his opinion of people as he received new information. He wasn't used to being as wrong in his initial assessment as he'd been about Margaret. Certainly not as wrong for as long. "I'll do my best to keep it brief."

"I suppose it's to do with"—she hesitated—"with Conte Vincenzo's death."

"It is."

"Am I obliged to speak to you? I have no knowledge of how these things work, but it seems you don't have any official authority."

"You know perfectly well I don't, Meg. You are quite free to tell me to go the devil. You've done it often enough in the past."

"And then?"

"I'd be obliged to take what I knew to the authorities, who can ask official questions."

Something flashed in her gaze. More, he'd swear, than just dislike of speaking to the Italian equivalent of a constable or Bow Street runner. "You'd better sit down." She dropped into a chair at the table and gestured him to the one opposite.

Raoul seated himself. He'd questioned Laura in a cell in Newgate during the investigation into the Duke of Trenchard's murder. This shouldn't be harder. Except perhaps that he'd been more confident in his judgment of what Laura was and wasn't capable of. "You didn't tell me you'd met Conte Vincenzo before yesterday."

Alarm flashed in her eyes, but she controlled it quickly. "Perhaps because I hadn't met him until then."

"Don't fence, Meg. I can understand the impulse. But I have it on excellent authority that you were seen leaving Vincenzo's bedchamber at the Grandisons' house party fifteen years ago."

Her arms closed her chest. "That's a preposterous—"

"I own I was surprised myself. But I'm quite sure the information is correct. I have no desire to share it with others more than is necessary for the investigation. You certainly didn't owe anything to me at the time. What you may have owed to Desmond is between you and Desmond."

Margaret wrenched her gaze away from his face. "Damn you—"

"Assuming of course that the obvious explanation is the correct one. I know full well it often isn't. And you've always had the ability to surprise me."

"Have I?" Her gaze shot back to him, her armor in place. "You grew bored with me quickly enough."

"Is that what you think? I didn't grow bored with you, Meg. But we each learned how different the other was."

Her mouth twisted. "At the very least, you learned how conventional I am. It can't come as much of a surprise to you that I wouldn't broadcast to you and the world that one of the other guests at a party happened to have been my lover. Or that Conte Vincenzo was gentleman enough to be discreet."

"No." Raoul watched his wife in the shadows of the orange tree that overhung the terrace. Her face was set, but ghosts lurked in her gaze. "But when Conte Vincenzo was murdered at that same party, you must understand my asking questions."

Margaret flinched at the word "murdered." "That had nothing to do with—"

"It's funny," Raoul said, "which things prove to be connected and which not. I'm not as much of an expert as the Rannochs, but I've seen that more than once in an investigation. Often even those in possession of knowledge don't realize what that knowledge may mean."

Margaret smoothed the sheer silk of her sleeve. "It's a commonplace enough story."

He sat back in his chair and crossed his legs. "There's never been anything commonplace about you, Meg. And you've always taken your promises seriously."

She gave a short laugh. "You, of all people, can say that? I

282

didn't take my wedding vows very seriously."

"You did while there was an actual marriage to go with them."

She looked at him for a moment. The careful shield in her gaze seemed to have slipped. "Are you saying that you—?"

"Was unfaithful first? No. Not until after I was sure about you and Desmond, as it happens. At least, not in that way. But our marriage was over, to all intents and purposes, some time before."

"Odd." She smoothed the lace frill on her sleeve. "That didn't stop me from feeling guilty. Not that it lasted a long time."

She flung that last out as a challenge. Raoul cheerfully ignored it. "I think you'd always loved Desmond."

"And that makes it hard for you to understand my seeking consolation with Conte Vincenzo? Perhaps I'm more cold-hearted or more of a wanton than you credited. Perhaps Desmond and I had quarreled. Perhaps I was bored and drank too much champagne."

"All of those are possible," he agreed.

"So why does the reason for my infidelity to my estranged husband and longtime lover matter a decade and a half later?"

"Because the man you strayed with was murdered. And anything connected to him could be relevant."

"Oh, God." She pushed herself to her feet and stood looking at the lake. Shifting waters, yet, unlike the open sea, they were enclosed, bounded by the elegant villas in which the key players in this drama resided. "There's a bit of truth in all of it. Desmond and I had quarreled. Not seriously, but he took it into his head that he wasn't good for me, and I resented being told what to do. I never liked that."

"Yes, I remember." Raoul smiled without calculation.

283

"It wasn't a serious quarrel, as I said, but it was enough for me to decide to accept Sally—Lady Grandison's—invitation. I thought some time away would do me good. And yes, I thought it might be good for Desmond to miss me." She looked down at her hands, resting on the balustrade. She still wore her wedding band. "It was intriguing meeting someone from Italy. I hadn't traveled at that point, though I used to dream about it."

"I remember that, as well." It was one of the things they'd planned, in the days when they'd still planned a future, seeing Paris, Rome, Florence, Vienna. Though, when they actually started to discuss it, Margaret had worried about the unrest on the Continent.

She cast a look at him over her shoulder. "The contessa wasn't with him. She was suffering from a chill, at least in theory. Vincenzo already suspected something was amiss with the marriage. He confided in me about it." She flushed. "I know, it probably sounds as though he was trying to seduce me—"

"Perhaps. Though that's on his head, not yours."

Margaret shrugged. "In any case, it got us talking. I told him I was a poor choice to give anyone advice on marriage, given that my own had failed years ago. But that I thought it could reach the point where two people realized they were so different they had no common ground anymore."

"A good way of putting it."

"It's odd." She hugged her arms across her chest. "I didn't suspect that the contessa would end up much like me. Separated from her husband and living with her lover."

"Save that the contessa is living in exile."

"Whereas I have all the comforts of my home and have managed to preserve the veneer of my reputation." She touched her fingers to the ring he'd given her twenty-three years before. "Don't think the irony isn't lost on me. I may blame you for a great deal, Raoul, but I'm not unappreciative."

He shrugged. "It's the least I owe you for not seeing the folly of our situation before you committed to it. Besides, I'd be an exile in any case."

"You love Ireland."

For a moment, loss bit him in the throat, and he caught a whiff of the longing he glimpsed in Malcolm's gaze in unguarded moments. "The country—the lack of a country—Ireland is now isn't a place I want to spend a great deal of time."

"At least it's still standing."

"Define still standing."

She drew a breath, then shook her head. "We'll just have the same quarrel."

"True enough." He sat back in his chair. "Did you talk politics with Vincenzo?"

"Do you think a man talks politics with a woman he's trying to get into bed?"

"Some men might. If they appreciated that the woman in question was out of the common way."

She gave a twisted smile. "And here I thought you viewed me as sadly ordinary."

"I never saw you as anything of the sort, Meg."

She glanced away. "Vincenzo saw the dangers in too much agitation. As I did." She cast a defiant glance over her shoulder.

"I expect that gave you common ground," Raoul said.

She met his gaze squarely. "Yes. At first it was merely that. Shared sympathies. Nothing that could be considered improper. But I suppose if I'm fair, I caught the admiration in his gaze from the first." Margaret had always been ruthless about not denying uncomfortable truths for all her care for appearances. "Except for Desmond, I hadn't seen that in a man's gaze for a long time. And Desmond was preoccupied and our quarrel was fresh in my memory. I was feeling he took me rather for granted. Vincenzo didn't seem to take me for granted in the least. And I suppose—perhaps I was tired of being careful, doing the right thing. I rebelled when I married you. But I'd learned caution. I hadn't rebelled since."

"All understandable."

"As I said, it's a sadly commonplace story. Tied up now in the tragedy of his murder, but hardly worth dwelling on."

"Did you see him again?"

"Once, in London. I went to stay there for a few days after the house party. But we both knew what was between us wasn't meant to last longer than a fortnight's pleasant dalliance. Isn't that how sophisticated people like you manage these things?"

"I make no pretenses to sophistication. And I've never been one for dalliance."

"Unlike your mistress."

"No." A simple word that covered years of far more pain than he'd have admitted to feeling at the time. "Arabella and I were alike in many ways. But certainly not all."

Margaret pressed her fingers against the sheer fabric of her sleeves. "I felt for Vincenzo when the scandal broke. I knew he would find public display as disquieting as I did myself. I'll own I was shocked when Thurston left England. I suppose the contessa must mean as much to him as what you call liberty means to you."

"An interesting way of putting it. He certainly seems to have come to terms with what he's given up."

"As do you."

For some reason the image that shot into his mind was of breakfast on the terrace that morning, the children laughing, the smell of coffee in the air. "One learns the folly of refining upon the past. Did you hear from Vincenzo again?"

"He wrote to me before he left Britain. I was back in Ireland by then. His letter was perfectly correct, the sort of thing that could safely fall into the wrong hands. But I could read between the lines. I wrote back wishing him well. I hoped he could also read between the lines."

It added up neatly. Too neatly? Or was he jumping at shadows? "Did Vincenzo ever talk to you about Carfax?"

Margaret's brows drew together in seemingly genuine puzzlement. "Why on earth would Vincenzo have talked to me about Lord Carfax, of all people?"

"It's possible Carfax has a connection to the investigation."

"Good heavens, is he in Italy too?"

"Not as far as I know." With Carfax, one could never be sure of anything.

Margaret smoothed her peach satin sash. "I don't think I've met him above a half dozen times. But the odd thing is the Carfaxes were at the house party, as well. Lady Carfax and I had some pleasant conversations about gardening. I don't recall exchanging more than a few words with Lord Carfax."

"Did Vincenzo?"

"Whatever was between us, I was scarcely living in his pocket in public. The gentlemen went out shooting. He could well have talked with Carfax then." She scanned Raoul's face. "Does it matter so much?"

"It could."

"Devil take it. You always do that. Say things that sound

287

like answers but fail to divulge anything."

"Don't think it doesn't take a lot of practice to master the art." He drummed his fingers on the tile tabletop. "Who else was at the Grandisons' house party?"

"Dear God, it was a long time ago. Alistair Rannoch. The Hardys. The Beverstons. Lady Frances—" She broke off and stared at him. "I heard Frances just arrived to stay with the Rannochs."

"So she did."

"And she's the one who saw Vincenzo leaving my room."

"No comment. But if it was Fanny, you can be quite sure she wouldn't broadcast another woman's secrets."

Margaret snorted. "The idea that Fanny and I would be on the same level—No." She put up a hand. "I have no one but myself to blame for this."

"How did Vincenzo get on with Alistair Rannoch?"

Margaret raised her brows. "Interested in how your wife's lover and your mistress's husband got on?"

"I've never cared to discuss Alistair Rannoch when I could possibly avoid it," he said with truth. "But if Vincenzo was close to Alistair, that could be significant."

"Why?"

"Surely I don't have to point out to you that though Vincenzo was killed in Italy, he was largely among British people when he died?"

"But Alistair Rannoch has been dead himself for more than a year."

"Meg." Raoul stretched out a hand across the table. "I expect you'll laugh if I tell you to trust me. But I presume you want to learn who killed Vincenzo. I think I know you enough to know you must have had some feeling for the man."

Margaret threw up her hands. "Very well. I don't know

why I should expect you to confide in me now, when you scarcely did when we were attempting to have a real marriage. You're a lot of things, Raoul O'Roarke, but if you're attempting to learn who killed Vincenzo, I suspect you'll succeed. And for once, I can say I want you to succeed." She returned to the table and dropped back into her chair. "As I said, I had little knowledge of what passed between the men when they were shooting or playing billiards or drinking port. I can't tell you whom Vincenzo spoke with. But—" She frowned. "I remember coming across Vincenzo walking with Mr. Rannoch in the garden. Not necessarily surprising, but they appeared deep in thought." Margaret's frown deepened. "I never knew quite what to make of Alistair Rannoch. I think I felt a certain solidarity because we were both caught in the same quadrangle. At the same time, I can imagine he must have been an appalling man to be married to. I had the sense he wouldn't have hesitated to go beyond polite flirtation with me if I'd given the least sign I'd accept it."

"Probably," Raoul agreed. "Aside from the fact that you're a beautiful woman, it's the sort of thing he'd have thought of to take revenge on me."

Margaret folded her hands on the table. "That afternoon, I had the distinct sense he knew what was between Vincenzo and me, which is absurd, because we could scarcely have been more discreet. It wasn't anything he said, so much as the way he said it. And the look in his eyes. I was very grateful that he left us before long, while at the same time I found myself wondering if it was dangerous to be alone with Vincenzo, while I hadn't worried in the least about it before the encounter with Mr. Rannoch. But then Vincenzo said—" She hesitated, as though conjuring up the right words. "That he hadn't been sure he'd wanted to come to this house party, but he'd be forever grateful that he had. Because he'd met me"—she colored—"well, he was gentleman enough he would say that, wouldn't he? And because he'd made a connection that might prove very beneficial for the future. I asked him what he meant before I could think better of it. He said we both knew the world was an uncertain, and likely dangerous, place. That one couldn't count on the future, and a prudent man, who cared about his future and that of his family, had to make his own luck. And I blurted out—" She shook her head.

"I'm sure you couldn't have said anything foolish."

Margaret's mouth twisted. "You're kind. I told Vincenzo I wasn't sure Mr. Rannoch could be trusted. Which is a bit odd, given that the main thing I knew about him was that his wife was your mistress. But—"

"You've always been a keen judge of people. What did Vincenzo say?"

"That sometimes the most dangerous people made the best allies." She rubbed her arms. "In that moment, Vincenzo almost seemed like a stranger. Then he shook the mood off, and I didn't ask any more." She looked at Raoul. "Have I answered all your questions?"

Raoul sat back in his chair and studied his wife for a long moment. In retrospect, he'd never been the best at reading her. Today's revelations had certainly emphasized that. But he knew her to a degree. He'd got her to open up, far more than he expected. And that, in and of itself, was curious. Curious and, perhaps, telling. "There's just one other thing. Was it pure coincidence that the first time you traveled outside of Britain, you just so happened to stay on the same lake as the man you had an affair with fifteen years ago?"

"What are you implying, Raoul? That I wanted to resume

290

the affair, at my age?"

"I'm not implying anything. And I don't see why age should have anything to do with it."

She gave a short laugh. "I wasn't the sort to go chasing across the Continent after a man fifteen years ago, let alone now." She swallowed and met his gaze, her cheeks tinged with color. "Desmond means a great deal to me."

"I don't doubt that. Which makes the question of how you happened to be here, of all places, particularly interesting."

CHAPTER 23

Frances stared at her nephew, his words reverberating in her head. "Suzanne married you to spy for the French."

"Her real name is Mélanie. But yes." Malcolm spoke in the same crisp, level voice he had used to recount the incredible truth of his wife's past. "I'm an agent. I was fair game."

"You—"

"I love her. Rather incredibly, she loves me."

Frances sat back in her chair, gloved fingers numb against the silk of her gown. Malcolm had asked her to come into the rose salon when she came downstairs from dressing for dinner. She'd known from his expression it was something serious, but she never dreamed how it would upend her world. "I suspected a lot of things, but not this."

"As Shakespeare would say, if this were played upon a stage now, I could condemn it as an improbable fiction."

"Oh, do stop it with your Shakespeare quotes. You use them like armor." She put a hand to her head. Her hair felt as though it was slipping from its pins, though that was probably just the effect of the story. "I should have seen it. I may not be a spy, but I've lived among spies. I know about Archie. He told me before he proposed. And I know what he and Raoul were doing in Ireland and against this Elsinore League—" Frances stared at her nephew. The obvious slapped her in the face, like a glove tossed down in a challenge that signals the end of a friendship. "What does Raoul have to do with this?"

Malcolm's gaze remained steady, but his skin seemed to have gone a shade paler. "He—"

Only this afternoon. She'd been sitting in Arabella's favorite spot with Raoul, talking about Archie and the baby and Laura Tarrington and contentment. "My God. I've half known he was a French spy for years." It was something she'd never quite let herself articulate, because it seemed better for all for her not to know. "But did he—"

"He was Mélanie's spymaster." Malcolm's voice was as steady as a ribbon pulled to the breaking point.

"He—" She jabbed a pin into her hair. "Raoul set up your marriage?"

"Not exactly. He sent Mélanie on the mission where we met. He didn't bargain on my proposing."

Fragments of the past swirled in her head. Malcolm's careful letter announcing his marriage. The rumors she'd done her best to dispel. The date of Colin's birth, six months after the wedding. "You offered her marriage because she was pregnant."

"That was part of it."

Frances squeezed her eyes shut. "And she wasn't pregnant as the result of an attack, as I always assumed. To think I thought it a lucky accident that you and Colin look so alike." So lucky she'd wondered sometimes if her reserved, chivalrous nephew had been Suzanne's lover months before

293

they married. Inchoate rage choked her. "Dear God in heaven, I could murder him."

"Please don't." Incredibly, Malcolm smiled. "I've grown quite attached to him."

Frances stared at her nephew, seeing the boy who had grown up too soon and been through so much. "Malcolm, this must have been—"

"Hell, at first. But it's an odd thing when one keeps looking at a situation. When one thinks about the loyalties that drive people to do what they did."

"I'm not particularly worried about Britain. Britain can take care of itself. It wasn't hard for me to come to terms with what Archie did. As I told him, being intimately acquainted with members of the government and royal family, I can understand the impulse to work against them. I'd look a terrible hypocrite blaming Suzanne and Raoul for doing the same. But for Raoul to have done this to you, to his son—" To the boy they'd both watched over, worried about, tried to protect.

Malcolm sat very still. His gaze, oddly, had softened. "It cost him an incalculable amount to give Mel up."

"And that excuses it?"

"No, but it's part of the equation."

Frances pushed herself to her feet and strode across the room. "I swear, the two of you are precisely the same, with your talk of equations when you should be talking about feelings."

Malcolm raised a brow. "Since when have you talked about feelings?"

"Since Raoul violated every one of them. No"—Frances put out a hand before he could speak—"don't say any more. This is between your father and me."

Archie walked beside Harry, gaze on Chloe, Livia, Colin, and Emily, who had run ahead. They had dressed for dinner and were on the path above the lake in the early evening. O'Roarke had disappeared, probably off on some piece of the investigation, and Malcolm was closeted with Lady Frances. Harry could guess what he might be telling her, and he suspected his uncle could, as well, but there was nothing either of them could do to help.

"You're very forbearing, Harry," Archie said. "I don't imagine this is the sort of news one expects from the parental generation."

"On the contrary. You can't think much of my skills as an agent if you imagine I was entirely surprised about you and Lady Frances."

Archie gave a slow smile. "Perhaps not. But for all your skills, I doubt you quite expected it to take this turn."

"Perhaps not. But I think I'm uniquely qualified to say that you'll make an excellent father."

Archie gave a rueful laugh and smiled again, an open smile, but almost shy. "It's the last thing I was expecting. But I confess I was—quite delighted."

"Having a child with the woman you love? How could you not be?"

Archie stopped walking. "You seem very sure."

"I've seen you together. I've never seen you look at another woman that way. And I've seen you with plenty of brilliant and beautiful women."

Archie gave a wry smile, though his brows drew together. "Some of my past was cover for my work."

"But not all of it."

"No, not all."

"I always wondered why you never married," Harry said. "Was it because—"

"Of being an agent? No, or at least mostly not. I was a confirmed bachelor long before I gave the Dunboyne information to O'Roarke. The truth is, I could never see the point of a marriage that was little more than a convenient alliance with both partners going their own way. A marriage such as—"

"My parents had?"

"If you like. And nearly everyone in my set. I was fortunate not to need a wife's dowry. I didn't feel the need for children. At least not until you came into my life. Much easier to be on my own."

Harry nodded. Until recently, it had never occurred to him how very alike he and Archie were in some ways. "If I hadn't met Cordy, I expect I'd have done much the same. Oh, not your string of beautiful mistresses. I've never been in your league. But, finding it simpler—preferable—to live life alone. And then I saw her and—" He shrugged, his gaze on Livia, though it wasn't a desire for children that had driven him to seek out marriage. Not at first. "You've chosen more wisely than I did. You and Lady Frances are much better suited than Cordy and I were."

"I don't know about that. I do know that what's between us took me by surprise, at a time in life when I thought I was long past it. And then marriage seemed the logical next step. The inevitable next step." He turned and met Harry's gaze. "I was going to ask her to marry me before I learned about the baby."

"Yes, Lady Frances put that in her letter to Suzanne. She

said you were most insistent she mention it."

Archie gave a faint smile, but his gaze remained serious. "I wouldn't want anyone to think I was marrying her to cover up a mistake. Or to do the right thing. I've seen enough of the world to know one can live without someone if one has to, but I'm damned sure I don't want to live without Frances." He cast a quick glance at Harry. "One can still feel that way at my age, you see."

"I wish you'd stop harping on your age, Uncle. It's going to be a bit odd when I'm the one giving you advice about babies."

Archie's face relaxed into a grin. "Scamp." He stared at the children for a moment. Chloe had bent down to scoop the puppy up in her arms. "Frances knows. About my past. And I don't just mean the other women."

"I wasn't going to ask," Harry said.

"No, you wouldn't, but you'd be pardoned for wondering. And I wouldn't want you to think—I told her some time ago. She took it without a blink. Said she was used to the people she loved being involved in intrigues. And that being intimately acquainted (which, with Fanny, means literally) with several in the government and royal family, she could understand the impulse to work against them."

"That sounds very like Lady Frances."

"Quite. Of course, there's still a risk—"

"Life's a risk, Uncle. As I imagine your betrothed would be the first to tell you."

Archie lifted a hand to wave to Chloe, who had turned back towards them. "But it gets more complicated when one drags others into that risk."

"Years." The words tore from Frances with an anger she would not have thought possible. "Decades. I wrote to you every week. I thought we shared secrets."

"We did." Raoul's voice was cool and level, very much as Malcolm's had been when he told her about Suzanne. Though his eyes held a desolation she hadn't glimpsed in her nephew's gaze. "Just not every secret. On either side."

Frances stared at her sister's lover. Her friend and confidant from the age of fourteen. She could see his bright gaze the day Arabella had introduced them. The way that intense gaze would follow her sister round the room. That same gaze focused on his son for the first time. She'd been the one who'd put the baby into his arms. The tenderness in the way his long fingers had supported Malcolm's head. "You're his father. You've thought of yourself as his father since he was born. Since before he was born." She could still remember writing to tell him of Malcolm's birth, knowing even at that young age how her words would be received and treasured. "And you betrayed him."

"Yes." His voice had the cut of a lash. But not directed at her.

"You *used* him, in your spy games."

"So I did. From any perspective, what I did was unforgivable."

"You loved him." Moments shot through her memory. Raoul carrying Malcolm. Laughing with him over a book. Throwing a ball with him. Raoul's intent face when she gave him a report on his son. Raoul's carefully worded letters that couldn't disguise his concern. Raoul looking at Malcolm in the

Berkeley Square drawing room in an unguarded moment a few months ago, wonder in his gaze. She might not use the word love easily but she could recognize the emotion. "For all your deceptions, I can't believe I was deceived in that. Don't try to deny it."

"I won't. Some things are beyond denying."

"And yet, you did this to Malcolm. Six years ago, of all times, when he was still so vulnerable." The fear of Malcolm's suicide attempt a decade ago shot through her. The helplessness. The longing to hold him close, the knowledge that she couldn't protect him in that way anymore. The jolt of terror, for weeks, whenever the post was delivered. She remembered Raoul's drawn face, like a man who is looking into hell. It was not as though they'd stopped worrying four years later, when Raoul would have set up the meeting between Malcolm and Suzanne.

"Malcolm is my son. He was also my opponent."

"It's not a cricket match, for God's sake."

"No. It was a war, with the fate of everything I believed in at stake."

"And that excuses it?"

"Nothing excuses it." His voice was contained but also rough in a way she had never heard it. "I don't have much conscience, but I have enough to hate myself."

She could almost taste the bitterness of his tone on her tongue. She had an odd suspicion he'd never admitted such self-hatred to anyone else. Certainly not to her, though he'd always tended to blame himself. Even for things that were quite beyond his control. "I was always inclined to think you had too finely tuned a conscience, " she said.

"You're an insightful woman, Fanny. But deception is my stock in trade."

"And yet, you had no need to deceive me by pretending to care." She thought back through the years. Sitting on the terrace at Dunmykel, the wind sharp about them. In her salon, glasses of whisky in their hands. Walking in Hyde Park, shielded by the lace of her parasol. What possible game could have been furthered by the raw pain he never quite let himself put into words? He'd been in London in the early autumn of 1812. That raw pain had been very much in evidence. "You weren't talking as though you were Malcolm's opponent six years ago." She could see him sitting in her dressing room, whisky glass in hand, the candlelight hollowing out his face and stripping away the mask he wore in public to show the shadows of strain. His words echoed in memory. *I could kill Carfax for dragging Malcolm into the spy game. But there's no denying it's given him a focus. At least, one that engages his mind. I tell myself that's enough to keep him going. Just because I'd find working for a man like Carfax hollow myself doesn't mean—*"Six years ago, you were talking as though you were as desperately concerned as I was. We were both afraid Malcolm was drifting." She gave a harsh laugh. "At the time, I actually thought Suzanne and Colin were his salvation. God, the irony."

"Quite."

She stared at Raoul. He stared back at her, his face with that set expression he got when he was most trying to conceal his feelings. "Is that it? Did you think Suzanne and a child would give him a reason to live?"

The few seconds' pause while Raoul drew in his breath revealed more than a stream of confession would from most people. "Whatever I thought, Mélanie took information from Malcolm that we used against the British."

"And that was important enough that you gave Suzanne up?" Frances stared at his familiar features, Malcolm's words in this same room, Arabella's favorite room, little more than an hour before, repeating in her memory. "Malcolm says it cost you an incalculable amount."

Raoul continued to sit very still, in that way he had, but his fingers had curled round the arms of his chair. She'd learned, through the years, to watch his hands. "Whatever it cost," he said, "it didn't stop me."

"No." She studied him a moment longer. His knuckles were white. Anger still choked her, but her brain had started to work. "The question is why. I suppose you loved Suzanne too. I rather think that should have been obvious to me years ago." She could see him, sitting beside Suzanne on a drawing room sofa, his arm very carefully not so much as brushing her skirts, but an ease in his posture that he displayed with few people. "I just didn't realize what I was looking at."

"I loved her." His voice was even, but stripped raw in a way she had never quite heard it. "I still do, though it's different now. It has been for some time. But I'm quite sure I always will love both of them."

"And when you gave her up—"

"Mélanie wasn't mine to give up."

Frances kept her gaze hard on his own. "Don't pretend you couldn't have stopped it."

"I could at least have tried." He pushed himself to his feet and drew a breath, as rough and new as uncharted terrain on which no human has ever set foot. "At the time, Mélanie would scarcely have acknowledged the existence of feelings. But it was already apparent to me that she felt something for Malcolm."

"So you decided she and Colin were safer with Malcolm?"

He leaned against the rose silk-covered wall opposite her, tension writ in every angle of his body. "So many different

301

motives aligned to support their marriage that I'll never be able to say what drove me the most strongly. But—" He hesitated, and she had the oddest sense he was speaking as he never had to anyone else. "If it had been anyone but Mélanie and Malcolm, I probably would have done everything I could to stop the marriage."

Frances stared at him, taking in the implications. "So it wasn't really about spying at all."

"I'm a spymaster, Fanny. Everything I do is about spying."

She got to her feet to face him. "Not everything, I think."

"Don't romanticize it, Fanny."

"My God, do you think I could? I know you far too well. Though in some ways, today I feel I never knew you at all." Frances spun away, her arms closed over her chest. "Perhaps I have no right to berate you. You never berated me for Alistair."

"What was between you and Alistair wasn't any of my business."

"He made Malcolm's life hell. And I let myself love him." Hot shame washed over her. She still couldn't think of Alistair without feeling shame. And grief.

"I don't think love is something any of us can really control."

She gave a harsh laugh, bitter with anger at both Raoul and herself.

He crossed to her side and put his arms round her. She pushed against him, then turned in his arms and clung to him for a moment. "They'll be all right, Fanny. That's what matters."

For some reason, tears prickled her eyes. She dragged her hand across them. "Colin—"

"Has two parents who love him."

She was acutely aware of the baby, already a vivid presence within her. Despite the day's revelations, she knew what Malcolm meant to Raoul. And, by extension, what his second son must mean. She drew back, her hands against his chest. "You must—"

"I get to see him. I'm a part of all their lives. I have far, far more than I deserve."

"I hate talking about deserving. I don't deserve a great deal, myself.

"Colin's having a happy childhood. So is Jessica. I think that will be true wherever they live."

"Will they really never be able to come home?"

"Malcolm thinks so. I think Mélanie harbors hopes. She's feeling the guilt of it."

"It's intolerable."

"I quite agree."

The thoughts swirling in her brain had begun to settle. The rage was still there, but it had moved to a new target. "Carfax did this to them. I could murder him."

"It's a possible solution, but there'd be no end of complications."

She lifted her head and looked at him. "God help us. I forget sometimes the world you live in."

"And yet, despite what everyone seems to think, I'm not a killer."

"You've been working against Carfax for years. Surely you have something on him."

"Not with incontrovertible evidence I could use to force his hand. Mélanie might risk going back without an iron hold on Carfax. Malcolm won't. He's too protective of his family."

"You're in danger, too. Possibly more even than they are.

I don't know that anyone would actually arrest Suzanne—though I wouldn't care to put it to the test—but they might well arrest you. Or simply have you killed. Don't spies do that sort of thing?"

"Sometimes."

A different kind of fear tightened her throat. He'd always been a madman when it came to running risks. Part of her was shocked he'd survived as long as he had. "You wouldn't—"

"Risk going back? I might on my own if the incentive were strong enough. I wouldn't with Laura and Emily. And I wouldn't want Mélanie to risk it, for her own sake and the children's."

She reached up and touched his face, something she'd have considered unthinkable a half hour before. "Arabella—hardly an example of prudence herself—used to despair of your recklessness. Has having a family finally made you learn prudence?"

"I make no pretensions to anything of the sort. But I am rather keenly aware of what I have to lose these days. Though if there were a way I could go back and thwart Carfax—"

"God knows the man has enough secrets. Pity he's never been the sort for romantic dalliance. I could help with those sorts of secrets."

"Fanny." Raoul put his hands over her own on his chest. "Talking of families, you have one of your own. And a new addition to worry about. Don't even think about going up against Carfax on your own."

"I'm not a complete shatterbrain."

"You're nothing of the sort. But you're also not a trained agent."

"Archie said much the same thing in London just after you left."

"He's right. And at this point, Carfax holds too damned many of the cards."

Frances frowned. She'd always hated to be boxed in. "I could talk to the Duke of York. Or even Prinny."

"And say what? My nephew's wife was working for the French, but please pardon her? I don't doubt your influence, Fanny, but I don't think even you could pull that off."

"Damn."

He pressed a kiss to her forehead. "Give it time."

"That's also what Archie says."

"Obstacles that seem insurmountable can change with time. We may understand that more than the younger generation."

"And I need to be prudent for their sake?"

"And your own. And Archie's."

Frances drew back and regarded Malcolm's father. Colin's father. Arabella's lover. Perhaps, more than anything, her own friend. "When Malcolm told me the truth, I wasn't sure I've ever known you at all."

"And now?"

She sighed and leaned against him. "I always knew you were an incurable romantic. And too clever for your own good."

CHAPTER 24

Mélanie looked up from dressing one of Emily's dolls as the French window from the rose salon opened and Raoul and Frances stepped back onto the terrace. They had pushed dinner back, ostensibly because of Raoul's absence, but also because sitting down with so many unexpressed feelings would be ghastly. The company were gathered on the terrace with olives, tomatoes, bread, and wine. For the past half hour, her chest had been tight the way it was when Malcolm or Raoul was off on a mission. Which, in a way, this was. Always harder to be the one waiting.

Raoul held open the French window. Frances stepped through it. Her arm brushed against him as she did so. Casual and accidental, but Mélanie released her breath at the ease it indicated. Malcolm, sitting across the terrace with Drusilla and Jessica on his lap, had gone still. So had Laura, who was refilling wineglasses.

Emily jumped up from the terrace floor and ran over to catch Raoul's hand. "Daddy, we're making a story. About a

306

princess who goes to a ball, only her stepsisters aren't mean and there's more than one prince. Come see."

Raoul smiled over his shoulder at Frances and let Emily draw him off. Mélanie moved to Frances's side. "Emily calls him that quite a bit now. I expect she'll be doing it more now she sees Chloe with Archie."

Frances nodded. She was watching Raoul settle down on the terrace floor with the older children. Incredibly, she was smiling, though her eyes had a thoughtful look.

Mélanie drew a breath. It hadn't been for her to tell Lady Frances. But she felt she owed Frances the chance to confront her. "Dinner should be ready in a quarter hour. Would you like a glass of wine? Perhaps we could take it into the salon?"

Frances met Mélanie's gaze and inclined her head. Mélanie would have sworn her husband's aunt was revising every moment they'd ever spent together. Which was probably the case.

Mélanie took two glasses of wine from Laura, who squeezed her hand as she gave them to her, and met her husband's gaze for a moment. Malcolm's smile was warm, but she could read the concern in his eyes. She returned the smile with determination and moved into the grand salon, all her attention focused on not sloshing the wine.

Lady Frances had seated herself on a straight-backed chair near the piano, facing away from the French windows so those on the terrace wouldn't be able to observe her expression. Mélanie put one of the glasses into her husband's aunt's hand. She'd been remarkably fortunate so far in the people who had learned the truth. Save for David. Her own glass tilted in her grip. But this was Frances, who in many ways had been like a mother to Malcolm, even before his own mother died. For all Frances might claim to take motherhood lightly, Mélanie had seen her act like a tiger in defense of her cubs. Not for the first time, Mélanie wondered what she herself would do to a woman who did to Colin what she had done to Malcolm.

Mélanie drew up a chair beside Frances, also with her back to the terrace. "Aunt Frances—"

"My dear Suzanne—I must learn to call you Mélanie, mustn't I?"

"You can call me whatever you wish, ma'am. I confess I'm quite relieved you're speaking to me at all."

Frances gave a faint smile, though her gaze was direct and more searching than usual. "I'm hardly in a position to talk to anyone about betrayal, given my past."

Mélanie returned Frances's gaze without flinching. "There are betrayals, and betrayals."

Frances took a sip of wine. "And yours had more reason behind it than some. I'm hardly a revolutionary, but, as I've told Archie, I can appreciate the logic behind the position. And I can appreciate commitment to something outside oneself, even if it sounds a bit exhausting."

Mélanie smiled despite herself. "That's more than I deserve, ma'am."

"On the contrary." Frances set her glass on the enamel-inlaid table beside her. "You're still the woman who's made my nephew very happy."

Mélanie took a sip of wine. A sparkling red Lambrusco with a hint of cherries, but she could taste the bitterness of what she had brought Malcolm to. "I don't know about that. I do know he's made me happy. He makes me happy. Happier than I ever thought I could be."

"What you make him is quite obvious to an outside

308

observer, my dear." Frances smoothed the striped lavender gauze of her skirt. "Given what I know about the man I am about to marry, who also happens to be the father of my child, I'd look a dreadful hypocrite for holding this over your head."

Squeals of childish laughter drifted through the French windows from the terrace. "Archie didn't marry anyone to spy on her."

"No. Though not on moral grounds, I think. I may be quite fortunate that he was never presented with the opportunity. It might be the one thing that would have persuaded him to try matrimony. Then he'd have turned honorable about it, and where would I be? Besides, I'm not sure I could have competed with the fascination of an agent."

"Lady Frances, it's quite obvious to an outside observer that no one could compete with you when it comes to Archibald Davenport."

Frances smiled, but Mélanie was sure she caught a spot of color beneath the other woman's rouge. "In truth, I sometimes think the lot of you who are agents belong to a fraternity as closed at the Elsinore League to those of us on the outside."

Mélanie took another sip of wine. She could appreciate the flavor more now. "It's more like we're all locked in a prison together."

Frances lifted a carefully plucked brow. "Don't pretend you don't enjoy it, my dear. I think that's part of why Malcolm loves you. Knowing your true identity, I can understand it even better. It's quite apparent Malcolm enjoys it as well, far more than he admits." She paused a moment. "He takes after his father."

Mélanie met Frances's gaze, the weight of all they had not

yet discussed descending on her shoulders. "Lady Frances—It was my decision. To marry Malcolm. Not Raoul's. Raoul may have gone along with it. But it was unequivocally mine."

Frances plucked a loose thread from the lace frill on her sleeve. "He didn't tell you he was Malcolm's father, did he?"

"No. I was furious with him for not telling me, when I first found out."

"And now?" Frances asked.

Mélanie fingered the white gold chain of her bracelet. "I know it sounds mad, but I think he thought he was protecting both of us. And Colin."

"It does sound mad," Frances agreed. "In precisely the way Raoul's always been a madman."

Mélanie stared at her husband's aunt's gaze. "So—"

Frances reached for her wine. "My dear Mélanie. I've known Raoul since before you were born. He has a great deal to answer for. But God knows, so do I, as well. It would take more than this to end our friendship."

A weight she'd scarcely been able to acknowledge eased in Mélanie's chest. "I'm so glad."

"Besides, I have a feeling Malcolm wouldn't forgive me otherwise."

Mélanie smoothed the skirt of her dinner dress, a patterned silk in shades of wine and black she'd had made up while they were staying with Hortense. Part of her new life. "They've—it's rather extraordinary. How they've learned to get on."

"Yes." Frances smiled. "And good for both of them. I've wanted Malcolm to learn the truth about Raoul for years. A bit ironic now."

The intricate pattern of the gown blurred before Mélanie's

eyes. "There's a lot between them. That goes back to before either of them knew me. The wonder is it wasn't smashed to bits."

"Perhaps airing the truth about you allowed them to share other truths, as well."

Mélanie fingered the clasp on her bracelet. It had been a gift from Malcolm, before he learned the truth. "I probably would have married Malcolm, even if Raoul had told me the truth. I didn't really understand what the marriage meant to Malcolm. And I've never been able to resist a challenge."

She was prepared to see a flash of anger or at least disquiet in Frances's eyes, but Frances nodded. "I expect you would have done. I rather think I might be disappointed if you said otherwise."

"Disappointed?"

"Men often assume women are swayed by emotions. I can admire your having the courage of your convictions."

Mélanie gave a smile, but she could taste the bleakness of it. "I don't know that I'll ever forgive myself."

"Oh, but you have to, my dear." Frances leaned forwards and squeezed her hand.

"For the children's sake and Malcolm's?"

"Yes, but mostly for your own. Trust me, I know. How on earth do you think I've managed to go on and be quite ridiculously happy, despite Alistair?"

The self-loathing in her voice hit Mélanie like a shock of cold water. She was used to it from Malcolm. From Raoul. From herself at times. But not from Malcolm's pragmatic aunt. "It doesn't sound as though Arabella blamed you for Alistair. I'm quite sure Malcolm doesn't."

"No, I don't believe he does." Frances tucked a loose curl into its pins. "And I don't think Arabella did. But that doesn't

311

mean I don't blame myself."

"So Alistair Rannoch recruited Conte Vincenzo into the Elsinore League?" Cordelia asked.

The children were in bed at last, and the adults, including Blanca and Addison, were gathered in the salon sharing coffee and information.

"It sounds that way from Margaret's account," Raoul said. He glanced at Archie.

Archie, sitting on one of the sofas with his arm round Frances, was frowning. "I know the League have international members. It's been a subject of debate, with some favoring a deliberate campaign to broaden the League's reach outside Britain. But I never heard Vincenzo mentioned specifically. Of course I don't know the names of a number of League members. Which makes those papers the Carbonari were trading to Carfax all the more priceless."

"And Sofia Vincenzo copied them from her father," Malcolm said. "Which means Vincenzo had access to high-level League information."

Archie stretched his bad leg out, a thoughtful look on his face. "Higher level than I have. One can't but wonder if Alistair simply saw an opportunity to recruit someone from abroad, or if he had a specific goal in mind when he recruited Vincenzo." He cast a glance at his betrothed.

Frances looked up at Archie, gaze frank. "Alistair never talked about the League to me. I'm not sure he appreciated my mind like you do."

Archie grinned, lifted her hand, and kissed it. "A lot was wasted on Alistair."

312

"Who do you think has the papers?" Laura asked.

"A good question," Malcolm said. "Sofia, Kit, and Enrico presumably would have no reason to have taken them, as they wanted Thurston to collect them and complete the exchange. Thurston doesn't have them—unless he's lying, but he could simply say he'd already sent them to Carfax if he didn't want to share them." Malcolm cast a glance at his father.

"No," Raoul said. "Not that I wouldn't have taken them in a heartbeat if I'd known of their existence. But I wouldn't have kept them from you."

Malcolm turned to look at Mélanie.

"Darling," she said, making her voice playful. "Why on earth would I have kept it secret, either?"

Malcolm grinned. "Just checking with the two people in this room most likely to have been able to pull it off. Considering that neither Archie nor Harry was present." He leaned forwards. "I need to talk to Percy Shelley tomorrow, to see what he and Vincenzo were talking or arguing about when Selena saw them. Though Shelley strikes me as an even unlikelier Elsinore League candidate than Byron."

"I could see Shelley or Byron or Mary taking the papers, though," Mélanie said. "If they'd known about them. Which doesn't seem likely."

Malcolm nodded. He looked at the others. "And we need to continue questioning the other guests and the servants."

"I spoke with Tomaso, Conte Vincenzo's valet, today." Addison set down his coffee. "A close-mouthed man. He quite refused to be drawn into gossip, despite all my best efforts. Admirable loyalty to his employer, but not helpful from our perspective. I did mention I'd heard rumors the conte might be involved in some sort of secret organization, and from his instant denial, I'd hazard a guess he knows

313

something about the Elsinore League, or at least that his master was involved in something secret."

"Interesting," Archie said, "given the League's level of secrecy. Though sometimes, as well you know, a man needs his valet to keep secrets. But it could suggest that Tomaso is something of an agent himself."

Addison nodded. "That was my thought. He did say that the button Mrs. Rannoch found quite definitely didn't come from any of the conte's garments, though he had no idea whom it might belong to. And"—he coughed—"reading between the lines, I had the sense the conte hasn't lacked for female company on his stay here, though I had the sense he was dallying with someone belowstairs."

"So do I," Blanca said, "I spoke with Rosa, the contessa's maid, this morning while Laura was with the children. Her eyes were red and she didn't try to deny being distraught over the conte's death. Apparently, she was with the contessa when the conte and contessa still lived together. She appears to have had a soft spot for the conte, and very likely more than that. She has long, dark hair untouched by gray. I suspect the hair Mélanie found in the conte's bed is hers."

"Good God," Frances said. "One likes to think one can trust one's maid. The thought of her betraying one with one's husband—"

"The contessa must be very soft hearted or very obtuse not to know," Cordelia said.

"Unless she doesn't care," Laura said. "She doesn't seem to have harbored ill will towards her husband, and I doubt she knew he was working against Lord Thurston."

"Yes, but I can't imagine she wanted him to know her secrets," Cordelia said. "On the other hand, I can't really see the contessa killing her estranged husband over an affair with her maid. And as for the maid—" She looked at Blanca.

"I can't swear Rosa didn't kill the conte, obviously," Blanca said. "But her distress and shock seemed genuine, not cover or the remorse of a murderer. But I wouldn't say she's overly loyal to the contessa. Mrs. Smythe's maid, Hibbert, by contrast, is fiercely loyal to her mistress. And quite blunt about Mr. Smythe's treatment of her." Blanca shivered. "She also insisted that Mrs. Smythe and Lord Byron aren't lovers, which fits with what they both told you. I can talk to the chambermaids tomorrow."

"And I can talk to the other valets and footmen," Addison said.

Raoul reached for his coffee. "I'll continue my rounds of the guests on the contessa's list. So far it hasn't yielded much, but at least it lets us rule some people out."

"A lot of revelations today," Mélanie said, "but in some ways it feels as though we're no closer to the truth."

"We know about the Elsinore League's papers," Malcolm said. "But damned if I have an idea where they are."

Harry grinned and leaned forwards to clap him on the shoulder. "It's only been one day, Rannoch. Even you have limits."

CHAPTER 25

Harry shrugged out of his coat in his and Cordelia's bedchamber at the villa. "With everything else, I never asked if you managed to get Caro's letter delivered to Byron?"

"Yes. And asked Byron to be kind. I hope I didn't do more harm than good." Cordelia unfastened the second of her sapphire earrings. The silver stuff of her gown fell about her in soft folds, reminding him of the night they'd met. "To be back in the midst of that insanity."

"Caro and Byron?"

"Caro and Byron, and who I used to be myself." Cordelia dropped the earring in her jewel box with a clatter. "Byron always drove me mad, for Caro's sake. But I have a horrible feeling I used to be far more like him than I care to admit."

Harry unwound his neckcloth. "You couldn't be like Byron if you tried, Cordy. I haven't spent that much time with the man, but I can recognize a poseur. And a brilliant poet, but that's another matter. You've always been true to yourself."

Cordelia unfastened the diamond bracelet he had given her, back before their marriage had fallen apart, before they had miraculously remade it. "I liked causing scandals. Flirting outrageously. Wearing the most outrageous gown I could find. Living down to people's expectations."

"Society had rejected you." Harry tossed the crumpled neckcloth on a chair after his coat and started on his waistcoat buttons. "I can quite see the impulse to reject society. I might have felt the same myself if I'd given a damn about society in the first place."

"But you were sensible enough not to, which rather proves my point." Cordelia put the bracelet in her jewel case. The diamonds flashed in the candlelight as she pressed the flower links smooth. "Even in reacting against society, I was playing their game. I'd probably have gone further if it hadn't been for Livia, and even then I wasn't as careful of my reputation as I should have been for her sake."

"I hope to God our daughters grow up knowing not to care for society's opinion. One could say you set a good example."

Cordelia gave a faint smile. "That's a shocking twisting of the facts from a ruthlessly objective scholar, Harry."

"There's not really such thing as objective scholarship, my darling. One just has to be candid about one's biases. And I fully admit mine are on your side. Because I know who you are."

Cordelia shook her head. For a moment her gaze looked almost wistful. "You've always seen me as better than I am, Harry. Caro and Byron ran roughshod over other people's feelings for the sake of the effect they could cause. And I did much the same."

Harry tossed the waistcoat on the chair after his coat and

317

neckcloth and turned, leaning against the chairback, to regard his wife. "You didn't cause the first one because you liked causing scandals. You caused it because you were in love with George."

Cordelia met his gaze. For a long time, he'd avoided all mention of George Chase's name. Then he'd realized that made it worse for her.

"I thought I was," she said. "And you're right, I thought that supposed love justified anything."

"I'm not sure you were wrong," Harry said.

"Harry!" Cordelia's fingers closed on her jewel case.

"It wouldn't justify leaving the children, but a husband you'd made it quite clear you never loved in the first place?" Harry stayed where he was, leaning against the chair, distancing himself from his wife as though she was at the other end of a telescope. "I wouldn't say that justifies deceiving said husband. But leaving him openly? You know I've never been one to hold a great deal of respect for the marriage tie simply on its own. I certainly don't think it should keep anyone in shackles."

Cordelia's fingers whitened. "Our marriage was never shackles, Harry."

"Wasn't it?" He subdued the impulse to cross the room and stroke his fingers against her cheek. They needed to talk about this, and they could only do it with distance. "It tied you, in the eyes of the world, to a man you really had no desire to be with at that point. Whatever's between us now, there's no sense pretending you'd have married me at all if you hadn't thought it was preferable to remaining single in your parents' household."

"That's not—" Cordelia bit back what she'd been about to say. She could have a scholar's ruthless honesty. "I'm not

318

denying I did you a great wrong in marrying you, Harry—"

"My darling." Every muscle strained not to take her in his arms. "I did you a great wrong in proposing to you."

"—But that year wasn't all unhappy. Not on my side, at least."

Images danced in his memory. Cordelia returned from a ball, startling him by looking into his study, dropping into a chair, kicking off her satin slippers, offering surprisingly keen insights into the bit of translation he was working on. Meeting her gaze over the morning papers, laughing together in unexpected, instinctive shared humor. Pulling her to him in her darkened bedchamber, awkward, terrified of putting a foot wrong, yet at the same time sure her response was not entirely feigned.

"Nor on mine," he said. "I could have lived on such memories for the rest of my life."

For a moment, their gazes held. Then she turned her head away, as though she couldn't bear the pressure of what she saw in his eyes. "And I threw it away for a mirage I thought was what is laughably called true love."

Harry's fingers tightened on the chairback. To see such self-torment in one's wife's gaze. To know another man—a man one despised—was the cause of it and be powerless to do anything about it. "For what it's worth, I think it was more than a mirage," he said. "You can feel real love for an undeserving object."

Cordelia's mouth twisted. "So one can. You felt real love for me."

"Cordy—It's not the same thing at all."

"Isn't it? Or wasn't it then?" She pulled a pin from her hair and stared at it between her fingers. "I hardly did anything to make myself worthy of your regard. I made an attempt to be a wife for a time, but ultimately I threw what you offered in good faith back in your face." She pulled another pin from her hair. "I always liked William Lamb. I used to bemoan Caro not seeing what was in front of her, and wasting her adoration on an undeserving object like Byron. But I never could quite admit I'd done the same myself. Though, for all his faults, Byron is hardly as undeserving as George." Her lips curled round her former lover's name. "I thought that when Suzanne told me the truth about her past. We both betrayed our husbands. But she betrayed Malcolm because she believed in something worth believing in. I believed in George, God help me."

Harry forced his hands not to close into fists. He remembered the look on O'Roarke's face when Laura had mentioned the Duke of Trenchard hitting her. Harry had planted George Chase a facer once when he first discovered Chase was Cordelia's lover. But that had been in anger over his wife's betrayal. Now Harry wanted to throttle Chase for what he had put Cordelia through, and for the ghosts that still lurked in her gaze in unguarded moments. "George has a great deal to answer for."

"Granted. But I wasn't his creature. I made my own decisions. Thinking back to what I put you through, I wonder how Archie could have not hated me."

"Archie's far too discerning to have done anything of the sort. He knew what I'd got you into by marrying you. He knew what George had put you through. He knew—what you meant to me." Harry drew a breath. They had talked more in the past three years than he once would have thought possible. But there were still myriad things they had never said. Things they probably never would say, some with good reason. And yet—"Even if I'd died at Waterloo, I wouldn't

320

have regretted a moment we spent together," he said.

Cordelia's gaze locked on his own. "Harry—"

"I was willfully blind to who you were and what you needed, for which I will never forgive myself. But for myself I have no regrets."

For a moment, it seemed as though the air between them might shatter like crystal if either of them moved. Then Cordelia closed the distance between them and put her mouth to his. "Do you have any idea how much I love you?"

She was in his arms, the warmth of her mouth, the scent of her skin, the brush of her hair against his cheek. But, for a moment, she seemed as far away as she had in the Devonshire House ballroom the night they met, her silver-beaded gown sparkling in the light from the French window behind her, her hair gleaming golden in the candlelight, her eyes blazing with life. A creature of moonlight and fire.

Because, of course, he'd never be sure which had come first, love or guilt. Which was strongest now. And what would have happened between them if he hadn't pushed her into marriage when she was vulnerable.

Which didn't change the fact that she was here in his arms now. Harry pulled his wife to him and returned her kiss.

Laura adjusted the tin shade of the nightlight in the night nursery, pulled the covers up about Chloe, and patted the puppy curled up at the foot of her bed. She turned to see Raoul touch his fingers to Livia's hair and then kiss Emily, who was sharing a bed with the older Davenport daughter. He crossed the space between the beds and kissed Colin, as well, something he wouldn't have let himself do a few months ago. In fact, a few months ago, before they left London, he'd hung back in the doorway while she kissed the children and tucked them in. Now he did it as automatically as she did. Though there was nothing automatic about the look of wonder in his eyes.

Laura slipped past him into their bedchamber. Raoul followed her and pulled the door to behind them.

"I can't tell you how relieved I was to see you and Lady Frances both come out of the rose salon smiling," she said.

Raoul leaned against the closed door. "It went far better than I had any right to expect. Frances has never been one to see things through rose-colored glasses."

"No, I'd say she's remarkably clear sighted."

He shook his head. "I think I benefitted from the glow of her current happiness." He drew a quick breath. "I never thought to see Frances so contented."

His happiness for his friends was plain in his tone and expression. Yet, along with it, so much else. Laura slipped her arms round him and leaned her head against his back. "Don't."

"Don't what?"

His voice was light, but she'd seen it in his eyes all evening, in and about everything else, when Archie kissed Frances's hand, when they discussed wedding plans, when Chloe talked about the new baby. "Don't dwell on the things we can't have. Please."

"I'm not given to flights of fancy." His voice was carefully even.

"Ha." She tightened her arms round him. "I'm very happy for Frances and Archie, but they aren't us. And even if it weren't for Margaret, you've said often enough you aren't made for a domestic life."

He turned round in her arms and set his hands on her shoulders. "Is that what you think? That I'm happier this way?"

Laura drew a breath. They were stepping on ground they had carefully avoided since their affair began. Ground that threatened to unsettle the basis of that affair. And yet, not talking about it wouldn't make the issues go away. And if she was right about certain things, those issues were only going to get more complicated. "I think your work is vitally important to you. I'd never want to get in the way of that."

His gaze moved over her face. "What do you want, Laura?"

Unvoiced, scarcely thought feelings and impulses welled up in her chest and tightened her throat. "Jack and I made a mockery of marriage between us. I told you at the start that after Jack, I couldn't imagine ever wanting to tie myself to anyone that way again." And that was still true. Mostly. Well, not that she couldn't *imagine* it...

"I know what you said then."

"I want you," she said. "But I'm not denying what I want for myself because of it."

And yet, there were moments. The unexpected glow in Frances's eyes. Seeing Mélanie's and Malcolm's gazes meet. Harry wrapping his arm round Cordelia, in a way only an acknowledged couple could do in public.

He slid his hands down her arms to gather her hands together. His gaze was open, as it seldom was. "These past weeks have been among the happiest I've ever known."

With some lovers, the words would be an easy platitude. With him, they were anything but. Laura tightened her fingers over his own, her throat tight with tears that were equal parts joy and sorrow. "For me, as well. But I don't think that

323

changes where you think you belong."

He drew a breath, rough with unvoiced feelings. "You can't think I don't feel I belong here. But—For years after Waterloo, I was reacting. Trying to protect my people, to salvage something from the wreckage. Now, in Spain, there's a chance of real change. For the first time in three years I've been building something, instead of reacting."

"And you need to be part of the change. Part of you feels guilty for being gone so long."

"Sweetheart—"

Laura reached up to smooth his hair off his forehead. "It's all right. You wouldn't be the man I love if you felt differently." And somehow, whatever was to come, they would find a way to make it work. She just couldn't bear it if she was the cause of making him be untrue to himself.

Raoul's gaze had gone unusually bleak. "Margaret was right. I'm in no position to offer a woman a settled life."

"Define 'settled.' Or, better yet, kiss me."

Malcolm closed the door to the night nursery. "I think we're through the worst. In terms of telling our friends and family."

Mélanie, who had already moved to her dressing table, met his gaze. She smiled, but the bruised look was back in the depths of her eyes. "I'll own to distinct terror, equaled only by some of our most hair-raising missions. In truth, she couldn't have been kinder."

"Not a word I often associate with my aunt."

"She has an amazing ability to see things from another's viewpoint. Perhaps not surprising, given that she is your aunt."

"She'd be able to see things from your viewpoint. She believes in women making their own choices. I was more worried she'd murder O'Roarke. And it would have been distinctly uncomfortable to have them at daggers drawn." It would, in fact, have cut him in two, which he suspected his wife saw all too clearly.

He moved to Mélanie's side and slid his arms round her. "One less thing to worry about."

Mélanie put her hands on his chest. "Your grandfather doesn't know."

Malcolm gave a wry smile at the thought of his grandfather, the Duke of Strathdon, a Shakespearean scholar who spent most of his time in Scotland. Strathdon had written to them once since they'd left Britain. Unlike Frances he'd made no attempt to inquire into the reasons for their abrupt departure but had merely said he trusted they were enjoying themselves and he'd be particularly interested to know what they thought of *Hamlet* in Italian translation if they got a chance to see it. "Judging by his reaction to the possibility of Alistair having been a French agent, I think Grandfather will take it in stride."

"I hope so. The world still doesn't know."

"We have our own world here. The rest of it matters less. Especially now so many of the people we care about are here."

"They won't be here forever."

"But they can come back." He shut his mind to Kit's questions about Parliament, and the longing they'd stirred. He drew his wife closer and kissed her forehead. "Not only are so many of the people we care about here, they're happy. And in charity with us and each other. We may be in the midst of a damnable coil of an investigation, but let's at least enjoy that."

Mélanie laughed. "Darling, you're an incurable optimist."

"Perish the thought," he said, and kissed her.

Mélanie returned his embrace with an eagerness that told of her relief at their having got through the day. But at length, she drew back and said, "We haven't talked about the other piece of news."

"Which other piece of news?" Malcolm asked, tucking a curl behind her ear.

"The other news involving Frances, I should have said. Frances and Archie."

They'd received Frances's letter revealing her betrothal and pregnancy only that morning, he realized. It seemed an eternity ago, yet he and Mélanie had scarcely had a moment to talk alone, and what time they'd had had been consumed by the investigation. "I've been guilty of thinking of her as my mother's sister."

"She is your mother's sister, darling. And I'm sure she wants you to think of her as such."

"Which doesn't make her too old for all sorts of new beginnings."

"Well, no. Hopefully no one's ever too old for that."

"It's not that I saw her as old." He dug a hand into his hair. "Fanny's never seemed old. But she's always been there, living in the South Audley Street house, with her string of lovers, whom she took lightly however exalted they might be. Cutting a swath through society, raising her brow at any hint of sentimentality or romanticism."

"You must remember when her first husband was alive. When Chloe was born."

"Oh, yes. I remember when all my cousins were born, even Cedric. But none of that really seemed to change Fanny.

Uncle George spent most of his time at his club. The house always seemed to be hers. I never saw her doing something as radical as—" He shook his head. "Falling in love."

Mélanie tilted her head back to look at him. "You had to have known her feelings were engaged with Archie."

"Yes, but I didn't realize how deeply. Falling in love's not the sort of thing my family do. I'm not sure my mother ever let herself fall in love after Peter of Courland, even with O'Roarke."

"I think Raoul would agree," Mélanie said. "But Allie undoubtedly loves Geoff. Gisèle loves Andrew. Judith loves her husband. I think you love me."

"You know perfectly well I love you to distraction, my darling. But look how long it took me to admit it."

"Perhaps Lady Frances has taken a lesson from the younger generation." Mélanie sat on the dressing table bench and drew him down beside her. "From things she's said, I think she's been able to enjoy being a mother more with Chloe than with the older children. The new baby should give her a chance to continue that. And watching Archie with Livia and Dru, I've always thought it sad he didn't get to raise a child from babyhood."

"Oh, yes." Malcolm slid his arm round his wife. "Perhaps they're the ones to have taught us a lesson."

"What?"

He dropped a kiss on her hair. "That one can remake one's life." He lifted his head and looked down at her for a moment. "Harry says David and Simon are thinking about taking the children and going abroad."

Mélanie's eyes widened.

"I know," Malcolm said. "There's been no hint in their letters. But then, they've both always been cautious in writing and they have extra reason to be so now. David only told Harry in confidence because he wanted advice on leaving secretly. Harry hasn't even told Cordy."

"It's probably the strongest move they could make to put Carfax in check," Mélanie said.

"Yes. I'm only impressed David saw it." His last, bitter confrontation with David in a sitting room at Brooks's echoed in Malcolm's head. "I've accused you sometimes of thinking I'm too much a prisoner of my background. I begin to wonder if I've done the same with David."

"You love David. It's easy to be afraid of losing someone one loves."

"And I should have given him the same credit I ask you to give me?" Malcolm drew a breath. Despite the cautious overtures in the last letters they'd exchanged, the pain of his parting with David still bit him in the throat. He didn't want Mel ever to see how strongly. She was burdening herself enough as it was.

"Well." Mélanie smiled, though her gaze told him she saw more than he wished. "You constantly surprise me, darling. In this, as in many things." She put her hands on his chest. "If David and Simon try to flee Carfax, they're going to need help."

"Yes." Malcolm put his hands over her own. "I only hope they'll let us give it to them."

CHAPTER 26

Malcolm came onto the terrace in the wash of early morning light to find Raoul alone at the table with coffee and the papers.

"Off to the Shelleys'?" his father asked.

"When it's a decent hour to call. I have a feeling poets aren't early risers any more than my wife is." Malcolm dropped down at the table and poured himself a cup of coffee.

"The Montagus and Vincenzos will be preoccupied with the funeral this morning," Raoul said. "But I can continue talking to guests who were at the picnic. The Lewises are next on my list."

"Even if all you can do is rule them out, it's an immeasurable help in getting the picture into focus." Malcolm took a sip of coffee. "I can't tell you how relieved I am that you and Aunt Frances are still on speaking terms."

Raoul gave a faint smile. "She was easier on me than I deserved."

"She knows you."

Raoul shot a look at him. "She had a right to be angry. You have a right to be angry, Malcolm."

"Everyone keeps saying that." Malcolm's voice cut with a force that surprised him. "But I fail to see what purpose my getting angry would serve."

"It might make it easier for you to manage all this."

"I'm managing perfectly well." Malcolm tossed down a swallow of coffee, a little too quickly. It stung his throat. "I know how you and Aunt Frances worry, but I'm not going to crack."

"I don't doubt it." Raoul turned his cup on the tabletop. "Malcolm, you're the most forbearing man imaginable—"

"You keep saying that, as well."

"Because it's true. That you even can meet me with equanimity is beyond wonderful. That you allow me in your home surpasses all expectation. That you actually have me living here—"

"Oh, for God's sake, O'Roarke. You're my father."

"I'm also the man who set the woman you later married to spy on you," Raoul said, in the same measured voice in which he might recite data about an opposing force. "Who let you marry her, knowing you are my son and that she was carrying a child I'd fathered. Who used the information she took from you against your side. Who met with her in secret—"

"Stop it."

"It's not a pretty picture." Raoul spread his hands flat on the table. "But it's the truth. An ugly truth that you must have to live with every day you look at me—at breakfast, at dinner, playing with your children. Mélanie was younger and she didn't know you were my son. I had two and a half decades more experience, I knew you were my son, I knew what we

330

shared. I played on the man I knew you were for my own ends."

Malcolm stared into his father's gray eyes, granite hard in the sunlight, even more implacable than usual. But he could read O'Roarke's deceptions better than he once had done. "You're trying to provoke me. Because you think it's good for me? Or because you feel guilty yourself? In either case, I fail to see where it gets us."

Raoul returned his gaze, then let out a rough laugh. "My God. You always see five moves ahead. Including moves some of us don't realize we're making."

"We're not chess pieces, O'Roarke. And I know you enough now to know you don't really believe we are."

Raoul leaned back in his chair, his gaze stripped unexpectedly open. It was unusual to see him that way. But not as unusual as it once had been. "We've talked about Mélanie. But you wouldn't be human if there weren't times you've hated *me*."

Malcolm met his father's gaze again, glanced out at the shifting waters of the lake, tried to cast his mind back. An elegant, anonymous hotel room. O'Roarke in a paisley dressing gown, admitting perhaps more than he had ever meant to about Mélanie and her marriage to Malcolm, and his own feelings, but still holding in most of what he felt and thought. The rage that had choked Malcolm, more biting because he had just begun to accept, with a sort of cautious wonder, that Raoul O'Roarke was his father and that the bond between them might possibly be more than mere biology. Yet also the understanding, by the end of that interview, of just what Raoul had given up when Mélanie married Malcolm, and what it had cost him.

"At the beginning," Malcolm said. "I hated the whole

situation, and I was angry at everyone connected to it. You. Mélanie. Myself. But even then I knew how you felt about Mélanie. In some ways it was rather a great trust, your deciding she'd be better off with me."

"That's a remarkably generous way of looking at it."

"That's a truth that was abundantly plain to me, even in the first flush of anger. As I said then, part of me knew how you felt about her without admitting it, even before I learned the truth about her working for you. It was hard enough for you to give her up. You'd never have done so if you hadn't thought she and Colin would be better off."

"I could have suggested she marry you and not spy on you."

"That would have been doing a disservice to a cause you believed in. Far more than I believed in my own. If working for Carfax can even be called a cause. Anyway, I doubt Mel would have married me without the incentive of spying. Not then." Malcolm frowned for a moment. "I think I'd think the worse of her if she'd been able to walk away so easily." He leaned back in his chair. "Mind you, I think you were a bit overconfident of my abilities as both a husband and father."

"Obviously not, given the results. I haven't ever thanked you, have I?" Raoul said.

"For raising your son? You have, in a hundred ways, without putting it into words."

"He couldn't have a better father." Raoul's voice was low and quiet and somehow more intense than Malcolm had ever heard it.

"I think he's happy," Malcolm said. "I don't think he ever doubts he's loved. Those are perhaps the most important things one can give a child."

Raoul drew an uneven breath. "Still. Rationality—for

which you have a genius—"

"—I wonder where I got that from?"

"—is one thing. Anger isn't the least rational."

Malcolm turned his head to stare at the enemy spymaster who was his father. "I loved you." The words spilled out with unexpected force, propelled by a tangle of emotions he'd barely acknowledged he was feeling. "As a boy—I wouldn't have put it that way, but I did."

"And I betrayed you."

"No. Yes, in a way, but I really do understand, for all no one can seem to accept that I do. It's all the years before—" His voice roughened with feelings he'd scarcely even articulated to himself. "You never told me the truth."

Raoul's gaze shifted across Malcolm's face. "About your birth?"

"Among other things. I can see why—But I didn't even know the truth of who you *were*."

Raoul's hand slid across the desk, then stopped. "I told you as much as I could."

"As much as you thought you could. But we were still close when I was no longer a boy. Why the devil didn't you—"

"Stay out of your way in the Peninsula?"

"Try to recruit me."

Raoul stared at him. The stir of the wind in the cypress branches echoed over the still terrace. "To spy for France? Against Britain? You wouldn't have done it."

"You sound very sure."

"I am. You're very loyal, Malcolm."

"So are you. So is Mélanie. The question, as you so often say, is loyal to what?"

"You love your country, Malcolm."

333

"England? I'm Scots. And I'm actually as much Irish and Spanish, thanks to you, and French, thanks to Arabella's mother."

"None of which changes where you grew up or how you view the world."

Images tugged at his mind. The plane trees in Berkeley Square. The rocks and roses tumbling down to the beach at Dunmykel. The walnut shells round the backbenches in Parliament. The glow of moonlight on the Thames. "Being loyal to a country doesn't mean taking on the burdens of the men who run it."

"I don't think you ever did that."

"I did their errands. And hated myself more and more. Until I realized that I agreed more with my wife who'd been spying on me, and my father who set her to spy on me, than I did with my own spymaster."

"Malcolm—I always knew you'd make a brilliant agent. But I hoped to God you wouldn't follow that path. You're much too decent."

"Don't. That's what Mel does. Don't put me in a bubble."

"I'm not. I've always admired you more than I can say."

"Even when I was doing Carfax's dirty work?"

"You didn't—"

"Damn it, O'Roarke." Malcolm's voice shook, raw with unvoiced feelings. "*You trusted me with Mel. But you left me to Carfax.*"

Raoul's gaze stilled on Malcolm's face. "Carfax probably saved your life."

Malcolm's gaze jerked to his wrists. The scars had faded to the palest of lines. He'd had bandages under his shirt cuffs that morning in Carfax's study when Carfax had offered him employment. "Giving me a sense of purpose? Perhaps. Other things could have done that."

Raoul drew an uneven breath. "By the time I knew—"

"That I'd tried to kill myself."

"—you were already on your way to the Peninsula. If I'd known in time—I'd have come back to see you. As quickly as I could."

"Would you have tried to stop me from working for Carfax?"

"I'm not sure." Raoul twisted his signet ring round his finger. "God knows I wasn't happy to learn you were working for him. I smashed a wineglass when I heard of it. But I could recognize, even then, what it meant for you to have a purpose and employment."

"And you still didn't think if you'd—"

"Malcolm—" Raoul leaned forwards. "It's hard enough to go on a mission, as you know. Only interacting with people for a few days, or even hours, the betrayals hit home. Harder still to do what Mélanie did. To get close to people over years—not just you, but your friends and colleagues and comrades—and reveal their secrets. But to spy on one's own people—That's not a life I'd wish on anyone, and certainly not my son."

"I wasn't working for Carfax yet. I could have gone to Spain and worked for your side without giving away British secrets."

"There'd still have been people you knew on the opposite side. People you went to school with."

"There must have been people you went to school with on the British side."

"There were." Raoul's voice held echoes. "On all sides."

Myriad past betrayals shot through Malcolm's memory. "So instead—"

335

"You'd have ended up hating yourself."

Malcolm watched a gull soar against the blue sky. "What do you think happened with my working for Carfax?"

Raoul drew a rough breath. "That should be on Carfax's head, not yours."

"My God, Raoul, you know it's not that simple. You know we're all responsible for our actions, to some degree. That's what you taught me. Mel would bite your head off for suggesting she isn't responsible for the choices she made. And Mel would never have worked for Carfax."

"Malcolm, we all made choices—"

"That we regret, and none of us sleeps well. But I made them in the service of a man I never agreed with. Who just tried to destroy nearly everyone I love."

"How Carfax used Mélanie's past isn't on your head."

"No. But it reinforces how disgusted I am with myself for working for him." Malcolm scraped a hand through his hair. "Kit Montagu didn't tell me about the Levellers, because he sees me as the enemy. An ally of Carfax. A representative of everything he's fighting against."

"Montagu's young. He doesn't understand—"

"No, but I can see his perspective." Malcolm studied his father. "You believed in your cause. You almost died for it, time and again. You fought for it at Waterloo. You gave up Mélanie and Colin and any thought of a life of your own. If it meant that much to you, and if I meant to you what you say—what I now believe—didn't you ever want to share it with me?"

Malcolm was ready for one of his father's expert fencer's deflections, but Raoul surprised him by meeting his gaze with the look of one who has let down his guard. "I wanted to share everything I believed in with you. Everything I hoped

336

for the world. The world I wanted for you. But I never wanted you to make the compromises I made."

"Christ, Raoul. Don't you believe one can't accomplish anything without some sort of compromise?"

"I suppose—I wanted you to have a chance to be a better man than I was."

Malcolm returned his father's gaze. "Whereas I'd have been quite proud to be remotely like you."

The words settled in Raoul's eyes. "My dear Malcolm. That's—"

"The truth." Malcolm drew a breath. The air was fragrant with the promise of the new day. "Instead, I became a man neither of us can be particularly proud of. To put a charitable construction on it."

Raoul's hand shot across the table to grip Malcolm's arm. "For God's sake." Malcolm had never heard such force in Raoul's voice. "I won't have you talk that way. I've always been proud of you, Malcolm. Never doubt that. The world would be a better place with more people like you."

Something unacknowledged tightened in Malcolm's chest. He gave a twisted smile. "Yes, well, you're a bit biased. You are my father, after all."

"Rannoch." Shelley held out his hand in the study of the villa he shared with his wife and Byron. "Last time, your charming wife called on us. Do you take investigating in turns?"

"We share a great deal." Malcolm shook Shelley's hand.

"Should I take your visit to mean that the questions are more serious this time?"

337

"Shouldn't Mary Wollstonecraft's son-in-law know better than to make the mistake of thinking a woman is less serious than her husband?"

"Touché, Rannoch. Or more dangerous."

"Oh, my wife's far more dangerous than I." Malcolm settled into the velvet-covered chair Shelley waved him to.

Shelley laughed. He couldn't have the least idea how much Malcolm was telling the literal truth. "A glass of wine?"

"Thank you." It was not yet noon, but in Italy they drank wine at all times of the day.

Shelley put a glass of red wine in his hand. "Dangerous or not, I assume this isn't a social call. If it's more about Byron—"

"It's not. It's about you."

Shelley's hand faltered filling his own glass. He set down the decanter. "You surprise me."

"Do I? I'd have thought you'd at least have been wondering if we'd find out."

Shelley stared at droplets of red wine spattered on the glossy wood of the table for a moment, then picked up a napkin and blotted them out. "Find out what?"

"Whatever you and Conte Vincenzo were quarreling about the day before he was killed."

Shelley gave a soft laugh, though it was rough with underlying tension. "I knew you were clever. Byron warned me of it yesterday, and I said I already knew. I should have realized. I should have had an answer ready."

Malcolm took a sip of wine. "Which would be a very clever answer to have prepared."

Shelley met his gaze. "You're the agent, Rannoch. I'm a poet."

"Anyone who's read your poetry knows you're a clever

338

man, Shelley."

Shelley dropped into a chair across from him, wineglass in hand. "We met Vincenzo in Florence. You know that. I suppose you could say he was part of the circles we moved in. Sofia was kind to Mary. Vincenzo himself was surprisingly sympathetic when our—when we lost our daughter." Shelley's fingers whitened round his glass. He stared across the salon for a moment. "He said it was every parent's nightmare. I remember thinking that love of our children, and fear of losing them, unites parents across all sorts of lines. Countries. Politics. Birth. Fortune." He tossed down a swallow of wine. "Vincenzo has—had—a handsome fortune. While Mary and I—It's cheaper to live abroad, but God knows one still has expenses. And if one keeps company with people like the Montagus and the Vincenzos, one has to keep up."

Malcolm began to have a glimmering of where this was headed. "Conte Vincenzo offered to loan you money after your daughter died?"

"No." Shelley set down his glass with care. "He offered to loan us money two months earlier, soon after we met him. We were finding Italy more expensive than we anticipated. We had Mary's sister Claire to care for. As well as our son and daughter." He drew a breath. "Vincenzo's offer came at a timely moment and seemed made in good faith. I accepted. He made it sound as though there'd be no hurry about paying him back. Then, when we saw him here—his attitude was very different."

"He demanded repayment?"

Shelley snatched up his wine and took a drink. "And wasn't kind about waiting. He said his own circumstances had changed and he needed immediate repayment. He reminded me that the terms allowed him to ask for it at any point, though at the time we signed the papers he had said it was purely a formality." Shelley drew a breath. "Needless to say, we don't have the money."

"And that's what you were quarreling about three days ago?"

"Not exactly." Shelley stared into his wine. "Vincenzo made the demand the day before. Three days ago, he offered me another option if we couldn't come up with the money."

Malcolm took a sip of wine. Even in death, Conte Vincenzo continued to surprise him. "Which was?"

Shelley moved his glass on the tabletop, studying the reflection of the red wine in the polished wood. "He offered to forgo the debt if I would get him information on the Levellers."

"The young Radicals currently active in London?" Of whom Kit Montagu was a member. "They put out some rather good pamphlets. I wouldn't have thought of them as particularly dangerous." More the sort of group to draw Carfax's fire than the Elsinore League's, he'd have thought. Though now there was the fact of Kit talking to the Carbonari.

Shelley shifted in his chair. "That's what I said to Vincenzo. He said his interest in them was his business, not mine."

"And he was willing to entirely forgo your debt if you got him this information?"

"No." Shelley reached for his wine. His fingers froze round the stem of the glass. "That was just the first part. He wanted me to write to a friend and get him to write back to me. About certain things."

It wouldn't have been such a surprising demand for the

Elsinore League to make to an agent. For them to have made it to Shelley was—bizarre. "What friend?" Malcolm asked. "I'm sorry, but in the circumstances I need to ask."

"I know. And you need to know." Shelley took a drink of wine. "He wanted to me to write to Simon Tanner and get him to commit—indiscreet facts—about his relationship with Worsley to paper."

Malcolm's fingers tightened. He forced them to unclench before he snapped his wineglass stem. "What did you say?"

"Do you think I'd do that to a friend?" Shelley scraped a hand over his face. "Not that I think Simon would have been stupid enough to put anything like that in writing, whatever I tried. I told Vincenzo that. He said he was sure I could pull it off."

"Did you ask him why he wanted this letter?"

"Of course. He said that was his business." Shelley shook his head, then stared at Malcolm for a moment. "Can you think why, Rannoch? Vincenzo hasn't been in Britain for years. Simon would only have been a boy. Why in God's name—"

"I'm not sure," Malcolm said, though he could hazard a fair guess. "How did you leave things with Vincenzo?"

"With me refusing to do as he asked, and Vincenzo telling me I had forty-eight hours to reconsider before he took legal action." Shelley met Malcolm's gaze. "I'm not stupid, Rannoch. I had an excellent motive to have killed him."

"Which is why you didn't tell me."

"Of course. I know I didn't kill him. No sense in your wasting time running after the wrong suspect."

"Thoughtful of you." Malcolm took a drink of wine. "Of course, I don't suppose you wanted to find yourself a suspect, either."

"No. Byron may find it romantic, but to me it merely seems devilishly uncomfortable."

"You're hardly the only one with a motive," Malcolm said.

Although Shelley's actually was one of the strongest they'd uncovered. On the other hand, if Shelley hadn't killed him, the revelations also meant he might have insights into the conte. "You saw Vincenzo twice in the days before he was killed," Malcolm said. "Did he say anything that might give you insights into why he was murdered?"

"Assuming I didn't kill him?" Shelley frowned into his wine. "Our conversations naturally focused on the debt and his demands. If he was afraid of anyone, I'm probably the last person he'd have confided in."

"Byron and Mrs. Smythe saw him meeting with a woman by the lake, but couldn't recognize who the lady was. Did you see him with a woman? Or hear him say anything that could help us identify who it was?"

"A woman?" Percy shook his head. "No. But I did see him talking with John Smythe."

"At the picnic? We know they quarreled then."

"No, I didn't see them at the picnic. I avoided Vincenzo as best I could. The day Vincenzo first demanded repayment of me. Vincenzo had sent a message asking me to meet him by the lake, and I wasn't in a position to refuse. I found him talking to Smythe."

"What about?" Malcolm asked. It wasn't necessarily surprising for the two men to have been in conversation away from the villa, but Smythe hadn't mentioned it, and it didn't fit with his dislike of Vincenzo.

"I don't know what they were talking about," Shelley said. "They went quiet before I reached them. But I saw Smythe put a paper in Vincenzo's hand. I have no idea what it contained, but the seal caught my eye. It was shaped like a castle."

Malcolm stared at Shelley. Shelley seemed to have no notion of the significance of his words, but if he'd wanted to turn attention away from himself as a suspect, he could scarcely have done better. For he'd just revealed that John Smythe had given Vincenzo a paper that bore the seal of the Elsinore League.

CHAPTER 27

Cordelia shook her head. "Why on earth would Conte Vincenzo have wanted an indiscreet letter from Simon to David? Did he want to blackmail them?"

"I suspect it's the Elsinore League who wanted it," Malcolm said. "And I don't think it's Simon or David they wanted to blackmail."

They were once again gathered in the grand salon. Malcolm had returned from his interview with Percy Shelley with a grim cast to his mouth and the light of the chase in his eyes. Even now, sitting beside him on the sofa, Mélanie could feel the tension running through him.

Raoul met Malcolm's gaze across the salon. "There's perhaps no better way to get at someone than through their children. Even if that someone is Carfax."

"But Carfax wants to separate Simon and David," Cordelia said. "If there was a scandal they might have to separate, at least temporarily."

"Carfax also wants David to be safe," Malcolm said. "If

344

there was actually proof in writing—As David pointed out to me a few months ago, it's still a hanging offense."

Cordelia paled. "Good God. People wouldn't—"

"Some would." Harry's hand closed on her arm. "You forget sometimes that not everyone thinks like you, my darling."

"No, I don't," Cordelia said. "But it's hard to believe anyone would actually go so far—"

"It's amazing," Lady Frances said, "what people will do. Even people one views as quite rational."

"You should have seen the look on Castlereagh's face when I told him my theory about Dewhurst framing Bertrand to separate him from Rupert," Malcolm said. "He called it 'unnatural.' I knew Castlereagh and I viewed much of the world differently, but somehow that brought home just how much. We're so used to Simon and David and Rupert and Bertrand that we forget—"

"That they're breaking a vile law simply by being with the person they love," Laura said.

"Quite."

"Simon and David are both careful," Mélanie said. "Even writing to us. It's clear reading between the lines, but they don't put things into words. Not that either of them is overly effusive, but one never knows when a letter may fall into the wrong hands."

Cordelia shook her head. Other than Frances, she was the greatest stranger of all of them to the world of intrigue, and the machinations still sometimes took her by surprise. "So the Elsinore League think they can use proof of David and Simon's relationship to blackmail Carfax? Into what?"

"I've been wondering just that ever since I heard Shelley's story," Malcolm said. "I don't know. But it appears the

345

Elsinore League are battling Carfax." He looked at Archie.

"I hear less and less," Archie said. "I wonder sometimes if they're on to me. Even if they aren't, Harry's friendship with you would make them view me as something of a liability. But I know there's been concern about Carfax for some time. And if they learned Carfax is close to getting his hands on a list of Elsinore League members—"

"Two of our enemies at loggerheads," Mélanie said. "And instead of watching from the sidelines, we seem to have ended up the middle."

"And by coming to Italy, we walked right into the crossfire." Malcolm tightened his arm round her.

"If Carfax and the Elsinore League are going after each other, the crossfire is likely to ripple across the Continent," Mélanie said. "Not to mention, throughout Britain."

"And apparently John Smythe is connected to the League, as well." Malcolm looked at Archie again.

Archie shook his head. "I haven't heard his name. But—I didn't make the connection at first because Smythe's a common enough name, but is he connected to Lord Beverston?"

"Beverston is John Smythe's father," Frances said. She might be a novice at intrigue, but she was an expert in the intricacies of the peerage. "And the Beverstons were at the house party where Vincenzo met Alistair. And Margaret."

Archie whistled. "I should have seen it sooner. Beverston is a League member. One of the founding members, I think." He looked at Malcolm. "He was at Oxford with your—with Alistair."

"Which makes him Vincenzo's ally," Laura said, "not his opponent."

"Except that the Elsinore League have been known to

346

turn on their own," Raoul said.

"I'll talk to Smythe," Malcolm said. "Not someone I relish spending time with, though at least probing his secrets doesn't stir feelings of guilt."

"Meanwhile," Harry said, "this gives Shelley a motive to have killed Vincenzo."

"Yes." Malcolm stretched his legs out and frowned at the toes of his boots. "Quite a strong motive. By his own admission, he didn't want to comply with Vincenzo's requests—didn't think he could comply with them—and they don't have the money to repay the debt. I don't know Shelley well. His poetry reveals quite surprising sensitivity, but God knows we've known sensitive people to kill before."

"He's not the only one it gives a motive," Laura said. "If Vincenzo pressed Shelley to repay the debt, it would impact Mary just as much as her husband. I like Mary Shelley, and she's been through an unimaginable hell. But I think she may be more ruthless than her husband."

Malcolm met Laura's gaze. "I suspect you're right. And for all we know, Vincenzo may have tried to pressure Mrs. Shelley when he couldn't make headway with her husband."

"And I can vouch for the fact that he can seem ruthless," Mélanie said. "And damnably smug. I can imagine him setting someone over the edge. If—"

She broke off as the door opened to admit Blanca, her loose hair windblown, her gown creased as though she had gathered up the skirt while walking quickly. "I'm quite a scandal with the Thurston maids," she said, pushing the door shut. "They can't understand how I still have my employment when I'm obviously with child. I said I didn't think you'd have turned me out even if I'd been unmarried, but, as it happens, my husband is Mr. Rannoch's valet. That confused them even more." She moved into the room and dropped into a chair. "But I did manage enough rational conversation to learn who the button you found in Conte Vincenzo's room belongs to."

"John Smythe?" Malcolm asked.

Blanca stared at him. "*Dios*. I thought I'd surprise you."

"Better than that, you've given us the confirmation we needed."

"How—"

Blanca bit back her question as a rap sounded at the door. "*Pardone*." Zarina came into the room. "Signora Shelley has called. She's asking for Signora Rannoch."

Mary Shelley turned to face Mélanie in the rose salon, into which Zarina had shown her. "Thank you for seeing me, Mrs. Rannoch. I know you must be busy, but I thought this shouldn't wait."

"Of course." Mélanie closed the door. "Please sit down."

Mary dropped into a chair. "When your husband called this morning, I realized you'd learned about Percy's debt to Vincenzo. I knew you would. I almost said something to Percy, but then I'd have had to admit I knew."

"How long have you known?" Mélanie asked, moving to a chair opposite Mary.

"Almost from the first. Percy tried to explain where the money came from, but really, for a writer, he's not very good at making up stories out of whole cloth. I can't deny the money was welcome. I'm more used to not having it than Percy is, but no one likes to scrape by. At the time I thought I'd let Percy enjoy the illusion and make use of the money. Now I wish I'd said something."

"You didn't trust Conte Vincenzo?"

Mary frowned. "He was always faultlessly polite, but something bothered me from the first. I couldn't understand his taking such an interest in people he barely knew." She gave a faint, half bitter smile. "Percy tends to think people will go out of their way for him simply because of who he is. But Conte Vincenzo never struck me as the sort to appreciate a great poet. If we'd been under less strain the past few weeks—" She shook her head, ghosts darkening her gaze. "As it was, by the time we left to come here I scarcely remembered the debt even existed."

"Understandably," Mélanie said. "I'm sorry—"

"No, it's all right." Mary curled her fingers round the arms of her chair. "You have to ask. To own the truth, I find it a relief at times to talk of something else, anything else. I understand why you're so drawn into investigations."

It was a remarkably astute comment coming in the midst of personal tragedy and present crisis. "When did you think of the debt again?" Mélanie asked. "When we started asking questions?"

"No, when Conte Vincenzo approached me about the debt." Mary folded her hands in her lap. "I expect you've already worked that out."

"I thought he might have done. I wasn't certain." Mélanie scanned Mary's face. "What did he say?"

Mary's lips curled. "That he could tell I was a clever woman. That he had no doubt I'd known about the debt from the first. That he was sure I would appreciate the need to make my husband see sense now. If I could persuade my husband to abandon his high-handed principles, there was no reason things couldn't end very agreeably for all of us."

"Did he tell you what he'd asked of your husband?"

349

Mary spread her hands over her lap, pressing the muslin of her skirt taut. "Not at first. But I told him if he expected me to intervene with my husband, he'd have to at least tell me what it was about."

"And did he?"

"A group called the Levellers. I've heard of them a bit." She drew a breath. Her knuckles whitened against the brown-spotted fabric of her skirt. "And Simon Tanner. I know Simon's words are considered dangerous by some, by why on earth would an Italian be so bent on destroying him?"

"I suspect he wanted to use the information against David's father."

Mary's eyes widened. "Dear God—I've heard of Lord Carfax, of course. I've heard rumors about what he does." She hesitated a moment. "Your husband works for him."

Mélanie smoothed the white gold chain of her bracelet. "Used to work for him. During the war. When Malcolm was an agent. Malcolm and Carfax could scarcely be further apart on policy." She watched Mary for a moment. For all the shock in the other woman's gaze, Mélanie would swear she was armored against revealing secrets. "You haven't said what you told Vincenzo?"

Mary's back stiffened. "What do you think? I'm not the sort to betray my friends. And though I'm not blind to my husband's imperfections, I know he wouldn't, either."

"What did Vincenzo say?"

"That we'd regret it." Mary's fingers curled inwards, the nails digging into her palms. "I told him it was up to him, but that he wouldn't get very far by pursuing us for debt. That only seemed to make him angrier. He was an unpleasant man, but not a subtle one."

"No," Mélanie agreed.

Mary twisted her wedding band round her finger. "I don't know what Percy and I would have done if Vincenzo had really pressed matters. We don't have the money. We don't have anyone to apply to for it. We've strained our relationship with Byron as it is. I'm sorry Conte Vincenzo is dead, but there's no denying it's a sort of relief." She looked up and met Mélanie's gaze. "It would be easier if I could have told you I didn't know about the debt. But the truth is I have just as strong a motive as Percy."

Mélanie returned her gaze. Mary Shelley was a formidable woman. One couldn't help but admire her directness. At the same time, Mélanie was quite sure she was aware that in giving herself a motive alongside her husband, she was muddying the waters. Which could help both of them. "Very true," she said. "On the other hand, you and your husband are hardly the only ones. In your dealings with Conte Vincenzo, here or in Florence, did you observe anything that could shed light on who else might have wanted the conte dead?"

Mary's fine brows drew together. "I can't claim to have known him well. He didn't strike me as a particularly kind man, so I can imagine any number of people disliking him. But enough to kill?" Her frown deepened. "There is the one woman."

"His mistress?" Mélanie knew Vincenzo had a mistress in Milan, though she hadn't heard the woman's name.

"I'm not sure about that. But I saw him with her in Milan. It looked more as though they were conferring than having an amorous interlude, though one can never be sure. And then I saw them together again by the lake four days ago."

"I think Byron and Mrs. Smythe saw her with Vincenzo by the lake, as well, but they couldn't see enough to identify her. Could you?"

"Yes, but I don't know her name. She was at the picnic, though I didn't see her with Vincenzo there. When we arrived she was talking to your friend, Mr. O'Roarke."

Mélanie drew a breath that grated through her. "I believe you mean Margaret O'Roarke. Raoul's wife."

Mary's brows rose. "Indeed. An interesting situation. Perhaps he can shed light on her acquaintance with Conte Vincenzo, then."

"I doubt it," Mélanie said. "He hasn't lived with her in twenty years, and I believe he knows her even less than he realized. Do you have any idea what they were conversing about either time?"

Mary shook her head. "Very little. Save—I can't tell you what it means, but when I saw them together in Milan the wind shifted and I caught a fragment of what they were saying with startling clarity. She—Mrs. O'Roarke—was talking. I heard her say 'Alistair started all of this.'"

CHAPTER 28

"Rannoch. I'm happy to talk to you again, but I think I told you everything possible yesterday."

Malcolm surveyed John Smythe across the Thurston library. He tried to remain as neutral as possible when dealing with suspects in an investigation. People could surprise you, and to get to the truth (or as close to the truth as was possible) of what had happened, it was best to keep an open mind. But, knowing what he knew now, it was impossible not to look at John Smythe as a particularly low sort of vermin. The sort of man who needed to prove his power by picking on those weaker than himself. Though in every way but the physical, Malcolm was quite sure Diana Smythe had ten times the strength of her husband.

"You weren't entirely forthcoming, Smythe."

"I beg your pardon? I admitted to quarreling with Vincenzo." Smythe's expression was as seemingly guileless as ever. Was it only his imagination, Malcolm wondered, that made him now see the hard gleam behind that open gaze?

"So you did. But you were less than honest about the reasons. Though I can quite understand that Conte Vincenzo's attentions to your wife might have been even more annoying, considering that you were allies."

"Allies?" Smythe laughed in a disbelief that rang like sterling. "With Vincenzo? I only met the man a few weeks ago. And I didn't much like him. Our only connection was through the woman my wife's father—lives with."

"So it seemed. And that explained enough of your dealings that no one—including me, to my regret—was inclined to look further. I expect that's why the Elsinore League thought it was clever to have the two of you working on a mission together. You had built-in cover."

"The what League? It doesn't sound very Italian."

"It's not, as you must know full well. I believe your father was a founding member. I know mine was. Though he never tried to recruit me to join their ranks. He never even told me about it. I suppose you're to be congratulated. Though I'd call it a dubious honor."

"Look here, Rannoch—"

"Smythe." Malcolm slammed his hands down on the Carrara marble table. "We know Vincenzo worked for the League. You were seen giving him a paper with the League's seal. You can't be so stupid as to think your denials will possibly convince me."

Smythe's gaze sharpened as it settled on Malcolm. "If you know anything about the Elsinore League at all, you must realize the last thing I would do is admit to a connection with them. If I had one. Which I don't."

"So the name Julien St. Juste doesn't mean anything to you?"

Smythe couldn't quite keep the flicker of response from

354

his gaze. "I don't know whom you're talking about."

"You want to find him."

"Are you saying you know this man, whoever he is?"

"If I did, I'd hardly put him in touch with you."

"Stop talking in riddles, Rannoch. If I had been working with Vincenzo—which I certainly don't admit to—surely I'm the last man who'd have killed him. If that's what you believe, why are you wasting time on me?"

"Because allies can turn on allies. Because the Elsinore League can turn on their own."

"You're saying they ordered me to kill Vincenzo? This group I don't even admit to knowing the existence of?"

"I think it's one possibility. A possibility I can't ignore. You and Vincenzo were arguing about something."

"His attentions to my wife."

"I don't believe you pay enough heed to your wife to have quarreled over her."

Smythe lurched forwards. "Watch your impertinence, Rannoch."

He was off his balance. Good. "Unless Vincenzo was telling you only a very weak man takes out his anger on women."

"God damn it, Rannoch." Smythe hurled himself at Malcolm. Malcolm blocked a blow to his jaw with a raised arm. "I begin to see what Diana is up against. What are you so angry about, Smythe? And why are you taking it out on your wife?"

"I'm not in the least angry." Smythe drew a breath and tugged his coat smooth, though his color was high. "And what's between my wife and me is our business."

"Normally, I'd agree. But not when someone is being hurt. If you have a scrap of sense, you'll realize that Diana has

355

a number of friends and that they now know what she's been going through. You won't take your petty insecurities out on her."

"My God, Rannoch—"

"Is that what this is? An attempt to prove you amount to something? I would think working for the Elsinore League would do that. Unless they don't really trust you, either."

"You bloody bastard." Smythe lurched at him again. "You sound just like my father."

This time Malcolm deliberately let the force of Smythe's blow knock him to the Turkey rug. "That's it, isn't it?" He stared up at Smythe's flushed face. "Your father is a League member. He brought you in, but he never really trusted you. They never really trusted you."

"You think they'd send someone they didn't trust, to deal with Vincenzo?" Smythe demanded. Then he drew a sharp breath.

"Quite." Malcolm sprang to his feet. "But now we can at least dispense with the charade that you aren't working for the Elsinore League."

Smythe stared at him, breathing hard. "You think you're so bloody clever, Rannoch. You don't know what you're in the middle of."

"That's true. But I know enough to realize just how much more there is to unravel."

"And you think you can unravel it? A man who was outwitted and cuckolded by his own wife?"

"Just outwitted, actually." Malcolm kept his voice level despite the chill that gripped him. He should have known Smythe knew about Mélanie, if Vincenzo had.

"All your Oxford brains, and a pretty harlot made a fool of you."

356

It took every ounce of Malcolm's willpower not to strike Smythe. That would have been playing his game. "It's a good thing she did. Or I wouldn't have my present happiness."

"Your—"

"It's amazing how happy a happy marriage can make one. But I don't know that I can expect you to understand that, Smythe."

Smythe gave a short laugh. "You're living in a dream world, Rannoch."

"Perhaps. But it's a very pleasant dream. Why should I wish to wake up?" Malcolm moved to the door. "I can't expect you to answer questions. But you can't expect me to stop asking them."

"He always said your compassion made you dangerous," Smythe said in a low voice.

Malcolm turned back. "Who did?" Though he already half knew the answer.

Smythe met his gaze and gave a hard smile. "Your father."

Why, when he knew conclusively Alistair hadn't even been his father, could the man still cut him from across the grave? "Yes, that sounds like Alistair," Malcolm said. "But then, I expect you knew him better than I did."

Harry glanced at Raoul, the only other occupant of the terrace. Suzanne—Mélanie—was still closeted with Mary Shelley, and Malcolm had left to talk to John Smythe. Cordy, Laura, Frances, and Archie had joined the children at the lake. Harry and Raoul had both lingered to see how Mélanie's talk with Mary Shelley went. Harry had been looking for an opportunity to talk to O'Roarke since they'd come to Italy, but now he had it, he fumbled for the right words. O'Roarke seemed to understand, because he stood quietly, arms resting on the balustrade, as though waiting for Harry to speak.

"I always knew you were remarkable," Harry said at last, gaze on the lake. "Even in the Peninsula, by reputation, before I met you. Certainly before I had the faintest understanding of who you really were."

"How long have you known?" Raoul asked.

Harry turned to look at him. "Didn't Malcolm tell you?"

"I know what Malcolm told me. I'm asking when you worked it out."

Harry gave a faint smile. "I suspected Suzanne—Mélanie—was the Raven last December during the *Hamlet* investigation. I didn't know for sure until Malcolm told me, the night they left Britain. That's also when he told me about you."

"But?" Raoul said.

Harry met that keen gray gaze, so like Malcolm's. "Archie more or less let it slip when I learned about his own activities in December. He said he'd gone from giving you information about Ireland to giving you information about France. Rather remarkably for him, I think he was too overset by what was happening to quite realize what he'd said. Given what I knew about your history and politics, it wasn't much of a step to see you as a French agent. Given the suspicions I'd just developed about Mélanie, it didn't take a leap of genius to suspect you were her spymaster."

"You underrate yourself, Davenport. But then, I knew you were a formidable opponent from the moment I met you. And that's quite without Archie's boasting."

Archie boasting didn't surprise Harry as much as it once would have done. "I was hardly at a level to give you cause for

358

concern. Or Archie."

"No? You have a gift for thinking outside the parameters that define most people. Malcolm has it, too."

Harry studied the other man for a moment. For all Malcolm had confided in him, there were certain things he hadn't said, and it wasn't Harry's place to push. Still—"Perhaps not surprising, given the influence you and my uncle had on us, growing up."

"Perhaps. Archie wasn't very happy when you went into the army."

"I can see that now. As always, he was measured in his response. He helped me get my commission."

"He knew you needed to get away. And he always thought it was important to let you go your own way."

"I don't imagine you were very pleased when Malcolm went into intelligence."

"No." Raoul's voice was even, but the turbulence in his gaze spoke volumes. "And not just because we were on opposite sides. It's not a life one would wish on those one cares about." O'Roarke drew a rough breath. "But I could recognize how good he'd be at it."

"It's funny," Harry said. "The things we say, that perhaps would be far better left unsaid. And the things we can never manage to put into words at all."

"Some things we don't put into words for a reason."

Harry looked down at his hands. "It's not a life I'd wish on anyone, either. God knows, not on my daughters. Or my wife, though as I told you last spring, I understand her being drawn to it. And yet—I can feel the allure of the game. Even now, I'm on the outside. Perhaps especially now."

"Oh, yes," Raoul said. "It's its own very particular form of seduction. I've always prided myself on my self-control, but

359

it's a seduction I've been far more vulnerable to than I'd care to admit. Still am, perhaps."

Harry cast a glance at the other man, seeing him with his arm round Laura or swinging Emily up in the air. If Harry had left the game behind—more or less—O'Roarke was still actively involved. But, though Harry had come to consider him a friend (odd that—not O'Roarke's being a friend—but having friends at all), they were scarcely on terms where Harry could ask about that.

O'Roarke's gaze moved over the water. Then he turned to look at Harry. "You're a forbearing man, Davenport. You could be pardoned for cordially disliking me. To put it mildly."

"Given what I've accepted, even embraced, in Archie? I'd look a hypocrite. Besides, I've never been a Crown-and-country sort."

"No, but you're a loyal friend. And Archie didn't manipulate you and spy on you."

"No." Harry turned and studied Raoul. His face was a cipher that would challenge the most brilliant codebreaker. But one could read a lot in his eyes if one knew to look. "There's a lot I don't know, O'Roarke. But I'm a reasonably good judge of people. And I can guess what Malcolm means to you."

Raoul's hands tightened on the balustrade. Like Malcolm's, his hands tended to give him away. "One could make a fair case that that makes what I did worse."

"One could make a fair case that I couldn't possibly blame you as much as you obviously blame yourself," Harry said.

Raoul met his gaze and gave a slow smile that seemed to break through the mask of reserve. "Have I mentioned that you're damnably acute, Harry?"

360

"Malcolm's my friend," Harry said. Funny, how easily that word now came to his lips. "And I can tell that he's happy. That means a lot."

"Yes, Malcolm has a remarkable ability to get past the past."

"He does. I've learned a lot from him. But what makes it so complicated, is that in large measure I think he's happy *because* of the past."

O'Roarke didn't move, but for a moment it was as though he had taken a step back. "You're a scholar, Davenport. You must know the risks of too simple a reading of the data. And that correlation isn't causation."

"It's more than correlation. The past is why he has Suzanne—Mélanie—and Colin and Jessica." Harry hesitated, his voice rough because, much as he wondered at his present happiness, he rarely put it into words. "I understand that, because my own tangled past is why I have Cordy and Livia and Dru."

Raoul's smile was at once distant and warm. "As I said, you and Malcolm have a great capacity to focus on what matters in life."

"And you have a great capacity to deny what's in front of you."

"I'm a realist."

"Archie says you're the world's last romantic."

"Archie is a good friend and a very astute man, but he has blind spots. Still, whatever the reason, I'm grateful you're still willing to put up with me."

"Talking of good friends, you're one yourself, O'Roarke. Besides—" Harry hesitated. He suspected O'Roarke's dislike of conversation that verged on sentiment equaled his own, but it needed to be said. "I owe you a debt of gratitude I can't

361

possibly repay. My whole family do. Without you, we wouldn't have our present happiness. Drusilla would never have been born."

Raoul went still. He was smiling, but a shade had closed over his eyes. "My dear Davenport—"

"Malcolm told me what you did at Waterloo. I realize I wasn't the one you were trying to save. But that doesn't change my being inestimably grateful that you were there."

Raoul drew in and released his breath. "I'd like to think I'd have acted as I did in any case. War is a hell in which honor has little meaning, and I fought savagely myself at Waterloo. But it's hard not to revolt at the thought of someone on any side striking down a wounded man and a civilian trying to help him. And if I'd known it was you—"

"You'd have intervened for Archie's sake?"

"Quite likely. But I was going to say I'd have intervened for your own."

"You scarcely knew me at that point."

Raoul grinned unexpectedly. "I'd only met you a handful of times. I'd been hearing your uncle's stories about you since you were at Eton. Archie can paint a vivid portrait. I felt I knew the lonely boy with the quick mind, and the brilliant scholar. And then the equally brilliant agent."

Harry started to turn the words aside and then nodded, not because of the praise, but because of the acknowledged bond. "Odd," he said, "the bonds that have been between all of us for so long, before we even knew it." He hesitated a moment. "I always found it a challenge, getting to know French soldiers undercover, sharing stories and glasses of wine and late-night confidences. At the time I'd have denied I had friends, but looking back, I formed friendships. With people I was fighting against. It must have been worse for

362

you, living so much of your life among the British."

"That's one way of looking at it," Raoul said. "Another is that I had to be particularly morally bankrupt to betray people I had known for so long and so well."

Harry shook his head. "Spying's a betrayal whichever way one looks at it. Funny, in a way. I ran away from my wife's betrayal and found escape betraying people myself."

"You're well out of it, Davenport."

"Do you ever wish you were?" Harry asked, before he could think better of it.

Raoul drew a breath. Harry almost fancied he could see the other man bite back the obvious, flippant answer. "Sometimes," he said. "More now than before. But at other times—it's hard to imagine—"

"Walking away from the things you believe in? I never really had that."

"That's part of it, yes. I keep having the illusion I can make a difference. But also—" Raoul paused. Harry had the strange sense he was saying something he'd never said before, not to Malcolm, not to Mélanie, not to Laura. "I'm not sure who I'd be without it."

Harry drew a breath. Raoul met his gaze and gave a faint, almost abashed, smile. "You were a scholar, Harry. You had that to go back to. Malcolm was on the way to a political career before the espionage sidetracked him. Sometimes I'm afraid the game isn't just what I play, it's who I am. Take it away, and I'm not sure there'd be much left."

"I don't think Malcolm thinks that. Or Mélanie. Or Laura. Or Archie. I don't."

Raoul laughed and clapped him on the shoulder. "That's because you're a remarkably decent man, Davenport." He hesitated a moment. "Harry—I'm glad Malcolm has you to

363

talk to."

Harry gave a faint smile. "I'm glad I can pay him back for all the times he had to listen to me blathering on."

"This has to be hell for him. I'm not sure any of us appreciate quite how much. Perhaps not even Malcolm."

"I'm sure he's missing home more than he'd admit," Harry said, "but I don't think he'd trade it. In fact, I rarely claim to know another person, but I know he wouldn't." He paused, then added, "I think David was starting to come round before we left."

"That's the best news I've heard in a long time," Raoul said. "If—"

He broke off as the French window from the salon flew open and Mélanie ran onto the terrace. Almost before Harry had taken in her presence, Raoul was halfway across the terrace. "What is it, *querida?*" He gripped her arms. "Mrs. Shelley—"

"Vincenzo tried to blackmail her, as well. But that's not—" Mélanie glanced from Raoul to Harry, then back at Raoul. Harry realized her gaze held not just shock, but concern. And that concern was directed at O'Roarke. "Raoul." She pulled free of his grasp so she could grip his hands. "I need to tell you something."

CHAPTER 29

T hurston stared at Malcolm across the desk in his study. "John Smythe is an agent for the Elsinore League?"

"Self-confessed." Malcolm gripped the arms of his chair, the same chair he had sat in that first morning when he warned Thurston about Vincenzo, and glimpsed the letter from Carfax. "And he was passing information to Vincenzo. He denies killing him, as one would expect. And says the fact that they were allies makes it even less likely he'd have done so."

Thurston fixed Malcolm with a level stare. "What do you think?"

"I think it wouldn't be the first time allies had turned on each other. Particularly allies of the Elsinore League. On the other hand, he's hardly the only one with a motive."

"But you told me."

"This has implications beyond Vincenzo's murder."

The implications settled in Thurston's gaze, though he scarcely moved a muscle. "Does this have anything to do with why he married my daughter?"

For all the control in Thurston's gaze and voice, Malcolm could recognize the concern of a father. "It doesn't seem likely on the face of it, unless the Elsinore League were playing a very complicated game with regards to you. And even if they were, Smythe married Diana before Waterloo, when it would have seemed questionable when or if your children would be able to see you. But—" Malcolm hesitated. For the sake of the investigation, it would be better to wait and not disrupt things. But much as he believed in learning the truth, some things came first. "It's become plain, however, that Smythe isn't the kindest of husbands."

Shock leapt in Thurston's gaze, closely followed by rage. "Are you saying—"

"He's a petty man," Malcolm said. "A man whose own father made him feel small, I think. And he vents that anger on those more helpless. Particularly his wife. Diana confided in my wife and Cordelia and Laura."

"She—" Thurston shook his head. His hands had gone white-knuckled. "Rannoch, are you telling me my daughter confided in virtual strangers—"

"Sometimes it's easier to admit such things to those one isn't close to. And I've found people often admit unexpected things in the course of an investigation."

Thurston gripped the edge of his desk. "I'll kill him."

It sounded like more than a figure of speech. "I'm entirely in sympathy," Malcolm said. "But we need him here until we conclude the investigation."

Thurston drew a long breath, fingers taut on the desk. At last, he gave a slow nod.

"Diana strikes me as a very strong woman," Malcolm said. "But she's going to need support. The law is lamentably not

366

on the side of women in such situations. But with money and the support of family, at least a legal separation can be secured."

Thurston nodded again, this time more crisply. "Being out of Britain handicaps me."

"Me, as well," Malcolm said. "But I have friends I can write to. I can put you in touch with a solicitor. I have a number of friends still in Parliament."

"If she wants a divorce?"

"I know the risks," Malcolm said. "But in this case—"

"If Diana wants a divorce, I'd certainly back her. I think her mother would be horrified."

"Lady Thurston is understandably wary of scandal. But there are worse things." He hesitated. "A decent man wouldn't hesitate to offer for Diana after she was divorced from a man like Smythe. He'd only be grateful that she was free."

Thurston spread his hands on the ink blotter. "I don't doubt that you would, Rannoch. I'd like to think the same is true of my son. I can take little credit for him, but I'm pleased with the man he's become. But from my memories of London society, I fear there are all too many men it would weigh with. Just as there were probably all too many influenced by the scandal of her mother's and my separation." He drew in his breath. "If that led to her accepting Smythe—"

"You don't know that, sir," Malcolm said. "All too many people choose a marriage partner mistakenly, without any lack of options. In any case, it's folly to refine upon the past."

Thurston had been staring at his signet ring, but at that he lifted his gaze to Malcolm. "When you get to be my age, Rannoch, you spend a lot of time refining upon the past."

Malcolm returned that keen blue gaze. "Believe me, sir, I

spend a great deal of time doing so myself. Much as I endeavor not to."

Thurston regarded him with a gaze that saw a great deal, but did not probe for more. "Then you'll understand my qualms."

"And you'll understand my advice not to dwell on them."

Thurston held Malcolm's gaze for another long moment. "Thank you, Rannoch."

They might not trust each other, but in this they were allies.

Raoul regarded his wife in the clear afternoon sunlight that slanted across the terrace of the Chipperfields' villa. Mélanie's words on the Rannochs' terrace still reverberated through his head. The very bones of Margaret's face seemed different.

"It's an old technique," he said. "Reveal secrets, genuinely embarrassing, perhaps damaging secrets, with just enough reluctance to make one's interrogator think he or she has succeeded. And thus protect far more damaging secrets that one is keeping. And yet, for all my own supposed skills, I didn't have the least idea of what you were doing. My compliments."

Margaret returned his gaze, her own as hard as fortified walls. The vulnerability she'd shown in their prior discussions was quite gone. "Is this yet another technique to get me to talk?"

"Only in the sense that it would be folly to waste more of both our time. I may have been shockingly slow, but certain facts are now clear in my head. Conte Vincenzo may well have been your lover. But you also helped Alistair Rannoch recruit him into the Elsinore League. The only thing I'm not sure about is whether or not you're still working for them."

"For the what? It sounds like a bit of undergraduate nonsense. You know I never had your taste for Shakespeare."

"Stop it, Meg." He slammed his hands down on the table. "I may have been an idiot where you were concerned, but I'm not a complete fool. Was Alistair your lover too?"

He'd meant to goad her, and he saw the words smash home in her gaze, breaking that granite reserve. "Is that what you think? That women only do things for a man if they're in his bed?"

"No, and if I had any such delusions the women in my life would quickly disabuse me of them. But knowing Alistair, it would have been his approach to recruiting you."

Margaret spun away, arms hugged across her chest. "Damn you. Why in God's name should I say anything to you?"

"For the same reason I gave you last time, when you so charmingly pulled the wool over my eyes. If you don't talk to me, I shall have to take what I know—and what I suspect—to other authorities."

"You wouldn't go to the Italian authorities about this Elsinore League of yours."

"Perhaps not. But I would go to Malcolm and Suzanne Rannoch." Leaving aside for the moment that it was Mélanie who had given him the information to piece together Meg's connection to Alistair and the League.

She flinched. "To think that a boy I saw you playing catch with would now seem a greater threat than you."

"Meg, if Alistair hurt you—"

"You think I'd only have helped him if I were coerced?

Dear God, I don't think you've ever appreciated the strength of my beliefs."

"Enlighten me."

"I imagine he'd have liked to get me into bed if I'd gone along with it. That part of what I told you before was true. As was the fact that he made my skin crawl. But in some things our interests aligned."

"Ireland."

Margaret shot a hard look at him. "Alistair at least appreciated the dangers of what was happening in '98. Even Desmond was inclined to underestimate the risks."

Raoul stared at his wife. "Dunboyne."

She hesitated, drew a breath, ran her fingers over the tiled surface of the table, tracing lines in the grout. "You still came home occasionally. You were careless about locking up your papers."

"You told Alistair where I'd be."

"I told Alistair where a rebel outpost would be."

"Knowing I'd be among them."

"I didn't wish you dead." She drew a breath. "No, that may not be true. Not then. I was—very angry."

Raoul released his breath. He felt as though he'd been dealt a blow to the chest. "I deal in information, Margaret. I can't blame you for doing the same."

"You keep your personal feelings out of it."

"I try to. I don't always succeed. You were angry with me and afraid for Ireland. Alistair offered you a chance to do something about both."

"He got himself invited to a party at Desmond's, of all places. He said straight out that we had something in common. The straying of our spouses, and their dangerous ideas."

"Did he tell you about the Elsinore League?"

"Not then. He said he had friends who were working to ensure Ireland stayed safe. I was longing for a chance to take action, not just to be the betrayed wife and worried landlord."

He could recognize the lash of self-hatred in her voice. "For what it's worth, I've hated myself enough to understand someone hating me."

Margaret watched him for a moment. "Does she know?"

"Does Laura know what?"

"The things you've done that you hate yourself for."

He returned her gaze steadily. "Some of them. More than I ever thought I could admit to anyone."

Margaret held his gaze a moment longer, then glanced away. "Desmond doesn't know. I think it would quite shatter his image of me if he did."

"Perhaps you underrate him."

"You defending Desmond, what are we coming to?" Her face turned serious. "I gave Alistair more information. I started to sense there was more to it. More to these friends he talked about. But I never knew the name of the organization. Not until you said it. It's rather silly. Alistair claimed to hate Shakespeare. That was his father-in-law's sphere."

"He asked you to introduce him to Vincenzo."

"He did. He didn't ask me to seduce Vincenzo. That was—what happened between Vincenzo and me was for myself."

"Why did Alistair care about Vincenzo?"

"He had interests in Italy."

"And then?"

"I stopped it." Her fingers stilled on the tile. "I didn't much like the person I was becoming."

"That happens to a lot of agents. But most of them don't

371

manage to stop."

"I wasn't an agent."

"No? You were passing information. That's rather the definition." He watched her a moment longer. "Why did you come to Italy?"

She drew a breath as though to deny the significance, then said, "I came to Italy to get away, as I told you. To give Desmond time, and to meet him later. But I came to Lake Como because Vincenzo asked me to. Well, actually, there wasn't a lot of asking about it."

"He blackmailed you?"

"It was made clear—obliquely, but clearly—that if I didn't do as he asked, Desmond would learn certain truths about my past."

"I'm sorry Vincenzo's dead, but I like the man less and less the more I hear about him. Had he tried that before?"

"No. I'd scarcely heard from him in fifteen years."

"Why now?"

"I didn't know until I got here. I met him in secret by the lake. I asked him. He said it was because you were here."

It shouldn't have been a surprise, given what they already knew. But the level of planning it suggested—"Did Vincenzo tell you what he wanted with me? What he wanted you to do?"

Margaret folded her arms in front of her, gripping her elbows. "He wanted to find a man named Julien St. Juste. He wanted me to convince you to find him."

Again, not a surprise. Again, the level of planning brought a chill of shock. "Did he tell you what he wanted with Julien St. Juste?"

Margaret shook her head. "I asked. I told him I didn't much care to be manipulated, and that I wasn't sure what influence I'd have on you, anyway. Unless he wanted me to let you know that the last thing I wanted was for Vincenzo and his friends to find Julien St. Juste. Whoever he may be."

"What did he say to that?"

"That he was sure I could manage. In this case, Vincenzo quite overestimated me."

"Did he ask you to do anything else?"

Margaret plucked at a thread on her sleeve, glanced out over the water, looked back at him. "He wanted me to find out if you were Suzanne Rannoch's lover."

Another chill shot through him. The pieces had all been there. The Duke of Trenchard had known about him and Mélanie. Folly to think he hadn't told others. But that this Italian aristocrat he had only met a month since, who had been his wife's lover, had known—

"Rather shocking, I thought," Margaret said. "Even with my mind broadened by the circles I've been moving in. Are you?"

"No."

Margaret watched him for a long moment. "Were you?"

"Never when she was Suzanne Rannoch."

Margaret drew a sharp breath. "Who is Julien St. Juste?"

"An agent for hire. A very dangerous agent for hire."

"And Vincenzo wanted to hire him?"

"I don't know what Vincenzo wanted."

"Mr. Rannoch." Selena met Malcolm as he emerged from Thurston's study. "Is there news? That is, I suppose you can't tell me—"

Malcolm smiled at her. "We know a lot of things that may or may not be relevant and we're no closer to arriving at an answer. Which is much the way it usually is at this point in an investigation."

Selena nodded. "I'm on my way to see Papa." She hesitated. "I'd never have thought this when we arrived, but I find it comforting to talk to him."

"People can surprise you," Malcolm said.

Selena gave a quick smile. "Yes."

Malcolm hesitated, then found himself saying, against all dictates of prudence, "The older I get the more grateful I am for the time I had with my father." And the time he still had. But he couldn't say so. He couldn't let Selena know that the man he was talking about was very much alive and working on the investigation.

In many ways it seemed a shocking half-truth, but Selena's eyes widened in understanding of the sentiment if not the facts. Then her brows drew together. "I suppose it's beastly to be grateful in the midst of all this tragedy—"

"On the contrary," Malcolm said. "I think one should snatch whatever one can from tragedy."

Selena considered this a moment and nodded again. "That's rather a lovely way of looking at it, Mr. Rannoch. Thank you." Her gaze flickered over his face. "Whom do you need to talk to next?"

"Enrico. I didn't speak with him yesterday. Do you happen to know where he is?"

"On the upper terrace, I think. He was with Sofia and Kit but then they went for a walk." Selena fingered her primrose sash. Malcolm had the distinct sense she was aware of at least some of what was between her brother and Sofia, but she didn't say more.

Malcolm found Enrico Vincenzo on the upper terrace, gaze on the lake. He turned at Malcolm's approach and

374

walked forwards, a purposeful look on his face. "Rannoch. I was hoping to see you. I assume you want to talk to me."

"Good of you, Vincenzo. I know this can't be an easy time for you."

Enrico gave a crisp nod. "My father and I didn't always get on well, but—" He glanced away and drew a hard breath. "Is your father still alive?"

Malcolm swallowed a laugh and a curse. "He died last year." Funny how those words now seemed an insult to Raoul.

"I'm sorry."

"We never got on well. It seems that should make it easier. But I think perhaps it leaves one with more questions."

Enrico inclined his head, as though he didn't trust himself to speak. They moved to a wrought iron table and chairs in the shade of an olive tree.

"Sofia and Kit told me about their talks with you yesterday," Enrico said. "Easier that we don't have to fence round the truth. I don't think I'd do very well trying to hide secrets from you, in any case."

"Actually, I was going to make you my compliments," Malcolm said. "You managed to hide the Elsinore League papers under the noses of several agents, with none of us any the wiser."

"That was Sofia," Enrico said. "I just gave her the papers. She's always been cleverer at such things than I am. And then the damned things disappeared. Under all our noses."

"Any idea who might have taken them?"

Enrico shook his head. "I've been wracking my brain, but I was trying hard not to seem to pay overmuch attention to the urn where they were hidden, so Thurston wouldn't suspect anything. God, talk about farce combined with tragedy." He stretched his legs out and contemplated the dusty toes of his boots. "I've been wondering if we should tell Thurston the whole, now."

"I haven't, for what it's worth," Malcolm said. "Though I can't promise it won't become necessary in the course of the investigation."

"Sofia wants to tell him. Kit isn't so sure."

"In many ways, I suspect you and your sister are closer to Thurston than his own children are."

Enrico frowned. "Yes, perhaps. I hadn't ever—He was always easier to get on with than my father. He didn't expect as much. But, more than that. He listens more. Not that I'd say I agree with his view of the world, either. I've heard enough about Lord Carfax to know he's not a man I'd care to do business with unless I had to." He shot a look at Malcolm.

"I used to work for Carfax," Malcolm said. "He wasn't a man I cared to do business with then. I don't work for him any longer."

"Difficult to break away, isn't it?" Enrico said.

"It was for a long time. But after the terms we parted on, I doubt Carfax wants my services any longer." Malcolm watched Enrico for a moment. "Carfax spied on my friends and me when we were at Oxford. We were nothing like as organized as the Carbonari. I'd say Carfax did us the honor of thinking us worth fearing, save that Carfax tends to fear dissidents of all stripes. His opposition to the Elsinore League is one of the few places I agree with him."

Enrico hunched his shoulders, gaze on the table. "I'm not sure how we made the initial contact with him. We don't share information unless we have to."

"The Carbonari's secrecy is impressive," Malcolm said.

Enrico met Malcolm's gaze, his own hardening. "It's

necessary. To combat men like my father."

"And the guns?"

"Words are a powerful weapon, Rannoch. But not the only one." Enrico stared out across the lake, gaze fixed on a heron soaring over the water. "I couldn't believe it when I learned Thurston was the one acting for Carfax. It made it easier to pass the information. But I was caught in the middle when the guns disappeared."

"The shipment of guns disappeared?" Malcolm said, trying to keep his voice casual.

"Not all of it. But not all of the first shipment reached us. Thurston claimed he sent them all. No one could figure out where they went missing. Of course, my colleagues thought I should know the answers because I knew Thurston. At the same time, I couldn't ask Thurston directly. I couldn't even let Thurston have a glimmering that I knew." He watched the heron dive into the water. "Either Thurston was lying or his own people double-crossed him, or someone on our end stole some of the guns. I never even saw the guns, but my own friends see me as a traitor."

"Not an easy position."

Enrico gave a defensive shrug. "It's not as though I'm the only one under suspicion. But ever since Sofia told me about her talk with you yesterday, I've been wondering—Father knew about the list of names. And he knew Thurston was trading guns for it on Carfax's behalf."

"But not that you and your sister were involved. As far as we know."

"No. But we don't know how long he's known about the papers and the trade for the guns."

"No."

"What if he knew months ago? When we made the first

trade with Carfax." Enrico sat forwards in his chair. "What if Father's the one who took some of the guns? To get Thurston and our side suspecting each other. The whole deal nearly fell apart then." He scanned Malcolm's face. "Does that sound mad?"

"On the contrary," Malcolm said. "It sounds like precisely the sort of thing the Elsinore League might do."

Mélanie stared after Raoul. He had gone to see Margaret almost immediately after she told him what Mary Shelley had revealed about Margaret's meeting with Vincenzo in Milan and their conversation about Alistair.

Harry touched her arm. "He'll be all right. If anyone is used to reevaluating situations and people, it's O'Roarke."

Mélanie saw Raoul's white face and the rare shock in his gaze when she'd told him. "It's not easy to learn you've been wrong about someone close to you."

"I imagine O'Roarke would say it's no more than he deserves. Not that I'd wish it on him, either."

Mélanie met Harry's gaze. "And I, of all people, shouldn't be worrying about it?"

Harry gave a smile that was quick and unexpectedly sweet. "One could say you're uniquely positioned to understand."

"You're kind, Harry."

"Don't talk rubbish." He offered her his arm. "Some time with the children might help."

Mélanie nodded. "You go down, I'll join you in a moment. I need to fetch my hat." And she needed a moment to order her thoughts. She'd seen Raoul go into danger countless times. Why was this worrying her so much? The danger

378

wasn't physical. But Margaret O'Roarke had gone from being a shadowy, not quite real, image to being a vivid presence. And now, someone she feared, for reasons she couldn't quite articulate.

Harry nodded, as though he understood. Better perhaps than she did herself. She went back into the villa, unusually quiet with all the children at the lake. But as she started across the entrance hall to the stairs, a sound struck her in the quiet. A faint scrape. She wouldn't have given it a second thought if it weren't that the villa should be empty, except for the servants who would be in the kitchen. She went still and she heard it again. From Malcolm's study. Odd how one's house could suddenly seem full of traps. But then, that had been her reality for so long she could scarcely remember anything else.

She moved towards the study, sliding her feet over the tiles. Roman sandals were almost as good for quiet movement as satin evening slippers. She paused by a Boulle cabinet and snatched up a bronze candelabrum. Sometimes one had to take weapons where one could find them.

She eased open the door of the study. A whiff of her husband's shaving soap greeted her. And another scent, too elusive to specify, but there. No other sign of an intruder. One of the windows was open. The bronze velvet curtains stirred in the breeze. Perhaps Malcolm had left the window open? Her senses prickled. She eased the door shut and stepped into the room.

The breeze accounted for the stirring of the long curtains. And yet—She moved towards them, gripping the candelabrum. She put a hand on the curtains.

A fist closed round the other end of the candelabrum. Mélanie tightened her own grip and fell backwards. Her weight pulled the intruder off balance. She lurched to the side

379

and twisted her arm, flipping the intruder onto his back.

The intruder stared up at her from the carpet with a sharp blue gaze, his fair hair gleaming in the light from the window. "*Buongiorno, cara,*" said Julien St. Juste. "Very adroitly done."

CHAPTER 30

Mélanie stared into that cool, maddening blue gaze. "You let me."

"On the contrary." Julien sprang to his feet. "You've always been a good physical match for me."

Mélanie set down the candelabrum, ignoring the memories his words stirred, which, as Julien knew perfectly well, had nothing to do with fighting. "You wanted me to find you."

Julien tugged his coat smooth. "Rather a leap."

"I wouldn't have been able to hear you in the room otherwise. Don't you ever think of just calling, like normal people?"

"I didn't necessarily want to see everyone else in the household." Julien flicked a speck of lint from his sleeve. "Besides, I wanted a look at the study."

"My husband's study."

He twitched his shirt cuff smooth. "Don't tell me you haven't gone through it yourself."

Julien had always known how to sting. "Not recently."

"More fool you. Malcolm Rannoch is obviously a clever man, and he doesn't leave papers lying about unnecessarily. He also keeps a miniature of you and his children where he can look at it easily. Despite the fact that you're in the same house."

"You'll have to accept that some things are beyond you, Julien. Like family feeling."

"Perhaps." Julien hitched himself up on the edge of the desk and regarded her. "You look well." He put out a hand and lifted her loose hair from her shoulder, then let the strands fall against her neck. "You were made for sunlight and liberty of all sorts. Italy suits you. Far better than stuffy, fog-bound Britain."

"I think you may be underestimating Britain."

"I rarely underestimate anything. You can't tell me you aren't enjoying Italy."

"It's a beautiful country. Though our stay here is proving a bit complicated."

"I'm sorry."

"For what?"

"Not checkmating Carfax for you."

Mélanie pulled her gauze scarf round her shoulders, despite the warmth of the sun. "Carfax is my problem, Julien."

"He's a problem I'd have liked to help you with, if I could. For what it's worth, I told you the truth in London in June, when I said I didn't know if Carfax knew the truth about you. If I'd suspected he was about to move against you, I'd have tried to protect you in my negotiations with him."

"Thank you, Julien. That's charming, even if I don't believe a word of it."

"Call it professional courtesy. I hate to see Carfax

382

manipulate anyone. Least of all, those I'm fond of."

Mélanie snorted.

"You've always underestimated my feelings for you, *cara*. Though I don't deny it's pleasant the change in your circumstances has brought us together again."

Nine-tenths of what Julien said was lies. The challenge was teasing out the one-tenth that was sincere. "The Elsinore League are looking for you," Mélanie said.

"Yes, I know."

Mélanie met that cool, mocking gaze. "How long have you been here?"

"You mean, did I get rid of Vincenzo?" Julien held his hand up to the light from the window and examined his nails. "You know I'd hardly have caviled at it, but do you really imagine he was enough of a threat?"

"That depends on what the Elsinore League want with you."

"An excellent question."

"Have you ever worked for them before?"

Julien gave a faint smile and crossed his legs at the ankle. "Let's say I've done business with them. I'm not necessarily averse to doing so again, for the right price. But they can be a dangerous group to work with."

"You aren't afraid of anything."

"I'm also not foolhardy."

"Had you met Vincenzo?"

"No."

"Do you know what the Elsinore League want with you?"

"I got in touch with them myself when I heard they were looking for me. Told them there was no sense being so roundabout."

"And?"

"On the surface, they want to engage my services."

"To do what?"

She had no very real hope he would answer, but after a moment he said, "To get rid of someone they think is in their way."

"Who?"

"An old friend of yours. And I suppose, one could say, of mine, if I owned to having friends."

"Not Hortense?" Fear tightened her throat.

"No. A more obvious target, though perhaps also more surprising. Your former lover. Raoul O'Roarke."

For a moment, reality spun round her. She put a hand against the wall to anchor herself. The walnut paneling was smooth beneath her fingers. "Why in God's name would they want—"

"I know you were in love with the man, but surely you can imagine reasons people might want to kill O'Roarke."

"But the Elsinore League? Now?"

"Yes, I confess I told them I thought O'Roarke was a somewhat dated target, unless they were particularly interested in Spain at the moment. Or Ireland, though he's hardly able to wield a lot of power there. Of course, Carfax is still afraid of him. But Carfax will jump at any shadow with 'Bonapartist' attached to it."

"What did the Elsinore League say?"

"They didn't. They said that it was their business. To which I replied that if I was going to be asked to turn on a former associate, I'd at least like to know why."

"Julien!" Mélanie managed to put a touch of raillery into her voice. "One would almost imagine you were admitting to feelings."

"I do have a certain code of conduct. And I rather take

384

offense to being treated as a mere killing machine." He examined his nails again. "Besides, Josephine was fond of O'Roarke. I believe you're still fond of him."

"Your point being?"

He looked up and met her gaze, head tilted to the side. It made him look like a beguiling schoolboy. She suspected he was very well aware of the effect. "I wouldn't say not causing you pain would entirely rule my actions, but it is something I'd seek to avoid."

"So you refused."

"Yes. Though I'm not sure they take my answer as final. Which may mean O'Roarke has a bit of time before they try something else."

"Why make such a point of reaching out to you? I know you know Raoul, but he also doesn't trust you. Surely others—"

"I think they had an ulterior purpose."

"They wanted you to do something else?"

"They wanted something else I possess. Secrets can be their own currency."

"About Hortense?"

"No. Older secrets. Potentially more damaging secrets. Which it doesn't suit me to have come to light just now. Certainly not in service of the Elsinore League's agenda."

Mélanie studied him for a long moment. She'd got to know him seven years ago, when they escorted Hortense Bonaparte into Switzerland to give birth to her lover's child in secret, more than she'd have thought possible at the start of the journey. And she'd probably revealed herself to him more than she'd intended, or certainly than was wise. But in many ways, he remained a cipher. "What are you going to do now?" she asked.

"Prudence dictates I should make myself scarce. But I've never been one to listen much to prudence. I find I'm rather curious to see how this drama plays out. My money's on you, but I wouldn't wager anything I couldn't afford to lose."

"Thank you, Julien. Your trust never fails to be endearing."

He reached out and brushed his fingers against her cheek. "You'll be able to find me if you need to, *cara*."

Much as Mélanie would have liked to say she wouldn't, she couldn't be at all sure that was the case.

"Well, well. Who'd have thought I'd be deemed important enough that the Elsinore League want to get rid of me?" Raoul looked round the terrace. Mélanie had run down to the beach to get Laura the moment Julien melted away. They'd gone back up to the villa to find Malcolm and Raoul both just returned. "I don't know whether to be flattered or appalled."

Malcolm cast a glance at his father. "Carfax calls you one of the most dangerous men in Britain."

Raoul lifted a brow. "It wouldn't be the first time Carfax was known to exaggerate the threat posed by Bonapartists."

"Julien said almost exactly the same thing," Mélanie said.

Laura had scarcely taken her eyes from Raoul since Mélanie recounted her interview with Julien, but when she spoke now, it was in a voice of suppressed calm. "The Elsinore League don't know how Trenchard died, so far as we know."

"And you think they might blame me?" Raoul moved to her side. The four of them were huddled together near the balustrade. No one had made a move to sit.

"You were investigating Trenchard at the time." Laura reached for his hand, though she spoke in the same controlled voice. "They could have learned that, with or without knowing Archie was helping you. They might well have known Trenchard was trying to blackmail Mélanie. You have a better motive than most of the obvious suspects. A far clearer motive than Louisa Craven. No one would suspect her without teasing out secrets we all hope to keep buried."

"They might even have thought that your being the murderer would explain Mel's and my keeping quiet," Malcolm said in a low voice.

"And as you pointed out, they avenge their own," Mélanie reminded Raoul.

"A number of them were quite angry with Trenchard when he died," Raoul pointed out, lacing his fingers through Laura's own. "We wondered if members of the League itself might have been behind his death."

"But other members weren't angry," Laura said. "And even those who were angry with him might have felt the need to avenge one of their own—one of their leaders—after he died."

Raoul glanced down at her hand where it curled round his own. "It's possible," he acknowledged.

"Or the motive might be that they knew about your work against them with my mother," Malcolm said. "Though one wonders why they'd seek vengeance now."

"Suppose they'd learned about Archie?" Mélanie asked.

Raoul frowned. "Then one would think they'd turn on Archie, not me. But we should warn Archie." He tightened his grip on Laura's hand and drew her closer, though he was still frowning in consideration of the evidence. "I'm more interested in what the League want to know about Julien's past. Particularly given that his past is such a cipher. But I'm not blind to the risks of the other threat." He drew a breath and looked from Malcolm to Mélanie. "It seems I didn't do you any favors by coming here with you." He cast a glance at Laura. "I'm rather at a loss as to whether I'd make things better or worse if I left for Spain."

"Don't." Laura turned to face him and put her hands on his shoulders. "Don't you dare think any of us would be safer without you. Leave when you need to, but not because of some threat. We can't live like that. Besides, we're all known to be connected to you."

He reached out and pulled her against him. "The more so because of the way we've been living."

"We've been living like a family," Laura said, her voice muffled by his cravat.

"Which we are," Malcolm said.

Raoul met Malcolm's gaze for a moment and pressed his lips to Laura's hair. "I couldn't leave now, in any case. Not in the middle of the investigation, with so much hanging over us and Julien and the Elsinore League in the wings."

Laura lifted her head from his shoulder. "So I won't wake in the middle of the night and find you've slipped from our bed for everyone's good?"

"Not unless I'm on the trail of the Elsinore League."

"Not entirely reassuring, but it will do for the moment."

"Oddly," Mélanie said, "I don't know that Julien is our enemy, at least at present."

"No," Raoul said. "I don't believe he is. Not that I think he'd cavil at killing me if he thought he had strong enough reason. But I don't know that he'd do it for the Elsinore League. And I'm quite sure he won't take kindly to being manipulated by them. Or to their attempting to manipulate

388

him."

"You've already been attacked since we've been here," Mélanie said.

"The bandit attack?" Raoul appeared to give it honest consideration. "I suppose it's possible they targeted me. But they weren't very effective."

"Perhaps that's when they decided they needed Julien St. Juste," Laura said.

"Julien's right," Raoul said. "He's an odd choice to go after me. He's a brilliant assassin, and he knows me, but the fact that he knows me means I'd be on my guard."

"Would you have been?" Mélanie said, remembering those moments in Hyde Park in June and countless other moments from the past. "If you hadn't known someone wanted you dead? You may not trust Julien, but you wouldn't have been expecting him to pull out a knife or a pistol." Or a wire, or poison in a glass of wine, or any of a number of other methods. Mélanie gripped her arms, trying to suppress a shiver. She'd faced danger. She was used to her husband facing danger. She was used to Raoul facing it, above all. But somehow, having the threat so immediate, and from someone they knew—

"Perhaps," Raoul said. "It's true I'm not as quick as I once was."

"Spare us," Malcolm said. "You aren't getting old, but that line is."

Raoul gave a faint smile. "In any case, I think Julien is right in this. It's more likely they chose him because of this information they want from him. I should very much like to know what that is. And if it's connected to the other things they're up to in Italy." He looked from Laura to Malcolm and Mélanie. "I need to tell you about my talk with Margaret."

389

Succinctly, he recounted what Mélanie already in part knew—Margaret's work for Alistair and the Elsinore League.

Laura stared at him and shook her head. "Good God. Margaret and I were both working for the Elsinore League."

"Not quite in the same way, though in the end, they were blackmailing her too."

Laura drew back to look at him, though she was still standing in the circle of his arm. "Do you think Margaret knew? Why they wanted to find Julien St. Juste?"

A shadow flickered through Raoul's gaze. "I'd have doubted it a week ago. But a week ago I'd have doubted a lot of things I've learned about Margaret since. She admitted she wanted me dead back in '98. A lot's changed since then. She certainly seemed more conciliatory when we spoke. But then that's precisely how she might seem if she knew about such a plot. And I could certainly see why she'd still be angry. Both politically and because she thinks I ruined her life."

Laura drew a breath. "You didn't—"

Raoul brushed the backs of his fingers against her cheek. "She doesn't have the life she could have had if she hadn't married me."

"She didn't have to accept you. Give Margaret the credit of having some responsibility for her own actions."

"Of course she's responsible. But—"

"Everything isn't your responsibility, Raoul O'Roarke."

"Family failing." Mélanie looked at Malcolm.

"I don't know what you're talking about." Malcolm grinned at her and pushed himself away from the balustrade. "We need to tell the others at least some of this."

"Preferably with minimal drama," Raoul said.

"You can't minimize this drama," Laura said.

"Perhaps not," Malcolm said. "But we can try."

Frances gasped, but she and Archie and the Davenports listened to Raoul's and Mélanie's accounts with admirable calm. Frances stared at Raoul. "I always knew you ran appalling risks, but—"

"Quite." Laura was sitting beside Raoul on the settee in the rose salon.

"And Margaret knew." Frances's brows drew together.

"She didn't necessarily know why the Elsinore League wanted St. Juste," Raoul said.

"Perhaps not, but she has a lot to answer for over the Dunboyne information," Malcolm said.

Raoul met his son's gaze. "She was extremely angry with me at the time. And she was working for what she believed in. It's hard for me to quarrel with that."

"Perhaps not, but I can," Malcolm said. His voice was grim in a way Mélanie seldom heard it.

"I can't say I'm much in charity with her, either." Archie stretched out his legs, feet crossed at the ankle. "Though with advanced years"—Frances hit him—"one learns to be tolerant of others' past mistakes. One finds one has made so many oneself. What interests me is the Elsinore League's current fascination with Julien St. Juste. That I haven't heard a whiff of." He looked at Raoul. "St. Juste was close to Josephine Bonaparte, wasn't he?"

"He was her lover," Raoul said. "Before she married Bonaparte. And close to her throughout the rest of her life. I think she's one of the few people he was loyal to."

"Julien claimed the secret wasn't to do with Hortense," Mélanie said. "He didn't say it wasn't to do with Josephine.

391

Not that he was necessarily telling the truth in any case."

"Do you think the Elsinore League want Julien St. Juste because of something he did or knows? Or because of who he is?" Harry asked.

"I've been asking myself the same thing," Raoul said. "And it's the more interesting because we aren't even sure of St. Juste's nationality. If this secret goes back to before his affair with Josephine, it's from very early in his career. When he'd have been in his teens. Before he earned a reputation. Or it could be that the truth of who he is is valuable information in and of itself. Which makes the question of who Julien St. Juste is even more interesting."

"And none of it gets us closer to who killed Conte Vincenzo," Laura said. She looked at Mélanie. "Unless you think—"

Mélanie stroked Berowne, who had jumped up in her lap and was kneading her stomach. She'd been going over her conversation with Julien ever since she left him. "I think Julien was telling the truth about not killing Vincenzo. Mostly because I think he's right that Vincenzo wasn't that much of a threat to him. But I could be wrong. Especially if Julien thought killing Vincenzo could conceal whatever this information is the Elsinore League were after. Are after." She looked at Raoul. "Do you think this means we were right to suspect Julien might be British?"

"Perhaps," he said. "But not necessarily. The Elsinore League's interests are international. As we've had driven home by recent events."

"Could he be—" Cordelia shook her head. "I know it sounds like a lending-library novel, but the bastard son of a prince or something?"

"That sounds rather annoyingly like Julien." Mélanie

392

scratched Berowne under the chin. "It would certainly explain his air of entitlement. Though I'm not quite sure what anyone would gain from the truth coming out."

"Embarrassment to his parents," Harry said. "In some cases he could even make a claim of inheritance."

"Blackmail is one of the Elsinore League's primary tools of power," Laura said. "Whatever it is, I'd hazard a guess it's something that would let them blackmail someone. Unless—"

Raoul met her gaze. "He's actually the heir to a throne? I've heard of stranger things. Though it's hard to see Julien abrogating such a role."

"It's even harder to see him in it," Mélanie said. "He'd be bored to tears by the protocol. And in a way, he'd have less power than he does now."

Raoul met her gaze for a moment. "As usual, you're an astute observer of character, *querida*. You make a good point. But for the moment, all we can do is speculate."

"And try to get Julien to reveal more," Mélanie said. "I don't think we've seen the last of him."

Malcolm exchanged a look with Raoul. "Nor do I."

CHAPTER 31

Malcolm slammed shut the bedchamber door. "Damnation."

Mélanie, on her way to her dressing table to dress for dinner, paused and turned back to her husband. "Julien is always a complication. You know how worried I was about him in London. But I honestly don't think he's a threat now. At least not a direct one. And I'm rather glad he's made contact. Easier to know where to find him. Or at least how to find him."

"Not that." Malcolm strode across the room. "He's not going to stop. He's never going to stop. He's not going to take half the precautions he should. And one of these days, he's going to get himself killed."

No need to ask who "he" was, and it clearly wasn't Julien. Mélanie folded her arms over her chest, the fears she'd been holding at bay downstairs welling up in her throat. "Raoul's always lived his life as though he could be killed at any moment," she said. "It's part of what makes him so

394

formidable. In the Peninsula, I'm not sure he really did expect to survive."

"I know." Malcolm had stopped midway across the room and was staring at a Renaissance oil of Persephone stretching out a hand to Hades. "It's part of why he wanted us to get married."

Mélanie drew a breath. Malcolm turned his head to meet her gaze. "He'd never have put it this way to you, but he wanted you and Colin to be safe. Another part of it was giving me a reason not to kill myself. And part of it, I think, was actually about spying."

Mélanie returned her husband's gaze. For all they'd discussed Raoul, they'd never quite talked about this. "Don't tell me you didn't realize," Malcolm said.

She stared down at her hands, fingers moving over her diamond and white-gold bracelet. "I did. About you, quite some time ago. But I never precisely thought he was trying to protect me." In those days, she'd seen Raoul as far more of a cold calculator. She'd learned in recent years, in bits and pieces, how wrong she'd been, but she'd never gone back and recast this part of the past in light of her changed perceptions.

Malcolm was watching her with a look that was oddly tender. "You've always been inclined to underestimate his feelings for you. I think he was afraid your own recklessness would get you killed, but he knew you wouldn't stop. In Lisbon with me, you were running risks, but they weren't physical. Or at least, not as much." He studied her a moment. "It doesn't change the impressiveness of what you did."

"No, it's not that." She studied the play of the evening sunlight on the tiny diamonds. "At the time I'd have been angry, and accused him of trying to wrap me in cotton wool. Thinking back, I'm rather grateful. I have thought—" She

395

swallowed, because it was hard to put it into words and they were still stepping on uncharted ground. "I think he sensed what was between us before we did."

Malcolm nodded, gaze still steady. "I think he did. And in the event he didn't survive the war, he thought we'd at least have each other. He's a master chess player. But his goals are personal far more often than he'd admit. None of which changes the crazy risks he runs."

Raoul directing a skirmish with a wound in his side, Raoul sauntering unarmed into a roomful of British soldiers and slipping out with a stolen document, Raoul with his scalp bloody from a sniper's bullet that took off a lock of his hair. "He doesn't run as many now as he used to. That is, he's not in constant danger as much."

"Hardly reassuring, given the dangers he still faces."

"We run risks, Malcolm. In Vienna we faced down assassins. In Brussels you were on the battlefield. In Paris, we sneaked a prisoner out of the Conciergerie, and Colin and I were held up at gunpoint. Even in London we were chased and shot at. Even here—"

"But we're a bit more cautious." He glanced at Jessica's cradle. "We don't forget we have children." His hands closed on the back of the sofa. "Just before we left London, Raoul told me he'd made provision for Laura and Emily should anything happen to him. And more or less asked us to look after them if anything did."

For some reason that sent a fresh chill through her. "He's being prudent."

"That's what he said. But I could see the reality in his eyes. I told myself what he's doing in Spain now is more tactical than what he did during the war. But now he's got the bloody Elsinore League after him. And, much as he gives the impression to the contrary, O'Roarke's not superhuman. All it would take is one misstep, one moment of distraction—"

"Raoul doesn't have those often."

"But everyone makes mistakes." Malcolm dug his fingers into his hair. "I don't know whether he's safer getting away to Spain—where the Elsinore League can almost certainly follow him—or here, where we can keep an eye on him, but we know they're plotting. I don't know—" He broke off staring across the room.

"What?" Mélanie asked.

"How the devil to protect him."

Mélanie stared at her husband. The thought of anyone protecting Raoul was laughable, and yet— "Darling, Raoul would be the first to tell you you can't make yourself responsible for protecting everyone. He'd understand, because he has precisely the same tendency."

"It's not that. That is, I do feel responsible to a degree, but that's not why—" Malcolm drew a breath. She could see him struggling for the words, the way he did when he spoke of the things that meant most to him. "I don't want Laura to lose him, of course. I don't want you to lose him. I don't want the children to grow up not knowing him. But—Damn it, Mel, you aren't the only one who loves him."

For a moment the world seemed to go still, as pieces of her understanding fell apart and reformed about her. It shouldn't be so surprising. She'd watched, with wonder and a lump in her throat, the bond growing between the two men. She'd seen their shared laughter, their quick, easy sympathy. But somehow the raw fear in Malcolm's voice and gaze, the actual words, took it a step further.

"The risk of caring for another person," she said. "Knowing one can lose them."

397

"Yes." Malcolm swallowed, hard. "But loving some people makes the risk particularly fraught. Just because I've turned thirty doesn't mean I've stopped needing my father. Quite the reverse, I sometimes think."

Even now, dealing with the complexities of her own relationship to the two men, she forgot sometimes the length and depth of the bond between Malcolm and Raoul. It went back far before she had met Raoul, before she had even been born. At moments, even before Malcolm knew the truth of her past, she would watch the two men and feel as though she had stumbled into a play in the midst of the second act without knowing what had come before.

Something eased in her chest at the thought that Malcolm's feelings about Raoul were so like her own. "I never used to say goodbye to him," she said in a low voice. "Because we were neither of us quite sure if we'd see each other again."

It was something she'd never have dared talk to Malcolm about before, but he nodded. "When he wrote me the letter from Les Carmes that Hortense gave to me, I'm quite sure he thought he was going to die in the Terror. We know how close he came to going to the guillotine. He almost died in Ireland. And God knows how many other times through the years I don't even know of."

"Darling." Mélanie went to her husband and knelt on the sofa in front of him, her hands on his shoulders. "Living on the edge is part of who he is. He may be hard on others in the service of a cause, but he's harder on himself. You'll never change him. Laura understands that, I think. It's part of why their relationship works."

Malcolm gave a bleak smile. "I didn't say I wanted to change him. I'm quite fond of him as he is."

"You said you wanted to protect him. But I don't think

the man Raoul is can be protected. The best one can do is try to help him face down threats." She reached up and threaded her fingers together behind his neck. "You're so good at seeing things through others' eyes. You need to try to see this through his."

"I am. That's what's so damnable. I'm enough like him that it isn't that much of a stretch. I can understand why he won't change. I just—want more time with him."

Her heart tightened with fear and love. "We have to appreciate what we have and make the most of it. And watch out for the Elsinore League."

"That goes without saying. But he can't have it both ways. He can't be in our lives, and Laura's, and the children's, and make us care and go through all sorts of high-handed machinations to protect us, and then act as though his safety doesn't matter. It matters to us. If he cares for us at all—and God knows I believe he does—it's going to have to start mattering to him. And he's going to have to put up with our interfering."

Mélanie stared up at her husband. "That's rather irrefutable logic, Malcolm. Turning his own actions on their head. It sounds quite like something Raoul might say himself."

Malcolm bent his head and put his lips to hers. "Yes, well, I am his son."

Carlo, the Thurston footman, well acquainted now with Malcolm, informed him that the family had finished dinner and were in the grand salon, save for Signor Smythe, who was in the billiard room.

"Thank you." Malcolm relinquished his hat to Carlo. "I'll show myself in."

He might not have got away with such behavior in London, but manners were more relaxed among the expatriates here. And Malcolm's role in the investigation was already well known. Malcolm pushed open the door to the billiard room, little caring that he rattled the hinges. "Why do the Elsinore League want Raoul O'Roarke dead?"

John Smythe straightened up, his grip on the cue he held not faltering. "You work quickly, I'll give you that."

Malcolm slammed the door shut. "Unless, of course, they don't deem you important enough to have let you in on the reasons."

Smythe reached for the chalk and rubbed the tip of his cue. "No comment, Rannoch. Save that you must realize your accusation didn't surprise me."

"Then you know the reason. Unless you find it as inexplicable as I do?"

Smythe gave a short laugh. "If you know O'Roarke half as well as you seem to, surely you realize there are a score of reasons people might want him dead. Including you, I would think."

Malcolm advanced into the room and leaned a hand on the billiard table. "The Elsinore League usually play higher-level games."

"Have you told O'Roarke that?" Smythe set down the chalk and examined the tip of his cue. "Whatever I think of him, I can't deny he's consequential. Or have you fooled yourself into thinking he's become domestic just because he dallies with pretty Lady Tarrington and plays in the sand with her daughter and your children?"

"I never underestimate O'Roarke."

"No? Is it to guard against him that you have your wife's former lover living in your household?" Smythe set down the cue and regarded Malcolm with a gaze as hard and steady as a sword's point. "Are you quite without self-respect, Rannoch? When you think of what that man did to you, what he's very likely still doing to you under your very roof, perhaps at this very moment—"

"Thank you, Smythe. You can leave my household to me."

Smythe reached for a glass of brandy that stood on a brass-inlaid cabinet beside the billiard table. "He really has you bamboozled, doesn't he? Hasn't it occurred to you that a man who would set his mistress to marry and spy on his son has no morals whatsoever?"

Malcolm willed his face to betray no reaction. He'd suspected Alistair had known Raoul was his father. It shouldn't be a shock. It shouldn't matter. It was something almost anyone who knew Alistair, Arabella, and Raoul should be able to figure out. Hardly damaging information. And yet—"I hardly think the Elsinore League would turn on anyone over morality."

Smythe tossed down a drink of brandy. "O'Roarke is a very dangerous man."

"You sound like Carfax."

"Lord Carfax is a lot of things, but he's no fool. He's not afraid to do what needs to be done. Like the Elsinore League. Like O'Roarke himself."

That was true, to a degree. But recent events had shown Malcolm a great many differences in the limits of Carfax, O'Roarke, and the League. "The League are looking for a hold on Carfax? To counteract the papers, if he gets them?"

"You can't expect me to comment on that. Except that

there are any number of reasons a hold on Carfax would be useful." Smythe returned his brandy to the cabinet. "You won't be able to protect him, you know."

"Carfax?"

"O'Roarke. Not against the League. You're clever, Rannoch, I'll give you that, but you're no match for them. You're not ruthless enough." Smythe pressed his finger over a drop of brandy that had splashed from the glass, blotting it out. "And losing him is going to eat at you. Though, knowing what he's done to you, I can't for the life of me understand why."

"Can't you? You seem fairly obsessed with your father yourself."

Smythe drew a sharp breath. Then he reached inside his coat and tossed a letter on the billiard table. "I found that the day of the murder. I've been trying to make sense of it, but I admit you're better suited to that than I am. If you really want to find Vincenzo's killer, instead of wasting time on me, you might want to take a look at it. "

CHAPTER 32

Malcolm pushed the bedchamber door to. "John Smythe is the sort of man who makes me regret I don't believe in dueling."

Mélanie looked up at her husband from the armchair where she sat holding Jessica, who had fallen asleep nursing. He hadn't actually slammed the door this time, but the tension in his shoulders was plain. Anger blazed from his eyes. The sort of unbanked rage she rarely saw on her husband's face. "He makes me regret women can't duel."

Malcolm strode across the room. "There has to be a way to get Diana away from that monster. Normally I try to stay out of people's personal tangles in an investigation—"

"Darling. We've never really managed to stay out of personal tangles."

"Perhaps not. But in this case, it seems imperative not to do so."

"Surely Kit and Thurston—"

"I hope so. I talked to Thurston earlier today, though it

may not be the best thing for the investigation. I think she needs legal protection. Smythe is both nastier and smarter than he looks."

"A lethal combination."

Malcolm crossed to her side and dropped down on the chair arm. She could feel the tension radiating off him. He touched his fingers to Jessica's head, then put a hand on Mélanie's shoulder. His touch was gentle but his fingers were taut with suppressed anger. "He knows about you, sweetheart. I learned that this afternoon."

Mélanie drew a breath that cut more sharply than she hoped her husband saw. "We had to assume he very likely did. It's not the threat it would have been in Britain." Though it made it all the harder for them ever to consider going back.

"No." Malcolm's gaze slid to the side, then returned to her face, at once armored and unexpectedly vulnerable, like smoky glass. "He also knows about Raoul. That he was your spymaster. And that he's my father."

This time the shock was a stab beneath the seafoam silk of her dressing gown and the linen of her nightdress. A reminder of a tangle they had learned to live with, but never really resolved. "We had to know that was likely too."

"Yes." Malcolm pressed a kiss to her hair. "And O'Roarke's being my father doesn't really put anyone in more danger. It's just more of our personal lives being dragged into public view."

"Does he know—" She couldn't quite say it.

"About Colin?" Malcolm slid his right hand behind her neck. "I don't think so, or I suspect he'd have taunted me with it." Malcolm kissed her hair again, then drew back and reached inside his coat. "Smythe also gave me this."

He put a folded paper in her hand. Mélanie smoothed it

404

open. A letter in Italian met her gaze.

Elena,

I won't waste time on recriminations now. If you wish to see your daughter in the future, I think you know quite well what you need to do.

Vincenzo

Mélanie stared up at her husband.

"Smythe found it," Malcolm said. "I think he was holding on to it, wondering how to best use it. Then tonight he decided to throw it to me to get me off the scent of the Elsinore League."

Mélanie nodded. "But that doesn't mean it's insignificant. If Vincenzo was blackmailing the contessa over Sofia—" She shivered. Because she liked the contessa. And she knew just how strong a motive a threat to one's child could be. "Perhaps it would be best if I talked to her."

Malcolm nodded. "I was hoping you'd say that. You can appeal to her as one mother to another. And she'll probably be far less on her guard. Though, God knows she shouldn't be."

He got to his feet and went to take off his coat. Mélanie put Jessica in her cradle. "Do the contessa and Thurston know about Kit and Sofia?" she asked. In the midst of the investigation and their own tensions, she'd lost sight of the personal drama others in the investigation were going through.

"Not that I know of," Malcolm said. "I hope they can confide in their parents. From what you've said about Sofia, and what I've seen of Kit, I think it might help them realize what they want."

Something in his words struck a chord. Mélanie turned and studied her husband, now unwinding his cravat from round his neck. The precise movements of his hands, the taut

405

control in his shoulders, the restless intensity in his eyes, not as well banked as it had once been. "Malcolm, what do you want?"

Malcolm stared at her, fingers frozen on his cravat. "What do I *want?*"

"It's a reasonable question. And, to my shame, one I don't think I've ever precisely asked you."

He gave a short laugh. "I'm not in Kit's shoes, thank God. I have what I want."

"We both know it's not that simple, darling. One doesn't get what one wants and settle happily into bliss. Life's too complicated."

"I want us to be safe. I want Colin and Jessica to be happy and secure."

"That's what you want for us. What do you want for yourself?"

"Christ, Mel." His voice cut with unaccustomed force. "We've just had to leave our home. We're in the middle of an investigation that involves both Carfax and the Elsinore League. Carfax is trading guns, the Elsinore League are trying to checkmate Carfax and kill O'Roarke, and are making use of his wife to do it. Not to mention dragging in David and Simon. We have a missing list of Elsinore League members, and Carbonari and the Levellers in the mix. And Julien St. Juste is caught up in the whole thing. This is no time—"

"That's just it, darling. There's never a time. Not in the lives we live. We tend to run from one crisis to another, with this one the worst of all, perhaps. But—"

Malcolm began to unbutton his waistcoat with quick snaps of his fingers. "I want to learn who murdered Conte Vincenzo. I want to keep O'Roarke from getting killed by the Elsinore League, or running off to Spain and getting himself

406

killed there. I want to extricate Diana Smythe from her brute of a husband. I want to find the list of Elsinore League members. I'd like to keep talk about my wife's past from getting any more public than it already is, though that may be a vain hope given the number of people who already know. In God's name, isn't that enough?"

"Darling—" She took a half step forwards. The edge in his voice shook her, yet it also told her how very much he needed to talk.

He tossed his waistcoat after his coat and cravat and unfastened his shirt cuffs as though he were ticking off items on a list. Or firing at a target. "We were both afraid we'd be bored here. Which certainly isn't the case. Perhaps that's a good thing. We're used to going from crisis to crisis, as you say. I begin to wonder if our current situation isn't too much, but all we can do for the present is try to get through it. If we get through the next week without anything adverse happening to anyone we care about, I shall count it a great success."

Mélanie moved to her husband's side and set her hands on his shoulders. The light from the candles on her dressing table caught the lines of strain about his eyes and mouth and the restless tension in his eyes. She'd seen him in so many moods, but she'd never seen his gaze quite like it was now. As though he he'd been cut loose from his moorings and wasn't sure where to seek refuge, and at the same time one word might set fire to tinder. "It's a challenge," she said. "But we've faced challenges before. We always find a way to muddle through. And that doesn't mean we should ignore what we're feeling." She touched his face. "Darling, you can't hold it all in forever. I'm not going to collapse. I can handle it. God knows I deserve it, but more than that, I'm your wife. You should be able to talk to me."

"Damn it, Mel." He jerked free of her hold and strode across the room. "This is no time to ask for emotional confidences. Especially when—"

"It's my fault we're in this situation in the first place?"

Her question hung in the air like pistol smoke. He stared out the dark window and drew a breath that cut like smashed glass. "It's Carfax's fault. But you, of all people, should appreciate that one can't wallow in one's own feelings at a time like this."

Mélanie swallowed. She could almost feel the tension vibrating off him. He was so close to the explosion she'd long thought he needed to give vent to. And now they were there, she couldn't tell if she welcomed it or feared it. "It may be precisely at times like this that one needs to talk most," she said.

He strode to the bed and snatched up his dressing gown. "Because it's worked so well in the past?" He jerked on the dressing gown.

"Malcolm, you can't deny that when we do talk—"

He spun towards her, eyes blazing. "When we do talk, every time we've talked for most of the past six years, I was confiding in someone whose purpose in life was to take information from me."

"Malcolm." She stared at him. Somehow for all her fears, she hadn't been suspecting this. The memory of his raw sobs when he finally broke down after Alistair's death echoed in her ears. She could feel the shudder of his breath against her chest and his fingers clenching her gown as she held him. "You can't think I was being an agent at those times."

He gave a twisted smile, though his gaze still burned. "I'm enough of an agent myself to know one never fully leaves off

408

being an agent." He scraped his hands over his face. "I love you, Mel. I'm not sorry I love you. God knows I'm not sorry I married you. I can't imagine a life without you. But there's no denying I was wrong to trust you. Wrong to trust you as an agent. Wrong to let my guard down as a husband."

Myriad moments came flooding back to her, cautious confidences, unexpected vulnerabilities, sudden leaps across the divide between two people who held the world at a distance. The moments that had forged the bond between them. For him to think those moments had been mistakes—"Darling. I can't tell you what it meant when you could share things with me. When I could share them with you."

"Which doesn't change the fact that I was a fool." He gave another hard laugh. "That's what Smythe called me. He was wrong about the reasons, but I can't deny he was accurate about my idiocy."

Mélanie studied her husband across an expanse of candle-warmed carpet. This explosion had been coming for months, but something had triggered it. Julien's revelations about the threat to Raoul had set Malcolm on edge, but it had got worse since his recent interview with John Smythe. "Darling?" she said, keeping her voice steady with an effort. "What did Smythe say to you? That you were a fool to trust me?"

Malcolm scraped a hand over his hair. "He was saying anything to wound."

"But you were talking to him about Raoul." She flinched at the sorts of things Smythe might have said, though she could not quite bring herself to put them into words.

Malcolm prowled to the chest of drawers and poured two glasses of whisky. "He was at great pains to say I was a fool to

409

trust O'Roarke."

Mélanie looked steadily at her husband. "You're the furthest thing from a fool, darling. But you have a remarkable capacity for forgiveness. What else did he say?"

"Oh, the expected." Malcolm put one of the whiskies in her hand. "He wouldn't say anything about the League's reasons for wanting Raoul dead. Just that he's a dangerous man. And that I shouldn't assume O'Roarke acting domestic meant he'd changed."

Mélanie studied her husband. His tone was just a shade too perfectly calibrated to display nothing but casual response. "We already knew that was true, darling. Laura knows it's true. A lot's changed—more than I ever dreamed possible—but Raoul's always going to be the man he is."

"Of course." Malcolm tossed down half his own whisky. "Smythe's long on insults but short on insights."

"But I expect he said the man that Raoul is a good deal more dangerous than the man we think he is."

"Hardly surprising, given that Smythe works for the Elsinore League."

Mélanie took a sip of whisky. "He said Raoul is quite devoid of scruples and you shouldn't trust a man who had so deceived you?"

Malcolm's fingers tightened round his glass. "Something like that."

Mélanie kept her gaze on her husband's face. "I knew him. Better than anyone I'd have thought in those days in Spain. I always loved him." She could say that now, without worrying about how Malcolm would interpret it. "But I don't think I properly understood him until much later. Bit by bit, and especially after I learned he was your father. I used to think he was much more ruthless. More Machiavellian."

410

"Yes, he likes to give that impression." Despite the recent explosion, Malcolm gave a faint smile. "It's a way of distancing himself. Protecting others. And probably himself too."

"And I suppose it's possible we're wrong," Mélanie said. "That he really is ruthless, even more than I once thought, and this is all a long-term ploy to win our trust, for some reason. But I choose to believe not."

"So do I," Malcolm said.

"Even though—" She couldn't quite say it.

"I was wrong to trust you once? Despite that, I choose to trust you and O'Roarke now. Because the alternative is unthinkable."

CHAPTER 33

Malcolm woke far earlier than had become his wont in Italy. His own words of the night before echoed through his head. Further sleep was impossible with that uncharacteristic outburst running through his head. And yet, for all that, he felt strangely easier for having put his tangled feelings into words.

Mélanie's hand was pressed to his chest, her face turned into the pillow, her dark hair tumbled about her. He brushed his lips over her hand and then slid from beneath the covers and dressed quickly. Breeches, shirt, waistcoat, no coat or neckcloth. Later, if he paid calls in the service of the investigation, he might add more, but he'd got out of the habit of formal dressing here. Even Addison was resigned to it. And just possibly relieved, judging by the days he omitted a neckcloth himself. Shaving could wait for later as well.

Jessica was asleep in her cradle. He touched his fingers to her hair and cracked open the door to the night nursery to see Colin, Emily, Livia, and Chloe all still asleep in the gray light of dawn. Berowne, curled up at the foot of Colin's bed, opened one eye, then curled his paw over his face. Chloe's puppy didn't even stir on her bed.

The villa was quiet as he went round the gallery and downstairs, cool and still in the early morning. The door to the kitchen was ajar and he saw a faint glow and heard the whistling of a kettle. It was early even for the servants to be up. He went through to see if he could help Zarina, and found Raoul lifting a kettle from the range.

Malcolm studied the man John Smythe had warned him was an incalculable danger and morally bankrupt. "A remarkably domestic sight."

Raoul grinned at Malcolm over his shoulder. He was also without a coat or neckcloth and also hadn't yet shaved. "I made the coffee myself for years. No reason I can't do so here."

"So did I, if it comes to that. Sad how one forgets how self-sufficient one can be." Malcolm dropped into a chair at the deal kitchen table while Raoul poured the hot water into a tin pot over a muslin bag of grounds. "I saw Smythe."

Raoul gave a dry smile in a cloud of steam. "Not a task I envy you."

"I managed to refrain from physical violence this time. Not that I wasn't tempted, in a way I almost never am." Malcolm looked sideways at his father. "He knows. Not just about Mel. About you being her spymaster. And about you being my father."

Raoul drew in and released his breath. "We had to know that was a risk."

"Quite. His knowing about Mel isn't as much of a threat now we're here. Now Carfax knows, in any case. And his knowing you're my father really shouldn't make a difference."

"Save that it's a damned intrusion."

"Quite." Malcolm regarded Raoul for a moment and smiled. "Not that I'm embarrassed to have you for a father. Quite the reverse."

Raoul's gaze settled on Malcolm's face for a moment. "If you knew the times I've wanted to call you my son—" He turned away and lifted a coffeepot from the shelf. The blue and yellow porcelain wavered in hands that were not quite steady. "Damnable the way convention forces us to lie about the relationships that matter most."

Malcolm watched Raoul set the coffeepot on the counter, wrap a towel round the handle of the tin pot and pour the coffee from the tin pot into the porcelain one, reach for two cups. Images teased at his senses, in a way that they had increasingly since their arrival at the villa. Sitting at this table, legs dangling off the edge of a chair, a steady hand giving him a mug of milk, a familiar smile. He looked up at his father. "I was here with my mother and you when I was small, wasn't I?"

Raoul went still, the coffeepot in one hand. "I didn't think you remembered."

"I didn't, until this trip. Perhaps being here with you again. Seeing Colin and Jessica and Emily here. Images started to come back. Playing in the sand. You carrying me down the steps on your shoulders. Mama playing the piano. Sitting at this table with you."

Raoul's gaze remained still, but Malcolm could see the shock of those same memories coming to life in his eyes. He poured out two cups of coffee, filling each to a meticulous point below the rim. "We came here every summer for your first four years," he said, in the easy voice Malcolm had learned he used to keep a lid on his deepest feelings.

414

"And then you were imprisoned in France."

Raoul put one of the cups on the table in front of Malcolm. "We'd probably have had to stop, in any case. You were getting old enough you'd have been able to talk about it, and you were too young to understand why you shouldn't." He hesitated a moment, then added in the same easy tone, "But those were some of the happiest days of my life."

"I'm glad," Malcolm said. His voice came out unexpectedly rough. "To have got the memories back."

Raoul picked up his own cup and moved to a chair at the table beside Malcolm. "You liked to count the balusters on the terrace. You had an affinity for numbers even then. I remember telling Arabella you were going to be a codebreaker. I had no idea how right I was."

"Addison and Blanca found a cradle for Jessica. Is—"

"Yes, that was yours. Arabella painted the animals on it. I helped a bit though mostly it was my job to clean the brushes."

Malcolm shook his head. He was reminded of moments he had seen Paul St. Gilles paint, blobs of color evolving into an image that slowly came into focus. The thought of his mother and Raoul, both master strategists, as young parents, painting a cradle, bent over a toddler, was unreal, yet for a moment the images were clear enough he could almost grasp hold of them. Strange to imagine himself so much a focus of both their lives.

Raoul was watching him, scarcely moving but with that gaze that saw so much. "Your mother was driven. But not at every moment. And she wasn't, thank God, incapable of knowing joy. You brought her a lot of that."

Malcolm nodded. For a moment he didn't trust himself to speak. "I'm glad I remembered. I'm glad we're here now. I'm glad we're here with the children."

Raoul blew on the steam from his coffee. "It's good. Realizing there are parts of the past one isn't sorry to remember." He took a sip of coffee. "This place has always been a refuge for me."

Malcolm watched his father for a moment. "You needn't feel guilty about being happy here with Laura because you were happy in the same place with my mother."

Raoul set the cup down with a faint, abashed smile. "I'm not. Or mostly not. Save that—" His gaze went to the window onto the terrace. "Then and now are the two times in my life I've come closest to glimpsing what it might be like to have a family."

"You do have a family, O'Roarke. Like it or not. We're none of us going anywhere."

Raoul's gaze moved back to Malcolm's face. "You can't imagine I'd want you to."

"You're better at facing down enemies than anyone I know," Malcolm said. "But when it comes to facing down the Elsinore League, just remember you aren't the only who'd feel the consequences."

"Malcolm—"

"Laura's probably hesitant to say how much she'd miss you. I know Mélanie is. I'm not."

Raoul met his gaze. "If you'd miss me at all—"

Malcolm took a sip of coffee. "Just about the only thing I don't think I could forgive you for is getting yourself killed."

Raoul held his gaze for the length of a heartbeat. " Given the life I lead, that's rather an extreme request."

"Believe me, I'm well aware of what I'm asking."

"Malcolm—" Raoul drew a breath, as though struggling for the right words. "I've never welcomed danger. And, given

416

the life I have now, you must realize I know how much I have to lose."

"I hope so." Malcolm reached for his coffee. Raoul picked up his own cup and blew on the steam, with the meticulous care of one walking on eggshells. They sat in silence for several seconds, the weight of what they had said, and of the things they had left unsaid, settling over them. Malcolm drew a breath, taking in the freshness of the morning air, the rich scent of the coffee, the memories he found he was glad to have regained.

But reality couldn't be held at bay indefinitely, especially in the midst of an investigation. And they were neither of them the sort of to linger on personal ground too long. "Smythe gave me a letter, apparently from Vincenzo to the contessa," Malcolm said. "Threatening to deny her access to Sofia if she doesn't go along with his plans."

Raoul set down his coffee, his brows drawing together. "Blackmail seems to have been a favorite tool of his. Perhaps not surprising in someone who was part of the Elsinore League. Was the handwriting genuine?"

"It looks like it, judging by the samples of Vincenzo's hand I've seen. Smythe was trying to divert me, but we need to follow up. Mel's going to talk to the contessa."

Raoul reached for his coffee, but stared into the cup instead of taking a sip. "The Elsinore League seem to have a particular affinity for using children against their parents. It's difficult to imagine a more loathsome form of coercion."

The contessa stared at the paper Mélanie had put in her hand. "You think this letter means I killed Vincenzo?"

"I don't necessarily think anything of the kind. But it does suggest a different story from the appearance of amity you and Conte Vincenzo conveyed to the outside world."

The contessa gave a twisted smile. "We did get on, for years. Or I thought we did. I begin to question if I knew anything about Vincenzo. I'm quite sure he didn't love me, but I think he may have been far angrier over the end of our marriage than I realized. He was certainly prepared to use any bargaining chip against me." She drew the folds of her Lyons scarf about her shoulders. "And nothing could make me quite as angry as the fear of losing my daughter."

"I can quite see Conte Vincenzo's not allowing you to see Sofia to be a great threat."

The contessa drew a breath, the sort Mélanie had come to realize often signaled the releasing of long pent-up secrets. "Not Sofia. My second daughter. Eliana."

Mélanie pictured Eliana bent over Emily and Colin at the picnic. A younger copy of her mother. Not much trace of her father in her features. She could hear Cordelia's anguished admission of uncertainty about Livia's parentage. "You said you left Conte Vincenzo in part because you were carrying Lord Thurston's child. But given the timing, and that you hadn't yet left Conte Vincenzo—You aren't sure?"

The contessa pressed her hands over the apricot-sprigged muslin of her skirt. "I told Bernard I knew she was his. I tried to tell myself I couldn't be sure. But the truth is there was nearly a month when Bernard was at his estates and Vincenzo and I were paying a visit to Scotland. He was still my husband. We—hadn't ceased to be intimate."

"That's usually true in such cases."

"It doesn't make it any less awkward or disagreeable." The contessa folded her hands together. "I imagine many women

418

in my situation would be relieved if it was possible to pass a pregnancy off as their husband's child. But when I found out I was with child, all I could think was that it was one more tie to a marriage I found intolerable, one more bar to being with the man I loved. I knew if I told Vincenzo the child was his, he'd insist on keeping it, out of pride, if nothing else. At the same time, I knew if I told Vincenzo I was carrying Bernard's child, he'd effectively end the marriage." She looked down at her hands and touched a ruby ring she wore, where a wedding band would go. "And I was quite sure that if he believed I was carrying his child, Thurston would not abandon me. We'd talked before about going away together, but without my pregnancy, I'm not sure it would have happened."

"No one seeing you with Lord Thurston can doubt he loves you."

"But many men love their mistresses without running off with them. Thurston gave up his family and position for me."

"You gave up your family and position for him."

For a moment, the reality of that loss showed in the contessa's dark eyes. "But I made the choice knowing the full facts." She ran a finger over the ruby in her ring. "I did Thurston a great wrong."

For a moment, Mélanie could feel the pressure of Malcolm sliding her wedding band onto her finger. Whatever their marriage was now, there was no mistaking that it had begun with a lie. She had wronged Malcolm the moment she met him. And she, too, had been carrying a baby that wasn't his, though at least Malcolm had known he wasn't the father. Still, it could be argued that she had used Colin. "Sometimes," she said, "one has to learn to forgive oneself. For the sake of one's loved ones, if not oneself."

The contessa met her gaze for a moment, unvoiced

questions between them even in this moment of understanding. "I caused my daughter to grow up a bastard."

"You caused your daughter to grow up with her mother. To me, that's far more important than legitimacy."

The contessa raised her brows. "You surprise me, Signora Rannoch. I would not expect a married English lady to talk this way."

"I'm not English. I'm married to a Scotsman. And I don't think like a married lady. I think Mary Wollstonecraft had much to say about the drawbacks of the institution. Happy as I am with my husband. I've seen Eliana with you. I'm sure she appreciates having her mother. And I suspect Lord Thurston is a better father to her than Conte Vincenzo would have been."

"Yes. He loves her."

Such a simple word that said so much about both men as parents. "How did Conte Vincenzo learn the truth about her parentage?" Mélanie asked.

The contessa closed her hands together. "Sofia mentioned Eliana's birthday to him. That wouldn't have been enough, in and of itself—babies can be early or late. But then he questioned my maid. Rosa was with me fifteen years ago. She always had a weakness for Vincenzo. I suspect she was sharing his bed then. I think he probably seduced her back into it. Deliberately or not, she revealed details of my pregnancy that led him to arrive at the truth." She loosed her hands but only to grip her elbows. "He threatened to try to get custody of Eliana."

"He'd have a very difficult time proving it now."

"So I said. But we're in Italy and he's Italian. The laws favor him and they favor men in these instances. In nearly all instances." She drew a sharp breath. "He doesn't really want

Eliana. It might be different if she were a boy. He wants—wanted leverage to use against me."

A common theme with Conte Vincenzo. "What did he ask you to do?"

The contessa drew a breath. "Spy upon my—upon Lord Thurston."

"Did he say why?"

"Only that he wanted information about dealings Bernard had with Britain. In particular, with Lord Carfax. He wanted me to go into his study, to go through his papers. To look for letters from Carfax and copy them out."

For a moment, Mélanie could see herself picking the lock on Malcolm's dispatch box. In Lisbon. In Vienna. In Brussels. "What did you say?"

"What do you think? Do you imagine me so lost to honor, Signora Rannoch? How could I do such a thing to the man I love? The father of my children? I've wronged Bernard by not telling him the truth, but I couldn't go that far."

The delicately scented tea the contessa had served her rose up in Mélanie's throat. "Your scruples do you credit."

The contessa drew a sharp breath. "It may seem that we live in a soap bubble here, but I'm not a fool. I know Bernard has dealings that are—secretive. I know, or can guess, that some might disapprove of those dealings. But those are his business. I know that may make me look like a fool—"

"Some would say it makes you a wise woman."

"I—we—live off his fortune," the contessa said. "So one could argue that whatever he does, I am complicit. But I have learned that asking too many questions can be fatal to a relationship. Sometimes secrets are necessary to maintain happiness."

Mélanie thought of the things she still kept from Malcolm

421

and the things she was quite sure Malcolm still kept from her. "I agree that at times honesty can have devastating consequences."

The contessa looked straight into her eyes. "Just so. So you can see why I refused."

"And so Vincenzo threatened to try to take Eliana?"

"Yes. As you say, he might not be able to prove his case. But he also threatened to tell Bernard about her parentage." The contessa drew a shuddering breath. "He deserves to know. But to see the love in his eyes change to anger—"

Malcolm's gaze in a dusty theatre stabbed through Mélanie's memory. She'd been certain she'd never see love in his eyes again. She had, far sooner than she would have dreamed possible. She saw it every day. She'd seen it hours ago when he kissed her goodbye before she left for the Thurston villa. But the ghost would always be there between them. "He loves you," Mélanie said. "He loves Eliana and she's unquestionably his daughter. It's amazing what people will forgive in the name of love."

Their gazes met and held again, unvoiced questions beneath the surface. "So I told myself," the contessa said. "But I can't deny that when I heard Vincenzo was dead, after the initial shock and horror, a part of me felt—relief." She glanced away, as though at a shameful admission, then looked back at Mélanie. "I wouldn't kill over that. I wouldn't kill in any case. But I can't deny I have a motive. And if anything could drive me to commit murder—" Her fingers closed over her ring. "You're a mother, Signora Rannoch. You must realize that a mother protecting her child is the strongest motive of all."

CHAPTER 34

"Dear God," Cordelia said. Across the rose salon, Mélanie could see her friend's own past playing itself out in Cordelia's gaze. "When I think of the women who pass their lover's child off as their husband's—This is the first I've heard of the reverse." She drew a breath and glanced at Harry.

"And then there are women like you, who are brutally honest with both their husband and their lover, Cordy."

"Harry—"

He reached for her hand. "Not a comfortable situation, I confess. But much less likely to lead to a tangle later on. This is the sort of thing that makes me appreciate how you've always been true to yourself." He lifted her hand to his lips.

Cordelia tightened her fingers round his own but shook her head, her eyes glassy. "I at least had control over where I lived and whom I lived with—or didn't live with. I can understand why she did what she did."

"So can I," Mélanie said. "But there's no denying it gives her a motive. Vincenzo threatened to take her daughter from

423

her and destroy her relationship with Thurston. She admitted as much. Very bravely. But she's strong enough and shrewd enough to do just that if she had killed Vincenzo."

"It also shows just how much the Elsinore League are targeting Carfax," Raoul said.

"Quite." Malcolm leaned back on the sofa beside Mélanie. "She obviously loves Thurston very much. I'm not entirely convinced Thurston deserves it. But I have no desire to spoil their happiness if we can possibly help it."

"If," Mélanie said. So often in investigations, avoiding collateral damage came down to "if."

"It gives Thurston a motive, too," Laura said. "Potentially. If he'd learned about Vincenzo's threats to the contessa. I don't think he'd want to lose Eliana, either."

"Not from what we've seen," Malcolm said. "And if he knew about Vincenzo's threats, he'd also know Vincenzo was trying to spy on him. Which is motive in and of itself."

Mélanie picked up a basket of Jessica's sand toys from the nursery table. Theoretically, she and Cordelia had come upstairs for the toys, but in fact, Mélanie had seen from her friend's face that Cordelia wanted to talk. As did she. Though now they were alone, they both hesitated.

Cordelia picked up Drusilla's favorite doll and gave a twisted smile. "That's my Harry. He always faces hard facts head on. Which, oddly, shows a distinct sort of delicacy."

"Malcolm does much the same, in his own way."

Cordelia spun away, fingers pressed to her face. "Dear God, the things that can bring it all welling up. I can go for hours, days, even weeks, forgetting what a cruel monster I was. And then something slashes open our careful reconciliation and brings it all welling to the surface."

Her hands were over her face, but her voice was choked with tears. Mélanie crossed to her friend's side and put her arms round her. "Dearest. We've all made mistakes. We're all learning to live with them." Though, after her talk with the contessa, her own mistakes resounded in her memory.

Cordelia squeezed Mélanie's fingers, then drew back and wiped her hand across her eyes. "Damn. I almost never cry. It's just remembering—"

"It can't but stir all sorts of memories. But nothing you did is remotely like—"

Cordelia turned to the French windows, her fingers closed on the flower links of her diamond bracelet. "I suspected I was pregnant when I told George we should end things and he should go back to Annabel." It was something she'd never before quite put into words with Mélanie. Her voice was steady, but Mélanie could hear the roughness beneath. Cordelia was frank to a fault, but she rarely spoke of her former lover, and Mélanie knew what talking about George Chase cost her. "And I knew I couldn't be sure who the father was. But by then, we knew Annabel was pregnant with George's child. And I knew that what George and I had wasn't what I had thought it was. That we were on the verge of falling out of love, if we hadn't done so already. Or at least, that I was. If I'd realized I was pregnant when I still thought George was the love of my life—" She drew a sharp breath. "I'm not sure what I would have done. I'd like to think I'd still have been as honest as Harry says I am. That I'd have realized Harry had a right to know the child might be his. But I'm terribly afraid I'd have simply wanted to pretend it was George's." Her fingers closed on the bracelet. "God, to imagine I could have sentenced Livia to having George for a father."

"The man you thought George was then was very different from who he turned out to be."

"All too true. I can't imagine loving the man George turned out to be. But my folly aside, I knew Harry was a good man. Part of my excuse for running off with George was that it would be better for Harry to know the truth and go on without me. It's hellishly uncomfortable not being sure about a child's parentage, but he had a right to that discomfort. And he was right just now, as he is so damnably often. It makes for fewer uncomfortable secrets later."

"Cordy." Mélanie watched her friend, searching for something to say that wouldn't be platitudes. "Take it from one who has more to torture herself over than you do. We have enough real-life actions to regret. It's folly to dwell on regretting what we might have done."

"Quite right." Cordelia turned to Mélanie with a firm, bright smile, though the light was at her back. "It's just being reminded of what George once was to me, I suppose. So often I tell myself he doesn't deserve consideration. But I was once as ready to give up everything for him as the contessa did for Thurston. I'm glad she hasn't been as disillusioned." She drew a breath. "I'm still not sure, you know."

"I thought not," Mélanie said.

"I keep thinking I'll see it as Livia grows older, half hoping, half dreading. At times, I think I catch a glimpse of Harry, but it could be expression and inflection more than her appearance. And as Harry says, she's herself, whoever her biological father."

Mélanie nodded. She could see Malcolm in Colin. Her heart stopped sometimes at how similar they were. Before

426

she'd known Raoul was Malcolm's father, she'd put it down to Colin picking up Malcolm's inflections and mannerisms. But now she knew biology could account for the resemblance just as much as living with Malcolm and taking him as a model.

For all Cordy knew of her secrets, she didn't know about Colin. At least Mélanie had never told her, though she'd often wondered how much Cordy guessed. The words welled up in Mélanie's throat, as they had so often in the past. But it wasn't just her decision. It was Malcolm's. And also Raoul's.

"No one seeing Livia with Harry doubts he's her father," she said. "Which he is, in every way that matters."

Cordelia nodded. "Still, if I'd kept anything back from Harry, and if I were threatened with his learning the truth now—" She shook her head, her blonde side curls stirring about her face. "We're so happy, and I know how hard-won that happiness is. Every so often, I draw a breath of sheer wonder. I'd like to think I wouldn't be capable of murder. But if anything could drive me to it—"

Mélanie met her friend's gaze. She'd seen her own hard-won happiness threatened so many times. It had never driven her to anything approaching murder. And yet—"Yes," she said. "The contessa has one of the strongest motives we've uncovered so far."

"Which is too bad," Cordelia said. "Because I quite like her."

"So do I, " Mélanie said. "But we've learned that's no guide to who may be guilty of murder. Of course, you could say the contessa has finer scruples than I. She said nothing would convince her to spy on the man she loved."

This time it was Cordelia who put a hand out and touched Mélanie's arm. "The situations are a bit different. You married Malcolm because you were a spy."

427

Mélanie tucked a strand of hair behind her ear. "Hardly a point in my favor."

"But it changes the dynamic. You went into the relationship with that expectation. You learned to love him. Quite different to go into a relationship loving someone and then learn to spy on him. It would be much more of a leap."

"Whereas I took the leap the moment I met Malcolm."

"You wouldn't have met Malcolm if you weren't a spy. I've lived with a spy myself long enough to realize Malcolm most likely wouldn't respect you if you hadn't been true to your mission. You wouldn't spy on him now."

"I don't think so," Mélanie said, throat raw with honesty. "I've been in enough compromising situations to know that one can never be entirely sure of what one would or wouldn't do. But I'd know what I was risking, if I did."

"Do you think he'd spy on you?" Cordelia asked.

Mélanie drew a breath, considering. She'd worried about their being on opposite sides, but she hadn't quite put it in those terms before. "I don't know. Not lightly. Not without being aware of the risks. But if he thought I was doing something he felt compelled to stop—I can't entirely rule it out. We both still think like agents, to a certain degree."

"Well, then," Cordelia said.

"But I'm quite sure he'd never have married someone to spy on her."

"If someone tried to blackmail you into spying on Malcolm, you'd react with just as much outrage as the contessa did to Conte Vincenzo. Perhaps more."

"Yes, I think that's true."

"You know it is."

"If my children were at stake—"

"You'd risk everything and tell Malcolm the truth.

428

Assuming there were truths he still didn't know."

"And assuming I couldn't get out of it otherwise. I was very good at getting out of things, for a very long time."

"You told Malcolm the truth, eventually."

"Malcolm worked the truth out for himself, eventually. If he hadn't—" She shook her head. "I wanted to tell him so many times, but I don't know that I'd have risked it. I was sure he'd never forgive me, and I couldn't do that to Colin and Jessica. Put their parents so at odds."

What if Malcolm hadn't worked out the truth the previous December? Malcolm's knowing had played no role in Carfax's decision to use her past in his effort to separate David and Simon. Which meant Malcolm might have learned the truth about her from David. They'd have had to flee Britain in the first flush of anger over the revelations. Assuming Malcolm had wanted to leave with her, with her betrayal still raw in his throat.

But even as she voiced the question to herself, she knew the answer. He wouldn't have abandoned the mother of his children when she was threatened by Carfax and exposure to the British authorities. He'd have thought it his duty to get her out of Britain to safety, even if he didn't think he could live with her afterwards. And because of the children, he'd have quickly realized that he had to live with her, however angry and bitter he might be. Which would have left them in exile, without the healing of the past months to build on. Probably without Raoul, because there'd have been no time for Malcolm and him to get to where they were now. How in God's name would they have survived, isolated, angry, with no one to turn to but each other, and so much they couldn't say to each other? If the events of the past few months had been difficult, they could have been so much worse.

"I can see why you couldn't tell him," Cordelia said. "If Harry hadn't known about George, I don't think I'd have ever told him after the fact. What purpose would it have served? I'd have been hurting him, and possibly Livia, to salve my own conscience. But I don't think I'd bow to blackmail, either."

"I'm quite sure you wouldn't, Cordy. You're much too much your own person."

The door opened and Laura came into the room, only to draw up short. "Sorry, I didn't—"

"It's quite all right." Cordelia turned to her with a smile. "It's just that the contessa's dilemma stirred ghosts."

"For all of us." Laura shut the door behind her and leaned against it. "I didn't have much of a relationship with Jack to fear losing. But I lived through the hell of his learning that Trenchard was Emily's father."

"Harder, in a way," Cordelia said. "I doubt Jack Tarrington had it in him to be as understanding as Malcolm or Harry."

"No," Laura agreed. "And we didn't have a reserve of—anything to fall back on. But if he'd lived, if we'd been raising Emily together, I'd have done a lot to keep him from learning the truth. For Emily's sake. And, I suppose, because I knew I'd wronged Jack, however little our marriage meant. Even now, I grow cold at the thought of Emily's learning the truth. Jack doesn't mean a lot to her, but to learn her father was actually Jack's father—"

"She'd cope if she had to," Cordelia said. "Especially as she has a quite decent man I think she's beginning to think of as her father. Or thinks of as her father already."

Laura colored, but gave a faint smile. "That helps. But I still fear it. I don't talk to her much about Jack, though I try to answer questions. I confess I don't really want her to feel a bond with him. But the truth couldn't but sting. Not to mention affect her view of me. I don't think I'd bow to blackmail, though, any more than either of you would."

"I'm quite sure you wouldn't," Mélanie said.

Laura moved into the room and stopped, staring at the dolls Emily and Livia had arranged round a tea table. "I let Trenchard blackmail me. Into spying on people I cared about."

"You didn't even know us when you started," Mélanie said. "And you were doing it because of Emily's safety."

"Trenchard had control of Emily. Vincenzo was threatening to take control of Eliana. It's not dissimilar. If the contessa really feared not just Thurston's learning the truth, but Vincenzo's taking Eliana—" Laura rubbed her arms. "The night I went into Trenchard's study and found him dying of a gunshot. I went there determined to get him to tell me where Emily was. I took your pistol. To threaten him. Even in my desperation, I wasn't thinking of murder. But if I hadn't walked in to find him already dying, if he'd refused, if we'd struggled over the pistol, even if I'd just got angry enough—I can't say it isn't possible."

"I don't think any of us can," Mélanie said. "And we can't say it isn't possible about the contessa, either. That's the thing about investigations. They can force one to confront what one might be capable of. And, as Malcolm says, one can never really know."

CHAPTER 35

Harry moved to stand beside Malcolm at the terrace balustrade. "What's our next move?"

"Damned if I know." Malcolm turned his gaze from the lake to his friend's face. "We have any number of motives, but nothing to point the finger at any one person. We're no closer to finding the Elsinore League papers. Or unraveling the threat to O'Roarke."

"We could break into the villa. Go through Smythe's things."

From Harry, that wasn't idle talk, it was a very real suggestion. Malcolm considered it. "He's not the sort to leave anything lying about. Especially now he knows we're on to him. But—"

He broke off as Raoul came out onto the terrace, shaved and buttoning his coat. "I'm going to see Margaret again. I want to gauge her reaction to the Elsinore League's plot to have me killed. Not that I have any illusions she'll confide in me, but I think I may be able to read something in her

432

response. Or perhaps that's an illusion, too."

It wasn't a bad idea, but Malcolm felt a jolt of disquiet at the thought of O'Roarke off on his own.

Raoul gave a faint smile. "Margaret's not going to pull a knife on me with a houseful of people within call. And the path to the villa is very public. Don't let Laura worry."

"Laura has nerves of steel," Malcolm said. "Which is more than I can say for myself. I'll come looking if you aren't back within two hours."

Raoul grinned, touched Malcolm's arm, smiled at Harry, and was off on the path along the lake.

"He's better able to protect himself than we are," Harry said. "And I'm not underrating our skills."

"I know," Malcolm said, looking after his father. "Which doesn't mean there's no risk. As to searching Smythe's room, I think it may be a worth a try. We'll need Mel and Cordy or Laura, or both of them, to create a diversion."

"I hardly think they'll object," Harry said.

"No, on the contrary. But—"

Malcolm broke off again at the sound of footsteps, this time from round the side of the villa. Kit and Sofia came into view, both a little breathless.

"I'm sorry," Kit said. "We heard voices, so we came round to the terrace instead of ringing the bell. I know—"

"Formality has rather gone by the wayside. If that's a byproduct of the investigation, I'd say it's a happy one." Malcolm gestured towards the table and chairs. "Do sit down. From the look of it, you have news."

Kit and Sofia exchanged glances as they sat at the table. From their flushed, windblown faces, the hasty knot of the ribbons on Sofia's hat, the rumpled fabric of Kit's coat, they had hurried from their own villa to impart whatever news it was, and now they had found Malcolm, weren't sure what to say.

"I can go inside," Harry suggested.

"No." It was Sofia who spoke. "This concerns the investigation, and you're part of that. We just aren't quite sure what it means." She drew a breath. "Last night, Kit and I met on the terrace after the household had gone to bed."

"To talk," Kit said quickly. "We're—trying to sort out what to do."

"It's all right." Sofia touched his hand with a familiarity that spoke volumes. "Reputations seem singularly unimportant just now."

"But they'll seem important again in the future," Kit said, with the assurance of one who had grown up in the beau monde.

Sofia tossed her head, making her hat slip back on her shoulders. "Speak for yourself. In any case, I'm quite sure we can trust Mr. Rannoch and Colonel Davenport." She turned back to Malcolm and Harry. "What's important is that the window to Lord Thurston's study was ajar. We heard voices." She glanced at Kit.

"To own the truth, we weren't sure whether to make ourselves scarce or try to hear more," Kit said.

"But needing information won out," Sofia said. "We couldn't hear a great deal, but it was Thurston and another man."

"We heard them say 'Carfax,'" Kit said, his voice grim. "But it sounded like they were trying to keep something from him. I can't swear to it, but I thought I heard my father say 'he's a dangerous man to double-cross.'"

Malcolm kept his gaze on Kit and Sofia, but he could feel Harry's quickening interest. "You intrigue me," he said. "Did you recognize the other man's voice?"

"No, and neither did Sofia. But when the conversation came to an end, the other man slipped out through the window."

"We were caught by surprise," Sofia said. "But we flattened ourselves against the wall of the house, and we were hidden by a hedge. I don't think he saw us."

"Did you see him?" Harry asked.

"Not much," Sofia said. "It was shadowy, and we didn't have the best angle. But the moonlight gleamed off his hair as he got to the edge of the terrace."

"Gleamed?" Malcolm asked, a suspicion beginning to take form in his mind.

"Yes," Sofia said. "His hair was a quite startling shade of gold."

This time, Raoul found Margaret by the edge of the lake, below the Chipperfields' villa. The villa had no beach but gave directly onto the water. Margaret stood near the gilded metal gates to the lake, beside a fountain surrounded by a manicured hedge. She turned at his approach, with none of the veneer of social convention that had been present at their other meetings. That was so much a part of who Margaret was. Who he had thought Margaret was.

She faced him. It almost seemed she was angling her body to make the most minimal target possible. "I hope you're here because you have new information, rather than to waste both our time with the same questions."

Raoul stopped a few feet off and regarded the woman to whom he was married. "When Vincenzo asked you to get me to find Julien St. Juste for him, did you know he wanted to hire St. Juste to kill me?"

Shock flared in Margaret's eyes. Two days ago he'd have sworn that shock was genuine. Now he couldn't be sure.

"Why on earth would Vincenzo want you dead?"

"An excellent question. I was hoping you could enlighten me."

"You can't imagine if I'd known, I'd have agreed. That I wouldn't have warned you."

"Like you did at Dunboyne?"

Margaret turned away. "That was different. I was angry. Everything between us seemed—closer. And your work put everything I believed in at risk."

"Whereas now you think I've ceased to be relevant? One could make a case for that. Which is why I find the Elsinore League's targeting me all the more interesting."

"That's not—Don't put words in my mouth. I don't think you'll ever cease to be relevant in that way. And, whatever you think of me, I'm not a monster."

"I know full well you aren't a monster, Meg. But you are a quite capable agent. I'm a fellow agent. I was fair game."

"Is that how you think about your son?" she demanded.

The words sliced open wounds that would never really heal. He managed not to flinch. "Even I have limits."

"So do I, whether or not you choose to believe me." Margaret folded her arms across her chest. "Vincenzo commanded, he didn't explain. I confess I didn't ask. I doubt it would have done much good. He was never much inclined to confide in me, even when we were lovers, even when I recruited him. Alistair actually told me more."

"Alistair, for all his faults, was no fool. He probably recognized your worth. I think Vincenzo tended to underestimate women."

"Vincenzo said—" She hesitated, gaze on the statue of Diana at the center of the fountain. "That I'd had a lucky escape. That you were dangerous. I said I wasn't really free of you. And he said—" She drew a sudden, sharp breath.

"That you might be?"

Margaret nodded. "I should have taken that more seriously. I thought it was just talk."

Margaret was either genuinely shocked or she was giving another very impressive performance. "One more question," Raoul said. "How soon did John Smythe come to see you after Vincenzo was killed?"

This time he could read the response in the tension that ran through her. Good to know he hadn't slipped entirely. "The next day. He had the correct codes. Don't ask me what they are."

"I won't. They'll change often anyway. What did he ask you to do?"

"To wait, for the moment. That we still needed St. Juste, but it was good to lie low for a time." She drew a breath. "He wanted to know what you suspected. At that point, I told him, nothing."

"Thus impressing Smythe with my stupidity."

"For what it's worth, Smythe told me not to underestimate you just because we'd been married."

"Have you seen him again since?"

"No. But—" Margaret hesitated. "The truth is, I told Smythe as little as I could. Because at the picnic, Vincenzo told me not to trust him."

437

CHAPTER 36

Malcolm pushed to the door of Thurston's study. "You're working with Julien St. Juste."

Thurston returned his gaze, blue eyes steady and unblinking. "I could say 'whom?' But then we'd spend a tiresome quarter hour in verbal fencing. And I suspect you'd get past my guard, in any case."

"I'm less sanguine about that," Malcolm said. "But I think we both have more important things to do than indulge in sparring."

Thurston picked up a blue glass decanter of brandy and filled two glasses. "If you know Julien St. Juste at all, surely you aren't surprised by the idea that we might be allies?"

"Not if Carfax brought you together. But I am a bit surprised that you've formed an alliance against him."

"I wouldn't say against." Thurston put a glass of brandy into Malcolm's hand. "We've both worked with Carfax. We're neither of us his creature. We discovered that we have certain interests in common that don't necessarily align with

Carfax's."

"Cut the line, Thurston. You and Julien were diverting weapons Carfax had purchased from you and committed to the Carbonari. Possibly others, as well."

Thurston settled back in his chair with his own glass. "I may have been born a baron, Rannoch, but I've become a businessman, of necessity. I sell to the highest bidder."

"You took money from Carfax, told him and the Carbonari some of the weapons were lost, and sold them to someone else."

Thurston took a drink of brandy. "You can't possibly prove that."

"In a court of law? I doubt it. To Carfax? I think I could make a case he'd believe."

"Once, perhaps. But then, Carfax isn't precisely talking to you just now, is he?" Thurston's gaze had sharpened, as though the tip had been pulled from a fencing foil to reveal a naked blade.

"I imagine Carfax would talk to me," Malcolm said, in a voice of deliberate ease. "It doesn't suit me to talk to him just now."

"As you say."

"He's a dangerous man to cross."

"So he is." Thurston turned his glass in his hand. "But by your own admission, you aren't working for him anymore. Whatever my relationship with him, I don't see how it can affect your investigation. So I don't really see what business it is of yours."

Malcolm took a sip of brandy. Pure theatrical gesture. His wife had taught him how effective they could be. "It's a funny thing about murder motives. Secrets almost always play into them. And not always in obvious ways. Investigations have

439

taught me to pay particular note to secrets."

"You think I killed Vincenzo because he'd learned I was double-crossing Carfax? Do you doubt Vincenzo was working for the Elsinore League?"

"No, that seems to be one fairly incontrovertible fact in all this."

"Then why on earth would Vincenzo have betrayed me to Carfax?" Thurston swirled the brandy in his glass. "I admit I had reasons to have killed the man, but I don't see how this makes them stronger."

"Nor do I," Malcolm said. "It could mean nothing. But it's still part of the puzzle."

"Look, Rannoch." Thurston sat back in his chair with one of his disarming smiles. "I freely admit to making compromises. I chose what was important in my life, and to make it work one could say I've betrayed my own honor. I was furious with Vincenzo. I didn't kill him, as it happens. But I had reason to have done. But not because of my dealings with Julien St. Juste. Don't get distracted by a side skirmish."

"Julien St. Juste is rarely involved in side skirmishes." Malcolm took a sip of brandy. "What do you know about him?"

Thurston raised a brow. "Do you expect me to answer that?"

"That depends on the nature of your alliance."

Thurston took a meditative sip of brandy. "I first met St. Juste through Carfax. Carfax sent him to negotiate a shipment. And then again to deliver a payment and collect the goods in exchange. Without knowing much about him, I realized his presence made the exchange even more important than I'd realized. St. Juste let slip that though he worked for Carfax, it wasn't an exclusive arrangement. And

440

that he'd understand if mine with Carfax wasn't, either. In which case, we might do some profitable business together." Thurston stared into his brandy for a moment. "I respect Carfax. But I have no illusions he's loyal to me. So I saw no reason why I should be loyal to him. As to loyalty to Britain—" He took another sip of brandy. "As I told you, I miss it at times, in ways I wouldn't have expected. But the longer I've been gone, the less British I feel. A country I couldn't live in with Elena, couldn't bring my children to—I saw no particular need to concern myself." He cast a glance at Malcolm. "That probably shocks you. I have a feeling you're still a loyal Englishman underneath."

"I'm Scots. As to Britain—I suppose I'll always be British, in a way, like it or not. But I certainly don't agree with many of the policies of Britain's government. I worked in support of those policies for far too long. I did things for which I'll never forgive myself. I've questioned the side I was on. So I'm the last person to judge you on that score."

"Though you judge me for doing it for profit, despite being too tactful to put it into words."

"I try not to judge, Thurston. We all have to make choices. Life's a complicated business, and life anywhere near the intelligence game tenfold more so. I am somewhat in awe of anyone making an alliance with Julien St. Juste." Though his wife and father had done so in the past. And they were the two people who had impressed on him just how dangerous St. Juste could be. He could still see Mélanie's pale face in the Berkeley Square library three months ago when she'd first spotted St. Juste in London, and Raoul's hand curled white-knuckled round the carved arm of the settee.

Thurston gave a faint smile. "There's no denying St. Juste is dangerous. And he plays upon that to ensure he's respected.

441

Not that he isn't fully capable of violence when he thinks it's necessary. We were attacked once in Milan . I saw him break a man's neck."

"Did you know Vincenzo was trying to recruit him to do a job for the Elsinore League?"

Thurston frowned.

"Afraid he turned on you?"

"I always knew it was possible. But I doubt the League wanted to use him against me."

"No. They wanted him to kill Raoul O'Roarke."

"What the devil—"

"My reaction. O'Roarke's, as well. O'Roarke's an enemy of the League, but one has to wonder why now. St. Juste seems to think they also wanted to make use of information he possesses. Which may have to do with the truth of his past."

Thurston took a sip of brandy. "Interesting."

"Who do you think he is?"

"My dear Rannoch. That's your department, not mine."

"But you've spent more time with him."

Thurston twirled his glass between his fingers. "An interesting man, St. Juste. Scrupulously careful not to reveal any clues to his past. But—" He frowned into his glass for a moment. "If I had to hazard a guess, I'd say he's English."

Malcolm sat forwards in his chair. "Why?"

"The instinct of one long-time expatriate for another, perhaps? His accent is flawless, at least to my ear. Elena says his Italian is without accent in various dialects. But one of the things one finds, living abroad for so long, is that people from other countries view the world differently, in subtle ways. There were moments I'd say St. Juste had the perspective of an Englishman. Which doesn't mean he's remotely loyal to

442

the country." Thurston ran his finger over the gilded rim of his glass. "And I'd say he's a gentleman. Or was raised as one."

"Yes, I'd agree with that," Malcolm said. "He's a good actor, but it's hard to counterfeit that innate arrogance."

"Of course, that doesn't mean his heritage is British," Thurston said. "Merely that I'd guess he was raised there. If you're thinking who he is by birth matters."

Thurston was a shrewd man. Malcolm nodded. "I wouldn't have thought it did. But the Elsinore League's interest changes things."

Thurston inclined his head.

Harry and Mélanie paused on the landing, as though taking in the view of the lake from the window at the top of the stairs. No creaks or stirs. They moved down the passage, casually, ready to give the impression that they were finding their way. The guest rooms were fairly obvious. The first they tried was Selena's, the next Kit's. The one after definitely seemed to be Smythe's. They slipped inside.

A tooled-leather writing case with his initials, to confirm they were right. A dressing gown on the foot of the bed, an open trunk.

"He doesn't share a room with Diana," Mélanie said.

"Good for her." Harry cast a glance round Smythe's room. "No sense in wasting time on anywhere obvious. Where would he hide sensitive information?"

"I always liked the finials on the bedposts," Mélanie said. "Or the back of the mirror. What about you?"

"I never used the same place twice," Harry said, pulling a finial off the bedpost. "Better not to have a pattern."

443

"You're brilliant, Harry." Mélanie turned the mirror over and examined the back.

"Quixotic's usually the word I get." He reached for another finial.

"It can amount to the same thing." Mélanie set down the mirror, which had yielded no clues, and cast a glance round the room. "Malcolm says people will make hiding places out of the things they use the most. But Smythe is something of a cipher." The room was spare, even for the chamber of someone who was traveling. No books, no personal items beyond a handsome dressing case and shaving things, which Harry was already checking.

"No false bottom in either," he reported.

Mélanie glanced back at the bed. Smythe was determined to exert control over his wife. In bed, as well? She thought of other men she'd known with similar tendencies. "Let's tip the feather bed off," she said.

Harry didn't question her. They removed the coverlet and slid the featherbed off the bedstead. God help them if Smythe returned abruptly. This would tax even their skills at putting a room back in order quickly.

Harry held the featherbed up. Mélanie felt along the bottom. And found a telltale crinkle. Also the puckering of hasty stitches. Smythe appeared to have slit the lining and then tacked it back together. Mélanie reached for her reticule. She hadn't brought her pistol, but she did have her nail scissors and a needle and thread for unexpected repairs to her gown. She clipped Smythe's stitches and drew out the papers inside.

A string of letters in code stared up at her from the top list. But more words showed through from the paper below. She glanced at it and went still.

444

"I think Smythe had the list of Elsinore League members."

"Christ," Harry murmured. "Well, that's one mystery solved. And we aren't putting them back."

Mélanie tucked the papers into her bodice, snatched up two spare feathers and tucked them back into the featherbed, then quickly stitched up the rent.

"My compliments," Harry said. "I confess, even at my best prepared, I didn't carry a needle and thread."

"One never knows when one might tear a flounce."

They got the featherbed back on the bedstead, replaced the coverlet and Smythe's dressing gown, glanced round the room for other signs they might have left of their presence. Only as they moved to the door did Harry murmur, "Why the devil did Smythe hold on to the list, instead of burning it? Surely the Elsinore League don't want it back?"

"I don't know," Mélanie said. "But I think I recognized the code in the paper that was with the list. It's one Malcolm devised for Carfax."

"I've only just realized Madeleine Lawrence-Hughes must be your cousin," Cordelia said, treating John Smythe to a dazzling smile. "She married my stepfather's nephew, so I suppose that makes us cousins of some sort."

"Quite. That is, how interesting, Lady Cordelia." Smythe regarded Cordelia and Laura across one of the small salons in the villa, where they had managed to corner him. He must wonder if they were here in the service of the investigation, Laura thought. But he couldn't be sure and he couldn't know how much they knew, so he had no choice but to play along.

At least, that's what they were bargaining on.

"So lovely to find these connections, don't you think? Especially when one is abroad. It makes it feel less isolating, somehow." Cordelia rested her elbow on the gilded sofa arm and leaned her chin on her hand, giving Smythe a good view of the bodice of her muslin gown, which was cut far lower than the styles his wife affected. "Do you miss England? My husband likes to travel, but I do find myself longing for sensible conversation and a good cup of tea."

Doing it much too brown, Laura thought, but Smythe nodded. "Even with the war over, the Continent's not the safest for English ladies."

"I quite agree. Harry, of course, is fascinated by old bits of pottery, so I think he's sometimes blind to the dangers."

Cordelia's tone suggested she wasn't entirely averse to those dangers herself. Smythe looked as though he was trying to decide if he'd understood her innuendo correctly.

"Your wife is fortunate she has you to protect her," Laura said. The words stuck in her throat, but she wanted to see how Smythe responded.

Smythe met her gaze squarely. "Quite. That is, I do my best to protect her. I pledged to do so when I married her."

Laura returned that intent gaze. "I've been without my husband for a long time. I hope Mrs. Smythe appreciates what she has in you."

"Diana made me the happiest of men," Smythe said in a voice without inflection. "I hope she feels equally blessed."

"I'm quite sure she recognizes precisely how much you are worth," Cordelia said, with a smile of sugared lemons.

Smythe inclined his head and pushed himself to his feet. "I'm sure you would like some tea. Very remiss of me not to have offered it."

"Oh, can't you ring for it?" Cordelia said. "We're so enjoying our conversation."

"As am I." Smythe's smile was as sweet as Cordelia's and convinced Laura that he suspected what they were up to. "But I'm sure Diana and Selena would like to speak with you both. The contessa and Donna Sofia, as well."

He moved to the door. Laura wondered if she should pretend to faint. The door swung open with a crack to admit Malcolm, followed by Mélanie and Harry.

Malcolm strode up to Smythe. "You're working for Carfax."

CHAPTER 37

S mythe raised his brows. "My dear Rannoch—"

"Spare us the denials." Malcolm folded his arms over his chest and put himself between Smythe and the door, though he knew Harry and Mélanie were guarding the door at his back. On the opposite side of the room, Cordy and Laura had gone absolutely still. They had Smythe surrounded, though with a man such as Smythe appeared to be, that wasn't necessarily reassuring. "We have the list you were keeping to send to him, instead of destroying it, as the League would have wished. Along with a coded communication you meant to send with it. I know that code. I devised it myself."

Calculations shot through Smythe's eyes. The chances of denial working, the wisdom of admitting the truth to gain the upper hand. "Does that surprise you so much?" he said. "You work for Carfax."

"Used to."

Smythe shot a look at him. "One doesn't really stop working for Carfax. If he wants you back, you'll come back."

"But I wasn't betraying the Elsinore League by working for him."

"Surely you, of all people, aren't going to accuse me of betraying the Elsinore League, Rannoch. Doesn't it improve things that I was actually working for my country?"

"I'm not casting moral judgments on your choice of employers. I am interested in the fact that you were betraying a group who are very dangerous to betray."

"Are you questioning my courage?" Smythe demanded.

"Your sanity, perhaps."

"Was it sanity for you to become an agent?" Smythe's gaze shot to Mélanie. "Or to stay married to a Bonapartist agent when you learned the truth about her?"

"Oh, becoming an agent was madness. The only thing that redeems the choice is that without it, I wouldn't have met Mel." Malcolm couldn't risk looking away from Smythe to meet his wife's gaze, but he was keenly aware of her presence a few feet behind him. "Marrying her and staying with her were probably the sanest things I've ever done."

"You're a madman, Rannoch."

"Undoubtedly. But my wife keeps me steady in an insane world."

"Your wife—"

"I advise you not to finish that sentence if you wish to avoid an altercation. Did Carfax send you to spy on us?"

Smythe gave a short laugh. "You have an exaggerated view of your own importance, Rannoch. Carfax values you. I'd even go so far as to say driving you from Britain left him as close to feeling guilty as is possible for Carfax. And he has a healthy respect for your wife and what she accomplished. But you're hardly what he sees as the greatest threat to Britain."

"I'm relieved to know he's still capable of that much

449

rationality. Did he tell you about Mélanie, by the way, or did the Elsinore League?"

"Both, actually."

"Who in the League told you?"

"Do you seriously imagine I'll answer that?"

"You obviously aren't loyal to them."

"I know the value of a bargaining chip." Smythe smoothed his coat sleeve, with the air of one quite heedless of being surrounded by opponents. "Carfax fears the League, as he fears few things."

"It borders on obsession with him."

"You've implied you think they're dangerous, yourself."

"Incalculably. And you?"

"You're questioning my working for my country?"

"And against your father."

Smythe examined his nails. "Well, you should understand all about that, Rannoch."

"A palpable hit." Out of the corner of his eye, Malcolm caught a faint flicker in Cordy's gaze. He was pretty sure Harry had worked out that Raoul was his father. He was less sure Cordy knew. There was really no sense in trying to keep it from either of them, though this wasn't the way he'd have chosen to make the revelation. "But I didn't work for my father and then turn on him. Or were you Carfax's from the beginning?"

"Does that matter?"

"Either way, it's not a parallel to me. I didn't knowingly oppose my father, let alone spy on him."

"No, the shoe is quite on the other foot."

"You could put it that way. I think O'Roarke feels guilty about it. Do you?"

"Guilty?" Smythe flung back his head and laughed. "My

450

father never took me seriously. Never thought I was up to much. Oh, I know lots of chaps complain about that with their fathers. But I actually heard mine say it. On a rare visit to Eton. To Thurston, of all people, before he left. The pater said Kit was shaping up to be a fine young man, and Thurston should count himself lucky. One couldn't always count on brains being inherited."

Malcolm regarded Smythe, face caught in the pangs of adolescence for a moment. Malcolm had nothing but contempt for the other man, on multiple counts, but for a moment he felt a flash of kinship with him. "I overheard Alistair say something similar about me when I was much the same age," he said. Though actually, Alistair had said he couldn't take credit for Malcolm's accomplishments. And Malcolm had already begun to suspect that Alistair wasn't his father. Which had been a strange sort of relief. "Still, your father brought you into the Elsinore League. Alistair never tried that with me."

Smythe gave a short laugh. "From what I saw of Alistair Rannoch, I suspect that was more because he didn't care for you than because he didn't respect you. But then, he knew he wasn't your father. No one, including the pater, has ever questioned my paternity." Smythe was standing with one arm resting casually on the back of the sofa, but his knuckles whitened against the gilded wood. "When he brought me into the League, I actually thought things had changed. It was the first time he'd come anywhere close to treating me—not even as an equal, but as a worthy heir." He contemplated the toes of his boots for a moment. "They gave me missions to undertake. It can mean a lot, being part of something."

"So it can," Malcolm said, without irony.

Smythe met his gaze for the briefest moment. "But then I

451

asked Father about a mission I'd been assigned to. A simple enough question, I thought. But Father said it wasn't my place to know, simply to follow orders. When I said that in the future—" Smythe drew a sharp breath. "Father said, did I seriously imagine I would ever be trusted with real authority? My place wasn't to make decisions, it was to follow orders. In other words, he'd brought me into the League not to be an heir, but to be a foot soldier. He practically said I'd make good cannon fodder."

"And so you went to Carfax?"

"Not right away. But I wondered how the pater could so underrate me, he'd trust me with sensitive information—because I did have access to that, foot soldier or no—and then insult me to my face. That's the problem with people like my father. And you. And the rest of you." His gaze shot behind Malcolm to Mélanie and Harry. "You assume people are idiots with smug self-satisfaction, and underrate them."

"You're a lot of things, Smythe, but I'm quite sure you're no idiot."

Smythe gave a short laugh. "I wanted to go where I could do the most damage. It didn't take long to think of offering my services to Carfax."

"I imagine Carfax couldn't have been happier."

"He finds me useful. He says I don't have your tiresome scruples."

"That sounds like Carfax. Was this before or after you married Thurston's daughter?"

"Diana? Oh, after. Not the smartest move, perhaps. Father wanted the alliance for the sake of the estates. If I'd waited—"

"You'd have spared Diana a good deal of unhappiness."

Smythe gave another laugh. "There weren't exactly suitors crowding round her. Taint of scandal, don't you know. If it hadn't been for Father and the estates pushing me, I'm not sure anyone would have come up to the scratch."

"I think you underrate your fellows, Smythe," Malcolm said.

"We'll never know, will we?" Smythe stepped away from the sofa. "This has been an edifying conversation, but it drags on. I know you have me outnumbered, but I don't believe I've admitted to anything but working for my country against an organization we all agree is a menace. I presume you don't mean to attempt to keep me from leaving the room?"

They were positioned to do just that, but Smythe was right, they didn't really have an excuse. Not without making accusations Malcolm wasn't quite prepared to make yet. Yet, if he was right, Smythe might well disappear from the villa before he could make them.

As Malcolm hesitated, aware of Mélanie and Harry poised for action at his back, the door burst open.

"You bloody bastard." Kit pushed past Harry, Mélanie, and Malcolm, as though quite unaware of their presence, and hurled himself on Smythe. "How dare you hurt my sister?"

The force of Kit's assault sent Smythe crashing into the sofa table. The table upended, sending a pair of Chinese vases to shatter on the tile floor. Kit and Smythe crashed to the floor, amid the wreckage of broken giltwood and smashed porcelain.

"Kit—" Smythe said in a strangled voice.

"Father told me. Diana admitted it. I swear to God I'll kill you." Kit drew back his fist and punched Smythe in the jaw.

Smythe took the blow, grabbed Kit's arm, and, with a dexterity that told of skills he had not hitherto shown, flipped

453

Kit onto his back. Kit's booted foot hit the andirons, which tumbled over with a clatter. Smythe scrambled to his feet, snatched up the poker, and swung it at Kit's head.

Malcolm lurched across the room and caught the end of the poker before it could smash into Kit's skull. Smythe lunged. The poker slid through Malcolm's hand and sliced through his coat.

The door banged open again. "Kit!" Diana yelled. "John! Stop!"

Smythe jerked back from Malcolm and caught his wife as she ran towards them. Suddenly the poker that had sliced through Malcolm's coat was at the base of Diana's throat.

The room went still.

"Diana and I are going to leave," Smythe said. "I advise the rest of you to stay here."

Kit sprang to his feet. "Don't you dare—"

Malcolm put out a hand to stop Kit, gaze trained on Smythe and Diana. Smythe was a man used to using violence to resolve issues, and used to taking that violence out on his wife.

"Give it up, Smythe." The quiet, steady voice was Raoul's. Malcolm realized his father had come into the room so soundlessly he himself hadn't even been aware of it.

Smythe's gaze went to Raoul, as Raoul must have intended. Malcolm kept his gaze on the poker tip at Diana's throat.

"Vincenzo was the enemy, after all, not you," Raoul continued. His voice was calm, friendly even. "We all count the Elsinore League an enemy. You can't think any of us would blame you for killing a man who was working for them."

Smythe's gaze fastened on Raoul's face. "He was on to

me. I didn't have any choice—"

"Quite," Malcolm said. Obviously, whatever Raoul had learned from Margaret had only confirmed his own suspicions. "It was very clever of you to take him unawares. Without you, the list of Elsinore League members would have been destroyed." Which was true, though it hardly excused murder.

"We're enemies in a lot of ways," Raoul said. "But in this, we're all allies."

Smythe's gaze shot between Raoul and Malcolm. Silence gripped the room again. Diana seized the end of the poker and spun away from her husband, jerking the poker out of his hands. Smythe's eyes widened in shock. He stumbled backwards and fell to the floor, cracking his head on the andirons.

Malcolm dropped down beside the fallen Smythe. Mélanie was there an instant later. She put her fingers to the base of Smythe's throat and shook her head. Even without that, the angle of his neck and the fixed glassiness of his stare told their own story.

Kit caught Diana in his arms. Diana clung to her brother, staring over his shoulder at her husband's face, frozen in death.

CHAPTER 38

"It may not be conventional," Thurston said, "but one can say justice was done."

They were in the grand salon, Thurston, the contessa, Enrico, Malcolm, Mélanie, Harry, Cordelia, Raoul, and Laura. And Kit and Sofia, who were sitting side by side, holding hands. It was, perhaps, a sign of the shocks of the day that no one, including the two of them, seemed to make overmuch of this. Diana was upstairs with Selena. Smythe's body had been moved to the same room where they had put Conte Vincenzo's three days ago.

"I never liked him much," Kit said in a low voice. "But I can't believe—"

"That he could have done what he did?" Sofia asked.

"That I didn't realize what he was doing to Diana," Kit said.

"Nor can I," Sofia said softly.

"He killed your father." Kit stared at Sofia, as though only for the first time processing that.

Sofia squeezed his hand. "My father had a lot to answer for."

"So did Smythe."

"Father—was worse than I thought." Enrico drew a hard breath. "Which is saying a lot. But I'm glad we know what happened to him."

"It's a tragedy," the contessa said. "But, pray God, Diana's life will be easier now."

"We must take comfort where we can," Thurston said.

There were still a number of unanswered questions, including why the Elsinore League wanted Raoul dead, and what Thurston and Julien St. Juste intended with the weapons over which they were double-crossing Carfax. But defending Carfax's interests was no longer his concern, Malcolm realized with a jolt of relief. And the Elsinore League were an enemy they were going to have to face on their own.

They took their leave soon after and returned to their own villa. After the children had been mollified for their parents' absence, they were able to update Archie and Frances on the events of the day.

"I might have known Carfax would be behind it," Frances said.

Malcolm smiled at his aunt, despite the tensions of the day. Or because of them. "In fairness, Carfax can't have had the least notion Smythe was going to kill Vincenzo. I doubt Smythe knew, himself, until he realized Vincenzo was on to him, either because Vincenzo confronted him or let it slip some other way. Though I have no doubt Carfax would have agreed with Smythe's actions."

"Carfax has lost yet another agent," Harry said.

"A minor setback from Carfax's point of view," Malcolm said. "He has an endless supply."

457

Cordelia reached for her glass of Nebbiolo. "Did the bandits who held you up when you arrived think you had the Elsinore League list?"

"I think so." Malcolm had been puzzling over this. "I think they were hired by the League. We know the League were interested in the Levellers. I suspect they knew Kit was one of the leaders and that the Levellers were reaching out to the Carbonari. The League thought—wrongly—that Kit had somehow got hold of the Elsinore League papers and was bringing them to trade in exchange for the guns for the Carbonari."

"So the bandits did mistake us for the Montagu party because they were looking for English travelers," Laura said.

"It seems the likeliest explanation." Malcolm twisted the stem of his own wineglass between his fingers. "Unless the League thought we had the papers and were bringing them to trade to Carfax on the Carbonari's behalf. But for better or worse, I think the League know us better than that."

"It could explain their sudden interest in Raoul." Archie patted Berowne, who had jumped up on the sofa beside him. "But I can't see them thinking Raoul of all people would trade such valuable information to Carfax."

"So we still don't know why the Elsinore League want Raoul dead," Frances said.

"No," Malcolm agreed. "But we have the list of names. Which may give us an upper hand."

"For perhaps the first time in a very long game," Archie said.

Raoul lifted his glass to Archie in a silent toast. "Quite."

Malcolm watched the look they exchanged. They had both been his mother's comrades. And perhaps, with the list, the quest his mother had begun might finally be coming to an end.

"This doesn't change anything," Laura said to Raoul in the privacy of their bedchamber. "You're still a marked man."

"I've always been a marked man, one way or another. I just have to be extra careful now."

"I'd be more sanguine if I thought you had the least grasp of what it means to be careful."

Raoul walked up behind her and slid his arms round her. "Trust me, I know what I have to lose. And Malcolm's right, the list gives us an advantage."

Laura turned in his arms and put her hands on his chest. This was perhaps not the best time to say it, but there was never going to be a good time. And he needed to know just what was at stake. "I have news."

His gaze flickered over her face. "Serious news from the look of it. Unwelcome news?"

"I don't find it so. There's no denying it's complicated, but I'm"—she drew a breath; how on earth to put the tumult of feelings since she'd been sure into words?—"rather excited." Talk about an understatement. She drew another breath. It should be a cause for joy, not anxiety, but so much hinged on his reaction. "I'm—we're—going to have a baby."

He stared at her for a long moment, eyes wide with a sort of stunned shock she'd never seen on his controlled face. Then something sparked in his eyes that sent relief coursing through her. "God help me. I should probably apologize."

"Apologize—"

He brushed his fingers against her cheek. "I'm sorrier than I can say for putting you in this situation, but—Sweetheart, how could I be anything other than delighted?"

Laura laughed, air rushing into her lungs. "The situation is as much my responsibility as yours. It's not as though we weren't both trying to take precautions."

His mouth twisted. "You'd think I'd have learned—"

"I don't think you could have done more, darling, except by abstaining entirely." He had, in fact, been scrupulously careful, from that first night he'd pulled out of her to later making sure she had a sponge securely in place. "And I'm quite glad you didn't do that."

He gave a wry smile. Then his face went serious. He looked down at her for a long moment, as though he was memorizing her features and at the same time seeing her anew. Then he dropped down on one knee and seized her hand. "I can't promise I won't get myself killed. But other than that, I won't fail you or Emily or the child. I pledge you my word."

Coming from him, such seriousness might have been comical, save that, coming from him, such seriousness meant so very much. And, she realized, this was probably the closest they'd ever come to wedding vows. She leaned down and took his face between her hands. "I know it. And the baby will be fortunate to have you for a father."

She put her lips to his. For a moment, in his stillness, she could feel the world humming round them. Then his arms slid round her and he got to his feet, holding her to him. The kiss deepened. She took a half step towards the bed and felt his hesitation. She broke the kiss to smile up at him. "I won't break. I was with child when you took me to bed the last time. The only difference is we know it. And it's not a bar to anything. On the contrary. Now we don't have to worry about

460

what's already happened."

He laughed and scooped her into his arms.

"Laura," he murmured a few moments later, as he laid her against the pillows.

"Mmm?" Coherent thought had a way of fleeing when she was in his arms, especially after the tensions of the day.

"It may be appallingly selfish, but I think at this point I do expect you to feel a sense of obligation."

She laughed and tangled her fingers in his hair. "I'd be distinctly insulted if you didn't, darling."

It was different. Not that they hadn't committed to each other before, but tonight they had crossed some sort of line. The sheer relief of telling him, the wonder of what lay before them, the fact that they were sharing it, whatever that meant. That they were sharing an uncertain future. That for all they had to fear, they had a great deal to hope for. He'd always made her happy, but she'd never known quite such intoxicating joy.

Later, lying against the pillows, his arm round her, he said. "Do you want to go away?"

She sat up to look down at him. His features were relaxed with odd, uncharacteristic contentment, but his gaze had sharpened. "Go where?" she asked.

"South America. The United States. The Canadian territory. Whatever the legalities, there'd be no one to know we weren't married."

She stared at him. He'd told her he'd asked Arabella to run off with him. But—"You didn't go away with Mélanie," she blurted out, before she could think better of it.

"I thought about it. I came very close. I wasn't sure she'd go with me. And I didn't want to leave the fight."

"You don't want to leave it now."

461

"No." He didn't shrink from saying it, which, in a way, made what he was offering all the more significant. "But I could. I might have done six years ago if it hadn't been for Malcolm."

She watched him. The tangle of his past, what he'd wanted then, what he wanted now, never failed to surprise her. "You don't want to leave Malcolm now. Or Mélanie, or Colin or Jessica."

"No. But I'm not as worried about Malcolm as I was then. God knows they have challenges, but he and Mélanie can look after each other and the children."

Between the carefully chosen words, images hovered between them. Raoul feeding Jessica strawberries. Building sandcastles with Colin and Emily. Playing chess with Malcolm. Making up stories with Mélanie. All of them laughing over morning coffee and glasses of wine at night. "You'd miss all of them."

"Of course." Again, the lack of denial made it clear just how much he was offering. "But—"

"*I'd* miss them. Emily would miss them. Perhaps I'm wrong not to give our child a clean start, but I'll be damned if I'll build our future on running away from the people we love."

He looked at her for a long moment and nodded, gaze serious, but a faint smile curving his mouth.

Laura pleated a fold of sheet between her fingers. "And I don't want to go off and invent a fictitious husband and come back a fictitious widow. We're managing very well, but I don't want one more child in this family to grow up not knowing who his or her father is."

Another sort of wonder shot into Raoul's eyes. He knew what it was to be a father. He didn't know what it was to be an

462

acknowledged father. "That means a great deal, sweetheart. But have you considered—"

She drew her knees up under the covers and linked her arms round them. "It would be harder if we were still in London. I'd worry about what we were exposing Malcolm and Mélanie and the children to. Here, we're all outcasts, in any case." She cast a quick look at him. "I'll offer to move out of the household, but—"

"They'll bite your head off at the suggestion, beloved. You might as well spare your breath." He looked at her for a moment. "Does either of them—

"You can't think I'd have told them before I told you."

"No. Which doesn't mean one or both of them hasn't guessed. I should have done."

"We've had a number of distractions. Besides, then you'd have denied me the fun of telling you." She rested her chin on her knees. "I don't mind living outside society."

"Do you mind our children living outside it?" He drew a breath, as though still dumbstruck from the wonder of it.

"I'd rather that than that they grew up lying to conform to society. A society their father, to a large extent, is fighting against. Surely you, of all people, appreciate that."

He reached for one of her hands and laced his fingers through her own. "Perhaps there's no greater test of one's ideals than having them come up against the reality of what one wants for one's children."

"What do you want for them?" It was something they'd never discussed. Emily was increasingly theirs, but he left decisions about Emily to her.

"For them to have as many options as possible."

"Outside society, in a way, they do. They won't be pressured to follow someone's idea of the done thing." She

463

tightened her fingers round his own and pressed her lips to his knuckles. "When I was Jack's wife I was almost a duchess. Emily would have been a duke's daughter. And we're both so much happier now."

CHAPTER 39

Raoul looked down at Laura, lying curled beneath the coverlet, her titian hair spilling over her face, one hand still resting on the sheet where he had lain, her mouth curved in a faint smile. His lover. The woman he loved. The mother of his child.

His fingers tightened on a fold of sheet. The wonder of it still thrummed through him. Joy mixed with cold terror. Considering he'd had to play this scene three times, one would think he'd be less dumbstruck by his lover telling him she was carrying his child. The circumstances were different, of course. Complicated, God knew, but not as fraught. Laura wasn't married. They weren't in the midst of a war. Laura wasn't Arabella or Mélanie. And he wasn't the nineteen-year-old lovesick boy who'd begged Arabella to run off with him or the forty-five-year-old agent in the midst of the crucial days of the war who'd weighed what he owed to Mélanie, to the child, to Malcolm, against how the next few months might shape the future of the Continent.

465

The third time, had he finally got the scene right?

He dressed quietly, went back to the bed, and touched his fingers to Laura's cheek. Her smile held calm certainty that all would be well. For all the possible dangers, to her, to the child, to Emily, that ran through his head, for all he questioned his own ability to be what all of them needed, he couldn't stop smiling himself.

He bent and dropped a light kiss on her hair. Laura stirred, her eyes half opening. "It's all right, sweetheart." He kissed her again, this time on the lips. "Go back to sleep. I'll see you at breakfast."

He'd said something similar that first night when he'd slipped from her room at the inn in Maidstone. Save that then it had still been dark out. Such a difference to be able to watch her in the daylight, not to have to sneak back to his room before dawn.

He drew the sheet over her shoulder, watched her settle into the pillows, then slipped from the room. He cracked open the door to what had become the night nursery. Colin, Emily, Livia, and Chloe were all still asleep, along with Berowne and the puppy. But when he went round the gallery and downstairs, he saw the door of the study ajar and caught a whiff of coffee. Malcolm was sitting at the desk, a cup of coffee at his elbow, papers strewn before him.

Raoul pushed the door open and leaned against the doorjamb.

Malcolm looked up with a quick smile. "One of the best times to get things done, before the children are up."

Raoul nodded. "May I speak with you a moment, Malcolm?"

It was an unusually formal way for him to begin a conversation, but Malcolm merely said, "Of course. Coffee?"

He poured a cup from the tray on a table beside the desk.

Raoul accepted the cup and took a grateful sip. Malcolm leaned back in his chair and watched him. Raoul realized he was still standing and dropped into a straight-backed chair beside the desk. He took a sip of coffee. It was strong and bracing, but didn't do much to clear the fog in his brain.

Malcolm took a sip from his own cup, gaze on Raoul, and didn't say anything.

Raoul took another sip of coffee, drew a breath, put the cup down, picked it up again. "Laura—That is, Laura and I—" Christ, it was harder than he'd thought.

Malcolm reached for his cup again. "It's all right. I'm a bit old to have a tantrum at the news I'm going to have a little brother or sister."

Raoul stared at his son. Malcolm looked back, a faint smile in his eyes.

"I don't know whether to be proud of your observational skills or horrified at my own," Raoul said.

Malcolm smiled and took a sip of coffee. "I have a few advantages. I've watched my wife through two pregnancies, I saw a lot of Cordy when she was expecting Drusilla, and I was reasonably sure about Blanca before she and Addison told us. And I think it's rather been on my mind because of Aunt Frances and Archie."

Raoul gave a wry smile. "It should have been on my mind, as well." And it had, save that he'd been more focused on what he and Laura couldn't have.

"If it's any comfort, I haven't suspected for long. And I wasn't certain until you told me."

"Does—" Raoul couldn't quite say it.

"I don't know if Mel's worked it out. She hasn't said anything to me, and I haven't said anything to her. I thought

467

you and Laura should talk about it before we did." He watched Raoul a moment longer. "My felicitations. I know it's complicated for you both, but I hope it's also a cause for joy."

"Thank you." Raoul drew breath. "We're both very happy." He took a sip of coffee. "I'm perhaps too happy, considering what I've exposed Laura to."

Malcolm turned his coffee cup in his hand. "Knowing Laura, I imagine she had little concern for much of what you're worrying about."

"Which doesn't mean I don't."

Malcolm smiled. "Suddenly concerned about the proprieties, after all these years?"

"I don't give a damn about proprieties. I do care very much about the options open to Laura and our children."

Malcolm inclined his head. "Point taken. It will be easier here. We're already living on the edge of society."

"That's what Laura said." Raoul took another sip of coffee. "Laura doesn't wish to—she doesn't want to pretend."

"That the child is someone else's? Thank God, we've had entirely too much of that, as it is."

"Again, that's what Laura said. But there's going to be talk, even with all of us living here. Laura said she'd offer to leave so it wouldn't reflect on you and Mélanie and the children—"

Malcolm slammed his hand down on the desk. "No."

Raoul felt himself smile, despite everything. "That's what I told her you'd say. And I love you for it. But the talk will get back to Britain."

"Anyone we care about won't pay any heed to it. Except to wish you well. Frances and Archie will be monstrously relieved to be a bit less the center of attention in this regard."

Raoul smiled, then reached for the coffeepot and refilled his and Malcolm's cups, mostly to give himself something to do with his hands.

"It's a startling thing," Malcolm said. "It's takes adjusting to."

"What does?"

"Realizing one is going to be a father."

Raoul set the coffeepot down, managing not to spatter drops on the polished walnut. "It's not as though—" He couldn't quite say it. For so many reasons, for all that had healed, the past was still too raw in some ways.

"You haven't faced it before? But never knowing you were going to have the chance to openly be a father. Speaking for myself, it's a wondrous and terrifying prospect."

Raoul met his son's gaze. Those moments almost six years ago hung between them. Malcolm's deciding to be a father to Mélanie's unborn child. Raoul's learning Mélanie was carrying his child, and almost simultaneously relinquishing fatherhood.

"Have I ever thanked you for what you gave up?" Malcolm asked.

Raoul swallowed. It was as though there was glass in his throat. "I could well be said to have abrogated my responsibilities."

"You made sure Colin was cared for. Perhaps in the best way you could, at the time. You're a father to him now, in many ways. But this is different. I'm glad you and Laura will both have the chance to experience it from the start."

Raoul stared into his half-empty cup. How odd when one's son became one's best confidant. "I don't want to—let them down. Laura and Emily and the baby."

Malcolm picked up his coffee cup. "I'm better qualified than most to say the child is lucky to have you for a father."

For a moment Raoul wasn't sure he could speak. "You

469

didn't need to say that."

"No, I didn't. I said it because I meant it."

For a long moment they regarded each other, past and future hovering and shifting between them. "I need to return to Spain," Raoul said. It seemed a particularly horrible thing to say after what had just passed between them, yet perhaps it was particularly apropos. "I should be back well before the child is born. If it's humanly possible, I will be."

Malcolm nodded without surprise or censure. "What I said to you in London three months ago still holds. Laura's part of the family. So are you. Mel and I will do everything we can for both of you. And your children. My word on it."

Mélanie was on the window seat nursing Jessica when Malcolm came into the room. She looked up with a smile. "We'll be down in just a minute. Is that coffee for me?"

Malcolm smiled and set the cup of café au lait down on a table beside her. "Have I ever mentioned you have a way of anticipating my every need, darling?" Mélanie shifted Jessica, picked the cup up one-handed, then went still, noting her husband's expression. "What's wrong?"

"Nothing's wrong. Quite the contrary." He sat on the window seat beside her. His expression, she realized, studying him in the wash of sunlight, was more bemused than disturbed. "I've just had a talk with O'Roarke."

Mélanie gave a sigh of relief. "Laura's told him."

Malcolm stared at his wife and gave a soft laugh. "You knew too."

"Guessed. The glow in her eyes and her skin. And she went swimming in a week she normally wouldn't have done."

Mélanie looked down at Jessica, recalling the moment she'd realized she was pregnant with her, then looked back at Malcolm. "How's Raoul taken it?"

"A bit stunned. But quite happy. Happier than he'll admit, I think."

Mélanie smiled. "I'm glad for both of them. To be able to experience it from the first."

Malcolm nodded. "A bit odd we've both been through what O'Roarke hasn't. At least, not precisely."

There was a time she'd never quite been able to imagine Raoul as a father. In recent years, with both Malcolm and Colin, as well as Emily, she'd seen what a very good one he could be. And yet—"He won't change," she said. "That is, he's changed in remarkable ways, especially since Laura. But he won't stop running crazy risks. Going up against dragons and tilting at windmills."

"No. But he's running somewhat fewer risks now. And he'll do his best to come back. He's always managed to."

Mélanie suppressed a shiver, despite the fact that she'd seen Raoul survive so much. Or because of it.

"Nothing's simple in this family," Malcolm said. "But perhaps the most remarkable thing is that we are a family."

Mélanie met her husband's gaze for a moment, myriad memories shooting through her mind. Accepting his proposal in a drafty passageway in Lisbon. Meeting Raoul at Hookham's Lending Library on their first visit to Britain, never guessing she'd one day be sorry to be exiled from that alien country. Standing with Malcolm over his sister's murdered body in Vienna. Copying out intelligence to send to Raoul before Waterloo, while fear for her husband glazed her senses. Telling Raoul about Fouché's threats in Paris. Meeting with Malcolm and Raoul and the Kestrel, Malcolm still not

471

knowing her past, neither of them knowing Raoul was Malcolm's father, none of them knowing the Kestrel was Bertrand. Malcolm confessing his betrayal of Bonapartist agents, a few hours before Jessica was born. Malcolm asking Raoul if he was his father. The moment in the Tavistock Theatre when she'd seen her marriage smash to bits in her husband's gaze. Facing Laura across a small room in the Brown Bear Tavern, Laura refusing to explain her finding the murdered Duke of Trenchard. Malcolm telling Raoul the Berkeley Square house was the closest he had to a home in London. The four of them in Berkeley Square, accepting that they had to leave Britain. "How in God's name did we get—"

"I don't know," Malcolm said. "But I'm grateful for it every day."

Mélanie nodded. In so many ways, the villa had become an island of safety. The real world was still outside it. She might talk about Raoul going off to fight dragons, but those dragons were real.

"Mel," Malcolm said.

Mélanie looked at her husband, trying to shake off her fears.

Malcolm hesitated. She could almost see him sifting through possible words. "It wouldn't be wonderful if this stirred memories."

It took her a moment to understand. "You mean, am I upset Raoul didn't raise Colin with me?" She shook her head. "It was a different time. The world was on fire about us. And we were both different people."

Malcolm nodded. "I think he came very close to asking you to go to South America with him."

"Which shocked me when I realized it. But I'm not sure I'd have gone. I was too focused on my cause. And, by the time I knew I was pregnant, I'd met you."

Malcolm's gaze settled on her own. "And you were too caught up in the spy game possibilities?"

"Partly," she said with honesty. "But I think I was also already on my way to falling in love with you. I didn't see it at the time, but I think Raoul did."

Malcolm smiled. "He has a damnable way of seeing things." He cupped his hand round Jessica's head. "Raoul's going back to Spain."

Mélanie saw the fear shoot through her husband's eyes. "He has to, darling. He wouldn't abandon a network."

"No, I know that. He says he'll do everything humanly possible to be back before the baby is born, and I believe him. I have to try to believe he can outwit whatever the Elsinore League may try. Meanwhile we have the papers. If we can't checkmate the League, perhaps we can at least put them in check."

Mélanie shifted Jessica in her arms. "I don't think we've seen the last of Julien. Mad as it sounds, I think he may be an ally."

"An ally we're going to need. Thank God the man's in love with you."

"Malcolm!" Mélanie sat up straight, eliciting a cry of protest from Jessica.

Malcolm grinned. "Only stating the obvious, sweetheart. It could be useful. We're going to need all the help we can get. Especially as we also don't know what Carfax's next move will be."

The Elsinore League. Carfax. Julien. Mélanie felt an improbable wave of laughter break over her. She put a hand on Malcolm's arm, drew him to her, and kissed him over their daughter's head. "At least we needn't fear being bored, darling."

"No," he murmured against her lips, "I think that's one danger we've escaped. Now we need all our wits and all our allies to escape the others."

HISTORICAL NOTES

I have, I confess, taken shocking liberties with Lord Byron's and Percy and Mary Shelley's chronology in Italy in the summer of 1818. Percy and Mary did visit Lake Como soon after their arrival in Italy in the spring of 1818 with the idea of taking a villa there for the summer and inviting Byron to join them. But Byron preferred to remain in Venice, and in the end the Shelleys, their children, and Mary's stepsister Claire Clairmont spent time in Milan, from whence Claire tearfully sent her baby daughter, Allegra, to Venice to live with her father, Lord Byron. The Shelleys and Claire then traveled south, stopped for a month in Livorno, and spent the summer in the spa town of Bagni di Luca, in the Apennine Mountains.

On 17 August, Percy and Claire left for Venice to try to see Allegra. They found Byron in an agreeable mood. He offered the Shelley party the use of his villa at Este for the summer where Claire could spend time with Allegra. The only problem was that Percy had told Byron Mary was with them, so that Byron, who could be surprisingly puritanical, wouldn't be shocked at Percy and Claire traveling alone. Percy wrote to Mary that she needed to join them at Este at once with the children. Their baby daughter, Clara, already ill, worsened on the journey. Mary and Percy took her to a doctor in Venice, but by the time Percy brought the doctor to the inn where Mary was with the baby, Clara was dying.

In *Gilded Deceit*, I have had the Shelleys and Byron in Milan over at least part of the summer, so they can meet the Montagu party. I have also moved Clara's death back about a month from the end of September to the end of August. And rather than Percy and Mary spending time in Este and Venice after Clara's death, I have the Shelleys go to Lake Como, accompanied by Lord Byron.

Byron later became involved with Carbonari (as, most likely, did Hortense Bonaparte's son, Louis-Napoleon, who appears in *Mission for a Queen*). Mary Shelley included an essay on the Carbonari by the exiled Italian revolutionary, Ferdinand Gatteschi, in her book *Rambles in Germany and Italy in 1840, 1842 and 1843* and donated the sixty-pound fee for the book to him.

Byron was drawn into Carbonari by the family of his mistress, Teresa Guiccioli. But if he and the Shelleys had met Sofia and Enrico in the summer of 1818 perhaps they would have played a role as well...

For further reading about Mary and Percy Shelley and Lord Byron, I recommend Miranda Seymour's *Mary Shelley* (New York: Grove Press, 2002); Florence A. Thomas Marshall's *The Life and Letters of Mary Wollstonecraft Shelley, Volume I* (London: Richard Bentley & Son, 1889); Daisy Hay's *Young Romantics: The Tangled Lives of English Poetry's Greatest Generation* (New York: Farrar, Straus and Giroux, 2010); and Benita Eisler's *Byron: Child of Passion, Fool of Fame* (New York: Alfred A. Knopf, 1999).

A READING GROUP GUIDE

The suggested questions are included to enhance your group's reading of Tracy Grant's *Gilded Deceit*.

Discussion Questions

1. Most of the central characters are expatriates or exiles, through circumstances or by choice. How does this shape their actions and the events of the book?

2. Mary Shelley says that her mother likened marriage to slavery. Diana Smythe's predicament shows the trap marriage could be for a woman in the era. In what other ways does marriage either constrain or liberate different characters? In what ways do the characters face challenges between being individuals and being part of a couple?

3. Malcolm says he'll probably be less British than Thurston in fifteen years. Do you think that's true? What do you think Britain means to Malcolm?

4. The threat of secrets being revealed drove the Rannochs from Britain. They arrive in a world that proves to be full of deceit. How do these deceptions, past and present, shape the actions of different characters? Do you think it would have been better if some secrets had never been revealed?

5. Mélanie was worried the quiet of life in exile would drive her and Malcolm mad. How do you think the Rannochs

are coping so far?

6. What do you think lies ahead for Kit and Sofia?

7. Do you think Malcolm, Mélanie, and Raoul will tell Colin the truth of his birth? Should they?

8. Who do you think Julien St. Juste really is?

9. How does being parents shape the actions of various characters and the different ways they define parenthood?

10. Do you think the Rannochs will ever go back to Britain? If they could go back to their old lives, how do you think they would feel about it?

11. What were your impressions of Margaret? Was she what you expected?

12. Malcolm and Raoul open up to each other and become very close in *Gilded Deceit*. How do you see their relationship impacting their professional lives going forwards?

13. How do you think becoming a father again will impact Raoul personally and professionally?

14. How do you think Mélanie will find purpose going forwards?

15. How do you think Carfax will react to David and Simon leaving Britain with the children?

16. At the end of *Gilded Deceit* we see Raoul planning to return to Spain temporarily for his work. Do you think Mélanie would be happier fighting alongside Raoul as long as she had her children with her?

MORE BY TRACY GRANT

Rannoch / Fraser Series
Mission for a Queen
London Gambit
Incident in Berkeley Square
The Mayfair Affair
London Interlude
The Paris Plot
The Paris Affair
The Berkley Square Affair
His Spanish Bride
Imperial Scandal
Vienna Waltz
The Mask of Night
Beneath a Silent Moon
Secrets of a Lady

Traditional Regencies
Widow's Gambit
Frivolous Pretence
The Courting of Philippa

Lescaut Quartet
Dark Angel
Shores of Desire
Shadows of the Heart
Rightfully His

ABOUT THE AUTHOR

Tracy Grant studied British history at Stanford University and received the Firestone Award for Excellence in Research for her honors thesis on shifting conceptions of honor in late-fifteenth-century England. She lives in the San Francisco Bay Area with her young daughter and three cats. In addition to writing, Tracy works for the Merola Opera Program, a professional training program for opera singers, pianists, and stage directors. Her real life heroine is her daughter Mélanie, who is very cooperative about Mummy's writing time. She is currently at work on her next book chronicling the adventures of Malcolm and Suzanne Rannoch. Visit her on the Web at www.tracygrant.org

© Raphael Coffey Photography

Printed in the USA
CPSIA information can be obtained
at www.ICGtesting.com
CBHW052154061124
17037CB00010B/75

9 781545 053393